Molly

FIGHTING THE FORBIDDEN

RUTHLESS & ROYAL #1

AUTUMN JONES LAKE

COPYRIGHT

DEDICATION

Love is a fight, but not everyone's a fighter.

Molly

CHAPTER ONE

GRIFF

My best friend's little sister Molly is the only person in the world distracting enough to make me miss a foot flying at my head.

The kick slams into my temple. Pain explodes through my skull. My vision blackens around the edges. I rock sideways but stay on my feet.

Stupid mistake.

Everything in front of me blurs for a second. I grit my teeth, refusing to give in to the throbbing ache. Shaking off the blow, I put my fists back up, and weave away from my opponent.

My wandering attention could've cost me the fight. But Molly's here. Watching. Even though she's what pulled me out of the fight, she's also the reason I'm diving back into it.

So she can watch me win.

I weave away from my opponent's next strike. He already had his shot. He's not getting another one.

Molly is my ultimate forbidden fruit—my best friend's little sister. She's sweet, shy, innocent, and gets good grades while I'm gruff, loud, definitely not innocent, and earn extra cash by beating the shit out of people in illegal underground fights.

Why is she even here?

The bloodthirsty spectators roar. This is a rougher scene than I'm used to. Dirtier fighting. Fewer rules. The dank, sweat-soaked air crackles with expectation.

My opponent—a skilled fighter, no doubt—goes in for another shot and that's when I retaliate, pummeling him with several calculated strikes. He sways on his feet, then crumples to the concrete floor.

Stay down, motherfucker.

He groans and flops his forearm over his eyes. The crowd erupts in chaotic cheers and shouts. The ref stomps over and toes my opponent in the ribs. The guy curls into a ball on his side, signaling he's done.

Breathing hard, I allow the ref to hold my hand in the air and show me off to the heavy bettors outside the cage.

"Give it up for Stonewall!" the ref shouts, using the ring name I was given years ago.

The people chanting my name are nothing more than a colorful, frenzied blur. My mind's already left the ring. I'm too busy searching for Molly to pay attention to the spectators, girls, or anyone else.

The organizer of tonight's matches approaches with a big smile stretched across his face. He hands me my stack of cash and slaps my back.

"Good match!" he shouts in my face. "Come back anytime."

Not likely. I don't plan to make a habit out of visiting Ironworks.

I nod to acknowledge his open invitation, then hustle out of the ring and into the fray. Need to reach Molly before the crowd swallows her. These aren't the sort of people she should be mixed up with.

I shoulder through the mass, bumping guys out of my way. *There.* No more than ten feet from me. She's in a shadowy area, waiting patiently against the back wall. My lips curve up as I recognize the logo of my fight club stretched across the front of her purple T-shirt. Brass knuckles and roses. Kind of like Molly and me.

Guys eye-fondle her as they walk by, but no one dares talk to her. They know better than to mess with Remy's little sister. Because she's my Molly—sweet, oblivious Molly—she doesn't notice their attention.

Her eyes are focused on me and nowhere else.

Unfortunately, a lot of ring bunnies are *also* focused on me. One approaches with a sway to her hips and her full, red lips curled into an enticing smile. My gaze shoots to Molly in time to catch the turndown of her mouth and quick glance toward the exit.

I need to reach her fast.

"Congratulations, G," Layla says. She waits for me to kiss her cheek. Give her some sign I want her to accompany me to the locker room or maybe my car so she can be my trophy for the night. Leaning in closer, she drops her voice to a conspiratorial tone. "Were you messing with him when you took that kick?"

I don't bother bending down to hear her better or return her smile. "Nope." My clipped answer's meant to satisfy her questions—both spoken and unspoken.

Layla knows a brush-off when it's happening. She's too proud to beg and too beautiful to bother trying to convince me. She lifts her chin and stalks away. On to the next fighter.

My eyes lock on Molly again. She's staring at the floor now, arms wrapped around her middle like she's trying to make herself as small as possible. She lifts her head as I approach. A tentative smile flickers over her lips.

"You didn't have to hurry up for me," she says, nodding in Layla's direction. "I know you have *fans* to attend to."

The words come with an edge of hurt—pain I wish I could erase from Molly's mind.

"Does your brother know you're here?" I ask, holding out my arms to her.

Instead of answering, she flings herself against me, wrapping her arms around my neck. I lift her up, hugging her tight, burying my nose in her cherry-vanilla-scented hair.

"You scared me when he got that kick in," she whispers against my shoulder.

No way will I explain she's the reason I took that blow. I'm too fucking happy to see her. And even though she shouldn't be here, I'm thrilled she came to see me.

Maybe too thrilled.

I need to let her go.

"I'm sweating all over you, girl." I squeeze her tighter, negating my warning. She's so soft and fits against me just right.

"I don't mind getting a little sweaty," she murmurs.

That takes my mind down a path it definitely should *not* travel.

Setting her down before I'm ready, I keep my hands on her hips. It's playing with fire. All the leftover adrenaline screaming through my system has me flirting with getting burned. Even though this isn't a fight club I visit often, I recognize plenty of people. Any number of them would be more than willing to report back to her brother that I had my hands all over his little sister. Her brother—my best friend and partner in crime—wouldn't hesitate to kick my ass.

I settle for a kiss on her forehead before taking my hands off her.

"You didn't answer me. Does Remy know you're here?"

"Of course not."

"Why'd you come?"

"Duh, to see you." She pokes her finger into my side. "I heard you were up against someone new. Sorry I missed most of it."

"You saw the best part."

Laughter spills from her lips, chasing away the leftover violent energy burning through my body from the fight. I glance around the open space. Still way too many people here to leave her alone while I go shower and grab my stuff.

"Follow me." I hold out my hand and she takes it, weaving

through the throng with me. The hallway to the private locker room is dark and deserted. Molly trots a little faster, catching up and wrapping her other hand around my arm.

"You don't have anything to be scared of," I assure her. "You're with me."

"I know." Her lips quirk up. "You'd kill anyone who touched me."

I return the smile. "*Kill* is a little strong." *Break a few bones, maybe.*

She squeezes my arm tighter.

It's not fear that keeps her clinging to me. It's trust. And that's not something Molly gives freely.

The locker room's deserted. My opponent probably took off as soon as the match was finished. To the other side of the building, the local hospital, or home—I don't know or care. No one else has a reason to be in here right now except me.

"Stay here. I'm gonna take a quick shower."

She touches her fingers to my head. "You're bleeding."

"Shit, really?" I glance at the mirror on the wall. She's right. It's a small cut, but a trickle of blood mingled with sweat slides down the side of my face.

Her fingers lightly rake through my hair and my eyes close. The shivery sensation sends my blood pumping south.

"Are there any Band-Aids around?" Her voice seems to come from far away and I sway on my feet.

"Yeah." I open my eyes and stare at the beat-up white metal cabinet next to the sink. "There should be something in there."

"Go shower." She presses both of her palms against my chest and lightly pushes. "I'll take care of the cut when you're done."

She turns toward the cabinet. The metal door creaks as she pries it open. Standing on her tiptoes, she reaches for the top shelf. The movement lifts her shirt, baring the skin above the waistband of her jeans.

I squeeze my eyes shut.

"First-aid kit," she announces. Something metallic clanks against the porcelain.

"Can't tell you if there's anything in it." I open my eyes. She's at the sink, head bowed, fiddling with the rusty lock on the kit. Her long, shiny brown ponytail reaches the small of her back. The urge to wrap it around my fist seizes me.

Don't you fucking dare.

"It's stuck," she mutters.

I'd help her open it, but I need to put some distance between us for a few minutes. Get myself under control.

"I trust you to figure it out." Without taking my eyes off of her, I reach into my open locker and grab my towel. "I'll be back."

"I'll be waiting," she answers.

I'm more eager to get back to her than I have any right to be.

Molly

I wish I had the type of confidence the ring girls have. One of them would strip down and follow Griff into the shower. Or surprise him once he'd been in there for a few minutes. If I were braver, I'd pull the curtain back, startling him, and then he'd realize I was standing there wearing nothing but a smile and offer to wash my back.

That's how the fantasy plays in my head.

In reality, the water starts up, the curtain makes that screechy sound as it's pushed aside to accommodate Griff's big body, and I stay right where I am. Playing with a bunch of Band-Aids that look like they've been sitting in this rusty tin since before I was born.

Is Griff using body wash or a plain bar of soap?

I couldn't get naked in front of him, could I? *No.* He'd probably laugh in my face, throw a towel at me, and tell me to cover myself.

A tap on my shoulder startles me so hard, I jump, throwing little yellowing packets of Band-Aids everywhere.

I've been so lost in figuring out the mechanics of soaping up my brother's best friend, I never heard the shower stop.

"What'd you scare me for?" I scoop the scattered Band-Aids out of the sink.

He's wearing a lopsided grin and not much else. Nothing but a thin red towel wrapped around his hips hides his skin from my curious eyes.

I've been witness to Griff shirtless plenty of times, but this whole-body tingling reaction is a new development.

I've known him since I was little. What feels like my whole life, really. He's my favorite person in the world besides my brother.

He's also a man now. Nothing like the boys I go to school with. He's cut and muscled in all the right places. Ruthless perfection honed from years of fighting, hard work, and pure survival.

The innocent crush on him I've nursed since kindergarten flipped to inappropriate a few years ago. Unfortunately, he still only sees me as a little sister. Probably always will.

This attraction is plain cruel. Even if he wanted me, I couldn't have him. He'd never do anything to piss off my brother. And Remy's made it clear many, many times his friends aren't allowed to date me.

"Didn't mean to startle you," Griff says, and I cringe. Was it obvious that I was checking out his body? "What were you thinking about?"

"N-nothing," I stammer. My traitorous cheeks heat, blushing hard enough to advertise *exactly* what smutty daydreams were dancing around in my head.

He squints, studying my face. "You sure *you* didn't take a hit to the head tonight?"

"No." I wave my hand at him. "Come here so I can fix your cut."

He steps closer to the small sink in the corner where I set out cotton pads and antiseptic liquid. Gently, I dab the cotton over his wound. A small hiss escapes him.

"Sorry," I whisper, hating that I'm hurting him even a little.

"It's okay." His low voice flows over my skin leaving goose bumps in its wake. I smooth some antibiotic ointment over the cut and seal it with a small Band-Aid. "All better. I think the bruise you're going to end up with will be worse than the cut."

"Won't be the first." He squints at me, a teasing smile playing at the corners of his mouth. "Or the last, I'm sure."

I can't laugh. Not when I hate that he loves risking bodily harm in these stupid underground fights all the time. My brother, too. And if it's not fighting, it's riding motorcycles or racing cars. It's like the two of them are bonded by a common death wish. Fear vibrates at a low, constant hum in the back of my mind that one of these days one of them will get seriously hurt.

Maybe sensing the change in my mood, Griff curls his hand around mine and playfully swings it side to side. "Thank you, Nurse Molly."

His gaze travels down my body. Mine takes the opportunity to do the same to him again.

I suck in a quick breath. "Oh." It's even harder to tear my gaze away this time, but I do.

"I'll, uh, let you get dressed," I mumble. It's a big room. Maybe there's a locker I can shut myself inside of to hide from all these weird tingly feelings.

"Wait." He reaches out, wrapping his hand around my arm. "Sit here." Leaning sideways, he swipes his clothes off the bench. "I'll be right back."

As I lower myself to the bench, my arm brushes against his stomach. His warm, flat, hard stomach. My hand whispers over the knot in his towel. So close. I could easily flick it open. My finger twitches against the terry cloth.

Why'd I do that?

My face flames even hotter.

Griff grabs my rogue hand and our eyes meet.

"S-sorry," I mumble, too embarrassed to hold his gaze.

"What are you doing, Muffin?" His low voice prickles over my skin.

Oh, I love when he calls me that.

"I didn't mean to," I lie. "It was an accident."

He groans.

"What?" My eyes snap to his.

"Nothing."

His mouth says *nothing*, but his eyes tell a different story, staring at me with an intensity that sets my entire body humming. His clothes fall to the floor in a whispered rustle. He curves his arm around my waist and presses his hand into the small of my back, pushing me forward against his hard body.

Holy...wow...oh my. What's happening?

My heart races. He stares into my eyes for a few seconds, like he's fascinated or surprised. He dips in closer, his fresh, soapy scent surrounding me. I stare at his mouth, his lips that look soft and kissable up close. Wait, *why* is he so close? He leans in and dusts a gentle kiss across my lips. Sparks dance and race over my skin.

Knees weak, heart pounding, I rest my palms against his chest and melt into him. He groans and brushes his knuckles under my chin, tipping my head back. His second kiss is slower and sweeter. My arms slip around his neck and his grip on my waist loosens, sliding down to pin me against his body, our connection so firm and complete.

I'm kissing Griffin "Stonewall" Royal. My brother's best friend. The love of my life. The only boy I've ever wanted to kiss.

No, this is more than kissing. We're exploring each other's mouths. Slowly, lazily, our tongues meet and slide against each other's. It's sweet, a little sloppy, gentle but passionate. His hand dives into my hair, cradling my head, deepening our kiss. The wonder fades, replaced by a jolt of electricity shocking my nerve endings.

Could I flick his towel off and find out what's poking against my hip? Would he show me how he likes to be touched? Would I really strip off all my clothes for Griff here in the locker room?

A needy moan eases out of me. I tighten my arms around his neck, raising myself higher on my tiptoes, close to climbing him like a tree.

Griff's body stiffens.

He pulls back, trying to break our kiss, but I cling to him, not ready for this to end. Not when I've wanted him to kiss me for so long. To look at me as something other than his best friend's little sister.

He stares down at me for a moment, his gaze lingering on my mouth.

"Griff?" I whisper.

"We can't do this."

No. No. No. We were doing fine.

Am I a bad kisser?

Would he rather be kissing someone else? Like the girl who so brazenly approached him earlier?

That's it, isn't it? By showing up here tonight, I stopped him from hooking up with one of the girls who love to bang the winner after a fight. Ring bunnies. Older than me. A lot more experienced. They'd know exactly how to keep Griff's interest.

My legs wobble. Humiliation washes over me and I try to wriggle away, but his hold on me tightens. I lean up, aiming to kiss him again, but he jerks his head to the side and I graze his jawline instead.

"Griff?"

He finally releases me and places a soft, passion-less kiss to the top of my head. The kind of kiss you'd give a kid after they skinned their knee or something.

Ouch.

Griff

Kissing Molly was something I swore I wouldn't do. Not yet.

I'm harder than steel. So close to taking what's mine.

Against my better judgment, I bury my hand in her hair, tilting her head back for another kiss. I have to taste her one more time before I stop this craziness. Her eyes widen in surprise. A soft, hesitant smile curves her lips for a second before I seal my mouth against hers.

This second kiss, I take my time, slowly teasing and tasting. She's as sweet as I always suspected but also spicy. Cherry lip balm and cinnamon candy.

Tearing my mouth away, I stare down at her kiss-swollen lips and dazed eyes. I did that.

Remy's going to kill me.

Fuck it. I go in for one more kiss, spearing my fingers through her hair and cupping the back of her head. One more kiss to remember how good she feels, to keep with me through the next few months. Her blue eyes flash with desire. She wants this as much as I do. I'd have to be blind and stupid not to know how she feels. Messing with her is a damn shitty thing to do, but I can't help myself.

Her soft fingers trace over my shoulders and down my arms, brush against my chest, reminding me a thin piece of terry cloth is all that stands between my cock and Molly. We could lose control any second. I don't want to fuck Molly in the locker room like she's some ring bunny I don't give two shits about. I want our first time to be special. I want her to *feel* how important she is to me.

"Molly, we have to stop." What I *want* to do is take her to my bed and learn every inch of her curvy little body. Figure out what sets her on fire. But I don't have that right. Not yet.

"No, we don't," she says with a firm authority I'm not used to hearing from her.

"Not here."

Not *anywhere*. What the hell am I saying?

Don't encourage this madness.

We can't.

I take both of her hands in one of mine and press another quick kiss to her forehead before releasing her. I grab my clothes off the floor and hurry the fuck away to get dressed and regain control of myself.

"Stay there," I call over my shoulder as I head for the showers.

Behind the curtain, I bang my head against the wet tile, willing my erection to go away.

I shouldn't be this worked up for my best friend's little sister.

My plan's solid and I need to stick to it. Slowly, I've been trying to show Remy I'm serious. Cleaning up my act. Holding down a decent job. Saving some money. Turning down every ring bunny who wants to jump on my dick. Subtly proving to him I'll treat his baby sister right and can take care of her the way she deserves.

She's eighteen in a few months. Graduating from high school. Headed to college in the fall. That's when I plan to claim my girl. By then, either Remy will accept us as a couple, or he won't.

I don't want to lose my best friend, but I refuse to lose Molly.

Molly

CHAPTER TWO

Molly

My whole body trembles while I wait for Griff to return.

We kissed.

He kissed *me*. Kissed me like he actually wants me the way I want him. Maybe I'm more to him than the annoying kid sister he feels obligated to look after because my brother is his best friend. Is that really possible?

"Ready to go?" he asks, striding into the locker room, fully dressed.

"Uh, sure."

He frowns at me. "How'd you find your way here tonight?"

"A friend dropped me off."

He growls out an unhappy sound that twists my belly. "You came in alone, though. You need to be more careful." His hand wraps around mine, and he tugs me toward the locker room door.

We're not even going to discuss what just happened? Or do it again?

"Wait, Griff. What was that?" I gesture toward the locker—the place where I want to build a shrine to our first kiss.

He lifts his eyebrows. "What was what?"

My heart sinks. He's planning to pretend the biggest moment in my life never happened.

But I'm *not* letting him get away with it. "Our kiss? If your memory's this bad at twenty-two, maybe it's time you start taking some vitamins."

He blinks. Slowly, the corners of his mouth turn up. Then he uses his bigger body to push me backward. My butt bumps into the tiled wall and I press my back to it. Griff slaps his palms to the wall on either side of my face, leaning down over me and staring into my eyes. "My memory is *fine*, Molly. I couldn't forget that kiss. Even if I wanted to."

"Then why are you pretending it didn't happen?"

"I'm not." His eyes close briefly. "But you just said the reason why we can't do it again...or anything else."

My body perks up at the *anything else*. Does he want to do more with me? I want to do a whole lot more with him.

"Wait." I frown. "What did I say?" *So I don't say it again.*

"I'm twenty-two and you're seventeen."

"So?"

"Molly," he says in that let's-be-reasonable tone that makes me want to stomp my feet, which I definitely won't do, because it would kind of prove his point.

"What does it matter?" Besides, he's wrong. "I'm going to be eighteen soon."

"It might not be a big deal when we're older. But now, it's a... problem." He tilts his head. "You want me to get in trouble?"

The thought of Griff being arrested or something because of me is enough to sober me up. He's been in trouble before. The months he spent in juvie a few years ago were some of the worst of my life. I sent him letters almost every day and eagerly waited for his responses—short letters that never said much about what he was going through but that I still have saved in my box of treasures. I'd die before I caused problems for him. "No. Never. I'm sorry."

He runs the back of his hand over my cheek. "Don't be sorry."

His forehead drops against mine, our noses lightly touching, and he stares into my eyes. "Don't ever be sorry. I'm not."

He's so close. I want to kiss him. Want him to take me in his arms again. I want to promise him I'll never tell anyone. What do a few more months matter anyway? It's not like I'll magically turn into a different person the moment I turn eighteen.

For a second, I think he's going to say *fuck it* and sweep me off my feet.

"Come on. It's late. Let's get you home before Remy loses his shit."

I groan, but take his hand. He's right. My brother's a tightly wound ball of protectiveness and rage. Three years ago, he stopped by and found our father taking his frustrations out on me with a belt. Remy packed up my stuff and moved me into his house that night, right after he laid our father out with a violent barrage of punches and the threat of more if he ever came near me again. Every day I live in fear Social Services will show up on our doorstep and try to force me to go back to my father's house. Although, the closer my eighteenth birthday gets, the more my worry eases.

Maybe now there's something else to look forward to after I turn eighteen.

Remy suffered so much guilt about leaving me alone with our father that he's a hypervigilant pain in my ass in the watching-over-me department. As his best friend, Griff also looks out for me. As much as I resent it, I understand why Griff thinks dating me would be betraying my brother. I even love him for his loyalty to Remy. I'd never want to be the cause of trouble between them.

Outside, we stop at Griff's shiny black 1970 Chevelle. I run my fingers over the purple-and-red pinstripes that I helped Griff pick out when he restored the car a few years ago. He even hands me the keys at his friend's racetrack sometimes.

He opens the door, and our bodies bump together. I reach up and touch his cheek. He turns his head and brushes his lips against my fingertips, sending a soft, shivery sensation to every part of my body.

"What are you doing, Molly?" he asks in a hoarse voice.

"How does your forehead feel?"

"Better."

"Good."

He holds my gaze for a few seconds before tipping his head toward the open door. "Come on. Get in."

I slide into the passenger seat and turn to admire the clean, black interior. My gaze lands on the shiny baseball bat Griff keeps behind the front seat—just in case. Griff's door opens.

"Still keep the bat back there?" I ask.

"Never know what might go down at these things." He shrugs as if having to beat someone with a bat to protect yourself isn't completely terrifying.

Once we're on the highway, Griff reaches over and takes my hand. My belly dips and swirls from the simple, sweet contact. It's romantic, a gesture from one of my favorite books. So many unspoken feelings bubble up inside me from holding his hand while he expertly guides the car along the roads that will eventually lead to my house. My only plan tonight was to see Griff in the ring. Never in my wildest fantasies did I imagine we'd kiss or end up holding hands.

"So, who drove you to Ironworks tonight?" he asks, casting a quick, questioning glance at me.

I shift away, unlinking our hands. "A friend."

"Who?"

"Uh, Wade? He's a friend from school."

A deathly sort of silence descends over us. Griff grips the steering wheel tight with both hands. "You were alone in some guy's car all the way out here?"

"I'm alone in *your* car right now," I point out.

"Molly." Disappointment bleeds into his voice.

"He's just a friend."

"That's not what I'm worried about."

I study him closely. The tight set of his jaw suggests that's exactly what he's worried about. I snort with annoyance. After all the ring bunnies and girls I've watched flirt with him at the racetrack over the years, he's worried about one of my classmates.

He glances over again. "How'd he even know where the fight was?"

I shrug. "His older brother knows someone who was in a match."

"Who?"

"I don't know, Griff." I huff and cross my arms over my chest. "I didn't ask a bunch of questions. I just knew *you* were going to be there, and I wanted to see *you*." I shrug. "So I asked if I could catch a ride, and he said yes."

The corners of his mouth turn down, like he's rolling something unpleasant around on his tongue.

"What'd you think of the place?" he asks, apparently deciding to let the Wade thing drop.

"Honestly?" My nose wrinkles. "It just looked like an old, dirty warehouse. I like The Castle better." The Castle's an old, rundown building too—the juvenile detention center Griff and a few of his friends were sent to years ago. Griff and my brother bought it when it went to auction and turned it into their own personal fight club. It's in the middle of nowhere, surrounded by overgrown wilderness. "Even though it's in rough shape, it has that whole romantic, gothic thing going for it."

"Romantic." Griff snorts, a dark edge creeping into the space around us. "Nothing romantic has ever happened there."

"Then why buy it if it has such bad memories attached?" I ask.

"I don't want anyone else having access to my ghosts."

I'm not sure what to make of that. Griff's never spoken much about the time he was incarcerated, even in his short letters. "But that's how you met Vapor and Eraser, right? So something good came out of being there."

One corner of his mouth slowly slides up. "That's true." He glances over at me. "Thanks."

Pleased I brought him back from whatever dark ledge of memories he was about to tumble off, I reach over and rest my hand on his leg. He sighs, clutches the steering wheel tight, then finally rests one hand over mine, giving it a gentle squeeze.

All too soon, he pulls up in front of the old Victorian home that once belonged to my grandparents.

"Tell your brother I'll be over in the morning to help him work on the railing." He nods toward the house.

My grandfather left the big, rambling home to Remy, and my brother's put a lot of work into fixing up the place—even more so after I moved in. Something's always breaking or needing to be repaired. But it holds warm memories of our grandparents, so I understand why Remy refuses to sell it.

"You know, if you're going to keep putting in so much work here, you should probably take Remy up on his offer to move into the guest room."

Griff releases my hand and stares out the window. "That's a bad idea."

"Why?"

As if it pains him, he tears his gaze from the house and focuses on my face. "I can barely keep my hands off you now. Under the same roof? It'd be asking for trouble."

"Oh," I whisper, completely shocked by his admission.

Guilt settles on my shoulders. One of the reasons my brother keeps asking Griff to move in is to help him pay the bills. I've offered to take more hours at the grocery store where I work two days a week, but Remy won't allow it. I'm sure it would make things easier on Remy to have a roommate to split the living expenses with. But because of me, the two people I care about most in the world have to struggle—and participate in dangerous, underground fights. Can't forget that part.

"I'd behave myself," I say.

The corners of Griff's mouth turn up and he lets out a soft snort. "I know you would, Muffin. It's *me* I'm worried about."

Oh, really?

"Why?" I ask innocently. "Are you worried I'd sneak into your room late at night and tempt you into doing something *inappropriate*?"

"What?" He frowns. "No."

"Are you *suuuure*?" I tease, enjoying watching *him* squirm for once.

"Yes, I'm sure."

"Really? You wouldn't like me waking you up in the middle of the night?" I unbuckle my seat belt, place my hand on Griff's shoulder, and twist my body until I'm straddling his lap. In my head it was a smooth, sexy move. In reality, it's awkward, and my knee slams into the door handle. He reaches down and eases the seat back but it's already as far as it will go. My butt rests on the steering wheel, and Griff wedges his hands between my cheeks and the wheel.

"What're you doing?" he asks, amusement coloring his words.

Somehow, I reach down inside myself and pull up some bravery. Maybe our earlier kiss altered my brain chemistry or unlocked my uninhibited side. "Giving you something to think about later tonight when you're all alone in your apartment." I swoop in and press my lips to his.

It's as if the touch of my lips snaps his self-control. He inhales sharply. His arms band around me, erasing the last few inches between our bodies. The tension in my legs melts away, and I realize my crotch is resting on his erection.

Oh, my. That feels *good*.

I move my hips, tentative at first. Experimenting. Griff groans, the sound vibrating straight to my core. I rock against him again and again. The sensation is both a tease and a promise of something more to come—if he'll let me.

"Ah," I sigh. "Oh."

"Molly?" His hands grip my hips to stop me, and I let out a cry.

"Don't." Oh God, if he stops me, I'll die. I need more. Something much, much more.

"Molly," he whispers. His hands leave my hips, sneaking under my shirt, grazing my skin.

"Griff, please," I whimper.

"What do you need?"

"Uh, I don't know...*more*."

His hands drop back to my hips, holding me down while he slowly grinds up against me.

"Oh. That. Right there." I wiggle against him, desperate for harder contact. "Please, Griffin."

Our harsh breaths fill the car.

"Say my name again," he begs.

Sweat beads along my forehead.

Hot, so hot.

"Griffin." So much agonizing need passes between us. Everything's so heightened and intense. My hands curl over his shoulders, digging in while a shot of white-hot pleasure rolls over me.

"Oh my. Wow." I moan and collapse against him, breathing heavily.

What was that?

My heart's hammering so hard I'm sure Griff can feel it.

"Griff?" I lift my head, staring into his wide eyes. "Was that...?"

His gaze roams over my face and he squeezes me tighter. "That ever happen to you before?"

"No. Did I...? Was that...?" My cheeks burn. Did I just grind myself into his lap until I...*orgasmed*?

His lips slide into a lazy smile. "Yeah, I think so."

Absolutely mortified, I bury my face against his neck and mumble, "I'm sorry."

"Why?" he asks, his voice low and strained. "You're beautiful. That was the hottest thing I've ever seen."

What crap. I pick my head up and stare at him. "Don't tease me."

"I'm not." He places a quick kiss on the tip of my nose. "Feeling pretty damn proud of myself for making you come while we're both fully clothed."

"Really?"

"Yeah, really." His lips quirk into an irresistible grin. "You make me feel like I finally earned my last name."

It's sweet but also somewhat sad in a way I can't express. I trace my finger over his bottom lip. "You've always been royalty in my eyes."

His hand cups the back of my head, pulling me closer for a long, slow kiss. "I'm glad I was the first one to give you that," he murmurs against my lips. "Want to give you all your firsts." After a few beats he adds, "And lasts." It's spoken so low, the words are a whisper over my skin.

His phone rings, the light from it brightening the interior of the darkened car.

Holy shit. We're sitting on the road in front of my house with my brother probably right inside.

"Wow. I forgot where we were," I mumble, untangling myself from Griff's lap and dropping into my seat.

"Yeah, me too." He eyes his phone but doesn't answer it. My gaze slides to the screen. *Ruthless.*

"Shoot," I whisper. "Tell me Remy's just calling to see how the fight went? He always checks in with you, right?"

He hits the *decline* button, and silence descends over us.

"We can't do that again, Molly," he says in a stern tone, so unlike the sweet way he just spoke to me.

Tears prickle my eyes. His strong, firm hand grips my chin, turning me to face him. "Please, don't make this harder. We just need to wait a little longer."

"Oh." He's not mad at me. I tilt my head, rubbing my cheek over his hand. "Do you care about me?"

"God, Molly. You know I do."

"Okay. I can wait."

The corners of his mouth tip up. Before he responds, his phone rings. It's Remy. *Again.*

We both stare at the screen.

"I don't think he's calling to see if I won. He's probably looking for you."

As soon as he says it, *my* phone rings.

My heart pounds as I also tap the red *decline* button. "Do you think he saw—"

Griff snorts. "No. If he saw what we just did, he'd be dragging me out of the car and beating the shit out of me by now."

"Oh," I say, at first relieved and then realizing what Griff actually said. "He better not touch you. What you and I do together is none of his business."

Griff nods even though his jaw locks as if he disagrees.

Griff

Maybe the kick I took to the head tonight was harder than I thought.

What was I thinking? Making out with Molly in front of her house where Remy could have easily walked outside and gotten an eyeful? No doubt in my mind he would've done exactly what I'd described to Molly.

Molly.

As soon as she bounds up the front steps and pushes inside the house, I throw my head back and squeeze my eyes shut.

Her cherry scent clings to my skin and the interior of my car. My cock's aching and my balls are probably bluer than a July sky. But it was totally worth it to see that look of wonder on her face. Her joy. To know I was the first one to give her that pleasure.

I wanted to give her so much more.

Fuck.

I'm so motherfucking fucked. Not twenty minutes after I swore I wouldn't kiss her again, I let her crawl in my lap and dry hump my dick until she came.

And it was fucking amazing. Better than any other sexual experience in my *life.*

When I'm finally calm enough to drive home, I turn my car around and head toward my apartment. I may have told Molly several white lies. I don't want to move into Remy's place, because once she turns eighteen, I want to be able to spend time alone with her without her brother in our business.

Does that make me a creep? Maybe.

A shitty friend? Definitely.

CHAPTER THREE

GRIFF

You'd think my aching balls would keep me awake on the short drive home, but fatigue and bone-weariness follow me to the small brick apartment complex.

I park in my regular spot and stop to check on my Harley at the edge of the parking lot. I really should start storing it at Remy's. Too tired to check anything major, I make sure it's in one piece, then head into the building. My mother's place is on the bottom floor, and I stop there first.

I knock softly—not that she's probably even lucid enough to comprehend what the sound means. I press my ear to the door. Nothing but the faint hum of a fan reaches me. A cold trickle of fear slides down my back as I use my key to open the door.

It's only a matter of time before I walk in and find her dead.

"Ma?" I call out as I step over the threshold. The fan whirring in the corner does nothing to clear the stuffy air. The apartment reeks of sweat, desperation, and chemicals with a sickly undertone of puke.

A blue-and-white glow flickers from the television, illuminating the room. I glance at the screen. *Intervention*. The sound's off, so none of the messages can sink into her drug-addled brain. Pity.

I'd laugh at the irony of how much my mother loves watching desperate families trying to get their loved ones sober if it didn't piss me off and depress the hell out of me all at once.

A pile of worn blankets are heaped on the brown, nubby couch. Then the pile moves. A pale, white arm flops out from underneath. My mother's face comes into view. She moans, sighs, and licks her chapped lips.

My mother was beautiful once, on the outside. Now, she's more like a husk or outer shell of a person. Her face matches the ugliness that's been inside of her since I was little.

"Why are you on the couch?" Why do I bother? Doubt she's even aware I'm here.

Her arm slides off the cushion, landing on the dirty carpet with a thud. A needle, still stuck in her skin, pokes from the crook of her elbow. A trickle of dried blood trails to her wrist.

My stomach rolls, bile burning the back of my throat. Taking a beating in the ring doesn't bother me. Needles and the destruction they cause do. Every damn time.

Disgusted, I pull the needle free and try not to retch. I toss it in the small trash can next to the couch. When she started, it was only popping a few harmless pills. Then snorting oxy but now, she's injecting herself as often as possible.

"Griff?" she slurs. "That you?"

"It's me."

"Sorry, baby. I had to."

I don't even bother asking. I just don't care anymore. "You pay your rent?" I ask instead.

"No. Lemme borrow some money?" she asks without opening her eyes.

I pull the wad of cash I'd earned from the fight out of my pocket and stare at it.

"Where's Larry?" Her loser boyfriend usually disappears around the first of the month, then shows up a few days later. Since he tends to keep my mom's habit in check, I tolerate his presence. It's nice to let someone else deal with her crazy for a change.

"Out," she mumbles. "Leave the cash on the table."

Yeah, that's not happening.

I plod into the kitchen, the shadow of sleep following close behind. Since she never eats, the kitchen's semi-clean. I find a glass, fill it with water, and bring it into the living room.

"Sit up and drink this." I hold out the glass.

She groans and squeezes her eyes tighter but finally peels herself into an upright position.

"Thanks," she whispers, taking the glass and tipping it to her lips.

"You eat anything today?"

Her bony shoulders jerk up. "Some eggs."

"Good."

"Did you win tonight?" she rasps, handing the glass back to me.

"Yeah." The fight was nothing. The real win for me was Molly. Finally letting her know how I feel. The warmth from being with her earlier is the only thing helping me cling to sanity now.

"Remy fight too?" she asks.

"No."

She lets out a muted hum that I don't care to interpret. The way she fawns over Remy became awkward years ago. While he'd never insult my mother to my face, he keeps his distance.

It's the disdain my mother's shown Molly that made me lose all respect for the woman who brought me into the world. When Molly's mom died, I'd thought maybe my mother would display a little compassion. It's not like I expected her to play new mom to Molly or anything. Just show some kindness to a motherless little girl. But no. If anything, Mom was even nastier than she had been before. I can't even blame the drugs. Molly's mom died years before my mother discovered the joys of opiates.

I glance at the clock. It's only getting later. "You good?" I ask.

"You leave the money on the table?" My mother flops her hand in the direction of the dining room.

"Sure." After rinsing out the glass, I search through the drawers until I find an envelope.

"Later," I call as I hurry out of the apartment. My mother groans but if she has any actual words for me, I can't make them out.

I jog to the basement and knock on the door of the only apartment down here. It's late, but the television's blaring, so the landlord has to be awake.

"You know what time it is?" he shouts from inside.

While I'm waiting, I stuff enough cash to cover my mom's rent into the envelope. I already paid my own a few days ago.

Seconds later, the door flings open, and Mr. Porter stands there in a blue bathrobe, white T-shirt, and boxer shorts. "Oh. Hey, Griff. Everything all right?"

"Yeah. Sorry to bug you so late." I hold out the envelope of cash. "Wanted to drop this off to cover Mom's rent."

He hesitates before accepting the money. "She's cuttin' it close, Griff." He waves me inside. "Come in. I'll write you a receipt."

"Thanks." I stand next to the open door while he crosses the room and picks up a small, spiral-bound ledger off of a bookshelf. He doesn't bother counting the money—just scribbles out a receipt, tears it out of the book, and returns to me.

"You covering her place and yours now?" He doesn't ask it in an unkind way—more like concern that he might have to fill a vacant apartment, or two, one day soon.

"Does it matter?" I ask.

He pushes the receipt toward me. "I guess not." His gaze narrows on my face and he taps his own forehead. "You all right?"

I reach up, my fingers flittering over the cut Molly bandaged for me. "Yeah. Took a kick to the head in the ring tonight."

"Griff..." He shakes his head but doesn't finish the thought.

I grab the receipt. "We good?"

"Yup." He runs his gaze over me again. "Get some rest, kid."

"Planning to. Got a long ride tomorrow."

He shakes his head but a smile twitches at the corners of his mouth. "God bless ya. To be young again and have your energy."

There doesn't seem to be a polite response to that, so I chuckle, thank him, then head upstairs to my own apartment.

As soon as I'm alone in my room, my thoughts return to Molly. Then Remy. How the fuck am I supposed to spend the day with him tomorrow without spilling my guts? He's my best friend. Like a brother to me for more than half my life. We've never kept secrets from each other.

But I guess I'll have to start now.

Molly

CHAPTER FOUR

GRIFF

Griff, nine years old.
Johnsonville Elementary School.

A ferocious roar rattled my stomach as I slid my tray toward the lunch lady.

Her uncaring eyes snaked over my bony shoulders. Contempt curled her sticky-looking orange lips. "One dollar."

The stiff denim of my too-tight pants scratched my knuckles as I jammed my hand in the front pocket. There was nothing but a nickel, a pebble, and a ball of lint at the bottom, but maybe the money would appear like magic.

With a hesitant smile on my shaky lips, I held out the nickel.

"Not today, Royal." She scoffed as she said my last name. "You still owe two dollars and fifteen cents in fines from last week."

As if it wanted to consume the lump of meat covered in red sauce before it was snatched away, my stomach lurched.

"Royal." Someone snickered behind me. "More like *beggar*."

I'd pleaded with my mother to call the school and pay my lunch bill. Her answer had been to swear no one would let such a "cute face" starve.

"Get out of the way, beggar!" someone else yelled.

Heat crawled over my skin.

"Shut the fuck up," a rougher voice said.

"Hey!"

"Watch your mouth, Holt!" another lunch lady behind the counter shouted.

Too embarrassed to turn around and check out the scuffle, I stood frozen. Maybe I could sneak away with my lunch tray without Orange Lips noticing?

A firm shoulder brushed against mine. I flinched and dared to peek at the intruder.

"Proud of yourself for lettin' a kid starve over two bucks?" My defender sneered at the lunch lady.

He was tall, wiry, and brimming with energy and anger. A fifth grader, maybe. I hadn't been at the school long enough to know everyone yet.

"It's the rules," she answered with an indifferent shrug.

He slammed his tray down in front of mine. Behind us, the crowd went silent.

"Here." Coins jingled and clattered.

I glanced at the kid again. The corner of his mouth slid up and he winked at me. My gaze dropped to the pile of change in his palm as he slowly counted out enough to cover our meals *and* my fines.

"There. That should be enough." He smirked at the lunch lady.

"Thank you, *Remington*." She swept the change off the counter, deliberately examining each dime and nickel as she dropped them into her drawer. "Now, beat it. You're holding up the line."

"Come on." Remington nudged me with his elbow and jerked his head toward the cafeteria.

Mortified, but grateful and curious, I grabbed my tray and followed. "Thank you for doing that," I said as I fell in step with him.

"It's bullshit." He lifted his tray. "Dogs shouldn't eat this garbage. Kids shouldn't have to *pay* for it."

"Uh, yeah." I hurried to keep up with him.

He banged his tray onto a table in the back of the large, crowded cafeteria, not bothering to ask the other kids if we could join them. Everyone seemed afraid of his presence, either offering a quick, mumbled greeting or looking away. Remington didn't seem to notice or care.

"How long you been here?" he asked, stabbing his plastic spork into the center of the glob of meat on his plate.

"Couple weeks." Switching schools mid-year had sucked.

"Is Royal your first or last name?"

"Last. It's Griffin...everyone calls me Griff, though."

He nodded once. "What grade, Griff?"

"Fourth."

"Sparks or Sheely?"

"Sheely."

He grunted. "She's a witch. Her grandson's in my class. Gonna kick his ass one of these days."

"What grade are you in, Remington?"

He flicked his ice-blue gaze at me. "Remy. No one calls me Remington except my asshole dad." He jerked his head toward the lunch line. "And the crusty lunch ladies."

I snorted and took a bite of my sauce-covered...meat. "Why's your dad an asshole?"

His icy stare settled on me again. "Why can't your parents pay your lunch tab?"

That shut me up.

My stomach rumbled, so I held my nose and choked down the gross food while Remy gave me tips about the school and neighborhood. Turned out, we didn't actually live that far from each other.

After I'd finished my last bite, Remy slapped the table. "Let's go."

I glanced at the wide, metal doors that led to the playground. "Outside?"

He followed my gaze with a blank expression. "Later. I want to check on my sister first."

"You've got a sister?"

"Yup. She's in kindergarten. Downstairs. Come meet her."

It wasn't like I had a burning desire to have kick balls thrown at me or slice open my leg on the rusty slide, so I shrugged. "Okay."

We grabbed our trays and dropped them off at the wide, metal window, then I followed Remy into the hallway.

"No one's gonna stop us?" I whispered.

He snorted. "No."

We jogged down the steps, our sneakers slapping against the concrete.

Bright, childish artwork lined the rancid mint-green walls. The window of the first door we encountered was dark. Remy peered in, then kept walking toward the library. I'd only been there once so far.

Loud chatter echoed from inside. Remy grinned and hurried to the open door. He peered inside and waved.

"Remmmieee." A little tornado dressed in baggy green corduroy overalls and a long-sleeved blue shirt with little cars all over it whirled out of the library and wrapped her arms around Remy's waist.

"Reading anything good?" he asked, smiling down at her as they moved into the hallway.

"Not yet."

Remy curled his arm around her shoulders and steered her toward me. "Molly, this is my new friend Griff."

"Hi, Gwith." The little girl wiggled her fingers at me and flashed a big, gap-toothed grin.

Tiny, navy blue Converse sneakers peeked out from under the hem of the too-long overalls. She was the cutest little kid I'd ever laid eyes on. So of course, I immediately tugged on the dark green bow someone had carefully stuck in her wild mass of dark brown waves. "Hey, Molly. Who put this dumb bow on your head?" I teased.

Molly pouted. Her big blue eyes filled with tears that made me want to hurl the mystery meat I'd just consumed into the nearest trash can.

Remy smacked my hand away. "Our mom fixed her hair."

The deathly way he said it made it clear that *that* topic was off-limits.

"Sorry," I mumbled, then caught Molly's eye. "I'm just kidding. It's cute."

"Fank you." She sniffled and touched the bow again.

Man, I felt like shit. I didn't know what to say to make it better.

She jammed her hands in her pockets and lifted her chin, somehow making her look like a three-foot-tall thirty-year-old. "What you doin'?" she asked her brother.

"Checking on *you*." Remy shoved his hands in his pockets, mirroring his sister's pose. "You eat lunch?"

"Yeff."

"Anyone bother you on the playground?"

"No." She turned her big blue eyes my way. "Are you walkin' home wiff us?"

I glanced at Remy who just drilled me with a hard stare, not giving me any hint of what answer he expected. It wasn't like I had anywhere else to go after school. My mom didn't care if I showed up or not. "Sure."

She beamed and something about her smile sent warmth and relief tumbling through me.

"Get back in there before someone comes looking for you." Remy jerked his chin toward the library and ruffled his hand over the top of her head.

She scurried away, throwing us a little wave over her shoulder.

"She's cute," I said to Remy as we started toward the stairs.

He chuckled. "Yeah. She's like the smallest kid in her class, though. The teacher treats her like a baby. And the other kids pick on her when they think no one's looking."

Well, at least now I understood why Remy sacrificed his playground time to check on his sister.

Recess was over by the time we returned to the lunchroom.

"Sorry if I cost you time on the monkey bars," Remy said with a smirk.

"Yeah, I'm not crying about it."

He slapped my shoulder. "Catch you out front after school?"

I nodded and we went our separate ways, lining up with our individual classes. Remy was in fifth grade. Like me, he was the biggest kid in his class. The other kids seemed to either try to joke around with him or avoid him altogether.

As I returned to my classmates, I realized most of them were now ignoring me too.

Fine by me.

School bored me for the rest of the day. The teacher covered stuff my old school had already done months ago. I doodled little race cars on the paper in front of me. Funny—that was what Molly had all over her shirt. Not rainbows and unicorns like most little girls. Was it a hand-me-down from Remy or did she pick it out herself?

After the final bell rang, I grabbed my stuff and hurried downstairs and out into the afternoon sunshine. My gaze ran over the herd of kids scattering away from the school like mice trying to escape a trap. No sign of Remy.

"Dere's Gwiff!" someone yelled behind me.

I turned and found Remy holding Molly's hand as he led her down the steps.

"You waited," Remy said. Had he been testing me?

"I said I would."

"We're down this way." He jerked his head to the left.

It wasn't the way I'd normally go home, but I could figure that out later.

Molly chattered about everything and anything the whole way

to their house. Once in a while, she'd pause long enough for Remy to ask her a question.

"Will Mommy be up?" Molly asked.

"I don't know," Remy answered in a tone way too solemn for someone all the other kids seemed to fear.

It didn't strike me as odd. My mom worked late nights and was rarely awake when I went to school in the morning. Sometimes she was still sleeping when I got home from school.

As we approached Remy's house, a frail-looking woman in a long blue-and-white-flowered dress waved to us from the porch.

"Mommy!" Molly shouted, trying to tug her hand out of Remy's grasp.

"Easy," Remy said in a low voice.

Molly nodded eagerly, then ran to her mother, giving the painfully thin woman a cautious embrace.

I almost opened my mouth to ask what was wrong with his mom but thankfully swallowed the question.

Mrs. Holt smiled warmly at me. "Who's your friend, Remy?"

"Dis is Gwiff!" Molly announced, jumping and pointing wildly in my direction.

"We met at lunch," Remy explained, leaving out the humiliating details. "Griff just moved here."

"Well, come in. Don't be shy." She shuffled slowly toward the front door, and Remy hurried to open it. "We've got snacks."

Inside, Remy's grandmother was in the kitchen, slicing apples. Molly had already pulled a stool close to the counter to help.

How often did Remy bring home strays? No one seemed surprised or bothered by my presence.

Mrs. Holt eventually left us to lie down, and her mother watched over us. Some time later, Remy's grandfather showed up too.

"Do your grandparents live with you?" I asked. The only grandparent I'd known had been my mom's father, and he'd lived with us for a while when I was younger. I still missed him.

"No." Remy shook his head. "They come over to help my mom while my dad's at work."

Again, I wanted to ask questions I shouldn't. Remy's warning stare forced me to swallow my curiosity.

Remy's grandmother invited me to stay for dinner, and I called my mom to make sure that was okay. When their dad came home, Molly and Remy barely acknowledged him. The man seemed perpetually annoyed, but he did help himself to dinner and a beer before disappearing out to the garage.

Nana Clary, as Remy's grandmother said I could call her, insisted I take a bag of apple crumb muffins when I left. I so badly wanted to eat them all on my way home, but I also wanted to save one for the morning.

"See you tomorrow," Remy said.

The Holt house was strange but also warm and welcoming. I didn't want to leave and return to the cold indifference of my own home.

It felt like I'd found a family.

Molley

Molly

I STILL CAN'T BELIEVE LAST NIGHT ACTUALLY happened.

Remy chewed me out for coming home so late without letting him know where I was, but I didn't even care. I was too high from my time with Griff.

Then the doubts settled in. Why'd I tell him I'd never done that before? Griff's used to all those confident, experienced girls that hang around the fights. He probably thinks I'm a weirdo now.

My spiral into the abyss of embarrassment is interrupted by the doorbell echoing through the house.

Griff.

It has to be him. He promised to be here to help Remy. Griff always keeps his word.

Should I hide in my room? Go see him? Can I play it cool? Or will my brother sense something's up? Can I even look Griff in the eye today?

I quickly grab a red tank top from my dresser drawer and slip it on. The straps are wide enough to hide my red, flowered bra but tight enough to be flattering, and the square neckline doesn't expose too much. I wiggle into a pair of dark jeans.

Nerves tie me into a knot again. I can't look at Griff in the daylight.

It'll be weird if I hide. Griff was just as into what we were doing last night as I was. I *have* to see him.

As if pulled by an invisible string, I grab a brush off my dresser and dash into the hallway. The need to see Griff outweighs any lingering embarrassment.

I hurry down the stairs, running the brush through my hair as I go. Ugh, I don't want Remy to open the door first.

Griff's in the living room, my brother nowhere in sight. I stop dead at the foot of the stairs.

"Morning, Muffin," he says, holding up a brown paper bag that has to contain at least one blueberry muffin from Busy Beans Cafe. He almost always brings me muffins on the weekends. The bag bulges with goodies, an irregular greasy stain seeping through the paper.

My mouth waters, and not from the plump muffins that will be bursting with sweet blueberries in Griff's hands. I rake my gaze over Griff's faded blue T-shirt and loose gray track pants. It doesn't matter what he wears though—he always looks good.

I toss the brush toward the couch and slow my steps. *Don't look too eager.* Chill. You've got this.

"Morning." My hoarse voice sounds like I just woke up. I take the bag from him and bounce it in the air a few times. "It's heavy."

"I brought extras for your brother and me." He raises an eyebrow. "If you're willing to share." A smile plays at the corners of his mouth.

His mouth. His lips. The memory of kissing him—no, *making out* with him last night slams into me, dampening my underwear. The rush of desire is quickly followed by a hot flush of shame.

Did I really grind on his lap until I came last night? In his car? Out on the street? What's the matter with me?

"Hey," he says in a low voice, crowding into my space. He brushes his knuckles over my cheek and stares into my eyes, concern darkening his expression. "What's that look for? You don't like muffins anymore?"

"No, it's not that."

His gaze continues searching my face, like he's trying to unlock my mind.

I swallow hard and slick my tongue over my dry lips. "Last night. I—"

"Griff, what the fuck, bro? You coming in or not?" Remy calls from the kitchen. At least I hope he's still in the kitchen. I don't think he'll appreciate Griff and I standing so close.

Touching each other.

I back away first, clutching the paper bag tight in my hands. Griff's forehead wrinkles in confusion. He looks so bewildered, I almost reach for him again.

"There you are," Remy says from behind me. "What are you two doing?"

Griff's mouth opens, but I spin around and flash a big smile at my brother. "Nothing. Griff brought muffins."

"No shit. He brings them every week." He narrows his eyes, staring at both of us.

Anxiety flutters in my chest. I can't stand Remy being suspicious of his best friend because of me. "Well, he brought enough for me to share today."

Remy focuses on Griff again. "Thanks."

"No problem," Griff finally says to my brother. About time he said something.

"Waitin' on your ass." Remy waves him outside. "Come on. We gotta leave for that party in a couple hours."

I trot into the kitchen where I drop the bag on the counter and set out three napkins. Remy made coffee earlier, so I pour some into a travel mug and add extra cream.

A few minutes later, Griff's heat whispers over my back and his arms snake around my middle, giving me a brief hug. "You all right?" he murmurs against my ear.

Tremors wrack my body. Why is Griff so determined to flirt

with danger this morning? My brother could walk into the kitchen any second now and catch us in this intimate moment. He'd lose it for sure.

But my body doesn't care about any of that. It wants to take Griff to a secluded location and do more of what we did last night. Preferably skin on skin.

Unless he thinks I'm a weirdo? Or too inexperienced. Why'd I have to admit I'd never done that before?

"Let's go!" Remy shouts from the front porch.

"Be right there!" Griff yells.

His hands grip my hips, and he turns me to face him. Only, I can't meet his eyes.

"Molly, look at me. What's wrong?" The distress in Griff's low voice undoes me and I lift my gaze.

Heat spreads over my cheeks and I can't answer his question. Instead I lift one shoulder. "Nothing."

I'm staring somewhere in the vicinity of his chest. He settles two fingers under my chin and tips my head back.

"Are you upset about last night?" he asks, quiet enough not to carry beyond the kitchen.

"No. Not really. It's not that." I force more conviction into my tone.

His forehead wrinkles in frustration. "What does that mean?" He cocks his head, listening for any sign that my brother might overhear us. "Talk to me."

"I can't." I wave my hand toward the front of the house. "Remy's right outside." I let out a long sigh. "It's nothing. I feel weird, that's all."

Griff doesn't laugh or tease me. "Molly, you have nothing to feel weird about. Last night was beautiful. Awesome. *Amazing*."

How does he just *know* what I was trying to say?

"Yeah," I mutter. "I'm sure the case of blue balls you went home with was so *awesome*."

He bursts out laughing. "I can't believe my little muffin said *blue balls*." He hooks his fingers in the belt loops of my jeans and yanks me closer. Leaning over, he brushes his lips against my ear. "Being with you was worth every second of pain. Thought about your beautiful face all night."

"You don't think I'm gross?"

His smile fades. "Absolutely not." He leans in again and lowers his voice. "When it's time, and you're ready, we're going to do that again. And a whole lot more."

My breath hitches. Tingles race through my veins. "What if I'm ready *now*?"

"You're not." He brushes his knuckles over my cheek, a pained expression twisting his face. "The fact that you're feeling this way the morning after means you're *not* ready. And I'm sorry. That's on me. That's my fault. I shouldn't have let things get so far."

Oh no. Oh, God. Panic thrums through my heart. That's not how I want him to feel at all. He'll never want to be with me if he thinks I can't handle it.

Vigorously shaking my head, I grab his hand. "That's not true. I'm sorry."

"Shh. I'm not going anywhere, Molly." His mouth quirks, and he gestures toward the front porch. "Well, I *am* going out there before your brother hunts me down, bags me, and nails me to the wall like a trophy."

Finally, I'm able to laugh.

Griff

"The fuck took you so long?" Remy asks as I return to the porch.

"Muffins from Muffin." I hand over one of the blueberry monsters and hold my cup in the air. "And coffee."

He grunts and swipes the muffin out of my hand, biting it almost in half and chomping on it like some sort of starved gremlin.

"Eat much, savage?" I joke.

"I'm starving." He squints at me. "What happened to your face?"

"Same face I was born with."

"Don't get cute."

I touch the small cut. I'd taken off the bandage and cleaned it again this morning. "It's nothing. Rico got a shot in last night."

"How? You're better than that clown every day of the week."

"Eh." I shrug. There's no way I'm confessing that Molly showed up at the fight. I know damn well *she* didn't tell him. "He's improved."

He crosses his arms and stares at me. Instead of running the tavern his grandparents left him, he should've been a drill sergeant. Still the same bossy bastard he was when we were kids. "I wish you hadn't gone without me. What if someone jumped you after the fight?"

"There were people I knew all over the place." *Hopefully none of them tattle to you about me rubbin' up on your sister.*

"Don't like you all the way over in Ironworks by yourself, though."

"Lost Kings hold that territory now. There's literally no other motorcycle club within a couple hundred miles. No one's gonna risk fucking with me."

"Why do you always have to argue?"

"Because you're not my mom."

He shakes his head, then flashes a dirty grin. "You hook up with Layla?"

"Fuck no."

"Why not?"

"Remy, I love you, but it's creeping me out that you're so concerned about where I stick my dick."

"Who's concerned, asshole? I just don't want to listen to you whine when it falls off from lack of use."

"Creeeeeepy," I sing in a fake, high voice. He cracks up laughing. I gesture to the pile of replacement wood for the porch railing in front of us. "Can we stop yapping and start nailing?"

"Yeah." His mouth twitches into another wicked grin. "That's what I was trying to talk to you about."

The only girl I'm interested in nailing is your sister.

No, he's definitely not prepared for that conversation. Neither am I. Not when he's got a nail gun, framing hammer, and several other possible instruments of death within arm's reach.

We work steadily for a few hours. When we're finished, Remy stands back and stares at the railing with his arms crossed over his chest. "Molly said she wants to paint it." He runs his hands through his hair. "The whole front porch looks like shit now."

"No," I say as patiently as possible. "It looks like you replaced a few pieces and are waiting for your painter to get to work." I slap his shoulder. "It'll be fine for a day or two."

He grunts in agreement and nods to the house. "Let's clean up."

Molly's in the kitchen. She must be fresh from a shower. Her long, dark hair's almost black, curling at the ends and still dripping water. My mind immediately shoots to picturing her under the running water. Naked.

Bad idea.

"Here. Eat. You two must be starving." Molly points to the counter where she's laid out what looks like a huge bowl of chicken salad, an assortment of bread, and other sandwich fixings.

"Thanks." Remy ruffles her hair, and she swats his hand away.

"Ugh. Don't rub your sawdust hands in my clean hair."

Remy chuckles. "Did you eat?"

"I picked at the chicken while I was making the salad."

"You're not going to eat with us, Muffin?" I ask.

Molly blushes and slowly meets my eyes.

Oh, shit. If she keeps that up, Remy's going to figure out something's going on between us.

"No, I need to dry my hair," she says.

I shrug, faking disinterest, even though I'm ready to follow her upstairs and hold the damn blow-dryer just so I can be close to her. "Okay."

It kills me to put my back to her, but I turn toward the counter and pretend to be fascinated by the chicken salad. By the time my plate's full and I turn around, Molly's gone.

Remy and I eat at the cleared end of the large dining room table. Molly's backpack, books, and mail cover the other end.

Fast and furious footsteps pound down the stairs a few minutes later.

"Remy! Dammit, did you use my hair serum again?" Molly stands at the end of the table and shakes a small, iridescent bottle in the air.

I bite my lip to hold in my laughter.

"What?" Remy flashes a wide-eyed *who, me?* face at his sister and runs his hands through his dark hair. "It makes my hair all soft and shiny."

"Ugh! You're a dude. No one cares about *your* hair." Molly storms past us and into the kitchen. Utensils clatter and drawers screech open as she searches for who knows what.

"Really, bro?" I cock my head and stare at Remy.

He shrugs. "What? I'll buy her another bottle."

"You always say that, but you never do!" Molly shouts from the kitchen.

I can't help it. A chuckle escapes and I cover it with a cough.

Remy grins at me. "Laugh it up. Ladies prefer a well-groomed man."

"Cool, you see any around here?" I make a big show of sitting all the way back in my chair and looking around.

Molly returns to the dining room, her teeth tucked into the corner of her bottom lip as she struggles to swirl some long, skinny, spatula-looking thing into her serum bottle.

God damn, she's cute. Even all red-faced, mad, and flustered, she's adorable.

Carefully, she drags the spatula out and smears the thick, clear liquid in her palm, then rubs it between her hands and smooths it into her hair, all while glaring at her brother.

"See? You're fine." Remy gestures to the bottle now tucked in the crook of her arm. "You'll probably scrape a few more uses out of it."

"Whatever. As long as it's *you* using it and not one of those braindead dingbats you're always bringing over here," she mutters as she twists the cap onto the bottle.

I choke on another laugh and cough again.

"You need a cough drop or something, bro?" Remy asks. "You getting a cold? Or just enjoy being a wiseass?"

"The last one." I grin at him, then turn toward Molly. "Is that why he always smells so girly?"

She sniffs the bottle. "It's not girly. It's nice." She walks over and leans against the back of my chair, draping her hair over my shoulder. "See?"

My heart stops. My brain stops processing any information other than her warmth being so close. Under the table, I curl my hands into fists to stop myself from grabbing Molly and pulling her into my lap.

"Get your hair out of our food," Remy scolds, half-standing and swatting at her with a roll of paper towels.

Molly sticks her tongue out at her brother and skips away.

Laughing and rolling his eyes Remy collects his plate, utensils, and glass. "We gotta get going if we're making it to Grinder's place on time."

I glance in the direction Molly just went. "Is she coming with us?"

"Fuck no." He scowls.

"Bro, it's his son's baptism, not an MC party. It's an all-family event. Dex told us the other day Molly could come. His girlfriend's sister's gonna be there. She's younger than Molly."

Remy's lips quirk, no doubt at the mention of Libby. Her big sister, Emily, had almost shredded Remy into confetti when she'd thought he was flirting with Libby. "Nah. It's too long of a ride for her."

"Did *she* say that or are you just assuming?" Last I knew, Molly was eager to go on a longer trip with us. And I sure as fuck want to figure out a way to have her ride on the back of my bike.

"Does it matter? I don't want her at an MC party."

"But it's *not* an MC party." Is he deliberately being stupid? "Shelby Morgan's gonna be there, for fuck's sake. Molly loves her music. Murphy's bringing his wife and kids. Molly likes hanging out with Heidi."

A brief scowl flashes across his face. "Maybe next time."

"If we're thinking of forming a support club for the Lost Kings, it would make sense to have Molly hang around with their women more often, you know."

"Yeah, I don't want them interrogating my baby sister."

I roll my eyes. "No one's gonna interrogate her." Finally, his reluctance clicks in my brain. "You want to go party at their clubhouse after the family party—is that why you don't want her with us?"

One corner of his mouth slides into a sly smile. "Fuck yeah, I do. Don't you?"

"Not particularly." I clear my throat. "I'm planning to come home tonight."

"Go ahead. I'll ride back with one of the guys tomorrow."

"Did Vapor and Juliet decide if they're coming?"

He picks up his cell phone and checks it. "No. Atlas is sick—they don't want to bring him around the baby. Eraser and Ella are out too."

"Fuck. Lost Kings are gonna start thinking we're not committed to this support club pretty soon."

"We're not all obligated to go to everything." He finishes cleaning off the table.

"You're gonna make me ride home all by myself, ya dick?"

"I'm not *making* you do anything. You should come to the clubhouse with me."

Why am I trying to talk him into coming home tonight? Let him go whore it up at the Lost Kings MC clubhouse.

I can stop by here and check on Molly. We can spend time together without Remy interfering. It's perfect.

She hates being alone in the house more than anything. Remy knows that. So it won't be weird if I stop by to check on her.

Maybe sleep on the couch.

No, that's a bad idea.

But now I can't get it out of my head.

Molly

I hate when Remy discusses me as if my opinion doesn't matter. Sure, I would've liked to go to the party, but now that he's decided I'll be in the way, I'll never tell him.

"Don't worry about me." I join them in the dining room.

Griff glances at me, then stops and does a slower inspection. I run my hands over the front of my short purple summer dress. It's still a bit cold for it, and I'm not even sure I'll end up wearing it tonight, but I enjoy the way Griff can't seem to stop staring. Holding his gaze, I curl my hands in the sides of my dress and lift it a few inches, swishing the fabric around my legs. I once overheard the guys teasing Griff about being a "leg man," and by the way his gaze follows the hem of my dress as it slides higher and higher, it must be true.

"Yeah, why's that?" Remy shouts from the kitchen. The smirk in his question is clear enough without seeing his face. But he pops into the dining room a few seconds later. Yup, smirking. *Jerk.*

"I don't want to go to your dumb party anyway." I try to keep my voice even, but my mouth twists into a pout. "Hayden's having a party. I'll be at her place."

Remy puts his hands on his hips, a sure signal he's about to say something irritating. "Is it a sleepover?" He dips his chin. "Is that why you're wearing your nightgown?"

"It's not a nightgown. It's a dress!"

Remy scoffs. "You're going to freeze your ass off."

"I'm just trying it on." I roll my eyes. "No need to read me the weather forecast."

"Who else is going to be at this party?" Griff asks.

"Yeah," Remy echoes.

I glare at Griff. Why is he siding with my brother? "I don't know. The usual crew. Jenn, Kyla, and Darcy. Wade said he's stopping by too."

"Little moneybags mingles with common folk?" Remy asks in a sarcastic tone. He glances at Griff. "I hate that kid."

"You've met him *once*," I protest.

"Once was enough," Remy grumbles. "And I know his dickhead older brother. The twatwaffle doesn't fall far from the toaster."

I side-eye my brother. "That makes no sense."

Griff's gaze shifts between Remy and me. He opens his mouth, then closes it. *Oh no*, is he going to rat me out for getting a ride from Wade last night?

But finally, Griff just shrugs. "Leave her alone." He lifts his chin at me. "You need a ride to Hayden's? I can drop you off on my way home." He pinches his T-shirt and pulls it away from his chest, reminding me of how warm and solid he'd felt when I was pressed up against him last night. "I gotta run by my place and change."

As much as I want to be alone with him, it's too early to go to Hayden's. "It's okay. The party's not until later. Hayden's picking me up."

"Seriously, it's supposed to be cold tonight," Remy says in his big-brother-dad tone. "At least wear a sweater with that. Maybe some pants."

I sigh and glance down, staring at my bare feet and the chipped red polish on my toes. Will I have time to fix them before Hayden gets here? "I'm going to save it for something more than sitting around, testing out hair styles for prom."

"Do *not* get into a car with anyone who's been drinking," Remy reminds me, as if I haven't heard that a thousand times.

"I won't. I told you, we're trying out prom hair looks." I cross my arms over my chest. "Sounds like you're going to be far away if I need a ride, though."

Remy blinks. *Ha!* Did I finally leave my know-it-all big brother speechless? "Call Ella or Eraser if you need a ride."

"I will."

Remy disappears into the kitchen. Griff watches the door for a second, then stands and slowly walks toward me.

My skin prickles as his gaze travels over my skin. He lifts his hand and runs his knuckles over my shoulder and down my arm, leaving goose bumps. My breathing speeds up.

"You look really pretty."

"Thanks," I whisper.

"Text me and let me know you're okay later? I'm not planning to stay late, so if you need something, you can call me."

Is that a sign? A hint that we can hang out without my brother around? "I can leave early too, if..."

"No." He clears his throat and jerks his hand away from me. "You should hang with your friends tonight. Figure out prom hair or whatever."

Why does he sound like he's yanking the words out of his throat?

"Yeah, Molly." My brother's razor-sharp tone borders on sarcasm and irritation. At me or Griff? I can't tell.

No, no. no. I thought Remy had returned to the kitchen. My mind races over the last few bits of my conversation with Griff. What did Remy hear? Was it bad?

He slowly walks up behind Griff. "You should spend time with friends *your own age.*"

Griff steps aside and turns toward my brother.

No. This isn't what I want.

The two of them staring each other down like bulls about to lock horns—all because of me.

Molly

I'M SITTING ON THE COUCH POLISHING MY NAILS WHEN Griff returns to our house an hour later.

"Hey," he greets me as he walks in the door. His gaze darts to the staircase. "Your brother ready to go?"

I flick my gaze to the ceiling. "He's probably doing a dozen wardrobe changes."

Griff snorts, then zeroes in on my hands. "What are *you* doing?"

I raise my arm in the air, wiggling my fingers to show off the layers of purple, red, orange, and yellow polish I've carefully sponged onto my nails. "Gradient manicure."

"Pretty." The corners of his mouth lift. "Looks like a sunset."

"Thanks." I beam, pleased he noticed. Most guys would probably roll their eyes and make fun of me doing something "girly" like painting my nails. Griff never belittles my interests. "That's what I was going for."

He glances at my supplies and picks up one of the bottles of polish. "*Mango For It.* Clever."

"Give me that." Laughing, I snatch the bottle of orange polish out of his hands. "Unless you want me to give *you* a mani before your party?" I wiggle my eyebrows.

"Nah, maybe next time." His happy grin fades. "You know I wanted you to come with us tonight, right?"

Ignoring the rapid fluttering in my chest, I shrug and focus on neatly swiping fresh rows of color on my sponge. "It's fine. I told you guys, I have my own party to go to."

He leans closer and lowers his voice. "I'd like having you on the back of my bike, though."

Forget fluttering. My heart's about to explode. "I like riding with you." I turn my head, and he's closer than I realized, our lips mere inches apart.

"Molly." Griff's raspy voice tickles every pleasure zone on my body.

Is he going to kiss me again? Would he risk it?

I part my lips.

A *thud, thud, thud* down the stairs shatters the moment. My brother with his perfect timing. I jump so fast, I jostle the polish bottles precariously balanced on my leg. Thank God, I twisted the caps tight.

Wait, some of the jostling was from Griff shifting his big body to the farthest end of the couch. As far away from me as the dimensions of our furniture allow.

Disappointment snakes through my chest. Why couldn't Remy stay upstairs for five more minutes?

"You spill nail polish on that couch, you're scrubbing it clean." Remy stops in front of me, a scowl creasing his brow.

I narrow my eyes and slowly run my gaze over my brother's outfit. According to my friends, Remy's "hot." Unfortunately, he's aware of his appeal, so it's my sisterly duty to keep him humble. "All that time spent primping in front of the mirror, and *that's* the best you could come up with?"

"Yee-ouch." Remy shakes his hands in front of him, like he's trying to put out a fire. "That stung, little sis."

What a liar. He's grinning from ear-to-ear.

Griff rumbles with amusement. I bite the inside of my cheek to hold in my own laughter.

"Stop running your mouth and look at how talented your sister is." Griff nods to my nails. "I should have her come into the shop and help me with some paint jobs."

Warmth from Griff's compliment slides over my skin. Then his words sink in. Does he really mean that? I'd love to work side by side with him at the garage again.

Remy snorts. "Yeah, just what those bikes need. Some girly colors."

It's like he thinks I'm still a little kid you'd ask to "help" hand you tools while you're working in the garage.

"You're an asshole." Griff glares at my brother. "I'm serious. She already helped me out with Black Beauty." Griff glances at me with admiration in his eyes. "Those sweet pinstripes were her idea."

The flutter of hope returns to my chest.

Remy's gaze slides between the two of us, then finally lands on me. "Aren't you going to your party?"

"Yeah." I wiggle my fingers at him. "What do you think I'm doing *this* for?"

"Fancy." Remy smirks. "Who you tryin' to impress?"

"Myself." I roll my eyes. "As if boys even care about this stuff."

"I care," Griff says.

I slowly turn my head his way. "You're not a *boy*."

"That's right." Remy's voice turns stern. Almost cold. "But *you're* still a kid."

Griff glares at my brother. I want to open my mouth and protest. *I'm not a kid.* I'll be eighteen in a few months. But I don't think it's numbers my brother's worried about. And what sounds more childish than whining that you're *not* a baby anymore?

My nervous gaze bounces between the two of them.

They have a long ride ahead of them tonight. Remy seems awfully suspicious. I don't want to be the reason for tension between them. My brother might be an overprotective pain in my ass, but he's not stupid. Maybe I should throw him off the scent. How, though?

"Who else is going to be at this party?" Remy asks.

"I already told you." I glance at my nails again. I need another layer of color before I seal them with a top coat.

The doorbell rings, saving me from this crappy conversation. I shake my wet nails at my brother and tilt my head toward the door. Blowing out an irritated breath, he leaves and answers it.

A few seconds later, Hayden sweeps into the living room wearing an aggressively pink dress and a grin stretched across her pretty face.

"Stop!" I shriek, throwing my arms up in front of my face. "I'm blinded by all the pink!"

"Shut up!" Hayden giggles and executes a spin, her golden curls fanning in a circle around her and settling over her shoulders. "I'm forever enjoying my Elle Woods phase."

"Elle Woods or Barbie?" Remy laughs, coming up behind her and giving the outfit a quick once-over.

She slants a cool look his way. "Both are awesome."

Griff shakes with silent laughter. "What's up, Hayden?"

"Hi, Griff," she sings. "What a *surprise* to see you here."

Oh, no, no, no. Hayden knows how I feel about Griff. I don't need her trying to embarrass me. She thinks she's "helping," but after some of Remy's comments to Griff today, the last thing I need is Hayden's less-than-subtle hints that Griff and I belong together being thrown around like grenades.

"He's always here," Remy says.

Hayden slides her gaze between Griff and me. Mischief brightens her eyes. "What are you wearing, Molly? Wade's *older* brother is home from college. He'll be there tonight."

My entire body cringes at the emphasis she puts on "older." *Please stop, Hayden.*

"You should wear that cute purple dress to show off your fantastic legs." She casts a quick glance at Griff, her lips twisting up ever so slightly. I brace myself for whatever else might fly out of her mouth. "Wade told me Wesley *specifically* asked if you were coming tonight like a dozen times."

"Doesn't that douche canoe have any friends his own age?" Remy grumbles.

Griff's gone so quiet, I'm afraid to look at him.

Say something, Griff. Stick up for me—for us.

Last night he confessed he has feelings for me. I understand that he wants to wait until after my birthday, but he could still say *something*. Why should we have to keep pretending just to make Remy happy, anyway?

Ignoring Remy's question, Hayden beams at me as if she's proud of her work here.

"I already tried the purple dress." I flick my hand up and show her my nails, and she nods with eager approval. "It's too cold to wear it tonight."

"It doesn't matter." She shrugs. "You look good in everything."

"Thanks." I jut my chin toward the bottles of nail polish. "Grab those? I'll finish this upstairs."

She collects the bottles with a soft clinking of glass on glass and heads upstairs. I follow without looking back at Griff *or* my brother.

Inside my room, Hayden hands me the nail polish bottles, then closes the door and leans her back against it.

"Are you blocking my escape?" I pull out the chair at my desk and line up the bottles, then uncap my fast-dry top coat.

"Nooo." She draws out the denial in a way that hints at her ulterior motives. "Did you see how jealous Griff looked when I mentioned Wesley's interest in you?" She cackles and rubs her hands together. "I sense there's been progress on the Griffin Royal situation. I'm right, right?"

Heat trickles over my cheeks and I turn my full attention to spreading top coat on each nail.

"Molly?" she prompts.

"Maybe a little." I concentrate on my pinky like my life depends on it, gently dabbing the wide brush over the nail.

"You're killing me, girl," Hayden groans. "Killing. Me."

Laughing, I cap the bottle and turn toward her. She crosses the room and perches on the edge of my bed.

My gaze strays to the door. "Griff and I kinda kissed a little last night."

"Kinda. Kissed." Her brow wrinkles as if she's disappointed with the most monumental thing that's happened to me in, well, forever.

Even though she's my best friend, I can't share more details about my stolen moments with Griff. They're mine. *Ours.* Precious memories. Not something to giggle over and dissect. Plus, no matter what Griff said, I'm still a little embarrassed about what happened in his car.

"You've gotta give me more, Molly," Hayden finally says.

She's listened to me whine about my feelings for Griff for years. I guess I owe her some small detail. "He admitted he feels the same way about me."

"Really?" Her eyes widen with excitement, and she rubs her palms together. "And?"

"He, uh, wants to wait until after my birthday to do anything about it." I shrug. "He's right. I don't want him in trouble because of me." My words aren't strong enough to convince *myself*, let alone Hayden.

"That's stupid." Hayden flicks her wrist in the air as if she's flicking my concern into the trash can. "The age of consent in New York is seventeen. Who's going to complain, anyway? Your dad? When was the last time he even showed his face here?"

"Uh, never. Thank God. Remy would probably kill him."

"Right." She tilts her head, staring at the ceiling as if she's working out a complicated math problem in her head. "Besides, just because you're a couple doesn't have to mean you're *screwing*."

"Hayden," I groan.

"What?" Her eyes bug out, emphasizing her point. "I'm serious."

"I don't want to mess up their friendship."

"Remy doesn't *own* you, Molly."

I groan and roll my eyes. It's not her fault. She doesn't have an older brother. "Tell *him* that."

"So you're never supposed to date *anyone*?" Her voice rises in pitch with each word. "*Ever*?"

"No, eventually I'll move out and do whatever I want." I glance at my hand and frown at a dent in my thumbnail polish. Too late to fix it now. "Besides, I've dated guys."

"Yeah, and Remy scared them away."

I snort. "With good reason. Kirk told everyone we screwed under the bleachers."

"I remember." She pats the space on the mattress next to her. "He was a jerk. I hope his life is hell in Ohio."

"Me too." I stand and relocate to my bed, falling against my pillows and pointing toward my closet. "I decided on red jeans and the black top with the roses on it."

"Pretty." Hayden stretches her arms behind her and leans back on her hands. She chatters about all the snacks she bought for tonight while I fling myself off the bed and open my closet door.

I wriggle into my jeans and pull my shirt over my head.

"Oh, I love those puffed sleeves." She squeals and sits up, clapping her hands together. "Nice cleavage too."

I glance down. "Too much?"

"Nope." She grins.

I lift the hem of the shirt. "It's a weird length. Looks silly out but tucking it in looks weird too."

"Ooo, let me try this trick I saw on TikTok."

Lord, what now? Hayden loves trying every "hack" she finds online. Makeup, clothes, organizing her tampons—if there's a hack for a problem she didn't know she had, Hayden will test it out and if it works, force it on all her friends.

"Do you have a cheap, thin bangle bracelet you don't care about?" she asks, squinting at my shirt. "And a hair tie?"

"Uh." I glance at my dresser. "I think so."

She swipes a silver bracelet off the top of my dresser and holds it up. "This okay?"

"Sure."

"Okay, take off your shirt and put it on inside out."

"What?" But I'm already lifting the shirt over my head. "Now what?"

She twists, tucks, and arranges the bracelet and elastic the way she wants without referring to her phone for the original inspiration. Hayden has an incredible memory for details. "Okay, take it off carefully." She helps me ease the shirt off and put it on again the right way, then walks behind me to inspect her work.

"Perfect. Look." She grabs me by the shoulders and steers me toward the full-length mirror next to my closet.

I peer over my shoulder and admire the neatly gathered fabric and "O" design my shirt's been pulled into without baring any extra skin. "That's kinda cute. Think it will hold all night?"

She shrugs. "If it doesn't, you'll be at my house, so I'll fix it. No biggie."

"Thanks. It really does look cute."

"And it makes your boobs look even bigger." She grins. "Let's go. I want to see Griff trip over his tongue."

I burst into giggles. "Please stop." I reach into my dresser drawer and grab a pair of thick black socks, then follow her out of my room.

"I'll do your hair and makeup at my house," Hayden says over her shoulder.

"Hair and makeup? I thought this was a low-key, hang-out-at-your-place kind of party?"

She scoffs but doesn't explain, just trots down the stairs.

Griff and my brother are still in the living room, and they both turn as Hayden and I enter.

"I thought you guys had to leave," I say.

"We do." Remy runs his critical gaze over me. "Wanted to make sure you're good before we hit the road."

Meaning he wants to make sure Hayden and I don't bring the party *here* while he's gone. How insulting.

"You're staying at Hayden's, right?" Remy asks.

"Yes," Hayden answers for me. "Don't worry. We'll be properly supervised, Mr. Holt."

I roll my eyes and heave out a sigh. Remy just laughs.

Griff's silently watching me and when I turn my attention to him, the heat in his eyes almost melts me on the spot. "You look good, Muffin."

Too tongue-tied to speak, I just stand there staring at him.

"She does, doesn't she?" Hayden gushes. "Wesley's gonna flip. He hasn't seen you since, what, Christmas, Molly?" Hayden focuses her sly smile on Griff. "They'd make a cute couple, don't you think?"

Subtle much, Hayden?

Hurt flashes in Griff's eyes for a moment. Then his features settle into a blank expression, devoid of the tenderness he showed me last night. "Don't know. Haven't met the guy."

A thousand pounds of disappointment steamroll over me.

Why can't he just say, *"No. Because Molly is mine?"*

Molley

CHAPTER SEVEN

GRIFF

The hurt in Molly's eyes chases me all the way down the Thruway. I could practically hear her plea for me to stake my claim on her in front of her brother and her best friend. Not twenty-four hours after I told her *why* now isn't the right time. After last night I'm so damn twisted up inside.

Part of me wants to be mad at her. But mostly I'm just mad at myself. And maybe annoyed with Molly's friend. She doesn't need to play matchmaker for my girl.

Party. Tonight's important and I need to focus. I'll talk to Molly tomorrow.

Grinder's house is full by the time we arrive. I was right. It's all family at the party. There was no reason Molly couldn't have come with us. I shoot a glare at Remy as he backs his bike into a spot near one of the garages but I'm not bringing it up again. If I keep bitching about it, Remy's big brother radar will activate.

"Nice ride." He holds out his fist to me, and I tap my knuckles against his.

"Always a good one when we don't get pulled over."

He chuckles and nods.

The back door on the patio slides open and Murphy, the vice president of the Lost Kings MC, waves us inside.

"What's up, brother?" He holds out his hand and pulls me in for a quick embrace, then gives Remy the same greeting. "How was the ride?" He steps aside so we can enter the kitchen.

"A little chilly, but good," I answer.

Murphy's face quivers with laughter under his full red beard. "You need better riding clothes then, goof."

He was the road captain for his club for years before he moved into the VP position, so of course that's his answer. "Good." I slap his chest. "How about I call you for a fashion consultation next time?"

He flicks his gaze to the ceiling. "Dex can help you out there."

Somewhere deeper in the house, a baby wails. Murphy cocks his head, listening for a second.

"Yours?" Remy asks.

"No, but I'm still gonna go check on Heidi." He slaps our shoulders. "Grinder and Serena are in the front room. Go say hi to baby Lincoln. Little dude's pretty chill even though we've been fussin' over him all day."

After Murphy leaves, Remy stares at the hallway leading into the rest of the massive house. His mouth twists, like he'd rather run outside and weed the yard with a pair of tweezers than say hi to an infant.

"Stop being a jackass." I smack his arm and scold him in a low voice. "You knew this was a family event. It's literally a party for a baby."

"I didn't say anything."

I shake my head and glance around the kitchen. I recognize Dex's girlfriend, Emily, and raise my hand to say hello but she's busy chopping carrots like her damn life depends on it. Remy flicks his gaze at her, then me, and rolls his eyes.

"Let's go," I say.

Walking through Grinder's big, modern house leaves me feeling like a wild boar who's been turned loose in a museum.

"He hasn't even been out of prison that long," I whisper to Remy. "How's he already have the funds to buy a place like this?"

He shrugs. "Lost Kings take care of their own. Reward loyalty and all that. Remember the bike they gave Vapor? And he's not even a patch holder."

"Maybe we should host more fight nights at The Castle. Start stacking more cash."

Remy stops and glances at me. "We do okay with that but it's not going to generate *this* kind of income. Especially when we've got so much overhead." He slides his gaze toward the living room where most of the chatter seems to be coming from. "I'm gonna talk to Teller about some investment stuff later if I can."

"Good luck. He can't stand you," I scoff.

"Nah, I'm growing on him."

"Sure you are."

We finally make our way to the formal living room. It's packed and while we're friendly with mostly everyone, I still feel like an intruder.

The corner of my mouth lifts as my gaze lands on Grinder. The older biker barely takes his eyes off of his fiancée as she carries their son from couple to couple. I lean in close to Remy. "I know he's a lot older than her, but they make sense together."

Remy chuckles softly and ducks his head. "Christ, first time I met her, I thought she was his daughter."

"You fucking said that to him too, didn't you?" My best friend has a bad habit of speaking before thinking.

"How was I supposed to know?" He snorts. "Thought he was going to murder me on the spot."

"Honestly, he kind of reminds me of your Grandpa Kip. The way he doted on Nana Clary, you know?"

A fond smile replaces his devilish one. "Yeah." His smirk returns. "Don't tell him he reminds you of my grandpa, though. He'll probably shoot us both."

"You're such a dick." I laugh and shake my head. "But yeah. I felt bad when I pretended to be the grandson of one of his friends to get his parole officer off his back."

"Nah, I bet he appreciated you helping him out." Remy's

head turns as he surveys the room again. "I feel like we give a lot more assistance than we get in return."

He's got a point to a certain extent. "They took care of the guys fucking around at Zips for us. We haven't asked them for much more."

Remy would rather gnaw off his fingers one by one than ask anyone for help. "I guess. I just want to be careful before we commit to too much."

"I hear you."

We finally get our chance to say hi to the baby. Despite his earlier complaints, Remy's happy to hold Lincoln and make goofy faces at him.

While he's busy with Lincoln, someone pokes my side. I glance down at the tiny, curvy blonde smiling up at me.

"Rooster said ya were gonna be here," Shelby says in her soothing Texan drawl. "Molly come with ya?"

I shoot a glare at Remy. "Nah, her friend was having a party tonight."

"Aw, that's too bad." She pats my arm. "Tell her I said hi."

"Will do."

Grinder clasps my shoulder with enough pressure to get my attention. "Thanks for coming."

"Thanks for having us."

"Z asked for a tour. You want to join us?" he asks.

"Sure."

"I'll talk to you later," Shelby says, throwing me a quick wave.

AN HOUR LATER, bored with touring the kind of house I won't be able to afford for who knows how many years, I plunk myself down at a long wooden counter in Grinder's finished basement.

I pull out my phone and send Molly a quick text.

Me: How's your party?

Muffin: Get there in one piece?

That didn't answer my question. My mouth tilts to the side as I reply to her text.

Me: Yup. Ride was good.

Muffin: Is Remy okay?

I lift my head, searching the area around me. I lost track of Remy near the sauna.

Me: So far, so good. How's your party?

Molly: Meh.

Agitation flickers through me. That's not a normal reply from Molly. She shouldn't be unhappy hanging out with her friends at Hayden's house. They're pretty tight. Shit, Hayden was trying to set Molly up with some douche canoe. Maybe that didn't go well. Would Molly tell him she already has a boyfriend?

No, why would she when I won't even tell her brother?

Why do I have to be so damn far away tonight of all nights?

Me: What's wrong?

I stare at my phone, willing her to reply.

"Too much home improvement info for you?" A gravelly voice interrupts my staring contest with the empty screen.

Recognizing the voice, I tuck my phone away. "What's up, Dex?" I slide off the stool and hold out my hand to the road captain of the Lost Kings MC.

"What's going on, brother?" He jerks me closer and slaps my back in greeting. "It's been a minute."

"It has," I agree. "Good to see you."

At least a conversation with Dex will take my mind off of missing Molly tonight.

Molly

The night started out pretty great. I helped Hayden fix snacks and lay them out on her long kitchen counter. Her cousin Jenn showed up an hour later with her giant kit full of hair tools, styling products, and barrettes.

Where Hayden is loud and bright, her cousin Jenn is sweet but plain—our friend group equivalent of vanilla pudding. She's even wearing a cream sweater and tan leggings tonight—plain as can be. We're friendly enough. Sometimes I feel like she's jealous of my friendship with her cousin and it makes our hangouts awkward.

But tonight Jenn and I are bonding over our search for the perfect prom hair style. "You should leave your hair down but maybe do some small, strategically placed braids," Jenn suggests, pulling a few strands away from my face and weaving them into a halo and pinning it in the back.

Kyla waves a packet of tiny clips shaped like little red roses. "I assume your dress will be red or purple?"

"Purple." I throw my hands up in an *of course* gesture.

"Don't get her started," Darcy warns. "She'll tell us all about how purple has been associated with royalty since ancient times, during the Bronze Age, blah, blah, blah."

My cheeks heat. I *did* probably say something like that—back in seventh grade. Of course, Darcy remembers.

"And she's going to marry Griffin Royal one day," Hayden sings. "So purple's her color forever."

I side-eye her pink dress. "Okay, Barbie."

Hayden falls into a fit of giggles. "It's my signature color."

"Indeed." Darcy flicks a small, pink satin bow at Hayden.

A thud resonates from the front of the house and a few seconds later, the doorbell rings.

"Guests are here!" Hayden jumps off the couch and runs to answer.

"What guests?" Jenn casts an anxious glance toward the front door. "I thought it was just us hanging out tonight?"

A slow smile curves Darcy's lips. "We invited a few extras to hang out."

Great.

It's not a "few" people. A bunch of seniors and a couple of

juniors stomp into the house. Loud, boisterous, and carrying cases of beer.

Jenn scowls. "Chris and James graduated like two years ago. Why do they even want to hang out with us?"

Kyla snickers into her hand. "You're going to a die a virgin, Jenn."

"Fine by me"—Jenn lifts her chin toward the two jocks babbling about some sportsball game—"if *those* guys are my only options."

I snort-laugh and pull myself off the floor. More and more people come in through the front door.

In no time, our fun night of braiding and curling our hair turns into a loud, crowded, noisy party.

"Your mom's gonna kill you," I warn Hayden when I pass her in the hallway.

She shrugs.

Annoyed and uncomfortable, I grab a can of seltzer from the fridge and wander through the house in search of a safe place to hide from the mayhem. Photos of Hayden throughout the years line the white hallway walls sprinkled with other family photos. There are a few blank spaces with the outline of a frame visible dotted throughout the wall of memories. Did Hayden erase her dad's existence from the wall or did her mom?

Bang. I collide with a body.

"Oh, sorry." Mortification heats my skin. Why am I worried about Hayden's family drama instead of watching where I'm going?

"It's okay. I was looking for you, Molly."

I lift my gaze and Wesley's utterly unremarkable face leers down at me.

"For me?" *No, no, no,* what did Hayden tell him? I'd thought she was kidding about trying to set us up to make Griff jealous.

He leans one arm against the wall and angles his body to block my escape, unless I want to trip over his big, white sneakers.

"Yeah, Hayden said you'd be here." He tips the bottle of beer in his hand toward his lips and takes a quick sip. "My buddies and I brought the beer."

Am I supposed to be impressed?

He points the bottle toward the kitchen behind me. "Wade's been yapping about Hayden all day. Ditched me to find her as soon as we got here."

Those two would make a cute couple, even if Hayden says Wade's too bookish. "She'll be happy to see him."

"Enough about them. What are you up to?" His gaze slides over me, stopping to linger on my chest for so long, I wish I'd worn a hoodie tonight instead of this dumb low-cut shirt.

I shrug and pull my hair over my shoulders, draping as much as possible over my chest. "School. Work."

"You still working at Miller's Farms?"

How'd he know that?

"Uh, yeah. Only a couple nights a week, though. My brother doesn't like me taking too many shifts."

His lip curls at the mention of Remy. "Yeah, how is Remington?" he asks in a snide tone that activates my little sister defensive shields.

I lift my chin. "He's good." *An overprotective pain in my butt who uses my hair products without permission, but I'm not letting anyone talk shit about him no matter what.*

"He still working at that dinky little pub off the Thruway?"

Anger flares hot and I glare at him. "Yes, he still owns and runs the tavern our grandparents left us when they died. Thanks for asking."

His jaw slides sideways in an *oh, shit* expression. "That's right. I forgot. I'll, uh, have to stop in one day."

You do that. "Sure."

"Sorry, I didn't mean it like that." He reaches out and touches my shoulder. I flinch and jerk away.

He holds up the bottle. "You want a beer?"

"No thanks." I raise my can of black cherry seltzer. "I'm good."

He squints at the can. "Is that hard seltzer?"

Any idiot can see it's a regular, fat can of traditional Polar seltzer—the same brand sold in every grocery store in New York—but I don't feel like explaining why I'm not pounding alcohol like all my friends. "Yup."

He leans closer, not even trying to hide that he's angling his head to stare directly down my shirt. "Where's Hayden's room?" he asks.

"Huh?" I frown in confusion.

"Wade claims her room's so pink it looks like the inside of..." his voice falters, "...uh, the inside of Barbie's dream house. Is that true?"

I chuckle uncomfortably. "She redecorated it, yeah." After her dad left, Hayden's mom let her do whatever she wanted to her room. Hayden chose wild hot-pink wallpaper and painted all her furniture fuchsia. "I'm not a big fan of pink, but it actually looks amazing. Hayden has a great eye for colors, patterns, and stuff. I asked her to come up with a purple and red scheme for my room..." Wesley's gaze is focused somewhere over my head. He's not even listening.

Why'd he bother asking?

Wesley's gaze wanders toward the stairs.

He seems to notice I've stopped talking and shifts his attention to me again. "So where are you planning to go to school next year?"

"I...I'm not sure yet."

His head tilts in this pitying sort of way that tightens my jaw with annoyance. "What do you want to study?"

"Communication disorders and sciences."

He shrugs and gives a blank expression. "Where?"

Good question. I don't have enough money to go too far from home. "Uh, I'm thinking of going to Greene Point, then transferring to Cortland or somewhere for the last two years."

"Greene Point? That's basically thirteenth grade," he sneers with all the assurance only a guy whose parents can afford tuition can muster.

I shrug like that didn't sting. "I don't want to go too far away."

"Yeah, I get that. It's nice coming home on the weekends." He grins. "My mom does all my laundry for me."

Of course she does.

"So, Molly." He pushes away from the wall and reaches for me, his hand hovering close enough for him to graze his scratchy thumb over my semi-bare shoulder.

I keep my gaze focused on the wall in front of me, not wanting to lead him on. "Yeah?"

"You wanna go upstairs?" he asks. "You can show me Hayden's pink *bed*room."

A mental red flag pops up at the unnatural emphasis he puts on *bed*. "Uh...I don't know if Hayden would like me giving tours of her room."

He stares at the ceiling for a second. "Yeah, but we could be alone." His thumb scratches over my shoulder again. "Maybe you could give me head?"

What?

My jaw drops and I stare at him.

Did he just say what I think he said?

Each word of our limited conversation replays in my mind.

What did I say that translated into *I want to suck your dick* in his addled brain?

"No."

"But we have such good chemistry." He grabs my hand and tries to push it against his crotch. "Look how hard I am for you."

That's supposed to impress me?

I yank my hand away before I encounter any "hardness" and shoot him a glare that I wish had the power to make his dick shrivel to the size of a rotten banana stem. "Guys get an erection if a stiff breeze tickles them. It's not exactly an accomplishment." I tilt my head. "Or a compliment."

He snort-laughs, then stops and frowns. "What?"

"I have a boyfriend."

"No you don't. Hayden said you're single." He lifts his chin. "You don't gotta swallow." He drops his gaze. "I can come on your tits."

Revulsion washes over me. "Charming," I scoff, and turn away.

A stiff grip encircles my arm, clamping down and yanking hard enough that seltzer bubbles and fizzes out of the top of the can in my other hand.

"You don't have to be such a bitch about it," he says.

"Get. Off. Me." My brother and his friends have been teaching me how to defend myself since I was the smallest kid on the playground getting picked on by the class bullies. Instead of following my natural instinct to yank my arm away, I push forward, twist, and pull down until I'm free.

He grunts in surprise.

An image of kneeing him in the nuts flashes in front of my eyes, but I don't want to escalate the situation.

Run.

Get away.

I bolt down the hallway in search of anyone at this dumb party that I trust. My arm stings from where he grabbed me, and I press the cool can of seltzer over the spot.

The music's so loud my head throbs. My panicked gaze pings around the house. The kitchen and dining room are crowded. A guy who's in my physics class is trying to execute a headstand on top of a keg. Apparently he learned nothing about the distribution of weight with respect to gravitational force. He lands on his back with a thud that shakes the floor. Beer pools around him and his friends howl with laughter.

"You okay?" I shout while his buddies continue to mock him.

He giggles and rolls onto his side. "Yeah. You want next?"

Idiots.

"Nope. I'm good." I just want to go home.

Trying to push the ugliness of what happened away, I take a few deep breaths and circle around the dining table to avoid passing Wesley in the hallway again.

In the living room, I find an unoccupied corner of the couch and fling myself into it. Does my shirt provide enough camouflage to blend into the floral upholstery?

I slowly turn my head, scanning the packed room. In darkened corners where they probably think they're invisible, couples are busy exploring each others' tonsils.

Still no sign of Hayden. Did she abandon her own party?

I spot Darcy across the room engrossed in a conversation with a guy on the football team. He keeps leaning in close, brushing his fingers against her thigh. *Doesn't he have a girlfriend?*

Oh, Darcy, no, girl. Don't go there.

I continue searching what I can see of the living room. No sign of Kyla or Jenn. Loud chatter and nonsensical conversations compete with the thumping music. If the party gets any louder, Hayden's neighbors are bound to call the cops. I can't be here for that.

Who the hell *are* half these people?

I cross my arms over my chest and swallow down my discomfort.

How can I be in a house full of people and still feel so alone?

My phone vibrates against my hip, and I shift lower in my seat, shove my hand in my pocket, and yank it out.

Griff: How's your party?

My lips curve into the biggest smile. I'm supposed to be having fun with my friends, but I'm happier about a text from Griff than anything going on around me.

Should I wait to answer? Let him wonder what I'm doing and who I'm doing it with, the way I always wonder who has his attention?

No, screw that.

I can't tell him what's happened, though. Or that I'm miserable and wish I was home.

Me: Get there in one piece?
Griff: Yup. Ride was good.
Me: Is Remy okay?
Griff: So far, so good. How's your party?

I could write a wall of text about how this isn't the night I'd expected. Or how some guy I barely know randomly asked me for a blow job and offered to spurt semen on my chest. No. I definitely can't tell Griff *that*. But if I don't answer, he'll know something's wrong.

Me: Meh

There. That sums up my whole night.

Griff: What's wrong?

My thumb hovers over the screen. Should I tell him my friends are all drunk and I'm bored?

Me: Just your basic snooze fest.

Something thumps against my foot, jarring me out of my thoughts. I glance up and find Wesley staring down at me.

My stomach drops. *Not again.*

"Why'd you come to a party just to sit on your phone?" he asks, totally normal. Like he didn't just try to rub himself all over me or offer to stick his dick down my throat.

"Texting my boyfriend." *There*, that should make him go away.

"I don't believe you." He grabs for my phone, but I tuck it behind me in my back pocket and glare up at him.

He smirks in return. "You're fast." His goofy expression fades. "Sorry about before." He wobbles his thumb in the direction of the hallway. "I'm kinda drunk."

I narrow my eyes and study him. Unfortunately, I have plenty of experience dealing with drunks. "Alcohol doesn't *change* your personality—it reveals it."

He drops into the narrow space next to me, forcing me to inch over. The couple making out at the other end of the couch turn and glare at him for the interruption, but he ignores them.

"Anyone ever tell you you're a buzzkill, Molly?"

"Probably." I shrug as if his words haven't hurt my feelings. "I don't give enough of a fuck to remember, though."

He rests his hand on my leg. My skin crawls. I glare at the spot where he's touching me—right above my knee. Thank God I didn't wear my dress. I'd scream if we were having skin-on-skin contact. I shift my leg away.

"Are you a virgin, Molly?" He leans in so close, his warm, sour breath mists over my cheek. *Ewww.* My entire body cringes from the stink. "Is that why you're so shy?"

My pocket buzzes again. Ignoring the gross question, I lean away from Wesley and pull out my phone, carefully angling the screen away from his prying eyes.

Griff: Why basic?

I respond with a shrug emoji.

Griff: Call Ella for a ride.

Me: I might.

"You really have a boyfriend?" Wesley asks.

"Yes," I answer in a tight, fuck-off voice.

Wesley squints. "Wade didn't tell me that."

"Why were you discussing my relationship status with your brother?"

"Because I like you." He traces his finger over my collarbone. A nauseating buzz vibrates through my stomach. "I've always liked you."

"Could've fooled me." I pull my leg away, dislodging his hand.

"Ah-ha." A triumphant grin that's more annoying than endearing spreads across his face. "So you *do* like me."

How did he get that from what I said? "Honestly, I nothing you." I squint and shrug as if I'm pained to reveal the truth. "I was pointing out that you're full of shit." Even if I once thought he was kind of cute, after the way he's behaved tonight, he might as well be a troll. "Asking girls you barely know to blow you is creepy as fuck."

"I never figured you were so bitchy."

I fake-yawn and pat my hand over my mouth. "So you've said."

He rocks and wobbles off the couch, then stumbles away.

The girl next to me, Jane, a junior, I think, leans over and grins in my face. "That was *epic*."

Embarrassed that she overheard our conversation, heat floods my cheeks. But I shrug and try to return a confident smile. "He was being so gross. I had to give him a dose of reality."

She giggles and throws her fist my way. "Good job."

I tap my knuckles against hers. "Thanks."

She returns to making out with the guy next to her and I pick up my phone again.

I hate bugging my brother's friends for rides, but I can't stay here another minute. Who knows when Wesley will return?

I tap out a quick rescue plea to Ella. She's married to one my brother's friends but she's like a big sister to me—someone I'm comfortable asking for help.

Me: Drunk guy won't leave me alone. Can you pick me up at Hayden's?

I stare at my screen, waiting for a response. She's probably working at the racetrack with her husband.

Am I being silly? Making a big deal over nothing? I promised Hayden I would stay over tonight. Is it rude to leave?

Ella: Be there in twenty.

I release a relieved sigh and stand, intent on finding Hayden to let her know I'm headed out. In the laundry room at the back of the house, I find her sitting on top of the dryer, waving her hands around and delivering a speech in a dramatic British accent, acting out a scene from...I have no idea what. Some rom-com she's probably obsessed with. I lift my hand and wave to capture her attention.

"Mollllleeee!" She slides off the dryer, landing in a pile of neatly folded sheets and blankets.

I slide my gaze to two girls in our class who are also sitting in the clean linens and shake my head. "Her mom's gonna kill you guys."

"What? Why?" One giggles and hugs a blanket to her chest. "They smell soooo good."

"Lord," I say under my breath. Louder, I add, "Hades! I'm heading home."

"What?" she screeches at top volume. "You can't go!"

Maybe I really am the buzzkill Wesley said I was. *Oh, well.* "I don't feel good."

"Go upstairs and sleep it off!" she shouts.

Not if you paid me a million dollars. I can't help thinking that if I fall asleep here, there's a chance I'll wake up with Wesley trying to rub his dick on me—or worse.

"Nah, I'm gonna head home."

"I'll ask Wesley to give you a ride." She thrusts her hips in the air and ends up falling over again.

Hell no. "Ella's already on her way."

"Oh." She pouts again. "Okay."

I bump into Wade on my way out of the laundry room. "Hey, Molly." He lifts his chin toward Hayden. "Is she okay?"

So polite—hard to believe he shares DNA with Wesley. "I think she's had too much to drink."

"Shit. I told Wesley we didn't need to bring so much beer."

I pat his shoulder. "I don't think you guys are the only ones who brought party favors."

"Wesley was looking for you."

"Yeah, we talked." *He's disgusting.*

I slip away before he can ask me anything else and make it outside without anyone questioning me.

A shiny black Chevy Blazer glides to a stop at the curb and I run to meet it.

"What's going on, McMuffin?" Eraser shouts as I slide into the back seat. I should've known Ella would bring her husband.

I groan at the nickname and slam the door shut.

Ella turns to look at me. "You all right?"

"Yeah." I sigh.

"Do I need to go in and kick someone's ass?" Eraser turns and lifts an eyebrow. Under his bushy beard he's really a big teddy bear. Well, to me, anyway. If he turns that scowl loose on my classmates, someone will end up peeing their pants. "I'll do it. Say the word."

I aim a pointed look at Ella. "Really? You couldn't come alone?"

"What?" Her eyes widen, and she flicks an amused glance at her husband. "He knows everything anyway."

Eraser glances in the rearview mirror at me. "Seriously, Molly. You okay?"

"I'm fine. I just thought it was going to be a smaller party." Knowing he'll report everything I say to my brother, I don't want to share too many details. "Some of the guys were drunk. I don't need puke on my favorite Doc Martens."

Ella chuckles.

"Thanks for coming to get me."

"Not a problem," Eraser says.

I cross my arms over my chest and stare out the window. With each passing street, the houses go from newer, modern styles with tiny, postage-stamp-size yards to older homes with more grass and fewer fences.

Eraser stops the car in front of my old but inviting house, the yellow porch light casting a warm glow over the front steps. "You want us to stick around?"

Oh, how I wish I could say yes. The thought of being alone in our creaky old house is so unappealing. But I can't ask them to stick around just because I'm a big chicken. "I'm too old for babysitters." I reach my hand forward and pat his shoulder. "But thank you for the ride. I appreciate it."

As I open the back door, Ella's door flings open. She bumps her shoulder into me as we head up the sidewalk.

"Sure you're all right?" she asks. "I can stick around."

"I'm okay." I glance at the car. "I didn't mean to screw up your night."

"Don't be ridiculous." She waves off my apology with a flick of her wrist. "We were closing Zips. No biggie."

"How'd it go tonight?" I ask. "Win any money?" Ella's tiny and dresses like Tinker Bell in her emo era. Guys who come to Zips to race look at her and assume she doesn't know how to drive. But she's a fearless competitor who ends up emptying wallets frequently.

"You know I did." Her lips slide into a confident smirk.

"Wish I'd gone there instead," I grumble like a cranky toddler.

She squeezes my arm. "Did you talk to Hayden?"

"I saw her before I left." I leave out the part about my drunk bestie rolling around on the laundry room floor. "I'll talk to her tomorrow."

"All right. If you need something, call." She reaches for me and pulls me in for a hug. "Sorry tonight was a drag."

"Eh." I squeeze her tight. "Thanks."

I lean against the door frame and watch as she slides into the passenger seat. Eraser won't drive away until I go inside, so I shut the door behind me and throw the deadbolt. The throaty rumble of Eraser's SUV intensifies, then slowly fades. I flick the porch light off and the hall lights on.

And then I'm all alone.

I escaped the party. Wesley's drunk at Hayden's, probably annoying some other girl now. I'm safe here.

So why did all those unsettling feelings from the party follow me home?

Molly

CHAPTER EIGHT

Molly

I'm too old to be scared when I'm home alone.

If I keep repeating it, maybe I'll believe it.

Every creak and sigh of our old house sends jolts of panic shooting through my body.

In my bedroom, I flick the light on. My purple and silver curtains are thick enough to block out the morning sun, but I still can't shake the feeling that someone could be watching from the street down below. They could realize I'm home alone and pinpoint exactly where I am in the house and—

Stop it!

I flick the light switch off and go to my closet. The door soundlessly slides open and an overhead light automatically brightens the interior. *Ugh.* I strip off my jeans and kick them into my laundry basket. I can't believe I wasted my cute outfit on such a sucky party. I should burn it all. The jeans feel tainted after Wesley put his grubby hand on my leg. Yuck.

I curl my fingers in the fabric of a pair of thick, flannel pants and pull them on. My bra's been annoying me all night, so I happily strip it off. I find a short T-shirt with a rib cage in the shape of a heart with flowers curling between the bones printed on the front and slip it on.

I'm still chilly, though. My fingers brush over soft fabric and I tug. Griff's hoody. One of many I've "borrowed" over the years and "forgotten" to return. My lips curve up and I bury my face in the fluffy cotton, inhaling what's left of Griff's scent. I pull it over my head and tuck my phone into the front pocket. My toes have turned to ice cubes on the old, polished hardwood floors. I grab a pair of woolly socks from my dresser and sit on the edge of my bed to pull them on.

Fatigue hasn't found me yet. Anxiety still hums through my brain. Go downstairs and watch television until I fall asleep? Or hide in my bedroom and watch videos on my phone under the safety of my blankets?

Cocoon of blankets wins. With my phone clutched in one hand, I burrow into my mattress and turn on my side. I tap on my YouTube app and start scrolling for something interesting to watch.

My favorite makeup channel, Tranquil Sparkle, has a new tutorial posted, and I settle in to learn how to perfect the puppy eyeliner trend.

The roar of an engine interrupts my viewing before the look is complete.

I pause the video, cock my head, and hold my breath.

Is that Griff's bike?

I toss back the covers and peel myself out of my warm, cozy bed. The rumble intensifies, then goes silent.

I'm frozen like a deer in the middle of my bedroom. My gaze pings between the door and my phone, waiting to see if he'll send me a text. Maybe it was someone else? No. Almost everyone in our neighborhood is over sixty and probably went to bed hours ago.

My phone buzzes in my hand, scaring the bejesus out of me. I fumble with it, trying to flick the screen on, then catch it and swipe my thumb over the screen.

Griff: *It's me. Are you up?*
Me: *Be right there.*

I race down the stairs, skid over the hardwood floors in the living room, and almost trip over one of the tasseled carpets on my way to the front entrance. Heart racing, I untwist all the locks and open the door.

"What are you doing here?" I step back so Griff can come in. The air's cooled since I got home. The spring night clings to his leather jacket as he crosses the threshold.

"I know you don't like being alone at night," he says in a hushed tone, as if he's afraid he'll offend me. But everyone knows I'm a big scaredy-cat. It's not exactly a secret.

Still, the fact that he doesn't want to hurt my feelings sends a warm shiver of pleasure through me. I shouldn't have been annoyed with him earlier for not telling Remy about us. Griff's shown me that I'm important to him in so many ways.

"And I brought you treats from downstate." He holds up a small, crinkled, white paper bag. "They might be a little banged up from the ride, though."

As if I care about the condition of the food. Griff was thinking of me while he was at the party. That's what matters. I snatch the bag out of his hand and peer inside. Two large, flamingo-shaped cookies, complete with sweet pink frosting, rest at the bottom.

"They look too pretty to eat," I say.

He chuckles and closes the door behind him. "Shelby brought them. There were cupcakes too, but I was worried they'd be mush by the time I got here."

Ugh. I'm so jealous. I would've rather gone with Griff instead of going to Hayden's tonight. I could've been hanging out with my favorite country singer—Shelby Morgan—instead of getting propositioned by Johnsonville High's creepiest alum—Wesley Chambers. "Thanks for thinking of me."

"Always." He turns away and slips off his leather jacket, then hangs it on a hook by the door.

I slide my hand into the bag and break off the beak of one of the flamingos and pop it in my mouth. Crumbly sweetness bursts on my tongue but the cookie's dry as sand. "Milk," I mumble. "I need milk."

"Lead the way." Griff raises his eyebrows, looking so damn irresistible my breath catches. Cookie crumbs lodge in my windpipe, choking off my air. I sputter and cough, my cheeks burning with embarrassment. Concern wrinkles Griff's forehead and he steps closer, patting my back. "Take it easy, Muffin."

"I'm fine." *Cough, sputter. Ack! Why won't it stop?*

"Come on. Let's get you something to drink." He presses his hand between my shoulder blades and steers me through the house into the kitchen.

Still coughing, I set the bag of cute but deadly cookies on the counter. Griff grabs a carton of milk from the fridge, fills a glass halfway, and hands it to me.

I take a few cautious sips, relieved when the annoying tickle in my throat subsides and I can breathe again without hacking. "Thanks," I wheeze. Why do I always do something embarrassing in front of Griff?

"You all right?" He crowds into my space, touching my elbow. Concern brews in his eyes. His square jaw's dusted with stubble that I want to brush my fingers against.

"I'll live."

His gaze drops to my chest, and a knowing smile spreads across his face. "Hey, isn't that mine?" He pinches the sleeve of my sweatshirt and gently tugs.

I set the almost empty glass of milk on the counter with a soft *thunk.*

"Do you want it back?" I grip the bottom of the sweatshirt and pull it up an inch, keeping my gaze focused on Griff's face.

He swallows hard, his eyes glued to the hem as I tease it up and down. His relentless attention twists me in knots. What will he do next? Kiss me? My lips part in anticipation.

He runs his hand over his chin. "No. You can keep it." His voice drops to a deeper-than-usual rumble as he slowly drags his gaze to my face again. "I like how you look in my sweatshirt."

"You do?" I release the fabric and curl my fingers around the ends of the ties at my neck, pulling them from side to side.

"Yeah." A slow and utterly cocky grin lights his face as he seems to emerge from his trance. "Why do you think I let you steal so many of my hoodies?"

"Steal?" I widen my eyes with fake outrage. "How dare you. I *borrow*."

"And never return." His teasing expression fades. "It doesn't matter, Molly. You can have anything of mine you want."

Even you?

If only I were brave enough to ask *that* question. Instead, I voice a different one. "Does that include Black Beauty?"

Shock widens his eyes for a second, then his expression turns thoughtful. "Yeah. If you really want her, I'll give her to you for graduation."

For a second, I can't breathe. And it's not from choking on cookie crumbs this time. Griff *loves* that car. He restored it himself. He jokes that I helped him do the rebuild, but he's being kind. All I did was watch and drool over how hot he looks working with his hands.

"I...I could never take your car, Griff. I was only kidding." I can't believe he said that. He barely hesitated too.

"Who said *take*? I said I'd *give* her to you."

"You love that car."

"I..." A thousand years seem to pass while I wait for him to finish the thought. "...know you'd take good care of her."

"It doesn't matter. I still don't have my license." I shrug, then slant a look his way. "If I'm ever able to afford a car, I was thinking..." I bite my lip. Will he think this is dumb?

"What?" he prompts.

"I'd like to restore a '71 Malibu Coupe." I shrug and lower my voice. "With you."

"Yeah? So, a fancier version of my car?" A teasing smile slips over his face. "I'd love to work on that project together. Then we'd have a matching set."

Yes, that's the point.

"I'll keep an eye out. See if I can get my hands on one in decent shape."

More time in the garage with Griff.

Don't faint. Be cool.

"Thanks. I'd like that." I finish my milk and set my glass in the sink.

"Why weren't you having fun at Hayden's?" he asks.

Ugh. This isn't a conversation I want to have. It's a waste of our precious minutes alone. Especially when my brother could walk in the front door at any minute and chase Griff away. "Why'd *you* leave your party early?"

"To see you." He jams his hands in his pockets.

I'm going to faint. *Deep breath.* I tilt my head toward the living room. "Mind if we sit out there instead?"

"Not at all."

In the living room, I plop down in my favorite corner of the couch and turn on the television. The home screen bathes the room in a soft whitish-blue glow. Griff drops onto the other end of the couch—about as far away from me as he can get.

"Why are you all the way down there?" I scoot closer and lean up against him.

A long moment of silence stretches between us. Griff's body remains rigid as if he's thinking through a range of actions.

"I missed you tonight." He flexes his hand, opening and closing it into a fist. "You really could've come with us. I don't know why your brother's so damn stubborn."

I can think of a few reasons why. "I wish I had."

Finally, he relaxes, sinking against the back of the couch. He stretches his arm up and over my head, curling it around my shoulders and pulling me more firmly against him. "You gonna tell me what happened at Hayden's?"

Hell no.

"Nothing bad." I cough and glance away, grabbing the old afghan I keep thrown over the back of the couch and dragging it down over my legs. A chill always lingers in the air of this house. "I thought it was only going to be a few of us hanging out. But it turned into way more people."

"What about that guy Hayden's so hot to set you up with? Wesley? Was he there?" he asks in a hard voice.

"I saw him, yeah." My lips quirk with annoyance to hide the unease that followed me home and only melted when Griff walked in the door. "He's kind of a jerk, though."

He frowns. "How?"

"I don't want to talk about him." It feels so good being pressed up against Griff. Too good to talk about bad things.

A few hours ago, I was sitting next to someone else on a different couch, completely uncomfortable, maybe even scared that Wesley might try to take something from me I didn't want to give. If I tell Griff that, or even hint at it, he'll hunt Wesley down and probably try to kill him.

So I cuddle up against Griff and keep the worst parts of my bad night to myself.

Molly

CHAPTER NINE

Molly

We had a moment back there in the kitchen. That's what I want to focus on. Not my crappy night at Hayden's.

I angle my body to the side and drape my leg over Griff's. The afghan slips off my lap, landing in a pile on the floor.

"Molly..." My name comes out like a warning. He tilts his head slightly and peers down at me. "What're you doing?"

The question slices my confidence in half. Isn't it obvious what I'm trying to do? He kissed me the other night. Said he had feelings for me too. Why can't I touch him? It's not like Remy's here to interrupt us.

Instead of answering, I recapture my bravery. Slowly, I raise my arm and rest my palm on his chest. His heart gallops under my touch.

We're still for a moment.

Then he covers my hand with his own, as if he's afraid my fingers will start exploring the hard contours of his body.

"What's wrong?" I ask when he doesn't say a word.

He twists his head to the side and peers down at me with a raised eyebrow—a look that pokes me like a silent scolding.

"We don't get to spend a lot of time alone like this," I murmur, my confidence slipping.

"I know," he rasps as if he's struggling to force out each sound.

"It's nice." I tilt my head to the side. "Being alone with you." *Hint, hint.*

He answers with a deep rumble of agreement that vibrates through my entire body.

"We should..." I'm not sure how to say what I want. I try to move my hand out from under his, but he clamps down harder, holding me in place.

"Molly," he groans and rolls his body sideways, so he's facing me. The movement dislodges my leg, and he releases my hand to cup my cheek instead. "What're you doing to me?" He brushes his thumb over my bottom lip. "We talked about this."

"Actually..." I flick my tongue against the pad of his thumb. His eyes flare and he sucks in a sharp breath. *Good.* Now I have his attention. "You gave me some excuses for why we can't be together at the moment. And now that I've had time to think about them, I want to tell you why they're invalid."

An amused but interested smile tilts his lips. "Is that right?"

I shift closer, sliding my hand over his ribs and curling my arm around him. To my relief, he mirrors the movement, pulling me closer, cradling me in his arms. It's awkward—our lower halves are sort of hanging off the couch. It reminds me of something my grandmother once told me about always keeping at least one foot on the floor when you're alone with boys. I never understood what she meant until this very moment.

His lips are so close. His beautiful, kissable lips that felt so good against mine before. As if he's reading my mind, he leans in closer and kisses my cheek, then the tip of my nose. Sweet but not quite what I had in mind.

I angle my head and catch his lips the next time he aims for my cheek. The contact unleashes whatever was holding him back. His hot, silken mouth devours me, his tongue pushing my lips open. I moan and bury my hands in his hair, holding him closer. I stroke my tongue against his and he groans. My pulse jumps with excitement.

Griff, always so in control, seems to be unraveling. Fire races over my skin, through my blood, burning with the need for more.

"Molly." He pulls my collar to the side and kisses my neck.

What was I going to say again? All the words have flown out of my brain.

Griff tugs at the fabric of the oversized sweatshirt. Why'd I have to wear his hoodie tonight? It's so big, it's like being encased in a sleeping bag.

Finally, he slips his hand underneath it and his fingers graze my stomach. All my senses are so heightened, his touch tickles. Laughter bubbles out of me into Griff's open mouth.

Between kisses, he smiles. "What's so funny, Muffin?"

"That tickles."

"This?" He raises an eyebrow and runs the tips of his fingers over my ribs.

"Yes!" I sputter. In between giggles, I tease my hand under *his* shirt and return the favor.

But it doesn't elicit laughter from Griff. My attempt to tickle him is more like igniting a spark. He reaches one hand behind his back and tugs at his shirt, pulling it up.

Oh, yes.

I eagerly help him take it off the rest of the way and toss it on the floor.

Much better.

My breath stutters. He's so, so perfect, his muscles straining to hold his weight off me, intensity burning in his eyes. I shift and wriggle myself underneath him, lifting my knees and pinning them to his hips.

He groans and the steely bulge in his pants presses hard against my center. A rush of pleasure pours through me. I did that to him? He could be with any girl he wants but he's excited to be here with *me*. He left his party early to see *me*.

I run my hands over his shoulders and down his back. His entire body shudders under my touch.

"Come closer," I urge, raising myself to kiss him again.

He groans into my mouth and settles against me. Why does my shirt have to be in the way? Doesn't matter. I can't separate our bodies again.

He shifts slightly to the side, putting more of his weight against the back of the couch. One of his hands skims under my sweatshirt again. Eagerly, I arch my back, encouraging his touch, silently begging him to explore wherever he wants. His rough hand brushes against the underside of my breast and I gasp.

He pulls back, wide-eyed, as if he's shocked to encounter skin instead of fabric.

"What's wrong?" I frown. My breasts certainly aren't small. I got teased mercilessly in sixth grade for already needing a C-cup when Cindy Adams stole my bra out of my gym locker and passed it around. Plenty of guys only spoke to my chest. And more than one date has tried to grope me the second they got the chance. Griff shouldn't be disappointed.

"Absolutely nothing." Gently, almost reverently, he touches me again. He leans down and presses a soft kiss to my mouth. His knuckles graze the side of my breast, lightly stroking. My nipples tighten, anticipating his touch. When he finally grazes his thumb over one peak, my body jumps and I whine into his mouth.

He answers with a low sound of approval and runs his nose along my jaw, raising the tension in my body another degree. "I thought about you all night," he murmurs as he trails his lips down my neck, stopping and nipping, then teasing his tongue against my skin.

"Me too," I whisper.

My whole body shivers and tingles when he gently teases his teeth against my earlobe. Under my sweatshirt, he strokes my breast again, lightly sweeping his thumb over the tip.

"I want you so much." He drops his head, staring down both of our bodies to where he's pressed against me. "Obviously."

I want him too but fear rushes in, colliding with my desire, and seals my mouth shut.

I'm not afraid of *Griff*. But of what comes *next*. Of what he expects. How I'll compare. Taking that next big step.

Making out in his car was different. We were on the street. In front of my house. It seemed unlikely we'd strip naked and go further.

Here in my living room, alone, we could do so much more. Am I ready for that?

If I'm not, will he go find someone who is?

Will it hurt?

Change everything?

"Molly?" He pulls back and frowns. "Are you okay?"

"Yeah," I whisper.

"Are you sure?" He leans in and nips my earlobe again.

"I, uh..." My mind blanks.

What should I say? What does he *want* me to say?

Griff

I'm not so far out of my mind that I can't feel Molly's body freeze. I lean in and kiss her neck again, inhaling her. God damn, she smells so fucking good. And she's soft. Fuck, everywhere my rough fingers roam, she's so soft.

"What do you want?" I kiss her again. "Tell me."

"Well..." Her voice cracks and she whispers the rest. "You know...We could maybe...if you want...whatever you want..."

Ah, fuck. That's not desire making her trip over her words. It's apprehension or confusion. *Nope.* I don't ever want her to have doubts. Not about us or anything that we do together.

I want *everything* from her. But I'm sure as fuck not an asshole who's going to talk her into something she's not full throttle into no matter how painfully hard my dick is.

Slowly, I ease my hand out from underneath her shirt and

stare down at her, studying her face. "If you can't say the words, you're not ready."

She blinks up at me. "No, maybe..." She closes her eyes, suddenly shy again. Is this the same girl who boldly threw her leg over mine and practically ripped my shirt off five minutes ago?

"A maybe isn't a *yes*." A mixture of amusement and disappointment wars inside me.

I take a breath. Close my eyes for a second. *It's okay.* This is fine. I'd rather stop now than keep going and have her be sorry later.

"Molly." I rest my finger under her chin, tipping her head back. "I don't want to talk you into anything. I want you to be one hundred percent sure. No regrets."

"But I—"

"No." I press a finger to her lips. "I've waited this long to be with you. I'm not going anywhere."

Her eyes widen and she blushes as if I've just voiced all her worries. "But you're..."

"No buts. When you're ready, tell me." I bite my lip and stare up at the ceiling. *What am I doing?* "Not in the heat of the moment when we're fooling around."

"We're still going to fool around?" She arches a brow in surprise.

"Fuck yes." I wipe the smile off my face. I'm older. The one with more experience. I need to slow this down. "I'm serious, though. I want you to be sure—not feel pressured because you want to make me happy."

"But I *do* like making you happy," she insists.

That's exactly why I need to slam on the brakes. "I know you do, Muffin. Taking things slow will make me happy." I lean down and whisper in her ear, "When you're ready to come on my cock, tell me. I want to hear the actual words from your lips."

Doubt seems to squinch her brows together. Then her head tilts with a sass I recognize. "What am I supposed to do? Greet you at the door in my underwear and hand over a signed contract?"

That's my girl. Whatever anxiety gripped her seems to be slipping away now. I snort and kiss the top of her head. "If that's what does it for you, sure."

Doubt stealing some of her sass, she bites her lip and frowns again. "But won't that ruin the moment?"

"No." Fuck, I'm getting harder just thinking about a completely confident Molly saying any variation of those words without hesitation. "Definitely not."

"I really like this." She strokes her hand down the center of my chest. "Being this close to you."

That Molly likes to cuddle doesn't surprise me one bit. "So do I." I slide my arm under her body and roll her toward me. "This is all I've wanted for a long time."

"Why didn't you say so?"

"You know why."

Her lips tilt into a teasing curve. "What were you planning to do? Declare your interest on my eighteenth birthday?" She tickles her fingers over my ribs, her fingers hot against my bare skin. "Wrap a shiny bow around yourself as my present?"

I rumble with laughter and touch my forehead to hers. "Would you like that?"

She runs her gaze over me, appreciation sparkling in her eyes. "Oh, yes."

"You like what you see?"

She nods quickly, then rolls slightly to the side, not showing off much since she's still swallowed up by my sweatshirt. "Do you?"

"Fuck, yes." As much as I love seeing her wearing my clothes, I wouldn't mind a whole lot less fabric in my way. Knowing she's not wearing a bra under all that material is playing havoc with my concentration. "You're beautiful, Molly." I don't need her naked to know that much.

"Thank you." She stares at my chest as if meeting my eyes is too much. Slowly, she traces one finger over my collarbone, then down my arm. "You know I was never planning to wear that dress to the party tonight. I just wanted you to see me in it."

Fuck me. Her admission steals my breath. I can't think of many girls my own age who would share that my approval meant so much.

"I'm honored." I kiss her cheek. "It made me crazy thinking some other guys might touch your legs, or hell, even look at them." I slide my hand over her hip and gently squeeze.

Instead of laughing, the corner of her mouth turns down and a wrinkle forms between her eyebrows. "You think I have nice legs?"

"Hell yes I do." I really want them wrapped around me again. Soon. "Will you wear that dress for me another time?"

The corner of her mouth slides up. "Where?"

Well, fuck. I'd actually have to take her out, wouldn't I? Somewhere besides the racetrack, a greasy garage, or an underground fight. "I'll take you out sometime. I'll think of a place." There aren't lots of options in Johnsonville. Maybe a restaurant in Empire?

"As long as I'm with you, I'll know I'm safe."

I frown at the strange comment. I'd protect her with my damn life. "Of course you're always safe with me. Come here." Keeping an arm around her, I drag us more firmly into the center of the couch and prop my shoulder on a cushion. "That's better." I hug her to my chest, then release her. "Tell me what's been going on with Molly."

She blinks and stares up at me, the corner of her mouth twitching. "You see me almost every day."

"Yeah, but I rarely have a chance to *talk* to you without your brother adding in his two cents."

She snort-laughs. "Valid." The smile fades and she seems thoughtful. "Nothing exciting. Miller's Farms will start spring hours again soon. So I'll be able to work four-hour shifts after school instead of three. *Whoopie.*" She twirls her finger in the air. "And eight hours on the weekend instead of six."

I'd worked for the Miller family for a few months when I was in high school too. Bunch of cheapskate weirdos. "I remember the thrill of Miller's. Is it still like working in your very own K-drama?"

"Nailed it." She giggles. "Stacy moved Ben to a different department because she thought he was flirting with Sarah, but he really likes Becky."

I only recognize one name in that story. "Shit, is Stacy *still* hitting on the front-end guys? She's at least ten years older than *me*, and she was doing that stuff when *I* worked there."

"Yup. It's kinda sad and awkward. She'll try to insert herself into our conversations and stuff. Like she's one of us. She's our manager but tries to act like she's still in high school. God, that's my worst nightmare. Thirty-five and still working there, trying fit in with the 'cool kids.'"

"Oh, so you're one of the cool kids?" I tease.

She rolls her eyes. "Yeah, right. I just want to collect my paycheck and go. They're all nothing but drama." Her mouth twists down again. "I've had enough of that in my life."

I hate that Molly's never really been able to be a kid. She's been working some sort of job since she was eleven or twelve. Babysitting, fast food, now the grocery store. She's never complained—it's just how it is.

"Enough about that dumb place," Molly says. "How's your mom doing since she moved back?" The sudden change in topic and her hesitant question twist my vocal cords into a knot. Molly's witnessed my mother at her worst. Scenes I wish I could erase from both our memories.

"Worse than ever." I exhale a slow, humorless laugh.

She lifts her chin, staring at me. The desire to understand shimmers in her blue eyes, encouraging me to continue.

"Every time I stop by her place, I'm afraid..." I can't quite form the words.

Molly doesn't laugh or crack a joke about me being scared of anything. She waits patiently, then finally prompts me for an answer. "Of what?"

Should I go down this road? She might think I'm an asshole for what I'm about to say.

"That I'll find her dead," I finally answer. "She'll finally have overdosed. Or gotten a bad batch. I dread going to her place. But I'm always worried that if I don't check on her..." I'm too ashamed to finish the thought.

Those are the most honest words I've spoken about my mother in years. To anyone.

"I'm sorry." Molly brushes her fingertips against my cheek. "That must be so scary every time. Not knowing what you might walk in on."

This is unfair to say when she lost her mother so young, but it eats at me late at night when I can't sleep. "Sometimes, I'm almost...disappointed. In a way, it would be a relief."

"Griff." She curls her arm around me tighter and buries her face against my chest.

I hide my face in her mass of dark hair, inhaling her sweet cherry scent. "That's sick and twisted, isn't it?"

"No," she says, so low I feel the word echo against my ribs. "All that fear and uncertainty has to wear you down. Numb you, after dealing with it for so long." She hesitates and peers up at me. "And even if it's hard to see it, she has to be suffering in a way too."

"Yeah. The older I get, the more I understand that. When I was younger, I hated her for not being able to just say *no*. I wish I knew what to do to help her."

"Addiction is powerful. And destructive." Molly speaks with more wisdom than she should have on this topic at her age. "If she could snap her fingers and be cured, I'm sure she would."

"Maybe that would be worse." I shift my gaze over Molly's shoulder. "She wasn't exactly Mother of the Year before she got hooked."

"That really sucks." Molly pulls back to look at me and cups my cheek. "She doesn't know how lucky she is to have you for a son."

I'm not sure how to respond to that, so I glance away. Shit, what if Molly worries I'll turn into a junkie like my mother one day? "She's taught me plenty about the kind of parent I *don't* want to be. That's for sure."

She lets out a sad laugh. "Yeah, I think my dad's done that for me and Remy too."

"He's always been a bastard," I grumble. Just thinking of Mr. Holt and the way he treated his family pisses me off.

"I know. I remember him being...angry all the time. The fights he had with Remy...I was always scared something I'd do would set him off and Remy would take the brunt of it." She swallows hard. "Not knowing what exactly would set off his temper always made me so nervous."

"You *couldn't* know because it wasn't rational or based in reality."

She hums softly. "Probably. I never feel that way around Remy." She taps my chest. "Well, unless he thinks I'm hinting at my feelings for *you*."

Fucking hell, that twists me up inside. That she feels that way at all. That she wants to risk telling her brother. She might be braver than I am. I haven't made much of an attempt to approach that topic with Remy. Not yet. "Do you? I mean, have you told him?"

"No, but he's pretty good at reading me." She lifts an eyebrow. "Have *you*?"

"No. I don't have enough to offer you yet. And he damn well knows that."

"Offer me?" She nuzzles her nose against my neck and drags her lips across my jawline. "You're everything to me. All I want is you."

I trace my finger over the curve of her cheek. "You mean that?

'Cause when we tell your brother, he's gonna have some opinions."

She snaps her head up so quick, she slams into my chin hard enough to make my teeth clack. "Why? He loves you. You're like a brother to him." Her eyes widen, and she rubs her fingers over my jaw. "Oops. Sorry about that."

"I'm fine. At least I didn't bite off my tongue." I work my jaw from side to side. "Anyway, I might be like a brother to him, but you're his *actual* sister. He doesn't want you tied down here." *Not to someone like me.*

She snorts and wriggles away then stares at me head-on. "Remy might need to readjust his expectations. My grades are good but they're not great. Not enough to earn me any meaningful scholarships for college. And since the situation with my dad is so weird, I can't ask him to fill out any paperwork. Remy's never been my official guardian or anything. I'm not emancipated. I'm basically in limbo."

Shit. Why hadn't any of that stuff occurred to me? "Any school would be stupid to pass on you."

"That's sweet but the competition is tough."

"I'll make sure you can go." I cock my head. "You still want to do the audiology thing?"

Her eyes shine and she lets out a soft gasp. "You remember that?"

"Sure. It was a big deal when your Grandpa Kip got his hearing aids. You always said you wanted to do the same thing for other people."

She snuggles up to me again. "Yes, that's still what I want to do." She squeezes me tight for a second. "Anyway, my brother doesn't have permission to weigh in on my love life."

Love. My heart thumps. What I feel for Molly goes way beyond love. "He's never said it, but I think he worries...with my mom..."

She tips her head back and frowns. "You don't touch drugs."

I should've known she'd catch on to exactly what I was trying to say. "True. But still..."

"Our dad's an alcoholic," Molly says. "A nasty, violent one who treated our mom like shit even when she was sick. So Remy better keep his judgmental thoughts to himself."

I snort. That's not how her brother operates. "The fights—"

"Remy's a fighter. His ring name is literally *Ruthless*," she points out. "For such a smart guy, he's got some weak arguments."

Laughter rumbles out of me. "He's never *said* any of that to me specifically."

"Oh, I seeee," she says in a teasing tone. "You're the one making up all the excuses for why we shouldn't be together?"

"No, just anticipating the discussion I'll have with him when the time's right."

"Ugh, you're not really planning some creepy 'can I have permission to date your sister' speech are you? That's so gross."

"Permission? No. But I can't disrespect him by saying nothing at all, Molly. You said it yourself—he's like a brother to me." I swallow hard. "Vapor, Eraser, Remy...you—our little circle's the only family I've got."

"It's the only family any of us have," she says quietly.

"True." Remy's dad kicked him out when we were in high school, but his grandparents took him in at least. Now they're gone. I had my mom, but I often wonder if growing up on the street might've been less damaging.

"I'd never want to come between you guys," Molly says quietly.

"I won't let that happen. That's why I want to do things right." It's dangerous getting carried away right now, but I kiss her forehead anyway. "I want to give us a good life."

"Mmm." She sighs. "*We* can make a good life *together*, Griff. That's what I want."

I like the sound of that way too much.

"No one comes between us. You and me," she murmurs, "against the world."

"You got it," I whisper.

Her breathing deepens and I peer down at her serene face. Everything in me wants to stay right where I am. To hold Molly all night long. But that'd be asking for trouble.

Soon.

But not tonight.

Carefully, I pull my arm out from underneath her and shift myself off the couch. I can't leave her downstairs by herself. And if Remy comes home in the morning to find us sleeping on the couch together, *lose his shit* won't begin to cover his reaction.

"Come on, my sweet muffin." I slide my arms under her small frame. "Let's get you to bed."

"Mmm," she sighs. Her body jerks as I lift her.

"Hang onto me, baby."

She links her fingers around my neck and murmurs, "Okay."

"That's it." I turn us toward the stairs and carry her to her room. Her door's only open a crack and I nudge it open wider with my foot.

It's too dark to see more than the outlines of her furniture. I cross the room, praying I don't trip over something. Thankfully, Molly's always been pretty neat.

I make it to the bed and gently set her down.

"You want the sweatshirt off?" I tug on her sleeve.

"No. Mine now," she mumbles.

Laughing softly, I turn away and click on the small lamp on her desk. It casts a soft glow in the corner of the room.

When I return, Molly's on her side with one hand tucked under her cheek. I chuckle under my breath. It's an improvement from the way she slept when we were kids—with her face shoved under the pillow. Remy teased her so much about smothering herself to death that she must've ended up breaking the habit at some point.

A fruity scent with a hint of something warmer lingers in the air. Like the cherries and vanilla scent of her shampoo, but softer. Her long, thick hair fans over her pillow.

She sighs and murmurs something I can't make out, then flips over to her other side, facing away from me. My lips quirk. How can my sweet girl be such a violent sleeper?

With her back turned toward me, it would be so easy to slide into her bed. Gather her in my arms. Bury my face in her hair. Kiss her shoulder. Wake up with her pressed against me.

One day.

Stillness settles over the house as the night eases toward dawn. I should go downstairs. If Remy decides to come home early and finds me up here, watching his sister like a creepy intruder, he'll kill me.

Keeping my eyes on Molly, I click the lamp off. To my relief, she doesn't stir.

As quietly as possible, I step out of her bedroom, leaving the door ajar.

Downstairs, I stretch out on the couch and close my eyes. Molly's enticing cherry scent clings to my shirt, teasing me with thoughts of returning upstairs, keeping me awake for hours.

No matter how hard I try, sleep continues to slip out of my grasp.

Molly

CHAPTER TEN

GRIFF

A SOLID *THUMP* RATTLES ME OUT OF SLEEP THE NEXT morning. Or is it afternoon already?

I blink my eyes open and find Remy looming over me.

He kicks his foot into the side of the couch again, jarring me further awake. "The fuck are you doing here?"

Slowly, I yawn and roll myself upright. My spine crackles in protest. Remy's lumpy old couch makes a lousy bed.

"I stopped by to check on Molly." I stretch my arms over my head and yawn again. "You know how much she hates being here alone."

Guilt flashes over his face. "Thanks for doing that."

"Not a problem."

"Eraser said he and Ella picked her up early." He cocks his head. "What happened? Someone bother Molly at the party?"

"Fuck if I know." I yawn again. Really would've preferred a few more hours of sleep. "She wouldn't tell me much about it."

"You talked to her, though? She was okay?"

She was more than okay. We were...I've never opened up to someone the way I did to Molly last night. And the stuff she shared with me...it's like everything between us changed or shifted.

Remy isn't the Holt I wanted to be woken up by this morning.

His foot slams into the couch again. "Where'd your mind wander, Griff?"

"For fuck's sake." I scrub my hands over my face. "I'm still half asleep."

He growls out something I don't bother interpreting and stalks into the kitchen. Ignoring his moody ass, I find my way to the downstairs bathroom.

A few minutes later, I join him in the kitchen, the scent of coffee pulling me along.

"So, how was the rest of the party?" I catch the mug he slides across the counter toward me, pick up a carton of half-and-half and pour a generous amount into the dark brew.

"I finally understand how Teller earned his road name," Remy says. "'*Tell-her-shit-she-doesn't-want-to hear.*' No fucking joke." He snorts and shakes his head.

"Why are you mad?" I try to hide my smirk with a sip of coffee. "Were you the girl in this situation?"

He stops, cocks his head, then laughs. "No, asshole. He tried giving me a lecture."

Well, now I'm almost sorry I missed it. "On what?"

"Let's just say..." He shakes his head. "Teller's got nerve lecturing *me* about who *my* sister dates," Remy grumbles.

What an interesting conversation. I lift an eyebrow. "He did? When?"

Remy shoots a glare at me. "After you ran out to see the garage."

I let out a snicker. What's he so pissed about anyway? Teller's always trying to pass on his wisdom to us; it's nothing new. "Bro, I wasn't even there."

He snorts in disgust.

I feel like I'm missing a few crucial pieces of information. "Wait, *why* did *that* topic even come up in conversation?"

"Never mind." He opens his mouth, then closes it and

frowns. "At least Dex put him in his place. Reminded Teller that everyone and his mother knows *he* didn't handle his sister dating *his* best friend very well."

Whoa. Dangerous territory we're creeping toward. "Uh, pretty sure Teller's over it by now." I swallow hard, uncomfortable pointing out the parallels in our situations. "Murphy's married to his sister. They have kids."

His dark stare intensifies. "Molly's too young to be worried about marriage *or* kids."

So am I. Although now that he's mentioned it, I can't stop picturing Molly in a white dress. Carrying red roses. She'd definitely choose red or purple flowers. Maybe both.

"I never should've let her hang around Heidi," he grumbles.

Christ, that's a stupid thing to say, and hell help him if he ever says that around any of the Lost Kings. Heidi's married to their VP, her brother's the treasurer, and every member of the club considers her a little sister. "Molly's a smart girl, capable of making her own decisions," I say. "She's not easily influenced by anyone."

Remy steps closer, challenge sparking in his blue eyes. "You have something you want to say to me?"

I don't flinch or move away. "I just said it."

He stares at me.

I stare right back.

"Why are you two snarling at each other like a pair of un-neutered pit bulls?" Molly's soft voice interrupts our matching fuck-around-and-find-out glares.

Remy breaks first, his face cracking into the warm expression he reserves for his baby sister. "Pit bull? I'm more like a big jungle cat. A panther, don't you think?" He throws his arm over her shoulders and tugs her closer. "How was your night? I heard you came home early. Everything okay?"

"Ugh." Molly shoots a glare at me.

I hold my hands in the air. "He already knew before I said a word."

"Hmm." Molly touches one finger to her chin. "Ella wouldn't rat me out. Must've been Eraser."

Remy chuckles and kisses the top of her head. "*You* should've let me know."

"Far be it from me to stop you from carving another notch in your belt." Molly flicks his side with her fingers and twirls out of his grasp.

The corner of Remy's mouth turns down. Jesus, if my best friend had any feelings, I'd say Molly just sliced one in half.

Even though he all but ordered me not to date his sister five seconds ago, I'll throw him a bone. "He actually had business to discuss at the party."

Remy nods at me and sends a smug look Molly's way.

Molly isn't fooled by our bullshit. "Suuuure you did."

"Seriously, are you okay?" Remy drops the smirky attitude. "You and Hayden have a fight or something?"

"Nothing like that." Molly shrugs. "More people showed up than I expected, and I wasn't feeling the vibe."

Remy's stare lingers on her face for a few seconds as if he thinks he's some sort of big brother lie detector. "So, no asses need to be kicked?"

"No." Molly's somber tone matches her brother's. "Nothing like that."

I shift my gaze to Remy. Does he sense something's off with Molly's explanation the way I did? He meets my stare and seems to be asking a similar question. I slightly shake my head and lift one shoulder.

"Thanks for sticking around, Griff." Molly's raspy voice reminds me too much of our conversation in the dark last night.

"No problem." If I turn my head and get sucked into her big, blue eyes, I'll be done. Remy will know everything.

Molley

CHAPTER ELEVEN

Molly

After the weekend I had, school seems rather mundane. Every day, the panic of looming graduation and the unknown of what comes next either has me wanting to stay in high school forever or hurry the hell up and get it over with so I can move on to the next chapter of my life.

Whatever that might be.

Well, after our talk the other night, I have hope my future includes Griff.

Hayden and I meet in the bustling cafeteria for lunch on Monday. I haven't had a chance to catch up with her since the party. I should be a better friend and ask how things went after I left. But I can't seem to shut off the annoyance simmering at the back of my mind. She never bothered texting to see if I was okay. We've been friends for so long, she should know I wouldn't bail early without a valid reason.

"Hey, girrrl!" Hayden trills. She tosses her lunch bag on the table and pulls out the chair across from me. Early afternoon sunlight streams through the large panes of glass lining the far side of the cafeteria. A beam of light catches Hayden's long golden hair, casting a halo around her head, making her look a lot more angelic than I know she is. She flashes a grin so blinding, it momentarily obliterates the negative thoughts crowding my mind.

"Where've you been all morning?" I ask.

"I came in late. But don't worry, I've got some stories for you." She leans across the table. "You missed a lot the other night. Why'd you leave so early, anyway?"

I shrug, not in the mood to discuss it here and now. Not when she's bubbling over with excitement, and we're surrounded by every junior and senior in our high school.

"What'd I miss?" My voice lacks enthusiasm. My mind's already wandering back to snuggling on the couch with Griff. Heat races over my cheeks. God, the way his warm breath coasted over my skin...the unrestrained desire in his eyes...the hoarseness of his voice. He wants me to be the one to tell him when I'm...*ready*. My skin tingles all over as I consider the possibilities.

I push the memory aside and try to focus on my best friend.

"Wade and I *talked*." She wiggles her eyebrows, indicating they did a lot more than *talk*. *Wow*. I bet Wesley was annoyed his little brother got some and he didn't.

"I thought you were just friends, and he was too 'studious' for you?" I tease, throwing back some words I'm pretty sure she uttered as recently as last week.

"He's not that bad." She shakes her head. "And he's a quick learner on other subjects. *If* you know what I mean."

I roll my eyes. "I think the table knows what you mean."

She giggles and uncaps her Coke. Brown, fizzy liquid foams, and bubbles over the sides. I toss a napkin at her and shift my notebook to the side.

Hayden and Wade, huh? Numbness snakes through my stomach. I'll be perfectly happy never being in the same room with Wade's brother again. "Be careful. Wesley's a creep," I blurt out.

She stops mopping up the spilled soda and stares at me, her bubbly attitude deflating like a two-week-old birthday balloon. "What are you talking about?"

Damn. I wasn't planning to talk about this at school. I quickly glance around but no one seems to be paying attention. No one's even looking at us over here at our corner table by the windows.

I suck in a deep breath and brace myself. Why am *I* embarrassed? I didn't do anything wrong. I certainly didn't encourage Wesley's gross behavior.

"Come on, Molly. Spill," Hayden insists.

"Nothing." I shrug like it's no big deal, trying to hang onto my dignity with my fingertips. "Wesley said some gross stuff at the party."

"He was drunk."

Sure, that explains it. I barely hold back another eyeroll. I lean toward her and motion for her to do the same. "He got grabby with me." Heat explodes over my cheeks. "And point-blank asked me to *suck his dick.*" The last part comes out as a forceful whisper.

Hayden bursts out laughing.

My embarrassment quickly shifts into anger. "It's not funny."

Hayden blinks, her expression unreadable for a moment. "Come on, Molly. Seriously? Wesley? Are you sure you didn't misinterpret things? He's always been so nice. And he's crazy about you."

He's crazy all right. Crazy disgusting.

My heart sinks at her reaction. Like it's no big deal. Or I'm overreacting. Frustration and hurt churn together in my chest. "Maybe it was the alcohol," I concede, even though I don't believe that for one second. "But he made me super uncomfortable."

"He's flirty. I'm sure he didn't really mean he wanted you to blow him."

I stare her dead in the eyes. "He offered to come on my tits if I didn't 'feel like swallowing.'"

That truth bomb lands with a sizzle. Hayden sits there, speechless.

"Yeah, okay," she says after a few seconds of uncomfortable silence. "That's a bit much." Her nose wrinkles. "Eww."

"Uh-huh."

"Well, what do you want me to do?" she whines. "I really like Wade."

"Nothing." I hold my hands in the air. "I'm putting you on notice—don't expect us to all double-date. Wade's brother is a walking red flag, and I don't want to be alone with him again."

"Okay, okay. Sheesh. Calm down." She blows out a breath.

Her dismissive attitude stings. But at least it's cured the guilt I felt about leaving her party early.

"Forget about him." She continues. "I only wanted you two to hook up so Griff would find out another older guy was interested in you. Then, he'd come to his senses."

I'm sure in her head that makes sense. But that's not the kind of relationship I want with Griff—one based on childish jealousy. "Sure," I mumble, just to move on from this topic. I wish I'd never said a word.

Kyla slams her tray down on the table next to Hayden. "I'm so done." She throws herself into a chair. "I can't wait to jet outta here for good."

Same, girl, same.

Darcy pulls out the chair next to me, making a less dramatic entrance. She sits and greets me with a quick elbow bump. I flash a faint smile at her.

I shoot a warning look at Hayden, but I shouldn't have bothered—she's rehashing the party with Kyla, my run-in with Wesley forgotten.

The cafeteria noises fade into the background. I'm so over this. I'm tired of feeling like I don't fit in anywhere—not even with the people who are supposed to be my friends.

Molly

CHAPTER TWELVE

GRIFF

Spending my day at the gym has become critical to my survival. I've always put myself through punishing workout sessions, but this is a whole new level. Other than jerking myself raw, there's no way to release the pent-up, explosive energy generated from all the time alone I've shared with Molly lately.

I squeeze my eyes shut as I push through one last rep. Picturing my Molly's pink cheeks sends another bolt of lust through me. This isn't going to cut it. My gaze bounces around the gym. Elliptical? Treadmill? Can I outrun this need?

"Focus," Remy barks from above me, guiding the bar back into the rack.

"I'm focused," I pant, wiping the back of my hand over my forehead. *Focused on defiling your sister as soon as she gives me the green light.*

Guilt forces my attention elsewhere.

"Looking good today, boys." Aubrey approaches us with a smile on her pixie face and a hand on her hip. What she lacks in height, she makes up for with her sweet personality.

Remy's mouth pulls into a suggestive smile. "When you gonna leave Sully and run away with me, short stack?"

Immune to his player bullshit, Aubrey rolls her eyes. "Never. But by all means, ask that again when he gets here."

Not deterred one bit, Remy smiles wider. "I'm just messing with you."

Ignoring him, she focuses on me—the one who doesn't harass her every time we work out at her fiancé's gym. For free. "How are *you* making out, Griff?"

With Molly, every chance I get.

I cough into my fist. "All right. How's business?"

"Finally picking back up." She sweeps her gaze over us again. "In fact, if you're down for it, I'd like to film one of your workouts for our YouTube channel again." She gives Remy a sly smile. "You're two of our most popular models."

I know for a fact Aubrey says this to everyone she talks into doing a spot on their channel. But Sully lets us work out here for free in exchange for the promotional clips his fiancée shoots, so I don't hold a little harmless flattery against Aubrey. The woman hustles hard to help her man make his business successful.

I'd like that kind of partnership with Molly one day. When I'm not thinking about when, where, and how to get my hands all over her again, I've been searching for the '71 Malibu Molly wants to restore as our project car.

"Any time." Remy runs his hands through his hair. "Just let me know so I can look my best."

Aubrey's mouth twitches. "You always look good, and you know it."

He smirks at her, then lifts his chin at me. "I gotta head out. You good?"

"Yeah. Thanks, bro." I hold out my hand and he pulls me in for a quick hug and slap on the shoulder.

"Catch you later." He nods to Aubrey, then heads for the locker room.

"Speaking of the channel..." Aubrey glances over her shoulder toward the front door, then focuses on me again. "A woman stopped by looking for you."

"Me? Here?" I swipe my towel over my face. "Who?"

"A Diane something." Aubrey bites her lip. "She left a card. She's from the city."

"New York City?" Or did she mean Empire, the closest *actual* city to Johnsonville.

"Yup. She's a television producer."

"Why's she looking for me?"

"Saw you in one of our videos. I looked her up. She's legit. She's putting together some kind of reality show for cage fighters." Aubrey shrugs. "She specifically asked for *Stonewall*." Not a surprise. For the public YouTube videos, available for anyone to see, I only ever use my ring name.

Aubrey slides her gaze toward Remy as he disappears into the locker room, then back to me. "She mentioned Remy, but she was the most interested in *you*."

"Why? Remy's a better fighter."

A brief scowl flickers over her pretty face. "I've seen both of you in the ring. I'd say you're evenly matched and skilled."

The corner of my mouth quirks. "Is that your professional opinion?"

"Yup."

Aubrey had never been to an underground fight in her life until I talked her into subbing in as a ring girl for us at The Castle. Sully still hasn't forgiven me for involving her in our deviant business. But it gave him the nudge he needed to break his rule about dating his employees, so really, he should be thanking me.

Amused by her assessment, I ask, "What'd Sully think of someone coming here to recruit *me*?"

"He was impressed. Thought it was pretty cool." She winks at me. "I think he's proud of you."

Sure he is. But I return her smile. "All right. Maybe I'll give her a call."

Aubrey's nervous gaze darts around as if she's about to impart some top-secret information. "I hope you won't be mad, but I kind of gave her your workout schedule."

"Why would I be mad about that? It'll make things easier to talk to her here."

She blows out a breath. "Good. She asked me for directions to where you guys fight 'for real.' She didn't mention The Castle specifically, but I think that's what she meant. I told her I had no idea what she was talking about."

Aubrey might be a good girl engaged to a guy who hasn't dirtied his knuckles in an underground fight since he was a teenager, but she's not dumb. I trust her not to spill our secrets. "Thanks, Aubrey."

Her lips quirk. "To be fair, if you told me a pot of gold was waiting for me at The Castle and handed me a map, I still probably couldn't find my way out there again on my own, but..."

I snort with laughter. "You underestimate yourself."

"You *overestimate* my sense of direction." She laughs and backs away. "I'll text you a pic of her card so you can reach out to her if you don't run into her here."

"Thanks." Flattery and unease war inside me as I step onto the treadmill. I participated in those videos to help Sully show off his gym, so he could attract more clients. It never occurred to me that helping out a friend might lead to my own opportunities.

A reality show, though? My face contorts with disgust. I hate those shitty drama circuses. I've had enough drama in my real life without making it my chosen form of escapist entertainment.

They'd pay me to be on the show, right? Probably not enough to live down the humiliation of taking part in an idiotic cheese fest that would be available on some streaming service for the world to laugh at for the rest of eternity.

Then again, if it's *enough* money I could use it to help Molly with her college tuition. Making sure her education's financially secure would be worth any potential embarrassment I'd have to encounter.

The front door opens, letting in noise from the busy street. Overhead chimes tinkle a short warning. A short, chunky woman with bright pink, spiky hair, and pink sunglasses strides into the gym. Aubrey stops in her tracks and glances at me. Tilting her head toward the woman, she mouths, *That's her.*

What should I do? Run over and introduce myself? Nah, fuck that. I stop the treadmill, hop off, and walk over to the long mirror against the back wall. I choose a dumbbell from the rack and face the mirror. Over my shoulder, I have a good view of the pink-haired lady talking to Aubrey. Both of them glance my way and I drop my gaze to my biceps, concentrating on my form as I slowly curl the weight up and down.

"Stonewall?" a scratchy voice rasps behind me.

I flick my gaze up and meet the determined eyes of the pink-haired woman who's maybe a few years older than me. Her lips stretch into a tight smile that seems more like a challenge than a friendly introduction.

"That's me," I answer slowly.

She sticks her hand out. "Diane Yurko." Her tone matches her confident demeanor. "Sidespeed Salmon Productions."

Side *what*? I roll the unfamiliar name around in my head, then toss it off. I take her hand and shake it. "Griffin Royal, classic car restorer, motorcycle enthusiast, and occasional brawler." Damn, this woman's grip leaves no doubt about her determination.

She lifts her eyebrows—also pink—with interest. "Nice hobbies. Perfect." Still holding onto my hand, she runs her gaze up and down my body—not in a sexually interested way. More like she's assessing how much money a thoroughbred she's planning to buy could earn her at the racetrack. "You're even more perfect than I thought."

I release her hand. "Uh, okay. For what?"

My heart thunders as I wait for her response. Shit, was Aubrey wrong? Is the woman casting a porno, not a reality show? Remy would be the better choice for *that* sort of entertainment. My fingers itch to whip out my phone and tap in a quick Google search.

She steps closer, her sneakers squeaking against the padded floor. "It's such a pleasure to meet you, Griff." Her smile's sharp, calculating. The hair and glasses might make her seem young, but her cutthroat business attitude suggests she's a lot older than I'd originally assumed. "I've watched all your videos on Strike Back's channel, and I just had to meet you. You'd be perfect for this new project I'm casting. Your moves are very impressive."

"Ah, thanks." I shrug, downplaying the compliment. "Just tryin' to help out a friend." I gesture vaguely toward the front desk.

Diane chuckles, the movement ruffling the fine pink hair framing her face. "You've got the moves of Volkanovski and the face of Alex Pettyfer, and yet you're so modest. Viewers will go crazy for you."

Heat crawls over my face. I glance toward the front desk. Aubrey seems to have disappeared, leaving me alone with Diane. It's not the first time a woman's complimented me, but this feels different. She's not trying to earn a ride on my dick. That situation I can handle with a quick "not interested." This one, I'm not sure what to say.

"Listen, Griffin." Her keen expression morphs into rapid-fire business talk. "I work for a company that's putting together a new reality show. It's going to be *Survivor* meets *Fight Club*."

I raise an eyebrow at the basic concept. "Brawling on a desert island?"

She cocks her head like I just gave her a great idea. "No. But I like that concept. Maybe *Big Brother* meets *Fight Club* would've been more accurate." She waves her hand in the air as if she's out of analogies. "Twelve skilled fighters—amateur, underground, bare-knuckle, street fighters—will live and train together. You'll compete against each other in various challenges, both physical and mental. There will be matches twice a week and the loser goes home. Last one standing wins a very substantial amount of money. However..." She lowers her voice, forcing me to lean in. "The three finalists *also* win a large cash prize."

Substantial. Large. Cash. Prize. Four winners are better odds than one. Molly's dreams of paying for college without the burden of crippling debt after graduation flash through my brain.

"How substantial are these prizes?" I ask. "Are we talking compact car money, down payment on a house money, or four years of tuition at an Ivy League School type of money?"

She snorts at the last one. "That's not exactly something you're worried about, is it?"

Ignoring the dig, I shrug. "Just trying to get a clearer picture of the stakes."

"It'd be enough to make a significant impact on your life. And maybe in the lives of your loved ones."

I don't want to seem too eager, and I feel like a monster towering over this lady, so I nod to one of the benches. "You want to sit down?" I ask.

"Sure."

She follows me over to the bench where I'd left my water bottle earlier. I grab it and take a deep swig, then sit next to her.

"So, what's the catch?" The money is certainly a big motivator but the reality of putting myself on television, allowing my skills and reputation to be judged by a bunch of arrogant fuckwads, leaves a bad feeling burrowing in my chest.

But the idea of winning a pot of money big enough to fund Molly's college education slices through my hesitation like an axe kick.

Diane switches into serious mode again. "You'd have to be away from home for up to eight weeks to film the show."

"Two months?" Shit. That's a long time.

"We'd pay you a small daily stipend to cover whatever you miss from work. No matter where you end up in the competition."

I might not have a job to come home *to* if I'm gone for eight weeks. Mr. Nelson is patient, but summer and fall are always busy at the garage. On the other hand, he's close to retiring and keeps hinting at how much he'd like me to buy the garage when he's ready to call it quits.

If I win this show, the money could be for Molly's future *and* mine. It could give us the start in life that neither of our families have provided.

"What do you think?" Diane prompts when I've been silent for too long. "You could transform this into other opportunities. You're a good-looking kid, Griff. Got panty-melter and heartbreaker written all over your insolent face and bad-boy swagger."

"Uh, thanks." I side-eye her. "I have a girlfriend."

"Slow your roll, kid." She snorts. "I'm not interested. But our audience, our sponsors, and other industry folks would *definitely* snap you up."

"I'm not a professional fighter." The places and reasons I learned to fight would make this woman's pretty pink hair curl.

"No shit, kid. We're not looking for professionals. And we don't give a fuck if the only fighting you do is underground. Hell, it adds to the mystery. As long as you stay out of trouble from the time you sign your contract until after the show airs, it's all good."

I glance around the gym, as if searching for answers in the weights and machines. "Give me some time to think about it?" Thank God, my voice comes out steady despite the turmoil rolling through me. "A time frame and dollar amount of the daily stipend would be nice too."

Diane nods, her fierce expression melting into something with more understanding. "Of course. I can email you those details and give you a month to decide. Then we need to start the pre-show prep."

"What's that entail?"

"Some interviews. Background checks. Psychological evaluations. All routine stuff. Some things you'll have to come down to the city for. We'll pay for the train ticket. Others we can arrange locally. I can tell you more once you've signed a contract and confidentiality agreements."

"Contract?"

"Of course."

Background check. My juvenile record should be sealed. Not that it sounds like it matters. Psych eval? Haven't been through one of those since I was a teenager getting tossed around the criminal justice system. Can't say I enjoyed the experience or ever want to repeat it.

This would be different, though. It'd be *my* choice. And for a purpose.

"I can tell you're a fighter." Diane taps her fist over her chest. "I don't mean in a cage. I mean in life. You haven't had anything handed to you."

It's not a question, so I don't bother agreeing or disagreeing with her statement. Besides, she's right.

"This could be a chance to level up," she continues. "I'm not saying it will change your life, but it could help you finally get ahead."

Get ahead? I've been trying to keep my head above water my whole life. What would *getting ahead* even feel like?

Molly

CHAPTER THIRTEEN

Molly

After school, Griff's waiting right outside the back entrance. His large, towering frame is hard to miss among the swarm of kids racing toward freedom. I lift my hand and wave, pushing through the wall of bodies to reach him.

"What're you doing here?"

He hands me a helmet. "You're working today, right? Thought I'd give you a ride."

"Thanks." If Remy or Griff are busy, I have to take two buses to get to my after-school job. Sometimes, I'll ask Hayden to drop me off if she's going that way, but our conversation earlier in the week left an unpleasant taste in my mouth. I'd rather walk the extra miles than ask her for a favor right now.

"I'm really happy to see you." In fact, this is the best part of my whole day.

We stop at his bike, and he faces me. "I missed you. Told Mr. Nelson I'd be taking a long lunch break this afternoon."

My heart flutters. As far as I know, Griff always eats lunch at the garage in between jobs. "I don't have to be at work until four."

"We can stop for dinner or something if you want."

"Sure." My voice wobbles. Why? Griff and I have grabbed fast food together before. But everything feels so different after the other night. I step closer, so we're almost touching. "How are you?"

He tips his head and one corner of his mouth lifts. "A lot better now."

"Me too."

"Come on." He nudges the helmet in my hands. "We probably have enough time to stop at Busy Beans for a sandwich. And maybe a muffin to take with you for break time."

I don't have the heart to tell him I don't get a break on the nights I only work three-hour shifts. Plus, I really want that muffin. Instead, I strap on the helmet and Griff helps me secure my backpack.

He straddles the motorcycle first. And oh, the thrill that runs through me when I rest my hand on his broad shoulder and boost myself onto the seat behind him. Some of my classmates—and a few teachers—stop and stare as Griff fires up the bike. But I don't care. I curl my arms around his middle and sit up straight. He reaches back and clamps his big hand over the outside of my thigh, checking that I'm secure. But his hand lingers. I squeeze him tighter and he slides his hand to my knee, his warm touch seeping through my jeans.

"We can go to the house instead!" I shout.

He shakes his head and releases my leg.

A few seconds later we rocket out of the parking lot.

Busy Beans is slow this time of the day, too late for lunch and too early for the dinner crowd. Griff and I walk right up to the counter.

The manager, Brantley, greets us and raises two expectant eyebrows, waiting for our order.

"Um... give me a second," I mutter.

Brantley taps his fingers on the counter. Too bad. The lighting is so weak, I can barely read the chalk menu above Brantley's impatient head.

"Turkey on a pesto bagel with mayo and sprouts," I finally say.

"Toasted?"

"Lightly."

"I'll have the same thing," Griff says.

"Be right back." Brantley whips around and stalks toward the back counter to assemble our meals.

"Copycat." I tease Griff, bumping my elbow against his side.

"Didn't want to risk his wrath and take too long." Griff gives a fake shiver. "Scary dude."

"I kind of miss seeing Aubrey here," I whisper.

Griff coughs and glances away. "I actually ran into Aubrey this morning."

"You did? Were you at Strike Back?"

"Yup. Met your brother there before he opened the bar."

I run my gaze over him. "Wish I'd been there to see that."

He lifts an eyebrow.

"You." My cheeks burn. "To see *you* working out. Not my brother."

He chuckles softly. "I don't mind hearing it."

What Brantley lacks in customer service skills he makes up for with quick, efficient meal prep. Griff and I have our orders a few minutes later.

We take a table by the window where he can keep an eye on his bike parked at the curb. Underneath the table, our knees touch. This almost feels like a date. We're alone together. Out in public. My heart beats a relentless happy rhythm.

"Hey, Griff." A silky-smooth woman's voice interrupts us.

I glance over at the blonde standing way too close to our table, wearing a cropped tank top, leggings so tight and thin they barely qualify as clothing, and flip-flops.

Mounds of dirty, hard-packed snow still line the sidewalks but she's wearing flip-flops. I side-eye Griff. Is this the type of woman he's usually interested in? Ones who don't know how to dress properly for early spring weather in upstate New York?

"Heather," Griff says hesitantly, as if he's praying that's her name. "How are you?"

"Good." She beams and thrusts her generous chest forward. "You?" Her gaze strays to me like she's waiting for an introduction.

Is Griff really going to pretend I'm not even here?

Fine. I'll introduce myself. I raise one hand and wiggle my fingers. "Hi." Damn. Why does my voice have to squeak like a little kid's? I sweep my hair off my shoulder and sit up straighter.

"Uh, this is my friend Molly," Griff says. "Remy's sister. Have you guys met?"

"No." She beams at me. "Gosh, you look so much like your brother." Her smile falters as if she's worried that's an insult. "But much, much prettier."

My nervousness breaks and my lips curve up. "Thanks," I answer, sounding less like a Smurf this time.

Her attention returns to Griff. "Well, I saw you and wanted to say hi. Are you looking for anyone to"—she casts a nervous glance around the immediate area— "work the ring this weekend?"

"We can always use extra bodies." Griff's jaw tightens and he glances at me before returning his attention to Heather. "You've got my number, right? Text me and I'll let you know."

I swear, she bounces up on her tiptoes. "Thank you. I'll see you then." She touches my shoulder. "Maybe I'll see you too."

"Maybe." I force what I hope looks like a friendly smile.

She spins around and flip-flops away. The noisy thwacking of her sandals sort of kills the sexy sway of her hips. If I tried walking like that, in those shoes, I'd trip and land on my face.

Griff acts like she was never there and focuses all of his attention on me. To keep myself from saying something childish, I stuff down my jealousy with a big bite of turkey and bagel.

"Sorry about that," Griff says. "She's not—"

"Dnrf," I mumble around my mouthful of food, then raise my hand to stop him from whatever explanations he's about to give.

He glances over his shoulder and leans closer. "She's not an ex or anything, Molly. Just a girl who helps us at The Castle on fight nights."

I shrug, as if I don't care, although the wad of turkey and bagel I'm trying to choke down says otherwise. "You don't have to explain to me."

He reaches over and rests his hand on my wrist. "Yeah, I do. I want you to trust me."

I swallow and take a quick sip of my iced green tea. "I do."

"I want you..." His hands ball into fists. "I haven't... I don't..." He sighs. "You're my girl. No one else."

What is he trying to tell me? "But you keep saying you can't date me," I challenge.

His jaw tightens but a hint of a smile ripples over his lips. "That doesn't mean I want to *date* anyone else."

I rest my hand on my hip. "Just how long have you had this moratorium on dating?"

"Moratorium?" He chuckles.

"A temporary pro—"

"I *know* what it means." He rolls his eyes and glances toward the front of the coffee shop. "They still have the picnic area at Miller's?"

"Yeah," I answer slowly. I wasn't done talking about *us* but maybe I need to drop it and enjoy the time we have together. "When it's warm enough, we take our dinner breaks out there."

"Good." He nods to my food. "Wrap that up. We'll finish there. I don't want you to be late for work."

I take another vicious bite of the bagel, then slowly wrap the rest of my sandwich and shove it in the brown paper bag. "What's the real reason?"

He reaches over, grabs the bag and my drink, then stands. I follow his lead, standing and pushing in my chair.

"We don't have much time together." He flashes a quick, warm smile. "I don't want anyone else stopping by and stealing my Molly minutes."

My heart soars at his sweet words, then stutters and takes a nosedive. "Because you don't want anyone reporting to Remy that we were out together?" One charming part of living in such a small town—rumors about the most mundane things spread fast.

Disappointment or frustration dulls his expression. As if to disprove my accusation, he wraps his arm around my shoulders and tucks me close to his body. "No. We come here all the time."

True. "You're not usually so touchy-feely, though." Why can't I just shut my mouth and enjoy this?

He leans in and kisses my temple. "I can't help it," he says against my ear.

His lips just touched my skin. In public. My heart's about to cartwheel right out of my chest. What am I even arguing with him about?

I'm a tangle of emotions on the way to work. I can't unravel Griff's words and dissect each of his touches. I'm too busy holding onto his body. He takes the roads slow and easy, lazily guiding the big machine with confidence.

The parking lot at work is half-full. It won't get busy until later. Griff roars up the steep slope to the employee parking lot on the side of the store and stops all the way at the end of the lot where the asphalt gives way to stone, dirt, a few dark-brown picnic benches, and finally, a ring of pine trees. It's a peaceful spot. Even in the winter I try to take my breaks out here, away from everyone. Sharing the spot with Griff makes it even more special.

I clamber off the back of the bike, hopping a little on one foot, almost losing my balance. Griff reaches out to steady me, resting his hand on my waist.

"I gotcha," he says.

"Thanks."

We settle at one of the benches and unwrap our food. A soft breeze rustles through the trees around us as we finish eating. Our conversation flows easily—well, mostly I talk about school, and Griff listens or asks me questions. Every now and then the metallic rattling of a shopping cart over the choppy asphalt or the rumble of an engine drifts up from the lower parking lot but otherwise, it's quiet.

"You want me to pick you up when you're done?" Griff asks.

My heart trips over itself. "Yeah. Of course. I mean, unless you have other stuff to do."

"No, I'll be done at the garage. I was planning to stop at the bar and help your brother close the place down."

I pick at the last piece of my bagel. "Remy doesn't like me there."

"He's not the boss of you." His lips quirk as he repeats words I've said many times. "But if you don't want to go there, I'll drop you off at home first." He shrugs. "I just want to see you."

Warmth replaces my uncertainty. "I want to see you too," I whisper.

When we're finished, I gather our trash and run to toss it in one of the garbage cans dotting the edge of the parking lot. Griff's already on his bike by the time I return. Shoot, yeah—he probably needs to get back to work.

"Hop on!" he yells over the loud purr of his engine.

"For a ride to the door," I shout, wildly waving my hands toward the store, "that's two hundred feet away?"

He flashes a lopsided grin. "Yup."

Shaking my head, I strap my helmet back on, hoist my backpack over my shoulders again, and straddle the bike.

He takes a lazy path through the parking lot, weaving in and out of the half-empty rows of cars as if he wants to prolong our last few minutes together as much as I do. The thrill of riding with Griff never gets old, even if it's only a short distance.

Finally, the bike rumbles to a stop by the door at the far end of the parking lot. More warmth fills my chest. He must have remembered this is the entrance I need to use to clock in. I brace myself on his shoulder and swing my leg over the seat, carefully lowering myself to the ground.

I unstrap my helmet.

"Keep it with you," Griff says. "I'll be back to get you later. Seven, right?"

"I have to count my till, so more like seven-ten."

"I'll be here."

My heart soars.

My afternoon rolls downhill after Griff leaves. My favorite coworker, Becky, called out sick, leaving me with no one to talk to. It's double-coupon night, so we're extra busy *and* short-staffed. Finally, around a quarter to seven my line thins down to only a trickle of customers.

I smile at the older man in front of me and hand him his change. "Have a good night."

He nods and grabs his bag. "Thank *you*. I hate those self-checkout things all the stores are installing these days. I prefer a real person ringing me out." His gaze shifts to the back of the store. "You tell ol' Mr. Miller that."

"I will. Thank you, sir." As if the Millers care about anything I have to say. They'd replace every last cashier with a machine if they thought it would be cheaper.

"Good night." He shuffles toward the exit, leaving his cart blocking my register.

Sighing, I scoot around the counter, grab the cart, and push it against the wall.

Something out of the corner of my eye moves—a person at my register. I hurry back, forcing a welcoming smile onto my tired face.

My gaze lands on Wesley. *What the hell is he doing here?* I glance at the few items he's stacked on the black conveyor belt. *Milk, cereal, gum.* He could've bought that stuff anywhere.

"What're you doing here?" I grab the carton of milk, my fingers slipping on the condensation rolling down the side and drag it over the scanner.

He lifts his chin. "Gettin' a few things for my mom."

"Shouldn't you be on campus?"

He shakes his head. "No classes tomorrow. I came home early for the weekend."

"Lucky you." My hand curls over the top of a box of Lucky Charms and I lift an eyebrow. "For your mom too?"

One corner of his mouth lifts. "Little brothers."

"Uh-huh. Why buy it here?" I wave my hand toward the center of the store. "All the grocery items are like double what they'd cost you at Wal-Mart." Most people only shopped at Miller's Farms for the fresh, local produce, grass-fed meat, and imported cheese. There's a good chance the best-by date has come and long gone on the overpriced grocery shelf items. Then again, Wesley's family doesn't exactly need to pinch pennies or clip coupons.

"Well, I also wanted to see *you*." He can't seem to meet my eyes and keeps shifting his gaze to the side. Either he really wants a package of beef jerky to go with his Altoids or he's wrestling with some guilt. "Wade said you'd be here 'til closing."

"Yup." I glance at the register and announce the total.

He slides a credit card into the reader. "Look, I'm sorry about the other night." A furrow forms between his brows. "I don't remember a lot of it, but I think I was rude to you."

"Yes, you were." I punch the *enter* key on my register. Why does the system always have to take so damn long to process credit cards?

I flick my gaze up. Unfortunately, no one's waiting in line behind Wesley. I can't hurry him along using the excuse that I have to ring up the next customer.

Finally, the register beeps and Wesley's receipt spits out. I turn to hand it to him and realize he hasn't bagged his groceries yet.

Are you kidding me? Nothing frosts my cookies like able-bodied people who can't bag their own damn groceries. I flick a paper bag out of the stack behind me and snap it open.

"Molly." Wesley gently takes the bag and the box of cereal out of my hands, holding them out of my reach. "Are you listening to me? I'm trying to apologize."

"Okay." I put one hand on my hip and raise my eyebrows. "And? You want a medal? I'm fresh out."

His lips twist—in amusement or anger, I can't tell.

He tosses the box into the bag and slides it down the length of my counter out of our way. Pressing both hands on the now still conveyor belt, he leans over so we're almost at eye level. His gaze drops to my chest—of course it does. Remembering the alternative he offered to coming in my *mouth* the other night makes me squirm. I wish I'd worn my sweatshirt over the deep-cut T-shirt with the store's logo on it tonight. The apron I have to wear doesn't provide adequate chest coverage.

"Please let me apologize."

"For calling me a bitch?" I lean in and lower my voice. "Or assuming I'd want to blow you? *Or* for your charming offer to come on my tits?"

He groans. "Can you blame me?" He sweeps his gaze over my chest again.

"I don't care."

"I've always liked you."

Weird way to show it. "Why didn't you ever say anything?"

"You were Wade's friend." He shrugs. "I don't know. And you were a couple grades below me."

"So why bother now, when you're away at school?" Something ugly dawns on me. "You think I'll be your hometown hook-up when you're not drilling sorority girls on campus."

A flash of guilt widens his eyes and his lips part. Yup, that was his plan.

"Not at all," he scoffs, and shakes his head.

"Really?" I cross my arms over my chest. "You seemed to think that was all I was good for at Hayden's party."

"Come on," he groans. "Okay, okay. I guess I *was* a jerk the other night. Now I'm trying to say I'm sorry," he says, as if I'm the unreasonable one. "And..." He pauses like he's about to offer something really great I shouldn't miss. "Maybe ask you out. I'll be home all weekend."

I open my mouth to laugh in his face.

"She's got plans," a deep, menacing rumble announces from my right.

Wesley honest-to-God jumps and lets out a short, strangled scream. It would be funny if my body wasn't going haywire.

Griff.

I turn my helpless eyes to him, standing less than a foot away from Wesley. All six feet, three inches of muscle glowering down at Wesley like he's ready to turn my checkout lane into his own personal cage match. Well, no, it wouldn't be much of a match. Griff could probably knock Wesley down with his pinky finger. Wesley played basketball in high school. He's tall and lean, but not lethal.

My heart thumps wildly as I take in Griff's expression. He towers over Wesley by a few inches. Wesley pulls himself up to his full height and slides his hands over his neatly tucked shirt. With a sneer, he runs his gaze over Griff's leather jacket, jeans, and work boots.

"Do I know you?" Wesley finally says.

Ignoring the question, Griff flicks his gaze to me, his eyes and expression warming immediately. "You almost done, baby?"

Baby. I'm going to melt into a puddle where I'm standing. I turn and glance at the clock on the wall behind my register. "I still have a few minutes."

I grab Wesley's carton of milk and stick it in the bag with the cereal. "I told you I have a boyfriend." I shove the bag at him. "Have a good night."

"But I'm not done talking to you," Wesley protests.

Griff did his version of polite. Wesley didn't take the hint. Now, Griff will use a different approach. I already sense it coming.

Griff steps so close to Wesley, I couldn't slide a piece of paper between them if I wanted to.

"Molly's done talking to you." Griff jabs his finger in the air toward the large plate-glass window behind the row of registers. "Parking lot is that way." He curls his hand into the edge of the paper bag, rolling it down. "You need help to carry this little baggie to your vehicle?"

Why couldn't Griff have been with me the other night?

"No." Wesley scoops the bag into both arms, cradling it to his chest. He throws a disgusted scowl at me, then marches out the door.

I smile up at Griff. "I had it under control."

"I know you did." He hands me a tin of mints to ring up. "I'm an impatient customer when it comes to my favorite cashier." He lifts his chin and purses his lips like he's about to blow me a kiss.

A flutter of heat fans over my skin. I mumble a total and he hands over a few dollars.

"Seems you forgot to tell me a few things about your party the other night." Griff accepts the change I hand him without taking his eyes off my face.

I swallow hard. "Did you bring your bike?"

He frowns. "Yeah, why?"

Because I want to avoid this conversation for as long as possible.

Griff

My preference would be to wait inside the store for Molly to finish her shift. Watching that smug asshole talk to Molly like he somehow owns her but doesn't respect her set off all my protective instincts. I couldn't hear their exact conversation but the parts I did get spiked my temper into the hot zone.

Am I being a jealous asshole because he's the dude Hayden was trying to set Molly up with? Did I read more into the situation? No, something wasn't right. Molly was so tense, her shoulders were practically hugging her ears when she was talking to him. Jealousy might have played a part in amping up my annoyance but my desire to protect Molly overrode everything else.

I'm leaning on my bike by the front employee exit, waiting for her to walk outside. I scan the parking lot every few seconds. Should I have followed Wesley out to his car and kicked his ass?

"Hey." Molly steps outside. Her sparkling eyes and half-smile erase my thoughts of tracking Wesley down and beating the smugness out of him.

I push myself off my bike and step toward her. "How was your night?"

The corners of her mouth tip up. "It got a whole lot better five seconds ago."

I slip my arms around her waist. She leans up on her tiptoes, pressing her hands against my chest. Staring up at me, she tilts her head. Expectation sparkles in her eyes.

"Happy to hear it." I lean down and brush my lips against hers.

I meant for it to be a quick, greeting kiss. We're standing in the parking lot under bright yellow safety lights—not exactly private. Every few seconds, the automatic door whirs open and closed for other employees leaving for the night. But Molly's fingertips dig into my back, urging me to keep kissing her. I groan and squeeze her tighter. Our noses bump together and she smiles against my mouth.

I touch my forehead to hers. "Let's get out of here."

"Okay." She rubs her hands over my back a few more times before releasing me.

Cold night air rushes in to replace the warmth of her touch. Now I wish I hadn't told her to stop.

"No one else bothered you after I left, right?" I ask as I take her backpack so she can strap her helmet on.

"No, Griff," she answers in a teasingly annoyed tone. "You didn't have to do that, you know." She turns so I can help her slip the straps of her backpack over her shoulders.

I curl my hands around the tops of her arms. "Do what?"

"Scare Wesley away."

The corners of my mouth turn up. "Not my fault he spooks easily."

She turns to face me, obvious disbelief twisting her lips into a sarcastic smile. "For real?"

"You're my girl and he was clearly making you uncomfortable—"

"I'm not your girl." Her smile fades. "You won't even tell my brother about us." She flips the visor down, obscuring her face.

"Molly." Whatever protest I was about to make dies in my throat. I flick the visor up and lean down so we're eye to eye. "You're mine to protect. Always."

"Why?"

"Why?" My eyebrows shoot up. "Because I *care* about you. No matter what." I take her hand and rub my thumb over her knuckles. "You're also my friend."

Her bottom lip quivers then stretches into a smile. She squeezes my hand. "You really mean that?"

"Of course I do." I frown. How can she doubt it? "Remy or no Remy, you'll always be my friend. I love being around you, Molly. And I hate anyone upsetting you."

Her smile returns. "That means a lot to me."

"That you're my friend?"

She nods quickly.

"Good." I sweep my hand toward my bike. "Your chariot."

She lets out a low laugh.

"Where to?" I ask. "Home? Or the bar?"

"Home, I guess. I don't want to listen to Remy complain about me being at the bar tonight." She lets out a dramatic sigh as she settles behind me on the seat and wraps her arms around my waist. "Nanna and Grandpa used to let me go there, so I don't know why Remy has such a bug up his butt about it."

I choke down my laughter and start the engine. "He worries about you."

Just like I do.

I'll get the full story from her eventually.

Molley

CHAPTER FOURTEEN

GRIFF

It's a clear, bright, but chilly afternoon. Perfect for the racetrack. I arrived early to help Eraser with a list of chores his uncle gave him to do before we could race.

Molly arrived with her brother not that long ago. No matter how I try to concentrate on scrubbing the grill grates clean, my gaze keeps seeking Molly.

Today, her long shiny hair, a shade of brown so deep it's almost midnight, tumbles down her back in loose, silky waves. Nothing like the wild puff of frizz she started high school with. She's always been cute but something about her tipped her into drop-dead beautiful not that long ago. High cheekbones, full pouty lips, button nose, delicately arched brows, wide blue eyes framed with dark lashes. Every time I look at her, my heart just —stops.

She's wearing another one of my stolen hoodies to the track today, and I can't stop thinking about the night on the couch with her. Touching her bare, soft skin—

"What are you thinking about, goofball?" Remy's voice is a violent splash of water on my fantasy.

"Nothing," I mutter, tearing my gaze away from Molly.

"You better finish cleaning that grill and get it fired up. People will be arriving soon." He points toward the big stone patio behind the racetrack. Usually Eraser's Uncle Pax mans the grill, but he's not coming today so I volunteered. So far, all I've done is clean one of the grates.

"Yeah." I tap my fist against Remy's arm. "I've got it."

I turn and walk toward the far end of the racetrack. Molly's talking to Vapor's wife, Juliet, by the starting line. I catch her eye and she nods. A few seconds later, she meets me.

"Wanna help me get the grill going?" I ask.

One corner of her mouth slides up and she bumps into my side. "Sure. I'll assist you in starting a fire."

Her low, honey voice gives me a better idea. I glance over my shoulder. Remy's way over by the stands, talking to two blondes now. They'll keep his attention for a while.

We enter the stone patio, enclosed by a low concrete wall to separate the food area from the racetrack. Molly and I weave between several weathered wooden picnic benches over to the grill-and-smoker combo Uncle Pax uses for our cookouts. Damn thing's the size of a Volkswagen Jetta.

I flip up the lid and replace the grate I just finished cleaning. "We need coal. I think Pax keeps the bags in one of the food booths." I jerk my thumb toward the first in a line of small, white, shack-type buildings. During the warmer months, different types of carnival food is sold from each building. Except for the one at the end, they're all locked and shuttered. I wave my hand for Molly to follow me inside the open door.

She flicks the switch on the wall, but the power's off. I leave the door wide, allowing some light to spill into the dark interior.

"It smells like stale fried chicken in here." Molly wrinkles her nose and lifts her chin. "Or sweaty feet."

"Maybe it's sweaty, fried chicken feet?"

She giggles and bumps into me again. This time, I curl my hand around hers and pull her to my side.

"I wish you'd do that out there," she says, so low I almost miss the words and the hurt behind them.

"Do what?"

"Hold my hand."

"Molly." I sigh and pull her closer. "I told you...please, just give it some time." I jerk my chin toward the door. "You heard your brother the other day. Did he sound real receptive to us dating?"

She frowns and lifts her hand, resting it over my heart. "He doesn't own me. He can't tell me who I can date."

I snort and shake my head. "It's cute that you think he won't have a *lot* of loud opinions about it."

"He can say whatever he wants. It's not going to change how I feel about you." She tilts her head, killing me with the innocent expectation written all over her expression.

"It won't change how I feel about you either, Muffin—"

"Don't call me that when you won't hold my hand in public."

"What?" I grab her by the hips and push her back until her butt hits the long, high metal counter in the center of the space, then boost her up on it so we're at eye level. "I've always called you Muffin."

"Yeah, but..." Her gaze slips to the side and she shrugs.

"I promise, this isn't going to be forever. I'll talk to him. Just... not yet."

She sighs.

"Hey, look at me." I trace my finger over her cheek and apply gentle pressure until she turns my way.

Our eyes lock. She throws her arms around my neck. Whatever words I had in mind dissolve into meaningless particles.

I lean down. She stretches up, pressing her chest to mine. Our lips meet, soft and gentle. She opens her mouth and I sweep my tongue inside, tasting cinnamon. She's tentative at first, then lashes her tongue against mine.

"Griff," she murmurs, tightening her arms around my neck and squirming closer to the edge of the counter.

Good God, she's at the perfect height. I'm painfully hard for her. If those jeans weren't in my way, we'd be in trouble.

I rumble an encouraging sound and she presses tighter to my body. I slide my hands from her back to her hips and flick my thumbs against the hem of her sweatshirt. Her legs wrap around my waist, trapping me in the best way possible.

She fuses her mouth to mine again, letting out a greedy little noise that sets me on fire. My hands slip under her sweatshirt and encounter another layer. I pull that up and finally graze soft, warm skin. Molly lets out another moan.

"Griff!" someone barks, shattering the secluded and steamy bubble Molly and I have created.

Busted. Caught.

"Fuck." I turn toward the door, shielding Molly with my body. Behind me, she curls her fingers in my shirt and rests her forehead between my shoulder blades. No time like the present to confess my sins to Remy.

But it's not Remy glowering at me from the doorway. It's Dex.

Thank fuck.

Maybe I shouldn't be too quick to offer up thanks. The Lost Kings MC's road captain has irritation carved into every line of his face.

Still, at least it's not Remy. I blow out a relieved breath. "Give me a sec, Dex."

He scowls, but I ignore it and wait until he walks away to turn to Molly again. I asked Dex to come find me so we could talk about a few things. I can't leave him hanging for long.

"Who was it?" Molly whispers.

"Dex. I gotta talk to him." I cup her cheek and press my lips to hers again—once, twice. Fuck, I can't stop.

But finally, I pull away and help her off the counter.

Her nervous gaze darts to the open door. "Is he going to tell Remy?"

Dex is a complicated but serious guy who doesn't seem to indulge in gossip. Involving himself in our personal lives seems beneath him. "I doubt it. But I'll ask him not to."

"Okay." She lifts her gaze to mine. "Because when Remy finds out—it'll be better coming from you than someone else."

"Yeah, Muffin. I'm aware."

She leans up and brushes a quick kiss on my cheek.

"Come on." I rest my hand on her hip and steer her toward the door.

Outside, she flips her hood over her head, as if that'll stop Dex from recognizing her.

Dex isn't fooled. He smirks as she scurries past.

"Hey, Dex," she says quickly, as if to say, *nothing to see here!* As much as she wants me to tell Remy about us, she wants to protect me and let me do it on my terms.

"I'll catch up with you in a few," I promise.

"I'll hang with Ella."

I nod and watch her until she reaches the girls over by the bleachers.

"Have you lost your mind?" Dex says, snapping me into the moment.

Yeah, a little.

Molly

My cheeks and ears still sizzle with embarrassment. I can't believe Dex caught us. Will he tell my brother? Griff said he won't. But what if he uses the information as some twisted loyalty test? Or he thinks it's a joke? Dex could think he's messing with Griff, not realizing the fuse he'll light if he says something about us in front of my brother.

Sweat trickles down the sides of my face. It's too damn hot for this sweatshirt. I flick the hood off the top of my head. The cool breeze swirling around my cheeks an instant relief.

"There you are!" Ella runs up and hugs me. "I was looking all over for you." She holds me at arm's length. "What's wrong? Are you sick? Your face is all red."

That only makes my cheeks burn hotter. I unzip my hoodie

and take it off, leaving me in my bright red T-shirt. I tie the sweatshirt around my waist for now.

"No. I'm fine." I jam my hand in my pocket, searching for an elastic, and pull my hair into a high ponytail while glancing around the racetrack. More Lost Kings have started arriving. Bikers in black leather vests and jeans dot the area. Greeting the guests and bullshitting about motorcycles will keep my brother occupied for a few minutes.

"If I tell you something, do you promise not to tell Eraser?" I ask.

Ella stares at me for a few beats, concern wrinkling her forehead.

I wrap my hand around Ella's arm and drag her over to the bleachers. "It's nothing bad."

"Eraser and I don't keep secrets from each other," she says in a more solemn tone than I expected.

I blow out a frustrated breath. I should've known that would be her answer. But I need to talk to *someone* about this and things aren't quite back to normal with Hayden, yet. "Just this once? For now? For me? Please," I beg.

She chuckles softly and seems to relent. "Okay. I promise."

"Griff and I—"

She cuts me off with a loud squeal of happiness and punches her fist in the air. "Finally!"

Frowning, I step back and stare at her. "What do you mean *finally*?"

"Come on, Molly. It's been so obvious for like...ever that Griff's into you and you're—" She lets out another *squee* and claps her hands together.

Utterly stunned by her reaction, I just stare at her. "Really?"

"Yeah." She whips her head toward the racetrack, then the parking lot. "Is Juliet here yet? She owes me twenty bucks."

"Wait, what?" I shout a bit too loudly.

"She said you wouldn't get together until after your graduation. I bet her that you'd be a couple before prom."

"Whoa, sister." I lower my voice to a whisper. "We're not *together* together."

"Give me a break." She flicks her gaze to the sky. "Oh, wait. Let me guess. *Remy?*"

"Well, yeah." I pull a *what else* face. "You know how tight they are."

"Geez." She bites her lip. "My man better step it up. Vapor too."

We're still talking about Griff and me, right? "Step up *what*?"

"Nothing." She snaps her mouth shut and widens her eyes as if she's completely innocent and isn't hiding a thing.

"Ella?" I prompt in my sternest voice.

"They've just, you know, here and there, the guys have been trying to plant some seeds in your stubborn brother's head." She sprinkles her fingers through the air like she's the romance fairy sowing seeds of love. "Operation Get Remy To Unclench."

I burst out laughing. "What?"

"About you and Griff."

"Aw, really?" I sigh. Damn. I better start offering my babysitting services more often so Vapor can take Juliet out on some stellar date nights.

"So, you think we make sense?" I fight to keep the hesitation out of my voice. "I'm not, you know, too young for him?"

She stares at me for so long, I twitch under her scrutiny. "You've been hanging out with us for years now. You're part of the group. You and Griff belong together."

That didn't sound like an endorsement. "Because it makes things easier on the group or..."

"Damn, Molly." Her face falls. "You know what I mean." She reaches out and squeezes my shoulder. "If you weren't still in high school, I wouldn't think of you being younger than me at all."

"Griff and I have known each other forever." I duck my head. "I've always kinda had a crush on him. But this feels different now."

"I know." Her gaze strays toward her husband. "When we

were kids, Easton was larger than life to me...my monster who kept all the other monsters away." Her voice takes on a wistful quality. "But when we were older and met up again, it was *way* different."

I'm not sure what to say to that. Griff and I haven't ever really been "apart." And even though my life hasn't always been easy, I've never been tossed around to different foster homes the way Ella was her whole life. I had my brother to take me in when I needed him.

And now I'm making out with his best friend behind his back. Worse, I can't wait to do it again.

"Hey, sorry." Ella squeezes my shoulder. "I didn't mean to go all melancholy on you."

"You didn't." I have the sudden impulse to hug her. I reach out, bundling her up in my arms, almost knocking her off her feet. "Thanks for listening to me."

"Any time, girl." She pats my back and I release her.

"What'd I miss?" Juliet calls out. I turn and she's walking toward us, carrying her son, Atlas.

"Aw, hey, little guy!" I hold out my arms and Atlas eagerly reaches for me, a sweet smile stretched across his toddler cheeks.

"How you doing?" I coo.

"No love for me, huh?" Juliet teases.

I lean in and give her a one-armed hug. "I've always got love for you."

"Operation Unclench needs to kick it up a notch." Ella leans toward Juliet and covers her mouth sideways like she's starring in some corny comedy.

"Oh, *reeeaally*?" Juliet clasps her hands under her chin. "Do tell."

Heat burns my skin from my forehead to my neck. "Nothing...just Griff and I..."

"Aww." Juliet throws a knowing glance at Ella.

"Uh." I tilt my head toward the shacks. "Your Uncle Dex kinda walked in on us. He won't say anything to Remy, right?"

"Walked in on *what*?" Ella practically shouts.

"Jeez, calm down." Juliet flaps her hand at Ella, and Atlas mimics his mother's movement, making all of us laugh.

"Nothing...just..." *Oh my God.* My face... How have I not burst into flames yet? "We were kissing but..."

"I doubt Dex is going to report to your brother," Juliet assures me. "He likes to stay out of everyone's business as much as possible."

"All right. Good." As much as I want Griff to tell Remy about us, I want *him* to do it—not have someone else do it for us.

Griff

Desire for Molly simmers under my skin. Our kisses in the dark still have me worked up. Not even my conversation with Dex erased the feel of Molly's warm, soft body under my fingers.

Sweet Molly in her tight jeans who seems to be trying to drive every man at this party insane.

Or maybe I'm the only one ready to lose my mind. My brain seems determined to wander into forbidden territory this afternoon, no matter how hard I try to wrangle it into more wholesome thoughts.

At some point, she shed the bulky hoodie she'd been wearing earlier, leaving her in a tight red T-shirt that keeps lifting and showing a peek of her skin every time she moves a certain way.

The party at Zips pulses with life—friends talking, music pumping, engines revving—and all my attention's focused on Molly.

And those jeans that curve to her body like a second skin.

I caught Spoons eye-fondling her earlier. The look on his face made me want to borrow his nickname as inspiration while I scooped out his eyeballs as a punishment for staring at my girl.

My girl. Mine. I gotta have this conversation with Remy sooner rather than later. I thought it made sense to wait until after her birthday but the disappointment in her voice before has me questioning that plan.

Molly's playing with Vapor's son, Atlas, while Vapor and Juliet take their new Jeep for a few laps on the track. Atlas brought a container of tiny toy cars with him, and the toddler seems determined to show off every single one to Molly. She playfully snatches one of the cars and hides it behind her back. Atlas's giggles fill the air.

I walk up behind her and steal the toy from her hand, then hand it back to Atlas.

"Hey!" Molly shouts.

"No!" Atlas shoves the miniature plow truck right back at Molly and shakes his head at me. Guess the little bugger's as enamored of Molly as I am. "Mow-wees," he insists with a scowl that looks exactly like his father's.

"It's all mine?" Molly gasps and widens her eyes with playful surprise, leaning down and blowing a raspberry on Atlas's cheek that makes him squeal with laughter.

She's killing me. A mixture of adoration and longing stirs in my chest. More than simple attraction—it's admiration for the way she connects with Atlas. It's a picture of our future suddenly becoming very clear. I've never thought about having kids of my own.

The impulse to claim Molly in front of everyone *tonight* seizes me.

She leans back, resting her head on my chest, and peers up at me. "Look what I've got," she teases, holding up the toy.

"Cute." Our gazes connect and the urge to kiss her pulls me down.

The playfulness in her eyes shifts into surprise, then desire.

I curl my arm around her waist. Just for a minute. No one's watching. Remy's busy talking to Jigsaw, trying to secure him as our bouncer at a few upcoming fight nights at The Castle.

Atlas doesn't seem bothered by my intrusion. The little guy's the best of both of his parents—Juliet's sweetness and smarts mixed with Vapor's curiosity and fearlessness. He happily returns to passing his toys to Molly while charming her with lengthy descriptions of each item. Molly seems to understand his toddler chatter and converses with him easily.

My arm's still around her waist. I like it there.

Someone slaps my back, jostling me forward.

Busted.

Twice in one day. What are the odds?

Pretty good if you keep groping Molly when literally everyone you know is within fifty feet of you.

My body tenses. *Let's do this.* I'll have it out with Remy here and now.

But as I glance over my shoulder, it's Eraser's big, bearded face —and he's grinning like a devil—not Remy's fist furiously flying at my jaw. "Hey, we've got a hornet's nest Uncle Pax can't get rid of out back." Eraser points toward the shacks where I'd been with Molly earlier.

Confused, I frown and stare at him. "Yeah, so?"

The fucker taps a finger against his bushy beard. "I was thinking, maybe it would be easier on you to just stick your dick in the hornet's nest?"

Vapor walks up behind his son and scoops him into his arms. Judging by the smirk on his face, he either planned this ambush with Eraser or caught the highlights of the conversation on his way over.

Molly snorts in disgust and wiggles out of my hold. "Is Juliet still on the track?" she asks Vapor.

"Yup."

"I'll take him to his mama," Molly says, holding out her arms for Atlas. He eagerly goes to her, wrapping his arms around her neck. "Since it seems you three have important *wasp maintenance* to discuss."

"Hornets!" Eraser corrects her.

She throws a quick smile at me, then takes off. Atlas waves at me over Molly's shoulder. If toddlers were capable of sarcasm, I'm pretty sure the smirk on his face would say, *Sucks to be you.*

"Why are you like this?" I turn toward Eraser and pull a sad puppy face. "Who hurt you?"

Vapor chuckles.

Eraser curls one of his python-sized arms around my neck and hugs me to his side. He points toward one of the food shacks. "Seriously, there's a hornet's nest on the overhang of the first shack. I'll get you a ladder. Drop your drawers and jam your dick in the hole. It'll probably hurt less than what Remy's going to do to you if he catches you mauling Molly."

"I wasn't *mauling* her." I shove him away. "Shut your oversized cake hole."

"The smarter move would be to, oh, I don't know, man the fuck up." Vapor's shrug takes the sting out of his "advice."

These two love fucking with me and now they have something extra juicy to needle me about, all because I couldn't keep my hands to myself.

"Why don't *both* of you mind your own damn business," I grumble, not in the mood for their bullshit today. Not after my talk with Dex, which hadn't been as reassuring as I'd hoped.

"It *is* my business," Vapor says, "when Juliet squeals so loud it makes my ears bleed. She thought you finally pulled up your big boy boxers. Now I'm going to have to disappoint her with the truth that you're still a coward." He narrows his eyes at me. "You know I don't like disappointing my wife."

Who knew Juliet was so invested in my relationship status? "I'll talk to Remy when I'm ready." I grip Eraser's wrist and unwind his arm from around my neck.

"Then you might want to put those baby-making eyes away, brother," Vapor says.

"Baby *what*?" This is the consequence of sharing a cell with guys who end up being your best friends—they know me too fucking well. "I was not."

"Yeah, you kinda were," Eraser says. "That's why I thought the hornets might help."

"Do you have some deeply disturbing obsession with hornets we should know about?" I ask.

"Don't try to change the subject," Eraser warns with a smirk.

"Fine. Yes. I'm planning to talk to him."

"When would that be?" Vapor asks. "When Molly's walking down the aisle, marrying someone else?"

I shoot a glare at him. "That's not funny."

"Hooo boy!" Eraser throws his head back and laughs at the sky. When he finally settles down, he slaps my shoulder. "You need me to do it for you?"

"No," I grind out. "I'll handle it."

"Handle what?" Remy asks, joining our circle of hilarity.

I glare daggers at Eraser that I hope he interprets as *shut yo' mouth*.

"Nothing." Eraser slaps my back, pushing me forward. "Griff's gonna help me get rid of that hornet's nest out by the shacks."

Seems like an appropriate punishment for a few seconds of daydreaming about my future with Molly. I hate insects. I'd rather cut an entire lawn with toenail scissors than deal with hornets.

"Let me do it, dipstick." Remy smacks my chest as if he wants to stop me in my tracks. "You're allergic to bees. What if you're allergic to hornets too?"

"Good call," I mutter, not at all surprised by his concern. He once watched me break into hives and swell up like Winnie the fucking Pooh after getting stung on the school playground.

Reality slams into my gut like a fist. Molly isn't a daydream. She's Remy's sister. My loyalty to Remy should come first. Every time I give in to my obsession with her, I'm betraying not just a friendship, but a brotherhood that's been my anchor since childhood.

Molly

CHAPTER FIFTEEN

GRIFF

WE'RE PLAYING WITH FIRE.

That's what the old country song currently spilling out of the speakers keeps reminding me.

No, *I'm* playing with fire. Every day since the racetrack, the flames seem closer and closer.

Almost getting caught should've been a wakeup call. I'm risking my friendship with Remy. Disrespecting him every time I'm with Molly—which is a lot lately. Behind Remy's back. Neither of us mention him but the guilt lingers.

I get plenty of adrenaline rushes from fighting, racing, riding my motorcycle. I don't need the added threat of getting caught fooling around with Molly.

Still, I can't help myself.

He's really going to kill me when he finds out I bought her a damn car. Giving it to her will be as good as announcing she's my girlfriend.

But I can't wait to see the look on her face when I hand her the keys.

And I'm really looking forward to spending a lot of time in the garage with her, fixing it up. Maybe I'll tell him the night before her birthday party? Give him time to digest the news.

Something more suitable for my mood blasts through the speakers.

I'm at work in the garage, lying on a creeper under a '65 Mustang, carefully loosening the bolts securing the shock absorber to the car's chassis. Each turn of my wrench punctuates the aggressive guitar riffs and growly lyrics of All That Remains' "The Air That I Breathe."

The *bing-bong* of the bell signaling someone has stepped into the garage breaks my concentration. I ignore the intrusion. The other mechanics come in and out all day long. Any customers should go into the front office and find Jerry. No one's gonna bother me in my corner of the garage.

A pair of pink leather high-top Chucks come into view.

My blood pounds.

Fucking pink sneakers get my heart racing.

Because I know they belong to one girl—Molly. I was with her when she bought them at the beginning of the school year.

I set the wrench on my chest and push myself out from underneath the car.

There she is, standing above me like an angel.

She flashes a shy smile and extends her hand as if to help me off the concrete.

"You think you can really lift me off the floor, Muffin?" I reach up and tickle my fingers against her palm.

"Lift? No. Assist?" She runs her gaze over me, and pink brightens her cheeks. "Maybe."

Whatever's making her blush, I like it. I take in her tight gray jeans, neatly cuffed above her sneakers, and her pink, flowery blouse. Somehow, she always looks cute, sexy, and innocent all at once. I grasp her hand but instead of letting her pull me up, I tug her down. The fender digs into my back as I sit up straighter and brace myself against the car. Laughing, Molly falls into my lap, straddling my legs and pressing her palms against my shoulders.

"What are you doing?" She gestures toward the office. "You're going to get in trouble."

"No one can see us here." I thread my fingers into her hair and palm the back of her head, pulling her closer. "I'm happy to see you." Lower, I add, "Been thinking about you all day."

"Me too," she admits. "Couldn't wait for school to end. I asked Hayden to drop me off."

"I would've picked you up."

"I wanted to surprise you." She curls one arm around my neck.

"You did. In the best way."

"She's coming back to get me in a bit. I know you have work to do."

Work's the last thing on my mind.

I pull her closer. The angle's awkward as hell and she's right—we shouldn't get carried away here. Plus, she's so clean and pretty while I'm all sweaty and dirty. It's a crime to rub myself all over her. She takes a deep breath as if she doesn't plan to come up for air any time soon and the second her soft lips brush against mine, any concerns about my greasy hands on her pristine outfit vanish.

In seconds, she's melting against me, parting her lips, and I sweep my tongue against hers. She sighs into my mouth as I slide my hand to her hip, my thumb finding the edge of her blouse and sliding it out of my way. Just one touch of her silky skin against my rough fingers—that's all I'll steal for now. But the moment I make contact, she squirms and moans. She rolls her hips, grinding herself against me.

And now we have a new problem. My cock's about to explode out of my coveralls.

Breathing hard, I pull away. "Easy," I groan. My lips tug into a crooked smile. "Why do you love to get me going in places we can't finish what we start?"

Innocent eyes blink at me and she squirms out of my lap, crouching on the floor next to me for a second before standing. "I don't know," she whispers. "I'm sorry."

"Hey." I stand quickly, dizzy from the lack of blood circulating in the head above my shoulders. "What's wrong?" I cock my head. "You got an exhibitionist streak I should know about?"

"What?" She stares at me, then a hesitant smile curves her lips. "I don't know. I guess it feels safer that way sometimes."

I frown and stare into her eyes. "Molly, what do you mean? You're always safe with me."

"Oh, I know that." She shrugs and shakes her head like she's trying to find the right words and coming up short. "Just, you know, we can't go too far if—"

"Someone might interrupt us?" I glance over my shoulder, but the small, box-shaped waiting room and office attached to the garage seem to be empty. "I promise you, I can control myself. What'd I tell you, anyway? I want a firm, intentional *yes* from you. When *you're* ready."

I can wait as long as she needs. When we finally get there, it's going to be amazing. I might be doubting a few of my life choices lately, but not that.

"Firm and intentional." She drops her gaze to my dick. "That describes *you* right now."

I groan and laugh at the same time. How does she do that? Shy one minute, cracking hard-on jokes the next. "Only for you, Muffin."

Her face pinches like I'm feeding her a line.

"Come here." I take her hand and pull her closer. She stumbles and slams into my chest. Her mouth opens, a soft *oof* passing her lips. "Easy, girl."

"You make my knees wobbly," she whispers.

I lean down and press my lips to hers. "Same."

She snorts. "Nothing about you is wobbly."

Maybe not, but my heart sure beats a hell of a lot faster whenever she's around.

"Griff!" my boss, a burly man in his fifties with a bald head, big gut, and salt-and-pepper beard, shouts from the doorway between the garage and the shop.

Molly jumps back like we've been caught with our pants off.

"It's okay." I curl my hand around hers. "Come say hi to Jerry."

Despite his gruff demeanor, Jerry's a friendly guy and a fair boss, and he's been a good teacher. He smiles when he sees Molly with me. At any other mechanic shop, I'd probably get chewed out for having a friend in the garage, but he beckons us closer.

"Been a while, Miss Molly," he says. "How've you been?"

"Not bad. I just stopped by to say hello to Griff. I hope that's okay."

Jerry shifts his eyes my way, mischief in them. "I'll let it slide today. You wanna work on some cars?"

Molly glances over her shoulder. "I don't think my skills are quite up to snuff."

He grins wider, his eyes crinkling at the corners. "I'm sure Griff will teach you anything you need to know. This kid's got a gift for restoring classics."

I duck my head, embarrassed by the praise. "I learned from the best."

"Yeah, and what Pax didn't teach you, you picked up quick here."

"I was talking about *you*," I correct, wanting Jerry to understand I appreciate everything he's done for me. "But yes, I learned a lot from hanging around Pax over at Zips. Still learning more every day."

Eraser's uncle collects delinquents like stray dogs. Any friend of his nephew's is a friend of his. When I was younger, he made sure we were fed, put us to work, and taught us basic skills. And when I needed a legit job, he sent me to his friend Jerry who hired me on Pax's recommendation. I could probably earn more working in the service department of a dealership or at a bigger garage, but Jerry lets me set my own hours, gives me interesting projects to work on, and hands me a cash bonus twice a year—on Christmas and my birthday. And he gave me work when no one else would take a chance on me—that alone is reason enough to stay. I dread telling him I'll need eight weeks off to film the reality show almost as much as I'm dreading telling Molly.

"Come." Jerry turns and waves his hand over his shoulder for us to follow him into the waiting room. It's small, with beat-up counters that are probably older than I am, chipped tile floors, several tall filing cabinets, and two chairs on either side of a nearly bare table with a coffee pot in the middle to give the appearance of hospitality. Jerry doesn't like to encourage customers to wait around while we're fixing their cars.

The phone rings, and Jerry lets out a string of curses. "Hang on a second," he grumbles.

"I'm probably going to be here late." I shift Molly toward the glass door leading out of the shop. "You hanging with Hayden tonight?"

"Supposed to do a girls' night in."

"Good." I brush her hair off her cheek. "Thanks for visiting me."

"Will you come over tomorrow? Remy says he'll be home early. I thought we could all do dinner and a scary movie together? Like we used to."

That much time in Remy's house, with him watching my every move? With Molly so close but untouchable? Sounds like torture. "Absolutely."

"Good!" She leans up and kisses my cheek just as a horn bleats outside. "Can I text you later?"

"Any time you want." I catch her hand, pulling her back. "Give me a better kiss goodbye."

She slides her arms around my neck and tips her head, waiting for me to close the distance. I lean in and brush my lips over hers. Way too short.

Like a puppy left at doggie daycare, I stand and watch her jog out to Hayden's car and fling herself into the front seat.

"Your buddy know about that?" Jerry asks.

How the fuck'd I forget that he's standing like ten feet away? "Not yet."

He whistles, low and teasing. "I don't want to be around for that conversation."

I jam my hands in my pockets and stare at Hayden's car until it disappears around the corner. "You and me both."

Molly

Most of my friends hate dinner-night at home with their families.

Not me. I love it when Remy's home for dinner instead of working at the bar until closing.

Even better when Griff's here too.

No fights at The Castle. No clandestine motorcycle club meetings. Just dinner and movies on the agenda.

Since we're all together, I pull out one of Nana's cookbooks to celebrate. I search through the cabinets and drawers until I find her prized blue enameled cast-iron Dutch oven. Many Sunday dinners for our family were made in this heavy pot. Fond memories of my mother and grandmother flow through my mind. I wish I'd paid more attention when Nana tried to teach me how to cook. Usually I preferred sitting on the stool next to the counter and chattering away.

Tears sting my eyes. Why couldn't we have had a few more years with my mother and grandparents? Why did cancer have to choose my mom? She was nothing but sweet, loving, and patient. Our father never really wanted kids and boy, did Remy and I feel it, especially after Mom died. As time passes, I remember her face less. Thankfully, all I have to do is look at the photos in the hallway to remember. Remy's changed a lot of things since he moved into our grandparents' house, but he's never touched the photos.

Damn, cooking shouldn't make me weepy.

"What's all the noise out here?" Remy grins at me from the doorway.

I sniffle and force a bright smile. "Since we're staying in tonight, I thought I'd make chicken and dumplings." I pat Nana's red-and-white cookbook with all the notes in the margins written in her precise script. Little tabs and sticky notes mark favorite recipes, and I flip through until I find the right page.

"Yeah?" Remy raises an eyebrow with interest. "You got everything you need?"

"I think so." I took the morning shift at the grocery store and brought home supplies. Chicken, celery, onions, carrots, half-and-half, butter, garlic, fresh thyme, sage, and rosemary. I scoop each item out of the fridge and into my arms, then carry them to the prep counter.

"Need help?" Remy asks.

"I could use someone to chop veggies."

"Griff! Get your ass in here!" Remy shouts.

I grab the bunch of celery and point it at my brother, fronds waving in the air. "God forbid *you* do any work in your own kitchen."

"What?" Remy widens his eyes as if he's perfectly innocent. "Two sets of hands will get it done faster than one, right? Then we can eat quicker."

Laughing I set the vegetables on the counter in front of him. "Sure, big bro. You've got an answer for everything."

"You called?" Griff steps into the kitchen, staring at me.

My lips part but no words form.

"No, I did." Remy throws a bag of carrots at Griff, who lifts his hand and catches it without taking his eyes off of me.

My lips curve slightly. "Impressive."

"Yeah? Try and catch this next." Remy waves a chef's knife.

"Don't you dare," I warn.

Griff stares my brother down, challenge glittering in his eyes.

"Am I really the youngest one here?" I snatch the knife out of Remy's hand and slam it on the counter.

"Chill." Remy pats my shoulder. "Griff knows I'm messing with him. I'd never harm his pretty, rugged face."

Griff snorts.

"Whatever." I shoot a sideways glare at my brother. "Are you chopping or yapping?"

"Aye!" He salutes me, grabs the knife, and moves down a few feet where he sets up a cutting board and lays out the carrots.

Shaking my head, I start laying out chicken breasts and seasoning them. Nana used to strip the meat off of a whole chicken for this recipe, but since I don't have one, I'm going to try it this way. And if Remy questions me, I'm going to stuff one of these raw globs of chicken in his pie hole.

The three of us work together efficiently. The boys discuss their schedule for upcoming fights at The Castle and who they want to entice into their ring of chaos. Which local underground fighter will bring in the heavy bettors. I'm rarely allowed to go there on fight nights, so I only half-listen to their conversation.

"Didn't Murphy used to fight up there sometimes?" I ask.

"His wife won't let him anymore," Remy says.

"Smart woman," I mutter.

"That's not true." Griff elbows my brother. "Molly doesn't realize you're kidding."

"Guys, I really don't care." I flip the faucet on with my elbow and scrub the chicken slime off my hands. Why didn't I find some rubber gloves or something before messing with raw chicken? Yuck. "Just trying to make conversation. What about Jake? Does he still fight up there? Or is he wifed up too?"

"No woman will have his horn-dog ass," Remy quips. Griff just rolls his eyes. My brother shrugs. "Jake would say the same thing."

Griff chuckles. "True."

"You know of any promising young athletes at school?" Remy asks me.

"Pfft." I snort. "No. Most of the guys in my class would probably pee themselves before the cage door shut behind them. Besides, they're all too busy playing video games. Actual physical activity might put them into cardiac arrest."

We continue like that for a while. For once, Remy doesn't try to shut me out of the conversation. Not that it's a secret he and Griff spend a lot of nights organizing bare-knuckle cage fights and supervising the spectators who come to bet on the fighters, but they rarely openly talk about it in front of me.

Maybe this is a good sign? That Remy realizes I'm not a little kid that he has to hide stuff from. And that I'm old enough to date his best friend.

Yeah, that last one's probably a stretch.

THE SAVORY AROMAS of sage and garlic still linger in the air as I clear the last of the dishes from the table a few hours later.

"Thank you, Molly." Remy catches my hand in one of his. With his free hand, he pats his stomach. "I'd help you but I'm too stuffed to move." His teasing expression slips. "Nana would be so proud. You nailed her recipe." He touches his fingertips to his lips and blows a quick kiss.

Happiness streaks through me. "Thanks."

I can't help glancing across the table at Griff. His eyes lock with mine. Electricity seems to crackle between us. So many unspoken desires flicker in his eyes.

Remy cocks his head and stares up at me. "You all right?"

"I'm fine." I sigh as I collect my plate, utensils, and the now empty breadbasket. Griff's never going to tell Remy about us, is he? Tonight would have been a perfect opportunity. We could have got it out in the open and not have had to hide how we feel.

Griff stands and picks up his plate. "You shouldn't do the clean up after all that cooking." He shoots a glare at my brother.

"What?" Remy shrugs. "I helped."

"Sure you did." Griff rolls his eyes.

"Can we still do movie night?" I ask. "Something scary?"

"Yeah." Remy slips his phone out of his pocket and flicks the screen on. "Whatever you want."

"Nothing with clowns, though." Griff elbows Remy as he walks past him. "We got our own Bozo right here."

"Har. Har." Remy swats at Griff but doesn't take his eyes off his phone.

Laughing, I carry my stuff into the kitchen and set everything on the counter.

"Thanks," I whisper to Griff as he sets his plate and utensils next to mine.

"Not a problem." He touches my shoulder. "Dinner was so good. Thank you."

A happy warmth spreads from my chest to my cheeks. "You're welcome. It's nice to have both of you home for a change."

Griff starts rinsing the plates. "Yeah, I'm shocked he left the bar early."

I open the dishwasher and accept a rinsed plate from Griff.

"What do you want to watch?" Griff asks.

"Well, I guess you ruled out *It* or any other clown movies."

He chuckles. "I'm surprised you even *want* to watch one, since you spook so easily." It's said with concern, not cruelty, so I don't bristle.

I stop and straighten, a damp dish still in my hands. "But you're here to protect me." Then reality crashes through my fantasies. I can't exactly toss a blanket over our laps and snuggle against Griff, using his strong body as a shield every time something on screen scares me. Not with Remy sitting right next to us.

"You could talk to him tonight," I suggest in a low voice.

"He's relaxed and apparently too full to move, so he can't chase you down."

My attempt at a joke falls flat on its face.

"We're all having a good night." He flips the faucet off and grabs a paper towel to dry his hands. "I hate to ruin it."

I swallow hard over the painful lump in my throat. Once it's out in the open, Remy will have to deal with us as a couple. Unless Griff has *other* reasons for not wanting to say anything...

What if he's embarrassed to admit his feelings for me?

"Sure. Whatever." I shrug and flip the dishwasher shut. It closes with a hard, metallic bang, and I turn away.

"Molly." Griff's fingers brush my shoulders, but I duck to the side.

"I'm going to make popcorn." Yup, all the popcorn-making supplies are on the other side of the kitchen. Away from Griff.

"What's taking so long, guys?" Remy sets a serving bowl and his plate on the counter with a clatter.

"Oh, shoot. I forgot those." I turn and vaguely gesture to the dishes. "I didn't start the washer yet."

"What are you two up to in here?" Remy casually bumps Griff away from the sink to rinse his stuff.

"Nothing," I answer in a flat tone. "I'm making popcorn for the movie."

"You sure you don't have some homework or something you need to do?" Remy asks me.

I frown at him. "I could work on a few things, but nothing pressing."

He finishes loading the dishwasher and slaps Griff's chest. "Come help me pick a movie."

"Let Molly choose," Griff says.

Sure, picking the movie will make up for not telling my brother about us.

Griff focuses his eyes on mine as if he's trying to have a separate, secret conversation with me. "She's the one who said she's up for something scary."

Remy eyes me playfully. "Naw, she's going to pick *Carrie* again."

"Hell, no, I'm not. Not with prom coming up soon. Hayden's gown almost looks like it came from *Carrie*. I chose something more modern. I still haven't decided if I'm going to wear my hair up or down..." I glance at Griff. He nods in a disinterested sort of way that clamps my mouth shut. I'd better give up on the idea of him ever taking me to prom. We wouldn't be able to hide *that* from my brother.

I find the air popper and a bag of unpopped kernels that I hope are still good. Ignoring Griff and Remy, I pull butter out of the fridge and chop it into small squares, set it in a bowl, and microwave it for thirty seconds.

When I turn around to find the big popcorn bowl, the guys are gone.

Good.

By the time I run out of kernels to pop, I have two huge bowls of popcorn drowning in melted butter and liberally coated with salt. I give both batches a final stir.

"If you guys want drinks, you better come and get them!" I shout.

They hustle into the kitchen to help me gather sodas and napkins. Together, we carry everything into the living room.

"Why only two bowls?" Remy asks. "Who says I'm going to share with you?" He pops a handful of popcorn into his mouth.

"You better share." I grab a fistful out of his bowl. "What'd you guys pick?"

"*Cabin in the Woods*," Griff says.

"It's horror and sci-fi so it won't freak you out too bad." Remy rubs his buttery fingers over the top of my head.

I laugh and swat his hand away, but he's right. Unrealistic horror movies don't scare me the way home invasion or stalker horror tropes do. "Thanks."

Griff side-eyes us but doesn't comment.

In the living room, I settle into my favorite corner of the

couch. Remy throws himself into his recliner. Griff eyes the other recliner and then the couch.

My breath catches in my throat.

He finally chooses the couch. Close enough for me to stretch my legs and poke his thigh with my toes if I want. I let out a happy sigh. Oh, how I'd love to snuggle up against him to watch the movie, but I don't dare.

He pulls the afghan off the back of the couch and arranges it over my legs. My cheeks warm as I remember sitting on this couch with Griff a few weeks ago and where we ended up. What he said to me.

Our eyes meet.

Desire sparks between us—simmering but forbidden. He studies me with an intensity that raises goose bumps over my skin. He's thinking of the same night, isn't he?

"Goofballs, we watching this or not?" Remy grumbles.

"Yeah, stop flapping your lips and start it." Griff tears his gaze away from me and flicks his hand toward the television. "Unless you're too scared?"

Remy huffs out a laugh and rolls his eyes. "What are you, eight?"

"Nah." Griff stretches out his legs and taps his socked foot against the arm of Remy's chair. "Size thirteen. Don't be jealous."

"Get your dirty feet off my furniture." Remy slaps at Griff's leg and laughs.

"Well, you're still having the same arguments that you did at thirteen and twelve, so at least you two are consistent," I joke but secretly, I love their brotherly banter. Why would I want to do anything to destroy their friendship? I shouldn't have tried to force Griff into saying something tonight.

Uncertainty settles over me like a black cloud. Am I being selfish for wanting Griff to tell my brother about us before he's ready? He knows Remy better than anyone. Maybe he has a reason for waiting until my birthday.

Griff squeezes my toe, pulling my attention back to the moment. He lifts the popcorn bowl and raises an eyebrow.

"Thanks." I take the popcorn and grab a handful, carefully tossing a few pieces in my mouth.

Aware of Griff's body so close to mine and my brother's presence, I barely concentrate on the movie—well, when Chris Hemsworth isn't on the screen, anyway.

The light from my brother's phone interrupts me occasionally as he checks or sends a text. I glance at Griff, who shakes his head. With Remy's attention diverted, I steal another furtive glance at Griff and move closer. He pulls my feet into his lap, gently rubbing his thumb over my toes.

As the credits roll, Griff's phone buzzes. He frowns and checks the screen, then scowls at Remy.

The doorbell rings, the sharp, unexpected bell shattering our quiet movie night.

No. No. No. My heart pounds.

Remy mutes the television. "You said you still have some homework, right, Molly?"

My stomach clenches. The movie just ended and he's kicking me out of my own living room? Did he invite someone over?

"Yeah, I guess." I don't bother hiding the annoyance in my tone. I toss the afghan off my legs and sit up.

Remy's bright blue eyes gleam as he bounds out of the living room, heading for the front door.

I turn to Griff, who just looks...troubled.

"What's going on?" I ask, even though understanding is rapidly closing in on me with painful clarity.

Griff shakes his head and glances away. "Who the fuck knows what your brother's up to."

But I don't believe him.

Giggling and shrill voices echo in the foyer. Blood pounds through my ears, mercifully drowning out the sounds for a moment. All of Remy's furtive texting now makes sense.

A few seconds later, three girls I recognize from The Castle strut into the living room. My brother trails behind them, his eyes glued to their asses.

Ring bunnies. That's who Remy invited into our home tonight. Girls who love hanging around the fights and screwing the winners. Actually, I don't think they're all that particular. Any muscled, sweaty guy who throws a few punches will do fine. They're like groupies who follow their favorite rock bands on tour. My brother always has a gaggle of them following him around at parties and invites some to our house on occasion, although not usually when I'm here. I sometimes have the pleasure of running into them the next morning as they're rummaging through our refrigerator or sneaking out the front door.

"Hi, Griff!" One of the girls lifts her hand and wiggles her fingers. "I haven't seen you in a while."

What's *this* girl's name? She looks familiar. The one with the small boobs, long, wheat-colored ringlets, and hips so narrow she looks like a pencil. She's circled Griff's orbit before. Have they...dated? Or whatever you want to call it. Did *he* invite her? Or did he ask my brother to invite her over?

Why would he do this to me?

Pencil-hips throws me a friendly wave. "Hey, Molly!"

Great, now I feel even worse for not remembering her name and wishing she'd burst into flames just for talking to Griff.

"Hi," I murmur and force what I hope seems like a polite smile.

My brother grins. "Griff, you remember Layla." He adds a knowing chin lift.

"Yeah," Griff answers slowly. "What's up?"

Great, so she really is some girl Griff's banged before? And now she's in *my* house.

I stand and side-step away from the couch. Any minute now, I'm going to be reunited with my popcorn, chicken, and dumplings.

The other two girls—Bunny #2 and Bunny #3—ignore me. They're too busy groping my brother. *Gross.*

"I'm gonna head upstairs." I jerk my thumb over my shoulder. Not that anyone's even listening to me. Finally, I work up the courage to make eye contact with Griff.

"You don't have to go," he says quietly. "Let's watch another movie."

The two bunnies who are apparently intent on banging my brother in front of everyone—including his younger sister—push him onto the loveseat. One straddles his lap and places her hand on his chest. I have to look away before I puke. Remy's always been a flirt and has girls begging for his attention, but this seems over the top. Even for him.

"Where?" I ask dryly. The only other television in the house is in Remy's basement sex cave.

Our perfect family night is now tinged with disappointment. I just want to disappear. My feet shuffle toward the stairs.

Griff glances at my brother and snorts in disgust.

Bunny #1 moves closer to Griff, murmuring something to him that I'm too far away to hear. He shakes his head, and she perches her tiny little behind on his leg and wraps her arm around his neck. Leaning close, she boldly whispers in his ear, so confident and secure that she has his attention.

I might as well be invisible.

Bile rises in my throat and I blindly turn away, groping for the staircase.

Griff's voice telling me to stay never comes.

His footsteps following me upstairs don't fall.

More giggles echo through the house. Someone squeals, "Threesome!"

Is that what Griff likes? Girls who don't even know how to count?

My stomach lurches.

How did our night go from family movie time to amateur porn set so quickly? Embarrassment and resentment chase me all the way up to my room. How could Remy do this? Why didn't Griff tell my brother to knock it off?

The familiar shameful, foolish ache blossoms in my chest. I'm nothing but a kid sister to Griff. I was kidding myself thinking we were a couple. Why should he publicly declare his feelings for me when girls like *that* are happy to jump in his lap any time?

I slam my door shut behind me, but it doesn't stop the shrill laughter and deep murmuring voices from sneaking through.

Screw this.

I grab my noise-canceling earbuds off my desk and jam them in my ears, sealing myself off from the nightmare unfolding below. It's a desperate attempt to protect myself from the familiar heartbreak threatening to consume me.

Furious and heartbroken, I tiptoe across the hall to the bathroom. Too scared I'll cry if I look in the mirror, I brush my teeth while staring at the shower curtain. It's a map-of-the-world design, and right now I wish I were anywhere on that map rather than in this bathroom holding back my tears.

When I'm finished, I hurry back to my room and shut off all the lights.

In the dark, I change into sleep shorts and a long-sleeved shirt. There isn't a single person I want to speak to. I'm too embarrassed to tell Hayden what happened. Not after I gushed about Griff all last night.

I put my phone on airplane mode and scroll through my favorite playlist, looking for something to drown out the painful noise in my head.

Slipping under the covers, I inhale deep, ragged breaths and force my mind to follow the meditative story flowing through my earbuds, intended to soothe and calm my troubled heart.

But the space in my chest where my heart should be feels hollow. I left it in a million pieces on the floor downstairs for everyone to stomp all over.

It's a long time before sleep shackles itself around my ankles and eventually drags me under.

Molley

CHAPTER SEVENTEEN

GRIFF

WHAT THE FUCK IS EVEN HAPPENING?

I should've known Remy was up to no good when he kept fucking around on his phone during the movie. But inviting these girls over to the house? This is bullshit.

Layla in my lap. In front of Molly. Remy implying Layla and I have a history in front of Molly.

Wait. Molly's gone. Shit.

"Um." Not wanting to put my hands on Layla, I slide myself to the side, out from underneath her bony butt cheeks. Unfortunately, she topples onto the couch, then slides onto the floor with a hard *thump*.

Shit. I wasn't trying to hurt the girl—I just wanted her out of my lap.

"Sorry." I'd offer a hand to help her off the floor, but I don't want to give her the wrong idea.

Too late. Seems she arrived at the house with plenty of her own ideas. She curls her fingers over my knee and pulls herself into a kneeling position in front of me. Licking her lips, she drops her gaze to my crotch, making it clear what she's after.

Nope. Hell fucking no. I jump off the couch like my ass is on fire, shooting a glare at Remy.

"What's the matter?" He has the nerve to smirk at me. "I think Layla wants to take care of you. Don't be rude."

"Fuck off," I snarl.

Layla's confused eyes dart between Remy and me.

I glance at the staircase. Molly must've gone to her room. Should I run upstairs and check on her? Will Remy stop me? Oh, I'd love to see him fucking try. Enough anger's burning through me that I'd probably relocate his jaw to his ass.

Just what I need to do—cause a scene in front of these girls and give them shit to gossip about later. Vile stuff that could get back to Molly and end up hurting her.

Should I get the fuck out of here and deal with Remy tomorrow when I'm not shaking with rage?

My feet are already moving toward the front door before I make up my mind. I grab my sneakers and jam them on.

"Where you going, bro?" Remy shouts.

I stomp into the archway between the hall and the living room to glare at him. "Home, asshole."

"More for me!" Remy's words and laughter follow me out the door.

CHAPTER EIGHTEEN

GRIFF

THE NEXT MORNING WHEN REMY OPENS THE FRONT door, his face has never looked so fucking punchable.

"Morning," he rasps. "Why're you here so early?"

"We need to talk."

He stares at me, then takes a step back. "What are you, a vampire waiting for a fucking invitation?" He opens the door wider.

I step inside and close the door behind me. Except for the faint scent of coffee, the house seems perfectly still. "Your fan club still here?"

"Nah." He waves his hand in the air and takes a sip of the coffee in his mug. His gaze drops to my empty hands. "What? No muffins today?"

"Busy Beans isn't open this early."

He yawns, loud and obnoxiously, blowing his rancid morning breath in my direction. "You should've just spent the night if you were going to be waking me up this early." He yawns again.

"Stop breathing on me, fucker." I wave my hand in the air. "I don't know if I should give you a breath mint or toilet paper."

He, of course, exhales in my face.

I shove him away and gesture to the mug in his hands.

"Obviously you've been up long enough to make coffee, jackass." Anger from last night still simmers in my blood and I can't keep it out of my voice.

"Christ, settle down," he grumbles. "Maybe if you'd let Layla blow you, you wouldn't be so fucking grumpy today."

"Stop being such a dick." I slept like shit. Sent Molly a bunch of texts when I got home, and she ignored every single one.

"What's got you so pressed, Royal?" He turns and lazily swaggers toward the kitchen, and I follow.

All night long I worked out what I wanted to say. How to phrase it so he'd understand Molly's not a hookup. What we have is real. Serious. And most importantly, I'm not asking for his permission to date his sister. This is a courtesy conversation to give him some information and that's all.

In the kitchen, he stops next to the coffeepot and sets his mug on the counter.

"I need to talk to you about something," I say.

Remy turns and raises an eyebrow. "You said that already." He rolls his hand through the air in a get-on-with-it gesture and leans against the counter. "Speak."

I take a deep breath and look him dead in the eyes. "Don't ever pull a stunt like last night again."

He lifts one cocky eyebrow. "What stunt?"

Is that genuine confusion or is he fucking with me?

Fuck, I'm tired of dicking around about my feelings for Molly. I'm tired of making excuses for why I don't want to fuck random girls after the fights and why I avoid the muffler bunnies who hang around the motorcycle clubs we've partied with.

Remy's my best friend. Even if I'm pissed with him for last night, he doesn't know *why*. So even if he uses those steel hammers he calls fists to beat the daylights out of me, he deserves the truth.

"Last night with the girls," I say in a calmer tone. "Don't ever spring something on me like that again. It wasn't cool that you did that in front of Molly."

Now he's on the alert. His eyes narrow, and he cocks his head. "What do you mean?" He says each word with slow deliberation.

Here we go. "I don't want you insinuating that I hook up with random girls in front of your sister."

He scratches the side of his head, like a cartoon character suffering from a case of confusion. A smirk twitches at the corners of his looking-more-punchable-by-the-second mouth. "I don't understand," he says, as slow as someone who just got kicked in the head by a donkey. "What's my sister have to do with anything?"

"Come on, Remy."

He crosses his arms over his chest. "No, explain it to me like I'm five. Why don't you want my sister seeing you with other women? I can't possibly understand the problem."

This motherfucker. He knows. He fucking *knows.* "You sure you're ready to hear this, bro?"

"Oh, I'm *dying* to hear it, *bro,*" he fires back with an extra dose of sarcasm.

"I want to be with Molly." I tap my chest. "No one else."

The amusement slides off his face and something a lot more deadly takes its place. He didn't end up with the ring name *Ruthless* by accident.

"You want to *be* with her?" He takes a step forward. "*My* sister."

"Yes."

"You and Molly?" Another step forward. "My *little* sister, Molly."

Another inch and we'll be toe-to-toe, but I stay right where I am. "Yes."

Since he seems to be working it out in his head, I wait with my mouth shut.

"You're serious?" His eyebrows crawl halfway up his giant forehead.

"More serious than I've ever been about anything in my life."

His gaze narrows as he studies me. "Then why aren't you with her?"

That's not the question I expected. Nope. On the absurdly long list of things I thought might come out of Remy's foul mouth this morning, that hadn't been one. "What?"

He shrugs and takes a step back. "There. Was that so hard?"

Utterly confused, I stare at him until his meaning sinks in. "You already knew?"

His mouth slides to the side. "How fucking stupid do you think I am?"

Shit. Exactly how *much* does he know? This could take a dangerous turn.

I jerk my shoulders up in a zero-fucks-given shrug. "Pretty fucking stupid."

He snorts, not offended, because he knows I'm lying.

"For one thing, Vapor and Eraser ain't as subtle as they think they are with all their, 'Gee, Griff sure is sweet on Molly,' hints," he says in the fakest, most sarcastic, high-pitched voice he's capable of.

I bust out laughing. "Neither of them talk like that."

"Close enough," he says. "Then there are the bunnies from The Castle."

"What about them?" I ask cautiously. I have a feeling I already know what he's going to say.

"Oh, just moaning and complaining about your lack of interest for months." He lifts his gaze to the ceiling. "Maybe closer to a year now? And let's not forget that you turned down literal porn stars when we were partying with the Lost Kings down in Virginia."

"Dude, *you* should've followed my lead and passed on the porn stars too. I'm pretty sure the prez of that charter's gonna gut you one day."

Ignoring that, he pokes me in the chest like he's not done dazzling me with his brilliant observation skills. "You've been working yourself to exhaustion at Sully's gym. And when you're not *there* or at work, you're helping me at the bar."

"I've always helped you out." I slap my hand over my stomach. "And I've been hitting the gym for years. That's why I look so much better than you with my shirt off."

"It's different, though." He squints, disregarding my attempt to distract him with insults. "You've been more focused than ever. Disciplined. Like you need to keep yourself *extra* busy. *Orrrr...*" He drags out the word like he's a bargain basement magician about to pull a quarter from behind my ear. "You're trying to burn off all the energy your dick isn't expending somewhere else."

Christ on a stick. Am I that obvious? "Your attention to my dick's social calendar is highly disturbing." I scoff and look away.

He huffs a sound full of tired sarcasm. "You asked."

"Not for that much detail." I shake my head, still confused. "Then why'd you try to push poor Layla on me last night?"

"Got you all fired up, didn't it?" He crosses his arms over his chest. "We're finally having this conversation today, aren't we?"

Reality slaps me in the face. "You did that on purpose?" Fury sends my voice into the stratosphere. I throw my arms forward and shove him. Hard.

He absorbs the blow, barely moving an inch. "It was time for you to man the fuck up and tell me the truth. Otherwise you're not good enough to date my sister."

"Seriously?" I blow out a long, irritated breath. "That was your weak-ass way of testing me?"

"Sure." He nods without a hint of shame or remorse. "If you'd fucked one of 'em, I'd have known you're not serious about Molly. *And* it would've finally killed her crush on you. Solved two problems with one blow job."

What the fuck? "Everything Molly did last night, making dinner..." I gesture toward the stove and the big blue pot Molly used, sitting clean on one of the back burners waiting for someone to put it away..."The good time we had hanging out, you ruined all of it just to force me into telling you about us?"

His smile falters.

Working up to a rage, I continue. "You're pissed at me for not being straight with you? I get it. You want to test me? That's fine. I don't give a shit. I can handle whatever you want to throw at me. And maybe you're right—I should've come to you sooner." I step closer and lower my voice. "But don't you *ever* fuck with Molly's head like that again."

Concern darkens his eyes. "Doesn't she trust you?"

"Yeah." I frown. After last night and all the unanswered texts, I'm not so sure she does. But that's for Molly and me to work out —in private. "We're not *together* together, and she—"

"What's stopping you?" he asks. "Don't say it's me. If you *luuuv* her so much, why aren't you together?"

Is he kidding? "Uh." My gaze slides to my shoes, and I run my hand over the back of my neck. "She still has some turning eighteen to do."

I meet his eyes again but don't find the anger I expected. He's more...thoughtful. And with Remy, that's scarier than his fury. "Her birthday's next month, ya dick. Our father sure as shit has no say in what either of us do." He scratches his chin. "And obviously you weren't planning to ask for *my* permission anytime soon."

I shrug. "She's not keen on the whole *permission* thing."

He snorts. "Yeah, I figured. So, what's the big deal?"

"Okay. Great." I take a step toward the dining room. "Glad we cleared this up."

"Whoa." Remy hurries to block my path and slaps his hand against my chest, stopping me. "Slow down there, cowboy."

I knew that was too easy.

"I'm cool with you *dating* Molly. But there'll be no sleepovers at your apartment. You treat her with respect." Remy's never sounded more like a dad in his life.

"You're sure you're okay with this?"

"Why? You going to give her up if I say no?"

My blood pressure spikes again. "Fuck no."

His face loses some of the hard edge. "I know you'll be good to her." He lowers his voice. "I *know* how much you care about her and wouldn't let anything hurt her."

That doesn't require an answer, so I just nod.

"By *anything*, I mean you too," he adds.

"I can't guarantee one of us won't get hurt but I'll do everything I can to make sure it's me."

"So will I." He stares at me.

"I hear you."

"Good. Then hear this too." He crosses his arms over his chest. For someone who acted so sleepy when I got here, he sure put a lot of thought into this conversation. "I want her to finish college. So you can date her on two conditions."

He's dead serious, so I wait for his "conditions."

"Don't get her pregnant, and do *not* stop her from going to school wherever she wants to go."

I swallow hard and focus on his second request. "I'd never do that. I want her to go to college as much as you do."

"Good."

Since we're being so open and honest this morning... "Now, I have something I need *you* to do."

"Letting you date my sister isn't enough?"

I glare at him. "It's not for me. You gotta do something to help Molly out."

"Help her with what?" He scowls. "I'm not giving her advice on how to date you."

"What?" I screw my face into a what-the-fuck expression. "It's not about *us*. It's about *her*. She needs financial aid forms filled out for college."

Remy blinks at me. How has none of this occurred to him yet? I didn't understand right away. But Molly lives with him, and he's fixated on her getting out of this town and going away to college. He's smart enough to know college isn't free or even cheap.

Then again, he's busy working his ass off every waking

moment, trying to maintain this house and his grandparents' business. "She can explain it better than I can," I say, not wanting to bring up their dad right now.

"All right. I'll talk to her." He holds his arms out. "Get over here, jackass."

How can I say no? He handled this a lot better than I ever expected. Still wary, I go in slow, accepting a brief hug. He smacks me on the back a few times—with more force than necessary.

Why the fuck didn't I come clean sooner?

After a few seconds, he pushes me away and drills me with a hard stare. "One last thing."

I lift an eyebrow and wait.

"You cheat on her"—he points a finger in my face—"I'll break you in half."

My anger bubbles to the surface. "The fuck is wrong with you?" I slap his hand away. "I just told you to stop trying to shove bunnies on my dick because I'm crazy about your sister."

He barely reacts to my outburst. "Still, I want you to understand, best friend or not, if you do anything to hurt or embarrass her in any way, I'll fucking end you."

"I'd *never* cheat on her."

He reaches out and slaps my cheek a few times. "Yeah, you're not like me. One girl's all your squishy, wholesome heart can handle."

I smack his hand away again. It's been a few months since Remy and I faced off in the cage. Maybe we're due for a round of sparring. "She's the *only* girl I want to *handle*."

"You sure she feels the same way?" He cocks his head, ignoring the dirty emphasis I put on "handle."

Is he still fucking with me or is that a serious question?

"We've, you know, talked." My mind flashes back to the night we made out in front of the house. And on the couch in Remy's living room. At the racetrack. At the garage...outside of Molly's job. My lips curl up. We've done a *lot* more than talk.

My dirty thoughts must register on my face. Remy rolls his eyes. "I don't want to know."

"Yeah, you really don't." I return his smirk.

"Better prepare yourself for prom. You heard her last night. She can't wait to get dressed up, get her hair done, all that stuff. She's been talking about it for weeks."

Dressing up has never been high on my list of priorities. But for Molly, I'll wear whatever puts the biggest smile on her face. "I can do that."

"Shit, bro. You didn't even go to your *own* prom."

Yeah, I was at Castle Correctional at the time. The only dancing happening there was with death. "I remember."

He lifts his chin. "She's probably awake. Go upstairs if you want to talk to her. Give her the good news."

"Which is?"

He grins like a fool. "That you finally found your balls and confessed your sins."

Man, I walked right into that one. "I can't believe I'm going to have such an asshole for a brother-in-law one day."

His jaw drops.

I grin and slap his cheek, then bounce out of the room.

After last night, he deserves that final jab.

Molley

CHAPTER NINETEEN

GRIFF

"Keep the door open!" Remy shouts after me.

Laughing, I hurry through the living room, sliding on the hardwood floors as I make the turn for the staircase.

Finally. The weight of sneaking around and pretending Molly's nothing more than a friend has *finally* been lifted from my shoulders. I should've done this weeks ago. Who knew Remy wouldn't flip his shit?

At the top of the stairs, I pause. What the fuck am I acting so cheery for? I should've punched Remy for the stunt he pulled last night. Diabolical fucking asshole.

Does Molly even know I left early last night?

She would if she'd bothered to check her phone.

The soft twang of country music reaches me in the hallway outside Molly's bedroom. My mouth turns up when I catch Molly's soft voice singing along.

"Sometimes your white knight rides a Harley,
Sometimes he saves you from drowning,
When you're only in three feet of water..."

The door's open a crack and I stop.

Pink socks. She's lying in bed on her stomach, feet in the air, and that's the first thing that comes into view. Pink socks with little red cherries dotted all over them. Long, bare legs. Loose, black cotton shorts with pink flamingos that show off every curve of her butt. Black, long-sleeved T-shirt, lifted a little, baring her skin.

I rap my knuckles against the door. She clicks the music off, closes her book, and glances over her shoulder.

"Griff?" She rolls to her side and sits up. "What're you doing in my bedroom at this hour?"

"Need to talk to you." I lift my chin toward the small red speaker on her nightstand. "Were you listening to Shelby Morgan?"

A quick grin stretches across her lips. "Yeah." She yawns and runs her hands over her hair, gathering it into one hand, then letting it loose. Her happy surprise at seeing me seems to fade into sadness. "Did...did you stay over?"

"No. I went home right after you left." I nod to her bed. "Last night."

She tucks one leg under her butt and her curious blue eyes meet mine. "Does Remy know you're up here?"

"Yup. Just saw him."

"Oh." Her gaze flits around the room, looking at anything but me. "Okay."

"Can we talk?"

This calls for me to be a hell of a lot closer, so I step all the way inside. Haven't been in her room since the night I carried her up to bed. Before that, it must've been when I helped Remy move her into the house. Once I realized my feelings for Molly had changed, it seemed like a bad idea to get too comfortable in her space—or anywhere near a bed whenever she was around.

As I approach, her lips twitch into a shaky smile. "What're you doing?" she whispers.

"Talking to my girl."

Another raised brow. "Your girl?"

I drop down on the bed next to her and take her hands in mine. "Yeah. My girl."

Her jaw tightens and she pulls her hands out of my grasp. Is she thinking about last night? About Layla in my lap? Is she mad I didn't chase after her?

It doesn't matter. None of that matters now.

"I'm not your girl," she whispers but then her voice gains strength. "Looked like *Layla* was your girl last night. She seemed awfully cozy in your lap." She glares at me. "Didn't look like her first time sitting on your throne, *Royal*."

Her jealousy's kind of cute. She has no idea that I felt nothing but annoyance when Layla touched me.

But Molly's tough-girl act is just that—an act. There's nothing cute about the hurt in her eyes.

"No other girl will ever touch my lap again," I swear with the solemn tone of a priest taking a vow. "I promise."

She presses her fist into the mattress and slides a few inches away. "Don't make fun of me."

"I'm not. I'm serious."

"What are you going to do? Toss her on the floor next time?"

"There won't *be* a next time." I reach over and curl my arm around Molly's waist, dragging her closer, rumpling her bedspread. In a smooth move, I sweep her up and into my lap, draping her legs over mine and clamping my hand over her thighs to keep her where I want her.

Remy said, "keep the door open." He didn't say anything about touching Molly.

"*You'll* be the only one in my lap from now on," I swear.

"Oh, please." She waves a dismissive hand in front of my face.

I capture her wrist and press her palm against my chest. "I'm serious. Last night was stupid, Muffin. I didn't know your brother planned to have those girls over. He caught me off-guard."

Her gaze flits to mine and then away. "You can do whatever you want."

"I *want* to be with you. And that's what I told Remy downstairs a few minutes ago."

She pulls back, wide, disbelieving eyes trained on mine, her hand still pressed to my chest. "No you didn't."

"Have I ever lied to you?"

"How would I know?"

That stings. I've always been honest with her. But I also understand she's still hurt from last night. "You know me, Molly." I press my fingers under her chin, tipping her head back.

"You really told him?" Her voice picks up a hint of excitement. "I thought you wanted to wait until my birthday?"

"Not after last night. I don't want to put you through that again. And if I didn't tell him, he'd—"

"Keep trying to fix you up with other women?"

Fix up sounds a lot kinder than what Remy had actually intended. But I don't want her to turn her anger on her brother. "Exactly."

She drops her hand from my chest and hooks two of her fingers around two of mine. She tilts her head, and her lips curve into a shy smile. "So, you and me?"

"You and me," I confirm. "No more sneaking around."

"I like how that sounds." She glances at the open door and a frown creases her brow.

"Your brother slapped a few conditions on us being together," I explain. "One was leaving the door open."

"Oh." She snorts and rolls her eyes. "Figures."

"So, you got a prom date yet?"

The sweetest pink spreads over her cheeks, and she ducks her head. "No. I'm going with my girl gang. Why?"

"Want to go with me, instead?"

Her eyes widen. "You know I do." Without glancing down, her fingers pull at the fringe of the blanket at the end of her bed. "I thought you were worried...I don't want to get you in any trouble."

"It'll be okay."

She raises an eyebrow, her face wearing an expression very

similar to her brother's. "You talked to Remy about taking me to prom too?"

"He suggested it."

"Wow. I didn't see that coming."

"Neither did I." I push her hair behind her ear. "I should've manned the fuck up and said something to him sooner." I blow out an annoyed breath. "You've been asking me to for weeks…" What else can I say that doesn't make me sound like the ball-less wonder Remy accused me of being?

"I understand." She curls her fingers around my hand and sets it on her leg. Her smooth, bare leg. The spot right above her knee that I love to grab. "Can we not talk about Remy for a little while?"

She shifts her body, positioning herself directly in my lap, her knees tight to my hips. Heat races over my skin. I tug at the collar of my shirt.

"Can I tell you something?" she asks in a low voice.

"You can tell me anything."

"I can't stop thinking about that night in your car."

I clear my throat as she moves in closer, her lips hovering near my neck. She doesn't have to say which night in my car. I already know. The same night plays over and over in my head too.

"You made me feel so good, Griff." She presses her lips to a spot below my ear I never realized was so sensitive. "I want to learn how to do that for you."

Liquid fire shoots through my veins. "Yeah?"

She nods slowly.

I slide my hand up her thigh, straight under her loose shorts, encountering nothing in my way. Just her warm, silky skin. I repeat the motion with my other hand until I'm clutching her bare ass. "You're not wearing underwear."

She laughs softly, the vibrations spearing me like jolts of electricity. "No, I'm not."

Testing a theory, I slide one hand out from under her shorts and tease it under her shirt. She arches her back, bracing her hands on my knees and giving me room to skate over her rib cage and finally cup her breast. "You're not wearing a bra, either."

"No, Griff," she says with teasing patience. "This is what I slept in. I wasn't expecting guests so early."

"I'm definitely not complaining." The discovery may have rendered me stupid, but no complaints. I palm her breast and sweep my thumb over her nipple. Her body jerks, and she lets out a soft gasp.

"You like that?" I'm aching with the desire to shove the material out of my way and tease her nipples with my tongue.

She nods slowly. "Yes."

I slide my other hand under her shirt and flick my thumbs over both nipples. A sweet mix of desire and nerves spreads over her face. She's so sensitive, jolting and gasping with every slight brush of my fingers against the hard tips. I circle one tight peak with my knuckle. "I want to kiss you here."

A slow shiver ripples through her body. "I want you to."

I lift her shirt a little, baring her stomach. "Wanna kiss you here too. And—"

"Griff." She closes the distance between us, forcing me to move my hands or have them trapped between us. Fine by me. I slide them up under her shorts again.

She lowers her mouth to mine. "Kiss me."

Her lips touch mine—warm and tentative. A thrill I only feel when I'm behind the wheel pushing my car to its limits, or winning a fight, rushes through me. At first, it's a soft, slow kiss. Then she spears her fingers through my hair, cranking up the intensity. Desire and the urgent need for *more* pounds through my blood. The kiss turns possessive and demanding, fueled by pent-up frustration. She flicks her tongue against mine and moans, the sound traveling straight to my dick.

She pulls away and stares at me. "You're really all mine now?"

That's the best question I've ever been asked. "Yes."

Someone clears their throat in the hallway.

Like a rocket, Molly shoots herself sideways and out of my

lap, kneeing me in the dick in the process. She sits straighter than a ruler and clasps her hands in her lap like a Catholic schoolgirl about to take communion.

I wince and press my palm over my broken dick.

"What did I say, Griff?" Remy growls from right outside the doorway.

I wheeze in a painful breath. "Uh…" I count off on my fingers. "No sleepovers. Keep the door open…"

He pushes the door all the way open and fires off a warning look.

I don't need the warning. I'd also never repeat the don't-knock-her-up and let-her-go-to-college parts of his "conditions." They're likely to either hurt Molly's feelings or piss her off. The don't-cheat-on-her warning isn't worth mentioning because it would never happen anyway.

Molly places her hand on my leg and scoots closer, like she wants to protect me from her brother's wrath.

Despite my throbbing groin, I flash a cocky-as-fuck grin at Remy.

"It's *my* room, Remy." Molly's forceful tone makes me grin even wider. "We can close the door. Especially if you're going to be hanging out in the hallway like a peeping creeper."

I cover my mouth and snicker into my hand.

Remy's lips twist with what I assume is a mixture of amusement and annoyance. "Is this what I have to look forward to if you're a couple? Public displays of—"

"We're in my room," Molly repeats.

"—and you defending him like he's a kid?" Remy finishes.

Molly laces her fingers through mine. "Yup." She adds a sassy head tilt. "Deal with it."

"My woman has spoken." I dip my chin.

"Fuck almighty," Remy grumbles and rubs his temples. "If I have to put up with this bullshit, let's at least go downstairs and eat some waffles."

"Waffles?" Molly lifts her chin, sniffing the air. "Who's making waffles?"

A sly smile curves Remy's lips. "I am."

I bite my tongue to cut off my laughter. Remy the mastermind. Luring us out of Molly's bedroom with one of her favorite foods.

"I could eat some waffles." Molly turns toward me and lifts an eyebrow. "How about you?"

"For fuck's sake." Remy groans.

"Sure." I risk death and lean in to kiss Molly's cheek. "Waffles sound perfect."

"Great!" Molly pushes me off her bed. "Go help Remy while I get dressed."

"Wait, what?" My eyes widen in surprise but I'm also laughing.

"Come on, bonehead." Remy shackles his hand around my wrist and drags me into the hallway.

Molly closes the door behind us.

"You think waffles are gonna keep me from making out with your sister?" I whisper to Remy. "That's adorable."

He smirks at Molly's closed door. "Worked, didn't it?"

Molly

CHAPTER TWENTY

Molly

Remy finally finding out about Griff and me went better than I expected. Almost *too* smoothly. Griff and I have been able to spend more time together without hiding it from my brother. It's a relief, but I can't help feeling like Remy hasn't *quite* given us his blessing yet, no matter what Griff says.

So when Remy's waiting for me one night after work instead of Griff, my suspicious little sister radar starts pinging like crazy.

"What are you doing here?" I yank open the heavy door to Remy's old Ford Bronco and hoist myself inside.

"Can't I pick up my hardworking little sister and treat her to dinner after a long shift at her thankless job?" He waits until my seat belt's buckled to shift into gear and roll the old beast forward.

Ignoring all the sarcasm, I glance over at him. "Usually you're too busy." Damn, I didn't mean to sound so critical.

"I know." He reaches over and pats my leg. "How was work?"

"Slow. Boring. I think Becky's going to quit, and she's my favorite person to work with."

"She the pretty blonde girl who's into horses?"

I roll my eyes. Is there a "pretty blonde" my brother *doesn't* notice? "Yes. She's smart and fun to talk to. Makes the night go faster when she's there."

"Everyone's gotta move on from Miller's Farm eventually." He shrugs.

I bite back a sarcastic reply. "I know."

My stomach rumbles and I glance at the clock in the dash. "Where are we going this late?"

He flashes a quick, apologetic smile at me. "The bar."

Happiness flutters in my chest. "Fine by me. I love visiting. Reminds me of Nana and Grandpa."

He quirks an eyebrow. "Living in their *house* doesn't?"

"Well, duh, yeah. You know what I mean."

He huffs a soft laugh. "Yeah, I know."

It's dark by the time we approach the old road leading to the bar my grandparents owned and operated for years. Neon lights cast a warm glow around the small, cabin-like structure. "Geez, I never realized how...deserted it seems out here."

"Tell me about it." He sighs and drums his thumb against the steering wheel.

"How does anyone even find the place?"

"They don't. Not since most of the factory jobs left." He pulls the SUV around the building and rolls to a stop by the side door. "I'm working on a few things to bring in more traffic."

I can't even imagine what that might entail. Remy has so much responsibility on his shoulders, and I don't do nearly enough to help him out. I'm another mouth for him to feed, another problem he inherited.

"Do you ever wish I hadn't moved in with you?" I ask.

Slowly, Remy turns toward me. Even in the weak glow from the security lights, I glimpse the pain flashing in his eyes. "No way, Molly. Never. Is that how I make you feel?"

I stop and consider our arrangement. Remy has never complained about me living with him. Because he felt like he no choice? "I don't know...Do you even like me? Or do you just feel obligated to take care of me because you're my brother?"

"Molly," he breathes out, hurt twisting in his voice. He reaches over and slides one of his hands over mine. "Yes, I *like* you.

You're one of the smartest people I know. And clever as hell. You're always saying something that makes me laugh, no matter how shitty or hopeless I'm feeling."

"What do *you* feel shitty and hopeless about?"

"Never mind." He pulls his hand away and stares at the building. "What brought this on? Why would you think I don't like you?"

"I don't." I shrug, feeling childish for letting one of the random dumb thoughts constantly circling my head escape my mouth. "I wish I were more independent." I force a laugh to lighten things up. "It's embarrassing I don't even have my license yet."

"Why? So you can run over to Griff's place?"

Anger tightens my jaw. Of course, that'd be what he thinks. "No. So I don't have to beg my friends for rides, or depend on Griff, or you, or take the bus. And how am I supposed to get to college next year without a car?"

"Fuck." He sits up and rubs his hands over his face.

"And speaking of college," I continue since I have his undivided attention, "unless I take a year off to work and save some money—"

"No," he snaps. "I don't want you doing that. It'll be too hard for you to go back."

"Remy, even community college is expensive."

"There's some money for you to go to college, Molly."

From where? "If I'm going to apply for any financial aid, I need a parent or guardian to fill out forms…I'm…scared to approach Dad about it—"

"Don't." He slaps his hand against the steering wheel. "Don't you dare go see him. Or ask him for a fucking thing. I don't want you alone with him again. Ever."

At first, his intense reaction pokes my defensive streak to life, but something about his tight expression says his anger isn't directed at me.

He's mad at himself.

"Remy," I say gently. "It's not your fault."

"The fuck it's not." He stops assaulting the steering wheel and stares at me. "I knew what a violent asshole he was...*is*. He treated Mom like shit, even once she got sick, but I never saw him put hands on her. I figured he beat my ass because I was a boy who could take it, and he wanted me to toughen up." He turns in his seat, reaches over, and takes my hands in his. "I never, ever thought he'd hurt you, Molly. I swear. I wouldn't have left you alone with him if I thought he'd treat you that way."

I squeeze his hands and rub them to chase away the chill in his fingers. "You think I don't know that? I've never been mad at you for what happened. Only grateful you put a stop to it and let me live with you."

"I would've sooner if..."

"You were busy taking care of Grandpa right up until the end." Tears prick my eyes. Remy's had to deal with a *lot* of death. We both have. But since he's older, and our mom was an only child, the responsibility of taking care of our grandparents fell on Remy's shoulders.

"You helped me." He pats the back of my hand. "More than you realize, kiddo. Grandpa loved having you around after school. Just sitting with him, talking to him, made him really happy."

I shrug and shift my gaze to the windshield. "I hope so. I still miss both of them so much."

"Me too." He lets out a sad, strangled sound and releases my hands. "Come on. Let's go inside."

We get out of the truck and Remy waits for me by the front bumper. He stares at the ground and toes his boot against a loose piece of gravel.

"I feel like I'm constantly fucking shit up here." He tips his head back and squints at the night sky. "I wish so bad Grandpa was around to tell me what the fuck to do sometimes." Remy's rarely ever so raw and honest with me.

I sigh and touch his shoulder. "Why don't you let me help? I could be working at night and helping my own family instead of the Miller family."

He slings his arm over my shoulders and hugs me to his side. "Honestly? I can't afford to pay you." He glances at the closed door and lowers his voice. "I gotta keep Lynette on. I promised Grandpa she'd always have a job. And I can't lose Anderson, otherwise I'd never get a night off."

Well, shoot. I didn't realize things were that bad. "You don't have to pay *me*. I'm family. I'll come in after work and—"

"No." He releases me and opens the back door, holding it open for me to go inside first. Dim, yellow lighting gives the hallway leading to the main part of the bar a dated but homey feel.

Remy steps in behind me and closes the door tight, then motions for me to follow him into the office on our right.

The second Remy snaps on the overhead lights, I'm flooded with memories of our grandparents. The double desk Nana and Grandpa shared is still covered in papers, although Remy keeps Grandpa's side neater now. Nana's side has cardboard file boxes lined up in a row. I spent many hours entertaining myself in this office when I was little. Sadness threatens to pull me away, but I drag my attention back to what Remy's sharing with me.

"...This thing we're setting up with the Lost Kings MC, it's already helping the bar a little." He glances at the paper-strewn desk and waves his hand over the clutter. "They've had a few... events here. Sent us new customers and stuff. Their treasurer is a really smart business guy. He's going to help me out with a few things." He rolls his eyes, but a smile curves his lips. "If I can stand listening to all his *other* life advice."

"Oh." I breathe out a sigh of relief. "So all these visits and road trips with the Lost Kings haven't just been about partying with a motorcycle club? It's business?"

"Yeah, some of it." He frowns and glances at the door behind me. "And that's more than I should tell you. Do *not* repeat any of what I said. To anyone. Not Hayden—no one."

"What about Griff?"

He rolls his eyes, but the corner of his mouth turns up. "Yeah, you can tell him. But don't give him a hard time if he doesn't share a lot of details, though, okay?"

"I won't." I hesitate. Maybe I should drop this since Remy doesn't seem to want to tell me too much. "I like the Lost Kings. I mean, you haven't let me hang around with them a lot, but when I have, it's been fine. Heidi's always been kind to me. And Shelby's so cool."

He stares at me for a long moment. "Heidi's never questioned you or anything?"

"Questioned me?" I cock my head and stare at him. "About what?" I frown, trying to remember our brief conversations. Cars, boys, school. Normal stuff. "No. She's fun to talk to."

"Good. I'm sorry I haven't let you come to more events. I just want to keep you safe." He pauses again. "It's a motorcycle club, you know."

"Because...a motorcycle club is more dangerous than all the cage fighters and degenerate gamblers you associate with?" I don't even bother to keep the sarcastic disbelief out of my tone.

"Good point." He snorts and actually smiles. "See? There's that clever mind I was talking about." His teasing expression melts. "Grandpa left some money for you to go to college. So don't worry about that."

"I thought I needed a lawyer to let me take the money out?"

"You do, but one of the things you can take it out for is school expenses."

"Oh." This is new information and would've saved me a lot of stress if I'd known about it sooner.

"It's not a lot," Remy adds. "You'll probably still need financial aid, but it should help. You're going to school. I don't want you trapped here helping me run the bar and working at the grocery store for a nickel above minimum wage."

"*Excuuuse* me." I draw out the words and add a silly face. "I make a whole twenty-five cents *above* minimum wage, thank you very much."

"Oh, well, in that case..." He rolls his eyes. "Seriously, though. I'm sorry I didn't think about the financial aid forms." He taps his forehead like he's stupid for not being aware of something that should be common knowledge.

"You're not a parent, Remy," I say gently. "And you didn't get the chance to worry about all the college stuff for yourself because you were taking care of Nana and Grandpa."

"That's not the only reason why," he scoffs. "I didn't have the grades you have."

I bite my tongue. Remy's just as smart as me, if not smarter. Our chaotic home life never gave him the chance to prove himself in school. But saying that might insult him, and that's the last thing I want.

"Well, why would *you* be worried about all these forms? I should've said something sooner, but I didn't want to stress you out over something I didn't know how to fix."

"Oh, I know how I'm gonna fix it." His hard-faced stare should chill me to the bone. If I thought it was directed at me, it would. "And don't walk on eggshells around me. You need something, say it. Stop acting like you're so grateful to live with me, you don't want to make a peep. It's your house too."

"Thanks," I whisper, a bit embarrassed he's nailed exactly how I feel. "Wait, how are you going to fix it?"

"Get me those forms. Whatever you need filled out. And I'll be the one to take them over to the house and have a chat with our dear old dad."

"Remy, no." Fear freezes my insides. Even when he's not drunk, there's no way to have a civil conversation with our father. "I don't want you getting into trouble because of me."

"I won't throw any punches," he promises in a less-than-reassuring tone. "Unless he gives me a reason to."

"That's little comfort."

"It'll be fine." Staring me in the eye, he walks around the edge of the desk and rests his hand on my shoulder. "I'll look into what we need to do about your license. Although, your birthday's so close—"

"I might as well wait until I don't need a parent to go with me," I finish for him. "You're right. I've made it this long. A few more weeks won't matter."

"You're a great driver. You won't have any trouble passing the test."

"Thanks." I bump my shoulder against his arm. "I mean it." I probably shouldn't open this can of worms. This is the best conversation Remy and I have had in such a long time. "And thanks for being okay with Griff and me."

He blows out a long, slow breath. "I wish you were a little older. I want you to experience life *outside* of this town. If you want to come back and settle down, that's one thing, but if you never get to leave at all…"

"So it's not me dating Griff that bothers you?" *Huh, who knew?* "You're worried he'll keep me tethered here?"

"I'm not thrilled about you dating *anyone*." He releases a bone-weary sigh. "But I've never heard you say entering a nunnery was on your list of ambitions, so no, you two together doesn't bother me the way *you* think it does. I know he'll treat you right." He holds up his hands. "Not because he's threatened by me. Because he's a good man—"

"He is."

"I know." His face twists with doubt. "Maybe it'd be better if you had more dating experience—"

I raise an eyebrow.

"Not *that* kind of experience. Ugh." He shakes his body side to side like he's trying to throw off a nest of spiders. "Just experience in general, so you don't have regrets later."

I open my mouth to protest, then stop as his words sink in. His concern makes sense. But I don't think there's a time in my future I could ever regret being with Griff. The few experiences I *have* had only make me appreciate our relationship even more.

"I've dated a little." I force some steel into my tone. "And..." *No one sets me on fire the way Griff does.* No, Remy won't be receptive to *that*. "I don't need to kiss more frogs to know Griff is a prince."

He chuckles. "Oh, man. I should've seen this coming *years* ago." He reaches over and flicks my ponytail. "As soon as he teased you about the bow in your hair, I should've known."

I grin so wide my cheeks hurt. "The highlight of my kindergarten days."

"Come on, let's scrounge up some dinner before it gets any later." Remy opens the door, and I follow him into the hallway.

We bump into Lynette coming out of the kitchen with a basket of chicken wings in her hands. The spicy hot sauce tickles my nose, and my mouth waters.

"Molly! It's been too long, honey." She holds the basket up and glances at my brother.

"Good to see you again."

Lynette hasn't changed a bit. Same short, black curly hair, tight jeans, tucked T-shirt, and bright smile. She reminds me of my grandparents—in a good way.

"Where you two sitting?" she asks.

Remy nods toward the bar. "The usual corner."

"Well, I got these ready when I saw your truck pull in." She lifts her shoulder and gestures with the basket of wings like the seasoned waitress she is. "Go on."

"I got it." Remy takes the basket from her. "Thanks."

I trail behind Remy like a dog watching her owner shaking a bag of kibble. Every time he stops to say hello to one of the guys perched on a stool at the long, wooden bar, my stomach growls in annoyance.

At the table, I shove myself into the far side of the booth. Remy sets the basket in the middle of the table, and I snatch a wing, biting into it with unladylike ferocity.

Instant regret. The sauce is *hot-hot,* not the medium I'd normally order. No drinks on the table yet. I cough and sputter then grab one of the celery sticks, scoop a big glob of blue cheese onto the end, and shove it in my mouth.

Remy chuckles. "Easy, kiddo."

I munch the celery quickly and mumble, "I'm so happy you still serve blue cheese instead of that nasty ranch everyone else is serving with wings lately."

He laughs even harder and shakes his head. "I'll be right back."

I twirl a carrot stick through the dressing and crunch on it while I wait for Remy to return with a pitcher of root beer and two glasses.

"Thank you." I pour the soda and take a deep gulp.

"Leave room for pizza," Remy warns, biting into his own chicken wing.

"You're the best."

We finish the wings and start working on the pizza Lynette dropped off. Every so often, Remy jumps up to take care of something behind the bar. Once I'm not so ravenous, I sit back and allow my gaze to wander around the small tavern. Remy wasn't kidding. Business is slow. It's the middle of the week, though. Maybe things are busier on the weekends?

No matter what Remy says, I need to help him out more. Another reason I should get my license. I could drive here after work, and he wouldn't be able to tell me to leave.

The last patron at the bar heads out and Remy returns to our table.

The door jingles and closes with a *whump*. I flick my gaze toward the entryway and spot Griff about the same time Remy notices him.

"Aw, look at that," Remy drawls. "It's our very own Prince Charming."

I assume he's using my earlier frog-kissing comparison to tease me. Under the table, I tap his shin with the toe of my sneaker. "Shut up."

Remy slides out of his seat and stands but Griff's eyes are

focused on me. I smile and wave, even though he's less than ten feet away.

"Good God," Remy groans. "You two."

"Hey, Muffin," Griff says.

"No hello for me, bro?" Remy holds out his arms.

"Hello," Griff says dutifully, stopping to give him a quick embrace.

Griff slides into the booth next to me. "Hey, baby," he says against my ear, planting a quick, sweet kiss on my cheek. The scent of the cool, night air folds around me. Griff must've ridden his bike here.

"Hey," I murmur, sliding my hand against his leg under the table. "I didn't know you were stopping by."

He cocks his head toward Remy. "Bonehead said you'd need a ride home."

"Ah." I flick my gaze to Remy, who shrugs. "I can stay and help out," I offer, even though I'd love to leave with Griff right this second.

"What'd I say about that?" Remy scolds.

"Yeah, but I'm already *here*," I protest.

"You already worked a shift at your job, *and* you need to be up early for school. I don't."

"Can I at least eat, and then you two can decide who's going where?" Griff reaches for a slice of pizza and a napkin.

"Bro, I'll get you something fresh." Remy jerks his thumb over his shoulder.

Griff mumbles a negative sound and bites into the slice. "I prefer it semi-cold."

Lynette hurries over, sets another pitcher of soda on the table for us, and stops to greet Griff.

"Thanks," Remy says as she hurries away.

"So..." Griff takes a sip of soda from my cup. "What'd you two talk about?"

"None of your business," Remy says.

Griff side-eyes me.

"Brother-sister confidentiality." I raise one hand like Remy forced me to swear on a bible. "I'll tell you later," I whisper loud enough for Remy to hear.

Remy chuckles. It's nice to see him in a more light-hearted mood. "We got some stuff sorted out, right?" He nods at me.

"I think so."

"Good." Griff slides his arm around my shoulders, pulling me to his side.

Remy rolls his eyes but keeps his objections to our display of affection to himself.

Despite my worries about college, talking it out with Remy gives me hope things will turn out okay.

As for the future of the nearly empty bar that's been in my family for decades, that's a different story. No matter what Remy says, I need to figure out a way to help him maintain our grandparents' legacy.

Molly

CHAPTER TWENTY-ONE

Molly

EIGHTEEN. IT DOESN'T FEEL AS MONUMENTAL AS everyone led me to believe. Just another day. Monday, I'll still wake up, go to school, sit through class, then go to work. Rinse, repeat until graduation.

"Hey, birthday girl!" Hayden shouts as I jog down my front steps and toward her new car.

The sun's weak beams intensify as I settle into the plush leather seat of Hayden's sleek black BMW convertible. Maybe Mother Nature knows it's my birthday and wants to turn up the wattage of the afternoon sunlight.

The soft purr of the engine fills the air. "This is really nice." I run my palm over the red leather under my thighs. I've been under the impression money is tight in Hayden's household since her parents divorced. Guess not.

"Early graduation present from my dear old guilt-riddled dad." She sighs and clutches the steering wheel. "Still not used to it yet."

My long hair ripples and tangles in the breeze. I slip a plastic hair claw in the shape of bright red apple out of my purse, gather my hair, and clip it back. The hour I spent curling each strand into perfect, beachy waves will be wasted by the time we get to wherever Hayden's taking me, but the day is too nice to ask her to put the top up. She's had *convertible* pinned to her vision board since we were twelve. There's no way I'll dampen her happiness because of my hair.

"I'm so excited." I bounce in my seat and clap my hands together.

"About what?" she asks with an innocent lilt to her voice.

I throw her a sideways glance. "I appreciate your commitment to this surprise party plan, but you realize I figured it out days ago." *Days ago* is a stretch. More like yesterday morning, when I caught Remy tucking red and purple party supplies into the back of his Bronco.

Hayden's laughter floats through the air as we speed along Johnsonville's tired old roads. "I don't know what you're talking about." Her lips twitch into a playful smile. "Just taking my best friend for a ride on her birthday."

"Suuure." I draw out the word in a teasing way.

Anticipation and sadness gnaw at me. The desire for a normal family flutters at the back of my mind, fleeting but still painful. Today, I miss my mom and grandparents more than usual. I miss "helping" Nana bake a heart-shaped cake for my birthday every year. The one living parent I *do* have is a violent disaster.

Wait, I *have* family. My brother and our friends. People I've *chosen* to be part of my life. That's way better than some man I share DNA with who never wanted me in the first place.

We pass the faded sign for Zips and my mouth curls into a smile. "Gee whiz. Look at that."

Hayden flips on her blinker and makes the turn. "Did you say 'gee whiz?'"

I lean forward and point at the sign. "Weird how we just happen to be going to Zips."

"*Huuuh.*" She frowns and draws out the sound. "That's *so* strange."

I run my hands over my short, purple dress, happy it's finally warm enough to wear it. I can't wait for Griff to see it on me. My legs are smooth and glowing after using my birthday-cake-scented sugar scrub, shave oil, and body butter on them this morning.

As much as I love Hayden, I wish I'd ridden to the party with Griff. He said he had work to finish at the garage this morning. But I suspect he was up to something else.

"Gee, look at all those cars and motorcycles I recognize." I tap my finger against my chin.

"Like Harleys and muscle cars aren't a dime a dozen out here?" Hayden says, driving past a bunch of vehicles and making her own parking spot behind the bleachers.

"Uh, that's Vapor's." I point to a Harley-Davidson with green flames painted along the tank. My gaze searches the area. More cars, trucks, motorcycles. I don't see Griff's Chevelle *or* his Harley. Isn't he here yet? Remy's Bronco isn't in sight either but they both could've parked inside the track.

"Please act surprised," Hayden begs. She pulls her cell phone out of her purse and taps out a message.

"I'll try." I grin at her and open my door.

There's a hush in the air. With all the vehicles we passed, there should be some noise coming from the area around the racetrack. I sniff, catching the scent of grilled meat. Eraser's Uncle Pax is usually bellowing out orders when he's manning the grill. Even from this distance, I should be able to make out his gruff rumble.

We follow the path to the racetrack area through a break in the bleachers and turn to the left, toward the barbeque area.

"Surprise!" a bunch of people shout. Shiny chunks of purple and red confetti rain down on me from above.

I burst into the biggest smile and can't stop laughing.

Hayden jumps up and down next to me, her long blond hair bouncing all over the place. "Happy birthday, Molly!"

Remy rushes up to me first, pulling me in for a hug. "We didn't surprise you at all, did we?"

"No, but that's okay." I kiss his cheek. "I'm so happy. Thank you."

Griff picks me up and spins me around. "Happy birthday, Muffin."

I pepper his face with quick, happy kisses. "Thank you." My whole body's buzzing from the excitement of the day. I throw my arms around Griff's neck and seal my mouth over his. This kiss is slower than a friendly hello. He tastes like spearmint, and I part my lips for more. He tightens his arms around my waist, lifting me slightly.

"All right. You've got other guests," Remy mutters.

I sigh and pull away.

Slowly, Griff releases me, letting me slide down his body while his hands push the skirt of my dress down so I don't flash the entire party.

"Thanks." I fuss with the swirling fabric, then perform a little spin. "What do you think?"

"You're stunning." He rubs his hand over his chin while staring at my legs. "Will you be comfortable taking a few laps around the track later?" He gestures vaguely over his shoulder toward a few cars parked near the starting line. One of the drivers steps on the accelerator so hard, the car rocks back and forth. The roar of the engine drowns out everything.

"I brought sneakers with me," I shout, lifting my foot to show off my silver, holographic, platform ankle boots. "These just went with my dress better."

His lips curve in amusement. "They look cute." His gaze travels higher, lingering on the hem of my dress at mid-thigh. He clears his throat. "Maybe cute isn't the right word."

"Griff, stop hogging our birthday girl." Juliet playfully elbows him aside and pulls me into a hug. "Happy birthday," she murmurs.

"Thank you." I squeeze her extra tight, so happy she's here. "Where's the little guy?"

"With Dex and Emily."

Griff raises a curious eyebrow and Juliet shrugs. "He offered."

"I'm glad you're here," I say.

Griff stays by my side while I meander around, saying hello to everyone and accepting birthday hugs. Someone decorated the length of the bleacher wall with red and purple streamers and a big "Happy 18th Birthday, Molly!" banner. The warm happiness glowing in my chest burns even brighter.

We finally reach the grill area, and Uncle Pax leans down to give me a hug.

"Happy birthday, Molly." He slides his gaze over Griff. "You need me to put him to work?"

"No. Thank you for letting them have the party here."

"It's Eraser's place more than mine now." Pax turns his head and coughs. "But you're always welcome here to celebrate anything you want."

I lean up and kiss his stubbly cheek. "Thanks."

He waves a spatula toward the party. "Don't even think of doing any work today. Go have fun with your friends."

My girl gang's hanging out with Ella and Juliet on the track near the starting line. Kyla squints in our direction, lifts her hand, and waves.

"Hey." Griff stops walking and turns toward me, resting his hands on my hips. "I have a special present for you later, but I couldn't bring it here." He nods toward the parking lot.

"Oooh, is it a present for both of us?" I wiggle my eyebrows at him.

His forehead wrinkles in confusion. "Sort of."

Okay, he didn't get that I was hinting at finding a secluded spot to make out.

"I don't want to take you away from your party and your friends," he says, "but I'd like to give it to you tonight."

My mind races through the possibilities. A ride on his motorcycle? Alone time at his apartment? *That* would be a perfect gift.

He glances at the parking lot again. Is he thinking of leaving right now? Then he leans down and kisses my neck. "I'd also like to have you to myself for a few minutes at least," he whispers.

The clear desire in his words rains over me in sparks of electric energy.

"I'd like that," I murmur.

"Yoo-hoo! Hate to interrupt!" Hayden shouts.

Griff chuckles softly and pulls away. "You're wanted at the starting line, birthday girl."

We join the girls. The scent of singed rubber and motor oil hangs in the air, triggering a flood of happy memories—afternoons learning how to drive, nights watching my brother and his friends race. This was the perfect place to celebrate my eighteenth birthday.

Excitement shimmers all over Hayden's eager face as I approach her. "Ella said I can test the BMW on the track."

I flick my gaze toward Ella, who shrugs. "I'll ride shotgun."

Griff keeps his arm around me while we watch Hayden ease her car to the starting line. Like she's done to me and everyone else she teaches, Ella has Hayden back up and approach the line several times until she gets it just right.

Laughing, I stare up at Griff. "Ella did the same thing when she taught me."

But he's not watching Hayden's BMW. His adoring eyes are focused on me.

"What's wrong?" I ask.

"Nothing." He leans down and kisses my cheek. "I love you," he whispers against my ear.

Emotion ties a knot around my throat. My heart thumps faster. Nothing will ever top this birthday. "I love you too," I rasp.

He pushes my hair off my cheek. "I don't think I've ever *not* loved you, but—"

"This is different," I finish for him.

He nods once. "Yeah, a lot different."

He's so serious. Almost sad.

"Is *that* my birthday present?" I tease, poking my finger against his side.

"Nope." He drapes his arm over my shoulders and tugs me closer.

"Wait, maybe we shouldn't?" I shift and pull away slightly. "Everyone's here."

He slides his hands around me and strokes the bare skin exposed by the low back of my dress. "Let them enjoy the show."

My heart thumps. "You don't mean that."

"Yes, I do."

"I don't want Remy mad at you."

"He'll get over it."

Remy gave permission for us to *date*. Getting cuddly in public, in front of all their friends, might be a different story.

Then again, I'm the birthday girl. If I had a cake and candles in front of me right now, *this* would be the wish I'd make.

I loop my arms around Griff's neck and pull him down for a long, slow kiss.

Griff

"This is now officially the best birthday I've ever had," Molly says when I release her.

"You mean that?"

"Yup." She leans up and kisses me again. "We can do this in the open today. And not just because of Remy." She raises her eyebrows and wiggles them a few times.

"It's not even my birthday, and I'm getting presents too, huh?" Finally telling her I love her and hearing it in return was enough of a gift.

She lowers her lashes and teases me with a coy smile. "I can think of one I'd like to give you."

Pure fire races through my veins.

My body goes completely still, absorbing her words. I lean down and brush my lips against her ear. "You know what you need to say to unlock *that* present."

A quick shiver races over her body. I pull away and stare down at her. Pink stains her cheeks and forehead as if the mere thought of asking for what she wants is making her blush.

My gaze lowers to the swells of her breasts, revealed by a dress that must've been sewn by Satan himself. Compared to other dresses, it's probably tame. But on Molly, it seems designed to drive my brain straight into forbidden territory. If I rest my hand on her back, I'm touching skin. If she twirls too fast, I get a glimpse of her thighs. It's nipped in to show off her waist and flares right over her hips, like it was made to highlight every inch of her I'm dying to explore.

"Molly!" Hayden calls.

Fuck, I've been trying not to monopolize her time at the party. "Now that she's run a few laps, you should go with her," I suggest.

She glances up at me, excitement dancing in her eyes. "Are you sure you don't mind?"

"Of course not. It's your day." My hand drops to her hip, and I give her a light squeeze. "I'll be at the grill helping Pax."

"Okay." She bounces up on her toes and kisses my cheek.

"Do you need your other shoes?" I ask.

"Nah, I'm just going along for the ride."

As she bounds over the grass onto the track, her hair billows behind her and her dress swishes around her legs. Before she ducks into the back of Hayden's car, she turns and waves at me.

"Where's Molly going?" Remy walks up behind me and slaps my shoulder.

"She's doing a few laps with Hayden in her new car."

"Aww, how nice of you to take your filthy mitts off my sister for a few minutes."

I roll my eyes and slowly turn my head toward him. "Are you okay with us together, or not?"

He holds out one hand, palm up. "In theory, I guess so." He holds up the other hand and pretends to weigh his options. "Watching it in real time, not so much."

"Would you rather have me be repulsed by your sister?"

"Honestly, yeah." He snorts with laughter and slaps my chest. "Whatever. As long as she's happy, that's all I care about."

"Thanks." My lips tilt into a dickish smile. "No fucks given about your best friend's happiness?"

He slow-blinks as if that never occurred to him. "Of course I want you to be happy too."

I nod once, not sure why I'm feeling defensive around him today.

Our attention returns to the cars. Hayden still can't seem to get the hang of rolling the car to the starting line.

Remy shakes his head. "A fucking BMW. I definitely can't compete with that."

"Thankfully, your sister doesn't expect you to," I remind him.

"I got the financial aid forms signed by our dad." Remy holds up a shiny pink legal-sized envelope that's been tucked under his arm.

"*That's* what you're giving her for her birthday?"

"No, there's something else in here." He glances around at the giant balloons, food, and decorations. "And the party itself." He casts a glance toward Hayden's car again. "Coordinating with Hayden wasn't exactly fun."

Molly's friend isn't *that* bad. "I'll give you credit. You did a nice job."

"Thanks." He jams one hand in his pocket and stares at the ground. "I had a fleeting thought about inviting him to the party *before* I went to the house."

He can't be serious. "Are you kidding?"

"It's her birthday. He's our dad." Uncertainty I'm not used to seeing on my best friend seems to surround him like a fog. "I figured we're all here to look out for her. Maybe..." He clenches his jaw and shakes his head. "It doesn't matter. He was wasted when I got there. Didn't even ask how she was doing. About her graduation. Nothing. Fuck him."

I let out a relieved breath. "I'm sorry. Your heart was in a good place, man." *But having your dad here would've been a fucking disaster.* I can't wrap my head around why Remy wanted to invite him.

Remy's quiet for a few beats, his gaze focused on the track even though I don't think he's watching anything in particular. "I don't want to turn into him one day."

I shift sideways so we're facing each other. "You're *nothing* like your father. I can count on one hand the number of times I've seen you shitfaced."

He seems to consider that. "You think if we stop fighting, though..."

"You want to stop?"

He flexes the fingers of his right hand. "Not really."

"You've got more of Grandpa Kip's personality traits than your dad's."

That doesn't seem to reassure him the way I'd intended. His expression doesn't change. "I should hope so. He certainly spent more time raising me."

I touch my fingers to my chest. "I don't exactly come from prime stock either. We learn better, we do better."

"Do better," he repeats, nodding slowly. "I like that."

"All the kids are saying it these days, grampy."

The corner of his mouth lifts in a wry smirk. "You would know."

"Ouch." I press my hands into my gut.

"Yeah, that was low." His smirk widens. "Your girlfriend isn't underage anymore."

"God, you're such a dick." I groan and laugh at the same time. "Come on. Let's go grab a burger. I'm starving."

"You're always starving."

I rub a hand over my stomach. "My metabolism is a finely tuned engine that needs fuel on a regular basis."

"Christ, you sound like Wrath." He falls in step next to me as we head toward the grill. "Are you going to lecture me about the evils of sugar next?"

I let out a derisive snort. The Lost Kings enforcer and former underground fighter gave up sugar and never misses an opportunity to preach the benefits to us. "Bro, I hope I'm still as jacked as he is when I'm forty. He could crack both of our skulls without breaking a sweat."

"You're probably right." He chuckles.

Proud of myself for cheering him up, I nudge him with my elbow. "What else did you get Molly?"

"Never mind. What did *you* get her?" He side-eyes me. "It better not be something inappropriate."

I stop walking. "Inappropriate, how?"

He stares at me.

Still confused, I shake my head. "Please don't ruin it for me if I tell you."

"How?"

I cast a quick glance around. Vapor, Eraser, Torch, Spoons, and Pip are all seated at a picnic table near the grill, heckling Pax. Molly's friends are over by the starting line with Juliet, waiting for Hayden's car to return.

No one who would run and tell my surprise to Molly is close enough to overhear me. "I found a '71 Chevy Malibu Coupe for us to restore together."

A wrinkle forms between his eyebrows. "You bought her dream project *car* for her eighteenth birthday?"

"I came across a good deal on it through one of Jerry's friends." Is the car too much? Nah, Molly's gonna love it. That's all I care about.

"Jesus, Griff. Even a 'good deal' had to be fucking expensive."

It *had* taken a large chunk of the cash I keep buried in a metal lockbox at the back of my closet but that's none of Remy's business. "It looks rough on the outside, but mechanically, it's not bad. The guy had been working on it for years, so it already has a lot of parts replaced."

"That's still going to be astronomical to restore."

No one asked you. "It's not gonna be much harder than the

work I did on my own car. She's driven mine, so at least it's something she'll be familiar with."

"I guess." He shrugs, still not sounding convinced.

"I'm gonna ask Vapor to do the paint and a few cosmetic things. I'd like to have it finished by the time her college classes start." That *was* my plan, but filming the show could throw off my entire timeline.

"I wish you'd asked me." Remy plows his fingers through his hair. "I was going to get her a car for college. Something built in this century with airbags."

"I thought you might say no, so..." My shoulders lift in an unapologetic shrug. "It was a good deal. I jumped on it before the dude changed his mind."

"That's a big undertaking."

"So?" *What's his point?* Restoring cars is literally what I do for a living. "It's not like I don't have access to the tools and parts. And a safe place to store it."

"True." His pinched face suggests he's still not pleased.

"I'm sorry, Remy." I force some apology into my tone. "I wasn't trying to step on your toes or anything."

"No, no." He cocks his head like he's preparing to give me bad news. "You realize she only wanted that car because of you, right?"

"What's your point? She still likes the car." I snort-laugh. "You wanna talk expensive? She saw a Mustang I was working on once too and said she'd like one. But that was *way* the fuck out of my range."

"So where is it? Are you giving it to her today?"

"Yeah, after the party. I've got it stored at the garage with a big red sheet over it and a little silver bow on the steering wheel." The steering wheel is currently sitting on the passenger seat, but it's the thought that counts.

He snorts. "Cute. I'm sure she's going to love it."

"I hope so."

"When are you going to find the time to work on it with her? She's got finals, prom, work—"

"I know." I can't keep the defensiveness out of my tone. "Weekends? I kinda expected to do most of the work myself, but I want to include her as much as possible."

"That might be a fun car for racing here. But I don't know if it's a practical daily driver for her. Especially if she ends up commuting to Empire or something."

I had already considered that possibility. As much as I love my car, it's missing a lot of modern creature comforts. "So what? Then she'll have a restored classic. She can flip it and buy whatever she wants."

He sighs and nods. "All right." A short, sharp alert blares from his pocket. "Fuck. Not now," he groans.

"Is it the bar?" I ask.

"Yeah. I gotta run in and help out Anderson."

"You need me to come with you?" The last thing I want to do is leave Molly's party, but Remy looks so stressed I can't help making the offer.

He casts a glance at the patio and then to where the girls are clustered together by the chain-link fence separating Zips from the woods beyond. They're dancing and singing along to the noise pouring out of the speakers in Hayden's car. "No," he answers slowly. "Did you see that asshole friend of Spoons showed up?"

"Everyone that guy knows is a chode. You'll have to be more specific."

"The one who looks like Eminem's long-lost hillbilly cousin."

I snort-laugh at the description but it still applies to more than one person who hangs out at Zips.

"Stay here and keep an eye on Molly," he says. "I won't be gone long."

"As if I wouldn't be looking out for her otherwise?"

He slaps my shoulder. "You know what I mean. Don't tell her

about this yet, okay? I want to do it." He holds up the envelope. "I'll give it to her when I get back."

"All right."

He turns and jogs toward the parking lot.

Shaking my head, I make a beeline for the grill. I wasn't kidding about wanting a burger. Hunger twists my stomach.

"Where'd Remy go?" Molly asks, hurrying to catch up to me.

"The bar." I glance over my shoulder. "You done riding with Hayden?"

"For now. Darcy and Kyla are with her."

"Hungry?"

"A little."

I twine my fingers with hers and head straight for Pax's grill. He grins when we approach and taps the side of his spatula against a plate piled high with greasy beef patties wedged between fluffy, golden buns. "All mine?" I ask.

"No," he says with the slow patience of someone speaking to a child. "For your table."

Molly gathers paper plates, napkins, condiments, and a few other items. "Where do you want to sit?"

I nod to a long picnic bench at the back of the patio. A line of trees behind it offers some shade.

I walk behind Molly as she navigates the maze of picnic benches and tables scattered on the patio. People wish her a happy birthday as we pass. She offers a smile and a thanks but keeps moving, much to my stomach's delight. The smell wafting off the plate of burgers in my hands is killing me.

I sit at the far end of the table, and Molly slides onto the bench across from me. "You don't want to sit next to me?" I ask.

"I'm always afraid these things will tip over if too many people sit on the same side." She pushes at the edge of the table.

I lean sideways and dip my head under the table. "Pretty sure it's bolted right into the ground."

"Oh." She laughs. "Okay."

I slide down so she doesn't have to step over the bench. Once she settles next to me, I rest my hand on her knee under the table. "That's why I wanted you next to me," I whisper in her ear. "This dress has been driving me crazy all day."

She lets out a slow, shaky breath.

I slide my hand higher, skating over warm, silky skin. "Your legs feel so good."

The corners of her mouth quiver. "I used my special birthday shave oil and body butter this morning."

I don't even know what the fuck body butter is, but it sounds like something I'd like to smear all over Molly. "Oh, yeah?"

"It's birthday cake scented."

Lord help me.

"I thought you smelled extra sweet today." I lean down and brush my lips against her shoulder. Vanilla fills my nose. My hand's still sitting mid-thigh, not quite under her dress but close. I fight the urge to travel higher into forbidden territory.

Not here. Not now. Too many people.

I slip my hand out from under the table and grab a paper plate from the stack Molly placed in front of us.

"What's wrong?" she asks.

"Nothing at all."

She turns her head and watches me for a moment.

"Molly," I say in a low voice. "I'm having a hard time not shoving that dress up around your waist to explore where you rubbed that body butter."

Her lips curl. "I used it almost *everywhere*, Griff."

I let out a long, low groan. "What are you trying to do to me?"

Still smiling, she reaches for a burger and drops it on my plate. "Eat your burger. You can have *cake* later."

"Careful what you offer, Muffin." I reach for another burger. "You think I'm only going to eat one of these?"

"Happy birthday, Molly." Torch drops onto the bench on the other side of the table without asking if we want his company.

"Thanks." Molly flashes a quick smile. "How've you been?"

"Not bad." He reaches behind him, pulls a small white envelope out of his pocket, and hands it to her. "I didn't know what you might want but thought that could be useful when you're running late for school or something."

"Aww, thank you," Molly squeals. She rips open the envelope and pulls out a birthday-themed gift card to Dunkin' Donuts. "This is perfect. I pass a Dunkin' on my way to school."

"Thought so." Torch nods.

"Thanks, bro," I say.

Torch cocks his head and stares at me for a second, then shifts his gaze to the nonexistent gap between Molly and me. His lips quirk. "Well, well, well. When did this happen?"

"Remy knows," Molly says quickly. That's my girl, always quick to protect me.

"Yeah?" Torch lifts one auburn eyebrow. "How'd that conversation go?"

"He was fine." My clipped tone's meant to shut down any further questions. Torch doesn't honestly expect me to spread gossip about myself, does he?

"Congrats." He shakes his head slowly. "Seems like all the finest ladies are getting locked down lately." He squints an exaggerated wink at Molly.

Don't kill him. He meant it as a compliment.

Molly lets out a nervous laugh and lifts her burger to her mouth, taking a small bite.

Spoons joins us, sitting next to Torch. He reaches over and grabs a burger from the plate but lingers way too long. Blatantly staring at Molly's chest, he hunches over the table, pretending to thoroughly inspect each burger.

"Are you planning to eat all of them?" Molly asks.

Spoons leers at her. "Do you want me to?"

"Well"—she points her plastic knife at his hand— "you're getting your germs over each one."

Germs are the least of the issues here.

"Sorry." Spoons gathers three or four burgers and arranges them on his plate in a circle, then returns to staring at Molly.

I want to tie a napkin around her neck to stop Spoons staring at her chest like a man who just got released from prison and rediscovered women.

Thankfully, *or not*, Molly doesn't seem to notice his leering. That's the only reason I haven't reached over and punched him, yet.

She turns toward me. "I'm going to grab more napkins. Do you need anything?"

"You're the birthday girl. I should get them."

She flicks her gaze across the table, her expression clearly saying she doesn't want to be left alone. She has a point. "It's easier for me to get up." She leans in and presses a quick kiss to my cheek.

Spoons keeps his eyes focused on Molly's ass as she weaves around the benches. She stops to talk to Juliet at a different table. *We should've sat over there.*

"Now that she's eighteen, you're definitely hittin' that, right, Griff?" Spoons drags his gaze away from Molly and curls his filthy top lip. *This dude's begging to lose his damn eyeballs if he keeps it up.*

"Fuck off." I reach over and slap his face two or three shades harder than a friendly tap. "Stop staring at her, asshole."

He holds his hands in the air like he meant no harm. "Come on. Can you blame me?"

"Keep it up and you're gonna wear your intestines home as a necklace," I warn.

"Show some fuckin' respect, man." Torch slaps his buddy on the back.

"I *respectfully* pointed out that his girlfriend is hot. What's wrong with that?" Spoons smirks at me. *Asshole.*

I'm not dumb. Molly's been a head-turner for years. I've admired her for longer than *I* should've, and helped Remy chase off the kind of boys who were only interested in her looks. She's kind, smart, and funny as hell. Spoons doesn't appreciate any of that. Guys like him barely think of her as a *person,* and I fucking hate it.

The bench dips as Eraser drops his heavy frame into the seat on my right. He reaches across the table and taps the back of Torch's hand with his fork. "You gonna stick around after and help me clean up?"

"Can't." Torch shakes his head, his stiff orange tufts of hair not moving a bit. "I have a date."

"Oh, yeah?" Eraser squirts ketchup on his burger. "Which hand?"

Spoons snorts out a laugh. "Lefty. Righty is all worn out."

I scowl at Spoons. "You're a fuckin' creep."

"You have no idea," Torch mutters.

Pip stops by our table and rests his hand on Eraser's shoulder. "I already told Remy I'd help with the cleanup," he says to Eraser.

"Thanks, lil' buddy." Eraser reaches up and runs his hand over the top of Pip's head.

"Knock it off." Pip takes a giant step to the side. "Or I'm gonna put all the trash in your back seat."

"We brought Ella's car." Eraser shrugs. "And I know you wouldn't do that to her."

Pip scowls. "Foiled again."

Eraser slides closer to me. "Sit. Eat a burger. I'm sure you'll think of some other way to get even with me."

Laughing, I grab a paper plate from the stack in front of me, drop a burger on it, and pass it down to Pip's end of the table.

"Thanks, Griff."

A guy ambles up to the table with his hands jammed in the pockets of his baggy jeans. Fuck, this must be the asshole Remy was talking about before he left. I've only met him a few times, and I've wanted to jam my fist down his throat on each occasion.

He hoists his ass onto the table we're eating off of and braces his feet on the bench. Spoons slowly glances over and gives a pointed look at the dirty sneakers almost touching his leg.

"Were you raised by raccoons?" Eraser reaches over and shoves the guy until he slides off the table. "I don't want to look at your ass crack while I'm eating, Buck."

Buck, how could I forget? Rhymes with *fuck,* which is what I say to myself every time this dude shows up at one of our parties.

Pip snickers. "That's insulting to raccoons."

"Chill, E." Buck raises and lowers his hands in a *calm down* gesture that's bound to infuriate Eraser even more.

"Don't tell me to chill," Eraser grumbles. "Pull up your pants. You look like you escaped the circus."

I sigh and take another bite of my burger. Maybe I should move to a different table.

Molly returns and sets a huge square piece of yellow cake with cherry-red filling and white frosting in front of me. "It's vanilla frosting and cherry filling." She beams, clearly pleased Remy chose the right cake.

I tip my head back and grin at her. "Thanks, Muffin."

Buck busts up laughing across from me and elbows Spoons who's cackling like a rabid hyena. I glare at them until they both shut the fuck up.

Molly's gaze flicks from me to the guys. I shrug slightly. Who knows what those jackasses are laughing about. I pat the spot she'd been sitting in earlier. "Sit with me, birthday girl. You barely touched your burger."

"I forgot napkins." She squeezes my shoulder. "Want anything else?"

She's standing so close, I "accidentally" brush my knuckles against her leg. A faint scent of vanilla teases my nose again. The cake on the table isn't the one I want to get my mouth on.

Eraser narrows his eyes and stares at Torch for a second. "You good, cuz?"

"I'm fine."

Eraser slaps my shoulder and pulls himself off the bench. "I'll be right back."

Molly follows him over to the table where all the supplies are.

"Yo, yo, Griff?" Buck waves one of his hands in front of my face. "You call her *Muffin*?"

Spoons ducks his head and coughs into his elbow, but it sounds a lot more like a laugh.

"Don't worry about what I call my girlfriend," I warn.

"Muffin?" Buck brings two fingers in a V shape to his lips and wiggles his tongue between them. "As in, you go muffin diving?" He grins and laughs like he's some sort of genius.

"What?" I stare at him in confusion then frown. "No. Shut the fuck up."

"Seriously..." Buck reaches around Spoons to tap Torch's shoulder. "He butters her muffin *gooood*."

"Bro, I'd stop if I were you," Torch warns.

"Take his advice." I growl. Under the table, my hands curl into fists. I really don't want to start a fight at Molly's birthday party. Maybe I can get Eraser to sign Buck up for a fight at The Castle next weekend. There's gotta be half a dozen guys eager to knock him around the cage for a few rounds.

"You're the one who calls her Muffin," Spoons says to me. "What're you gettin' so pissed about?"

Buck shifts his gaze toward Molly. "I'd lick her muffin—"

Blind rage seizes me from the inside out.

I jump out of my seat, shaking the entire table, and reach over the wide, wooden surface, then hook my fingers into the neck of Buck's shirt. I yank hard until he's balanced on my arm, hanging in the air, caught between the bench and tabletop.

I press my face close to his. "Wanna say that again?"

"Dude, chill, chill!" Buck flails his arms in the air. His sneakers thud against the underside of the bench as he tries to free his bottom half. "Muffin's slang for pussy," he hisses. "How do you not know that?"

Horror washes over me.

That's not true. Is it? The sweet nickname I've been calling Molly since she was little isn't something perverted. It can't be.

Remy would've told me to knock it off if it was. Someone would've said something by now, right?

People are staring at our table. Just what I don't need—more attention drawn to the situation. I definitely don't want Molly to overhear anything this deviant says.

I throw Buck into his seat. He flies backward, almost falling off the bench. I lift my shoulders in a casual shrug, even though I'm feeling anything but calm. "Guess I'm not familiar with all the creepy pervert lingo like you are."

"You're an idiot." Pip glares at Buck. "You're thinking of *muff*, not muf*fin*. They're two different words with completely different meanings, you absolute fucking dolt."

"Thanks." I frown in Pip's direction. "Couldn't have piped up sooner?"

"And miss you choking him? Nah." Pip holds out his fist to me, and I tap it quickly with my own.

"Shut up, Pipsqueak," Buck grumbles. "You're just mad girls don't want you to eat their *muffins*."

"That's what you think," Pip mutters.

Relief replaces my previous horror as I tune out their back-and-forth insults. What if Buck's the only asshole stupid enough to say that to my face? There are plenty of dumb fucks walking around the planet. Maybe I shouldn't call her muffin anymore in case it gives someone else perverted ideas about my girl.

Molly

"Why are boys so weird?" Juliet says, staring at Griff and Pip's table. "I wish Spoons would stop inviting Buck to stuff. He never knows when to shut up."

"Yeah, they both creeped me out." I shrug and turn away. "That's why I'm staying here at your table."

"Eraser threatened to drag Buck behind his truck if he didn't watch his mouth." Ella rubs her hands together with wicked glee. "Maybe tonight's the night."

I snort with laughter and poke my fork into the corner of Juliet's slice of cake.

"Sooo..." Juliet nudges me with her elbow. "You and Griff? Finally."

Ella titters with laughter and slaps her hand over her mouth.

Juliet shoots a glare at Ella, then returns her big sister eyes to my face. I brace myself for whatever's coming.

"Seriously," Juliet says. "How's it going?"

"Good."

"Everything's...okay?"

I turn my head and stare her dead in the eyes. "This convo's giving *your changing body* lecture vibes, Juliet."

"Do you *need* a birds and the bees talk, Molly?" she asks in her most serious mom tone.

Ella bursts out laughing.

"Shush, I'm serious." Juliet reaches over and taps Ella's arm. When she turns to me again, her face is all sisterly concern. "I've birthed a tiny human. Nothing embarrasses me anymore. You can ask me anything."

I open my mouth to protest but a catch in my chest stops me cold. There are so many things I wish I had my mom around to talk to about. Or my grandmother. She always listened, even if a lot of the advice she gave was of the generic "don't let boys talk you into anything" variety, without ever explaining what the *anything* might be.

Nothing immediately springs to mind though. "I can't think of anything right now." My gaze shifts toward the racetrack where Vapor and another guy are walking around an old green Camaro.

"I won't say anything to your brother," Juliet promises. "Or even to Vapor."

I doubt she keeps many secrets from her husband, so I appreciate the offer. "Thanks."

"I know what it's like not to have a mom around, and first love...is a big deal." Juliet sighs, then chuckles. "Although I *did* have a best friend who gave me a 101 Sex Positions guide."

Ella whistles. "Vienna's a smart chick."

My nose wrinkles, and I turn begging eyes on Juliet. "Please don't do *that*."

"I won't." The corners of Juliet's mouth twitch with humor. "Promise."

I breathe out a sigh of relief.

Juliet's expression turns back to serious. "I mean it, though. Anytime, just call me. I promise not to judge."

"I will." She's someone I *would* feel comfortable talking to about relationship stuff. I reconsider what she said and frown. "A book of sex positions? Like with pictures?"

Bright pink spreads over her cheeks. "Oh, yeah."

"One of the foster homes I was in, the dad just passed around old issues of Penthouse or showed us porn on his phone." Ella shrugs and looks away. "He was super gross."

Juliet stares at Ella with wide, pained eyes for a second. "That's not a healthy way to learn about *good* sex. What happened to him?"

Instead of answering, Ella gets up and leaves.

Juliet watches Ella for a few seconds as she jogs over the asphalt toward the middle of the track. "Damn," she mutters.

"Is she okay?" I ask.

"Yeah, I think so." Juliet refocuses her attention on me. "Look, I love Griff. He's always had Roman's back. He's a good guy. And we all know how much he cares about you. But he *is* older. Don't let him talk you into anything you're not ready to do."

My mouth opens and closes while I search for the right protest. "He's not. He hasn't."

"Okay. I'm just saying, as much as we love the boys..." She bumps me with her elbow. "Sisters gotta look out for each other."

Tears mist my vision. I love my brother and I can talk to him about lots of things. But sex with his best friend? Absolutely not. "Thanks."

I glance around the immediate area but most of the people are focused on the racetrack or stuffing their faces. Ella found Eraser, and he's got his arms wrapped around her tight, his chin resting on the top of her head.

Juliet turns her head, following my line of sight, and smiles with relief. "Good." She shifts her gaze back to me. "So you two are okay?"

"We're great." I lean in closer to Juliet. "Actually, um, he made a big deal...well, not a *big* deal, but he said he needs a firm and enthusiastic *yes* from me before we, you know, do anything." I whisper the last word. "Not like a 'yeah, okay, go ahead' when we're... when... well...*you know*." Heat sears my cheeks, and I'm not even sure that made any sense.

Oh, God. What if she tells Vapor and the guys rag on Griff because we're *not* doing it?

"Oooh." Juliet's eyes widen and she fans herself with one hand. "He wants you to green light a premeditated sexcapade? That's so hot."

I squint at her. Is she making fun of us?

"I'm serious, really," she insists. "That's good. Sex can make you crazy." She twirls a finger next to her ear. "You've got so many things to worry about in the upcoming months. If you're not ready, that's okay. You don't need a guy pressuring you." Her gaze shifts over my shoulder toward Griff's table. "That's actually really sweet."

I glance down and pick at pieces of pollen on my dress. "I want to, you know." I shrug, unsure of how much more to say.

"Of course you do." Her tone implies it's the most obvious thing in the world. "When you're ready, you'll know. Do you want the number for my doctor's office? She's really great."

I frown at her. "For what?"

"The pill?"

"Oh." I blush even harder. "I'm supposed to go to the clinic with Hayden in a couple weeks."

"Okay. That's good." She hugs me again. "Proud of you, Molly."

"Really?"

"Yup."

"Thanks." A relieved smile spreads over my face.

"I'm back, kiddo." Remy's deep rumble sends a shock of fear straight through my stomach. Did he overhear what Juliet and I were talking about? I doubt he'll find the "premeditated sexcapade" thing as adorable as Juliet did.

"Everything okay at the bar?" I ask.

Remy flops a large pink envelope on the table and waves his hand in the air. "Yeah, it's fine." He steps over the bench and sits across from me.

Juliet picks up her cake and stands. "I'm going to find Vapor." She squeezes my shoulder. "If you need me..."

"Thanks." I pat her hand and flash a grateful smile.

"What'd you guys talk about?" Remy asks after Juliet leaves.

"Nothing," I answer too fast. I reach under the table and smooth my dress over my legs.

Remy nudges the pink envelope across the table. "This is for you."

"Me?" My eyes widen, and I eagerly rip the sealed tab open. Inside, there's a bunch of papers. "My financial aid forms! Wait." I stuff them in the envelope. "You went and talked to Dad? When?"

"Couple days ago." He taps the envelope. "If you need anything else filled out, just tell me. We came to an understanding."

That doesn't sound good. "What does that mean?"

"Don't worry about it."

"Did he..." Am I really going to let Remy know how pathetic I am? "Did he ask about me?" I ask in a small voice.

Remy's leg starts bouncing under the table, shaking his whole body. He clenches his jaw. Finally, he blows out a long breath. "Not really," he answers.

Why do I even care? "Thanks."

"For?"

"Not lying to me." I circle one finger in front of him. "The leg bouncing and teeth grinding. You're pissed. And you were considering lying to me so you wouldn't hurt my feelings."

He stares at me in disbelief for a few seconds. "You know me that well, huh?" he asks without his usual humor.

"Thanks for telling me the truth."

"Dad's an asshole, Molly. It's got nothing to do with you."

"I know."

He jerks his chin. "Take out the other thing in there."

I slip my hand in the envelope and search until my fingers brush against a small, thick square of paper. I pull it out and stare at the cream business card. "Advanced Hearing Center." My brows knit together. "Won't *you* need their services long before I do?"

"Funny," he scoffs. "I ran into Mr. Fisher. Grandpa's hearing aid specialist," he reminds me.

"Oh! Really? Where?"

"At his office."

"Are you okay?"

"I'm fine. He told me once if I ever needed something to let him know." He spreads his hands in front of him and stares me straight in the eyes. "I told him you're about to graduate, and you want to go to school to be a hearing aid specialist too."

I sit straight to absorb what he said. "You did? Why?" It feels weird. Like he exposed my secrets to a stranger or something.

He considers me carefully. "I think it'll help you get into school. You're already going to be applying late. Working there will look better than ringing up groceries at Miller's Farm."

"Oh. But I'm probably going to end up going to Greene Pointe for the first two years, then transfer."

He rolls his eyes as if I'm being dense. "So? It'll still help. Maybe you'll decide you don't like it and want to do something else. Or maybe you'll love it and decide you want to go on and get your master's in audiology or whatever. At least it'll give you some experience."

Someone touches my shoulder. By the feel of the body behind me, it's Griff. I tip my head back. "Hey."

"Can I join?" Griff lifts his eyebrows. "Or is this a confidential talk?"

"Sit," Remy says. "Talk some sense into your girl."

"Talk some sense?" I bristle.

"Yikes," Griff mutters as he climbs onto the bench next to me. "What's going on?"

"I got Molly an internship at Fisher's hearing clinic and she's making up excuses for why she can't do it."

"I didn't say that!" I shout louder than I intended. "I just don't have any experience or anything."

"Yeah," Remy says slowly, as if I'm an idiot. "That's the whole point. To get experience." He flicks his gaze at Griff. "Am I speaking another language?"

"Won't I have to like dress up or something though?" A medical office isn't going to let me wear jeans and T-shirts the way my cashier's job does. "It's an office."

Remy's clearly exasperated with me. "So we'll buy you a summer business wardrobe or whatever the fuck. Why are you being so difficult?"

"Hey," Griff snaps. "Ease up." Griff slides his hand over mine. "What's wrong?"

Feeling helpless and unable to put the words together, I stare at him and shake my head.

"You're worried because you don't have experience," Griff says.

I bob my head up and down.

"Okay," Griff says calmly, shooting a scowl at Remy. "Everyone has to start somewhere, Molly." He glances at Remy. "It's Fisher's place? The guy your grandfather saw?"

Remy nods.

Griff takes my hand again. "So, Fisher knows you're just graduating from high school, and that means you won't have any experience." He flicks another questioning look at Remy. "Does he want her to come in and interview or what?"

"He wants to talk to her, but I got the impression she has the job." Remy's tone softens. "He remembered you right away. Seemed happy that's what you want to go to school for. I told him your grades are excellent, that you're more than book smart, and that you're serious, and a hard worker."

A ray of hope pokes through all the clouds of doubt in my chest. Remy said all that about me? "Really?"

"Yes," Remy groans.

I stare at the card in my hands. "Wow. Okay. When should I call him?"

"After school on Monday," Remy says.

I step out of the bench and hurry to the other side of the table. "Thank you." I throw my arms around Remy's shoulders and rest my forehead on the top of his thick, curly mop of black hair. "I'm sorry," I murmur.

He reaches up and pats my arm. "It's okay. It's not like we have lots of responsible role models to help us out with this shit. I'm swimming in the dark here, Molly."

I hug him tighter. "I know."

Click.

Remy and I both focus on Griff, who has his phone pointed at us.

"Say, birthday!" Griff flashes a big, cheesy grin.

Molley

CHAPTER TWENTY-TWO

Molly

"YOU'RE REALLY NOT GOING TO TELL ME WHERE WE'RE going?" I reach over and rest my hand on Griff's leg as he guides his car out of the Zips parking lot and onto the road. "We could go to your apartment."

"We can stop there later if you want." He flips the blinker on and smoothly turns the steering wheel. The old muscle car rumbles under us like a content jungle cat.

"You think Remy's still mad at me?" I ask.

"He wasn't mad *at* you," Griff says. "Just frustrated with the situation."

I fiddle with the fabric of my dress, twisting it between my fingers then releasing it. "I don't know why the idea of the internship made me so scared."

"Change is always scary."

"But I'm not scared about graduating from high school. I can't wait to do that." It's all the stuff I have to figure out *afterward* that leaves me frozen. "What was going on with Spoons and that weird guy?" I ask to change the subject. "It looked like you were going to kill him for a minute."

"Nothing." He answers so smoothly, I know he's lying. "He needed a lesson in keeping his mouth shut."

I run my hands over my dress again, pressing out the wrinkles. "Were they making fun of you for dating...me? Because I'm younger than you?"

"What?" He glances over, his face scrunched with concern. "No. Why would you think that?"

Because I thought I overheard them teasing you for calling me Muffin. "I don't know."

"No. That wasn't it. And it wouldn't matter if they did. They're both fucking idiots." He glances over again. "What'd you and Juliet talk about?"

Thank God it's dark in Griff's car. I'm blushing from head to toe. "Nothing much."

"Secret stuff?" he teases.

"I guess." My voice falters for a second. "She asked how we were doing."

He chuckles softly and rubs his hand over his chin. "Juliet's good people."

He's not worried or even curious about what specifically she asked? No. Griff has nothing to hide.

"You mind if we stop by the shop?" he asks. "I forgot something when I was there this morning."

"Sure. It's not still open, right?"

"No, Jerry closed hours ago."

A chance for us to be alone. My heart thumps with happy anticipation.

The old gray building with several garage bays lined up on the side is dark as we pull into the parking lot.

Griff stops right in front of the glass front door.

My gaze darts around parts of the dark, empty parking lot where the glow from the security lights doesn't reach.

"Can I come in with you?" He probably won't be in there long, but I don't want to sit in the car all by myself.

"Yeah, of course." He shuts off the engine and opens his door. "Wait there."

I dig in my purse for my lip balm and slick it over my lips quickly. My door swings open and Griff holds out his hand to me.

"Thanks."

He pulls me into his arms and stares at me with so much longing, my heart flutters. I raise up on my toes, tilt my head, and purse my lips.

An engine roars by on the road in front of the shop. The driver honks their horn, startling me out of Griff's arms.

"Jackasses," he mutters. Shaking his head, he sifts through the ring of keys in his hand until he finds a short silver one on a red ring. He slides it in the lock and opens the door.

Inside, it's dark, but the mix of moonlight and the lights spilling through the wide glass windows highlight where we're going. Griff moves quickly to the right, opening the door leading to the garage bays.

The familiar, sharp scent of motor oil stings my nose as we enter the garage. Griff flicks on an overhead light that shines down on an old Ford pickup in the first bay.

"I like this. Are they keeping the mint-green paint?" I ask, running my fingers over the shiny chrome front fender.

"Yeah, I just replaced the clutch," he says over his shoulder.

He keeps walking. My platform boots had been cute and comfy when I'd gotten dressed this morning but now my toes squish and rub with every step. I limp and struggle to keep up with Griff's long strides.

Griff stops and turns. "Are you okay?"

"My feet are starting to hurt. I should've changed into my sneakers."

"Come here." In two steps, he's in front of me and scooping me into his arms. His loving eyes roam over my face for a few heartbeats. "Birthday girls should be carried, anyway."

I loop my arms around his neck. "Thank you."

The last bay holds a car-shaped lump under a big red blanket of some sort. It looks too new to be something Griff uses often.

"Did the owner bring their car's blankie from home or something?" I joke.

Griff chuckles and gently sets me down on the hood. "Hang on."

I slide on the material. Afraid I'll scratch whatever's underneath, I jump off and stand in front of it. The lights flicker above. Definitely a car under there. Wide black tires peek out from under the edge of the red cloth. Griff walks up behind me and slides his hands over my eyes.

"What're you doing?" I laugh.

"Keep your eyes closed for a second."

"Okay."

The warmth of his hands on my face disappears. His body brushes against mine, his footsteps a quick shuffling over the concrete.

There's a ripple through the air. A rush against my cheek. A rumpling of fabric.

"Open," Griff says.

My heart pounds. I peel my eyelids open and stare at the beat-up black-and-copper Chevy Malibu in front of me. My jaw drops and a squeak of surprise scratches out of my throat.

"Happy birthday."

My scrambled brain can't comprehend what's happening. My gaze flits between the car and Griff's questioning face.

"It's yours."

"What do you mean it's mine?" I ask, my voice full of surprise and anticipation. He remembered that I said I wanted to restore a Malibu with him? Then went out and found one for us? Am I dreaming?

Griff flashes a crooked smile, and my heart skips. "Correction —when we're finished with the restoration, it'll be yours."

"Really?" I squeal with delight and throw my arms around his neck. "You remembered that's what I wanted?" I pepper his face with happy kisses.

"How could I forget?" He slides his arms around my waist,

lifting me and catching my lips with his own. He sets me down and takes my hand. "Come on."

As we walk around to the driver's side, I realize the back panel's actually a glossy blue and the trunk lid's a dark matte red with a dent in the center.

"The frame's straight," Griff explains. "The damage is from them swapping panels with a different car."

"I was wondering about the color scheme," I tease. "Copper with black stripes up front and blue and red in the back."

"That's easy to fix. What's important is the panels are in good condition." He squats down and runs his fingers along the bottom. "Minimal rust. Floorboards and trunk bottom are solid. Glass in the doors and quarter panels are intact."

"Important parts." I nod as he stands and opens the driver's side door.

"Now, the interior..." He pushes the door wider and leans inside to grab a black steering wheel off the front seat. He turns and holds it out to me. A silver ribbon's twisted through the three spokes and tied into a bow. "Needs work."

"Aww." I grip the wheel with two hands. "Can I keep the bow?"

"Of course."

I peer farther inside.

"The vinyl needs to be reupholstered." Griff reaches in and flicks a piece of the black cracked front seat. The passenger side's even worse. Discolored chunks of yellow foam spill out of several long, wide cracks. The headliner's ripped and hanging from the ceiling in spiderweb-like tatters. "I can find replacement foam and covers or swap in new seats. Needs a new headliner and sail panels, too. We can order whatever you want. No radio but the A/C has been replaced," Griff says in an almost apologetic tone.

"I can bring my Bluetooth speaker with me; I can't lug around an air conditioner," I say.

"It needs work—not gonna lie." He slams the door shut.

We stand side by side next to the shell of the Malibu. The

harsh overhead lights really do reveal how much work the car needs. Excitement bubbles up inside me. This is *our* project. That means spending lots of time working together. As he explains everything he thinks the car needs, my excitement grows.

"How long do you think it'll take?" I ask.

He rubs his jaw and studies the car. "I'm hoping we can finish it in time for college in the fall."

"Wow," I breathe out. "That's quite a present. I can't believe you went to so much trouble."

"It's not trouble when it comes to you." The concern in his eyes shifts to something a bit happier. "It's in better shape than it looks." He runs his gaze over the blue rear panel. "Vapor can do the paint and bodywork. You and I will do the rest."

"This is the gift that keeps on giving." I can already picture us working side by side in the evenings, slowly bringing the car back to life.

"Because we'll be constantly working on it?" he asks.

"No, because I'll get to spend more time with you." I don't know how to explain to him that it's about more than the car. It's something for just the two of us, separate from his friendship with my brother. A start to this chapter of *our* lives as a couple. Rebuilding this car with him feels like a symbol of the new direction our relationship has taken.

"I can't wait." He leans in and brushes a gentle kiss against my cheek. "You like it?"

"I love it."

He settles his hand on my waist. "You'll need to wear a little more to work in here with me."

A volatile concoction of love and desire explodes inside me. "I thought you liked my dress."

He drops his gaze to my shoulders, then my chest. I hold my breath while he lifts his hand and skims his knuckles over the tops of my breasts. A trail of tingles follows his touch. "I like it very much."

He's so close, his intoxicating scent swirls around me. Smoke from the grill, a hint of fuel from the racetrack, and sweat from spending the day in the sun—all mixed with something unique to Griff.

He dips his head and crashes his lips to mine. It's not the sweet, soft, gentle kiss of before. He's demanding. Intense. He slides his hands into my hair, tilting my head back as he deepens our kiss.

Yes, yes, yes! This is what I've wanted all day, every day for the last two-thousand-nine-hundred-and-ninety days of my life. Give or take.

I open my mouth and hook my fingers in the belt loops of his jeans, inviting him closer.

He groans low in his throat and pulls back. "I've wanted to do this all day."

"Me too." A relentless throbbing shoots straight to my center. I rock sideways in my boots.

Griff frowns. "Are your feet okay?"

"Huh?"

Before I have a chance to remember what feet are or that I have two of them attached to my body, he kisses me again. He slides his hands over my hips and lower, bunching my dress in his fingers and dragging it up.

He bends at the knees and lifts me as if I weigh nothing. "Wrap your legs around me," he demands, kissing my jawline and then my neck. Eagerly, I hug my knees to his hips and curl my arms around his neck. Primal instinct has me writhing against his body. He's hard behind his jeans.

He only takes a few steps. My butt hits the hard metal hood and I brace my feet on the bumper. He slides one hand under my dress, dragging it over the outside of my thigh. "You're so soft everywhere," he whispers.

Bathing myself in the appreciation shining in his eyes, I lie back against the hood and stretch my arms over my head against the cool glass of the windshield. "Look. No hood scoop in my way."

"Molly," he groans. He bends and half-climbs onto the hood with me. The metal thumps under our weight. He braces himself over me, his broad, hard, sturdy body pressing into my softer, smaller one. "What do you want?" he asks.

"Touch me."

He strokes his fingers against my thigh. "I *am* touching you."

I reach for him, hooking my arm around his neck and dragging him closer. He answers with a searing kiss. My blood pounds through my ears. I slide my foot along the fender, opening my legs.

Griff groans against my neck and kisses a path to my breasts. I raise myself a few inches. "Zipper. In the back."

Between my hair being in the way and the awkward angle we're splayed in on the car, it takes a few quick jerks to lower the zipper enough that I can push the straps of my dress off my shoulders, baring my sheer purple bra.

"Your bra matches your dress." He cups one of my breasts with his hand, leans down, and sucks my nipple through the thin material.

"Oh God," I gasp, as sparks fly over my skin.

He releases my nipple and blows air over the damp tip.

"Griff." I moan his name and work one bra strap off my shoulder, then the other, baring myself to him completely.

"Molly," he breathes. "You're so pretty." He grazes his knuckles against my straining nipples. "I knew you would be but...damn."

I arch into his touch and he leans forward, wrapping his lips around my other nipple. My body trembles, and I let my head fall back with a *thump*. Little daggers of pleasure travel straight to my center.

"Griff."

He sucks harder and teases his tongue over the tip, driving me wild. Then his hand returns to my thigh, pushing my dress as he slides all the way to my hip. The dress is too tight for him to move higher without me taking it all the way off. But he follows the waistband of the seamless boy shorts I'm wearing underneath. Not the sexiest underwear for this encounter. When I dressed this morning, I was thinking of how short my dress was and how I didn't want to flash anyone when I climbed in and out of cars at the track. I never dreamed I'd end up *here* with Griff or I would've chosen differently.

Griff explores carefully, like he's measuring the boundaries of my underwear while mapping the contours of my body. Pulses of pleasure race over my skin with every touch.

"Molly, look at me." He kisses my cheek.

I open my eyes as he slides his hand along my inner thigh. "Please keep touching me," I whisper.

Staring at me with a burning intensity so powerful my skin prickles, he wedges his hand between my legs and strokes his fingers along my center. The throbbing at my core intensifies.

"Oh." I squeeze my eyes shut.

"Eyes," Griff reminds me. One finger firmly slides over my underwear, following the seam of my lips. He lets out a low groan. "You're drenched, baby."

My breath stutters in my chest. "I—"

He kisses my cheek and whispers in my ear, "You can be as loud as you want. No one's here."

"Don't stop," I beg, my voice full of desperate need.

He focuses all of his attention right over my clit, first rubbing in circles, then making strong up and down movements.

"Oh shit!" My back arches, and I push against his hand.

"You like that more than this?" He returns to the slow, circling movement.

"I don't know. I like it all."

"Greedy girl," he says with teasing approval. His fingers return to the other strokes.

Squeaks and moans pour out of me as the tension slowly builds. A wave of heat rolls over my body. Griff keeps increasing the pressure until I burst.

"Oh!" I squeeze my eyes shut and whimper a bunch of nonsensical noises.

"Yes." Griff's voice is a whisper over my skin. "You're incredible. Keep going."

I press my palms against his chest. The sensations pulse through my body over and over. I curl my torso off the hood, gasping for breath, chasing every last bit of release.

Spent and with sweat misting my forehead, I fall back. Griff catches me with his arm behind my shoulders, and I curl into his body. He slips his hand out from under my dress and grins. His skin glistens from my arousal, and I bury my face against his chest. Words escape me. All I know is that I want to spend the rest of the night with Griff, exploring each other.

"Happy birthday to me," I finally whisper.

"You're amazing." He kisses the top of my head.

Feeling bold and curious, I slide my hand down his body, cupping his erection through his jeans. He groans and closes his eyes briefly.

"Griff." I lean up and kiss along his jaw.

A distant rumble from the road grows louder and louder until the garage doors rattle.

That's more than one vehicle. They have to be right outside.

"What the fuck?" Griff helps us up and off the car while I stuff my breasts into my bra and slip the straps of my dress in place. Helpless, I turn my back to him for the zipper. My thighs feel slippery. My underwear clings to my skin.

"Griff! Where you at?" someone shouts. The bell on the door between the garage and office *bing-bongs*.

"You've got to be kidding." I run my hands through my hair.

"Fucking hell," Griff grumbles under his breath.

"Yo, Royal!" another voice shouts. "We know you're here."

"Guys, maybe we should wait for them outside," a woman's voice says.

"That's Juliet," I whisper. "What are they all doing here?"

"Nah, Griff won't mind," Remy says.

Oh, this is the worst.

"I'm going to kill your brother," Griff seethes. He pulls my body in front of him. Something hard pokes into my back. "Please don't move. Or this is going to be even more awkward for everyone," he whispers against my ear.

He loosely drapes his arms over my shoulders, so we're standing in an awkwardly casual pose. As if I wasn't coming on Griff's hand five seconds ago. *Nope, nothing to see here.*

I spot my brother's tall frame first. Then Vapor and Eraser. Juliet and Ella follow them, hanging back and pointing out different things that seem like an attempt to slow the guys down.

"Hey, guys. What's up?" I ask in a way-too-chipper tone.

Eraser stops in the open space between this bay and the one next to it. "Is this a good time?"

"No," Griff rumbles. "But don't let that stop you."

Remy scowls at us. "I thought you wanted us to see the car?" he says to Griff.

Something about his tone and the question feel off. He almost seems sincere, but not quite.

"Nooo," Griff says slowly. "I said I was bringing *Molly* to see the car."

Vapor and Eraser turn and frown at Remy. Juliet rolls her eyes. Ella mouths *sorry* at me.

"Everything okay, Griff?" Eraser flashes a cocky grin over my head. "Why're you using Molly as a human shield?"

Griff lets out an annoyed rumble and tightens his hold on me.

"This it?" Remy asks, gesturing to the car.

"You see any other '71 Malibus in here?" Griff asks with a snarky edge.

The guys crowd around the car, peering inside, opening the doors, giving it a much more thorough examination than I did.

Griff squeezes the top of my arm and releases me. "Thank you," he whispers in my ear before joining the guys to show off my gift.

Juliet shakes her head, but her lips are pressed so tight

together, I think she's fighting off laughter. "I'm so sorry," she whispers. "Remy said we were supposed to stop by and see the car."

I shoot a glare at my brother, but he's not paying attention.

Ella reaches for me and smooths the back of my hair down. "Did we interrupt anything good?"

"Yeah, kinda." I lift my eyebrows to punctuate my annoyance but they both laugh.

"Poor Molly," Ella whispers. "Remy's gonna cockblock her until she's thirty."

I snort and glance down at my dress. "I'm *divine*," I mutter. "Griff's the one who's going to be hurting."

Juliet holds up her hand in a *please stop* gesture.

"He'll live," Ella assures me.

"Hey, Molly!" Vapor shouts. "You have quite a few choices in colors to go with here. Any idea what you want?"

I walk over to meet him by the trunk. "I told Griff I wanted red, but now I'm thinking purple with big red stripes up the front of the hood." I sweep my hand through the air, even though Vapor knows what I mean.

Vapor side-eyes Griff, who returns the look with a warning scowl. "Whatever she wants," Griff says.

"Unless that offends the rules of classic restoration colors or something?" I tease, not really caring if purple and red weren't official production colors.

"Your car. Your colors." Vapor taps the hood. "Besides, it's just paint." His mouth slides into a smirk, and he glances at Griff. "I'll add little black pinstripes, then when your cars are side by side, they'll be perfectly color coordinated."

"That sounds lovely." Juliet elbows her husband in the side.

"It looks good," Remy says to Griff. "I was worried but you're right. It's not in bad shape from what I can see."

"Gee, thanks," Griff says with a healthy dose of sarcasm. "It's almost like I know what I'm talking about."

We spend a few more minutes talking about the car.

"All right. It's late," Remy announces. "Let's go." His gaze lands on me. "Truck's out front."

"But..." I glance at Griff, but he's staring at the ceiling with his jaw clenched tight.

Remy hits a button on the wall that lifts the big garage door. It rattles and inches upward.

Griff touches my shoulder, and I turn around. "Go ahead. I need to put some stuff away and lock up here."

"Are you sure?"

"Yeah, I'm sure." He touches his thumb to my chin and tips my head, then leans down. I eagerly meet him halfway, slamming my mouth against his.

"Thank you for the best birthday ever," I whisper in between kisses. "I love you so much. I can't wait to work on the car with you."

A slow smile slips over his face, chasing away the irritation from Remy's intrusion. He presses his forehead to mine. "Me too."

My gaze slides to the front of the car. "Thank you for my other present." My voice drops so only he can hear me.

"That was for me too, baby." He grins.

"Well, I really wanted to give *you* a gift." I angle my body to accidentally brush my hand against him but he captures me by the wrist.

He lifts my arm and, staring into my eyes, brushes his lips against my knuckles. The soft, gentle kiss feels like a promise that we'll do a whole lot more in the future.

CHAPTER TWENTY-THREE

GRIFF

A few days after Molly's birthday, I get a call from Diane.

"Where are we on the show, Griff? You in or out?" she says instead of a normal hello or how are you.

"I think so." I'm ninety-nine percent sure I'm in, but I don't want Diane to think I'm too eager. No reason to give her the idea that she has any kind of leverage over me.

"Lukewarm enthusiasm." She laughs. "I'll take it."

She emails me a list of instructions and I spend the next few days running around, trying to collect the information they want and sending it to Diane's assistant.

The last item on Diane's list stops me cold.

We suggest contestants speak to an attorney and have a will drawn up before competing on Supreme Underground Fighter.

Supreme's the name of the show today. So far, I've seen several variations. I can't decide if this is the dumbest one yet.

But a will? For what? My collection of vintage graphic T-shirts? Despite all the stuff I enjoy doing that could get me killed, I don't think about dying on a regular basis.

I do have some money saved, though. I own my car and Harley outright. Who gets that stuff if something happens to me?

My mother, probably. Fuck that. She'd take the money and shoot it into her veins. I'd want whatever I have to go to Remy and Molly.

A will.

Damn, what a gut-punch reminder that this could be dangerous.

After the night of Molly's birthday, I'd rather punch Remy than seek out his advice, but I'd better tell him I'm planning on leaving for two months.

I shoot him a text and he tells me to stop by the bar. It's a slow night. So slow, he must've sent Lynette home early. His Bronco's the only other vehicle in the parking lot. When I walk in, he's sitting behind the bar, reading a magazine.

The swish of the front door opening and closing draws Remy's attention to me. He grins and tosses the magazine on the counter.

"Where've you been?" he asks.

"Busy."

My clipped tone doesn't give him pause. "Not too busy to pick Molly up after school every day."

I duck my head and shake with laughter. "You got me." Between school, her job, my job, and all the extra stuff Diane's had me doing, I haven't had as much time as I would've liked to spend with Molly this week.

"Hope you found time to order your tux," he warns. "Prom's around the corner."

I burst into welcome laughter. "Thanks, Dad. I've got it under control."

"You better. You disappoint her, I'm gonna kick your ass."

I pull out a stool at the bar and knock my knuckles against the counter. "I never knew you had such strong feelings about high school dances."

"I have strong opinions about my sister's happiness." The severe expression on his face loses some of its edge. "Thanks for taking her to that interview with Mr. Fisher."

"Yeah, no problem."

He rests his elbows on the table and leans forward. "We still hosting fight night this weekend?"

"Hell, yeah. Why?" I grin at him. "You need me to knock you around?"

"In your dreams."

"One thing, though." I plow ahead to cut off the sarcastic *what* he's about to ask. "I want Molly to come with us."

"Why?"

"Because she wants to see the fights."

"You mean she wants to see *you* fight?"

"No, I'm not going in the cage this weekend." Diane specifically asked me *not* to take on any fights until the show starts filming. She hadn't been amused when I'd asked if that was supposed to be the fighter's version of revirginizing myself.

"I'll need you to help me call the fights and ref," he says.

"That's fine. She can hang with Eraser and Ella."

His face twists with doubt, but he lets out a sigh of resignation. "Most of the challengers on the roster so far are kids from Greene Pointe, Empire U, and that academy in Ironworks. So I don't expect it to get too rowdy."

"Is that going to draw in enough betting action?" I rub my fingers together.

"Yeah, it should be good." He pushes away from the counter. "Did you eat?"

I glance around the empty bar. "Is the kitchen even open?"

"Not really, but I have a sub in the fridge if you want to split it."

"Yeah, sure."

He jerks his head toward the booth. "Grab a drink and go sit."

"Thanks." I duck behind the bar and open the small black fridge under the counter. I'm not in the mood for beer or soda. After those two options, pickings are slim. I pull out a small, unopened bottle of cranberry juice and take it to the corner table we usually use.

Remy returns a few minutes later and sets a plate with half a roast beef sub and a handful of pickles on it in front of me.

"Looks good." I reach for my half. "Where'd you stop? Harry's?"

"Yeah." He drops into the chair across from me. "I threw some wings in the oven too. Won't be as crispy as the fryer—"

"Nah, I like 'em any way I can get 'em. Thanks for doing that."

After a couple bites, Remy sets his sub down and stares at my face. "What's up? You seem extra pinched and squinty-faced tonight."

"That's rude." I grab a napkin and swipe the rough paper over my mouth.

"Yeah, but I'm right. What's going on?"

Is this like the Molly situation? Does he somehow already know? Aubrey could've let it slip when Remy was at the gym without me. Should I have told him sooner?

I sit back and take a swig of juice, then brace my hands against the table. "This has to stay between you and me for now. Seriously. I'm not supposed to talk about it."

The cocky attitude vanishes from his expression. Concern wrinkles his forehead. "Are you okay?"

"I'm fine."

He picks up his soda and slowly sips it without taking his keen blue eyes off my face. "You're not planning to propose to Molly, are you?"

"What? No. Not yet." Why would he even think that? "Do you *want* me to?"

"Absolutely fucking not. But she's eighteen now. I can't stop her."

I roll that around in my head and set it aside. "We haven't been together that long. We haven't even... No. Neither of us are ready to get married."

He blows out a relieved breath.

"To be honest..." I lean forward and lower my voice even

though we're the only two here. "I'm a little insulted by your obvious relief that I'm not here to ask for your sister's hand in marriage."

He snorts with amusement. "I'll be thrilled to have you as my brother-in-law. When the time is right."

That doesn't sound as reassuring as it should. "Molly and I will decide when the time's right, bro. Not you."

"Noted." He lifts his chin. "Go on."

Here it goes. "I got contacted by a production company to appear on a reality show about amateur cage fighters hoping to go pro." I force out the words quickly, feeling stupider by the second. Remy doesn't have any more regard for reality television shows than I do.

"A reality show?" Remy stares at me with his jaw unhinged and a deep frown squeezing his forehead. "Did you learn nothing when we watched *Cabin in the Woods*?"

"What?" I blink, not making the connection at first. "Fuck, Remy. I'm serious. This is a huge opportunity for me."

His face slowly shifts into an insufferable smirk. "To get eaten by a family of zombie cannibals?"

I grit my teeth and start counting to ten. *One, two, three...*

"All right, all right. Settle down. I'm joking." He groans. "I heard there was a producer scouting local fighters. Knew they were interested in you, but I didn't think you'd bite."

"Well, I did. I still have to sit through a psych exam or some shit but I'm ninety-nine percent sure I'm in."

"Psych exam." The smile slides off his face and the frown returns. "Griff, you gotta be real careful what you tell those fuckers."

"You think I don't know that?"

"No," he insists. "I'm not talking about the shit we do at The Castle, the racing, or the motorcycle club." He reaches across the table and taps the side of my head. "I'm talking about *you*. Be careful what information you give them about yourself. They'll use whatever they can as ammunition against you."

"Remy, the show's focus is fighting, not some *Bachelor* dating bullshit."

He cocks his head like I'm stupid. "You ever talk to Shelby about what she went through on *Redneck Roadhouse*? That show was supposedly about singing but they fucked with the contestants personally."

"No. When and why did *you* talk to Shelby about it? Rooster doesn't like you anywhere near his girl."

He rolls his eyes. "Jigsaw mentioned it when we were down in Virginia helping out the club. He said she went through all sorts of shit that left her kinda messed up."

"Well, she's a successful singer touring with Dawson Roads now, so I guess it worked out okay for her," I argue.

He shrugs. "Okay. If you trust this producer—"

"I don't even *know* her. And I don't trust anyone outside our circle." I blow out a breath. "But there's a lot of money at stake."

"You've never wanted to go professional."

"Maybe I *would* if I had professional training."

He stares at me. "I thought you wanted to buy the garage from Jerry one day?"

"Yeah, and how am I gonna do that working hourly? He pays me well, but it's not enough."

He holds up his hands in surrender. "I thought you'd work out some sort of arrangement with him when he's ready to retire."

I sigh. "Maybe. It's just every time I get money saved up from the fights, my mother hits me up for a 'loan' or to pay her rent or whatever."

"Jesus, Griff." Disappointment and defeat grind through his voice. "If it's that bad, why are you spending all that money on Molly's car?"

"Because it makes her happy." Why am I explaining this to him? Shouldn't he *want* Molly to be with someone who'll do anything to make her happy? "What's the point of doing *any* of this if I can't put a smile on my girl's face and give her something she needs? She supposed to sprout wings and fly to college in the fall?" I hold out my arms and flap them up and down to punctuate how dense he's being.

His jaw works from side to side. I can't tell which thing I said put that irritation on his face, so I ignore it.

"I told you I was planning to get her a car for school," he says.

"We're having fun doing the restoration together."

His hands shoot across the table, connecting hard with my chest. "Don't be a dick."

"Get your mind out of the gutter." I shove him back. "It's fun working on a project with her. That's all I meant." So far all we've had a chance to do together is order the parts we need for the interior, but I love how seriously she takes every decision.

"Jesus, you've got it bad," he grumbles.

"No shit. I've told you that like a hundred times." I cock my head and choose my words carefully. "I know this is a difficult concept for you to understand, but I actually *like* Molly. As a person." I raise one hand in the air and tap my fingers together like I'm working a sock puppet—maybe a puppet show *would* be the best way to get my point across. "I *like* talking to her and doing things with her."

His harsh expression fades. "She's not driving you nuts with all her questions?"

"No." I snort. "She asks smart questions." Hell, even if she didn't it wouldn't matter—I love listening to her voice.

His big brother tantrum finally seems to pass. A genuine smile spreads across his face. "I'm not surprised."

Relief that I've finally told Remy about the show settles over me, but it's short-lived. "I haven't told her about the show and how long I'll be gone for filming. So, can you please not say anything to her?"

Big brother protector returns. Remy's eyes narrow. "What the fuck you waiting for?"

"Jesus, Remy." I stab my fingers through my hair and turn away. "We just got together—"

"But you were sneaking around behind my back," he adds in a let's-be-honest dry tone.

"We weren't *sneaking*." I grit my teeth and swallow the rest of my argument. He's fucking with me.

"Did you tell your mother you're going to be away?" he asks.

Talk about conversational whiplash. "No. What the fuck for?"

"They're probably not going to let you have access to your phone. If she needs to reach you and can't..." He doesn't finish the thought. Doesn't need to.

"I'll call her." That'll be an annoying conversation. One my mother's bound to forget five minutes after it ends, too.

"Tell her to contact me if she needs something."

"Bro, you don't have to do that." I'd ask Remy to help me bury a body before I'd ask him to deal with my mother's craziness.

"Yeah, I do," he insists. "If you're doing this, you need to give it your full attention. No distractions or worries. I can deal with your mom."

"If she reaches out, it's just gonna be to ask for money."

He shrugs. "Well, I don't got any, so that'll be a simple conversation."

The front door's bells jingle, announcing customers. Remy shoves away from the table. "Shit, hope they only want extra crispy wings," he mutters.

"You want me to go take the wings out of the oven while you deal with the customers?"

Remy doesn't have a chance to answer. The customers round the corner and we recognize the two Lost Kings MC members right away.

"Teller." Remy dips his chin. "Jigsaw, what brings you into my fine establishment this evening?" He holds out his arms wide.

I stand and move around the edge of the table. "Teller." I hold out my hand and he shakes it quickly. Teller's blond hair, sharp jaw, and easy smile give him the appearance of someone who should've been cast in those *Magic Mike* movies Molly and her friends went nuts for. But I've witnessed him casually dispose of the body of someone who hurt his sister, so to say I maintain a respectful fear of the Lost Kings MC's treasurer is an understatement.

"How you been?" he asks.

"All right." My gaze slides to Jigsaw, and I search my brain for random small talk that won't piss him off. "You've been hanging out in our neck of the woods more than usual lately."

"What's it to you?" Jigsaw growls, sounding as deadly as his serial killer road name suggests. His cold, calculating eyes always remind me of the Terminator. The jagged scar through one eyebrow adds to the menacing vibe always surrounding him. He's fought at The Castle a few times but most of our regulars are too scared to enter the cage with him. That makes him perfect for helping us with security, though.

He lets my hand dangle for a minute before gripping it tight and flashing a smile that's more terrifying than friendly. His best friend's girl, Shelby, claims Jigsaw's a "sweetheart" but I haven't seen that side of him. The few times we've ridden with his club, his MC brothers have relished sharing stories of how Jiggy collects the fingers of their enemies. I never got the impression they were joking.

"Have a seat." Remy sweeps his hand toward a larger corner booth. "I was about to bring out some wings. Don't really have much else tonight."

"That's fine." Teller nods. "Thanks."

While Remy runs to the kitchen, I slip behind the bar, grab a pitcher, and fill it with soda. I return to the table with the pitcher and a stack of cups.

"You always here?" Jigsaw asks as I slide into my seat.

I casually rest my elbows on the table and pretend I don't feel like I'm sitting across from a cobra and praying it won't strike.

"I come in after work some nights and try to help out." I shrug. "He pays me in subs and chicken wings."

One corner of Jigsaw's mouth twitches with what might actually be amusement.

Remy returns and sets a plate with a heaping pile of chicken wings on the table. He sets smaller plates in front of each of us and drops a tub of blue cheese dressing in the center of the table.

"Thanks." Teller grabs a wing and bites into it.

Jigsaw studies the wings carefully before selecting one and dropping it on his plate.

"They're not poisoned, bro," Remy says.

Jigsaw flicks his soulless eyes Remy's way. "When did we become bros, kid?"

I wish Remy had better control of his mouth.

Teller elbows Jigsaw.

"So, what brings you by tonight?" Remy asks.

"Checking up on one of our businesses in Pine Hollow," Teller answers. "Wasn't far. Thought we'd stop in and say hi."

I side-eye Remy. Lost Kings paying us a visit is nothing new. They've been slowly recruiting us to form a support club for a while now. Couple of brothers fight at The Castle. They've helped us at Zips. They've used Remy's bar to have a few meetings with other assorted criminals. We usually get a heads-up though.

"Always good to see you." Remy gestures to the plate. "Sorry I don't have more available at this hour."

"This is fine," Teller assures him.

When his buddy doesn't drop dead, Jigsaw must determine the chicken wings are safe and digs in.

I sit back and wait. Is there some other reason for their visit tonight? Or is it a sign from the universe?

"Teller." I wait until I have his attention. "Your wife's a lawyer, right? Does she do wills and stuff like that?"

"Well," Teller says slowly, picking up a napkin and wiping his hands.

"Charlotte's busy with the two tiny humans she popped out, so probably not," Jigsaw answers.

Teller scowls in his MC brother's direction. "She's still on maternity leave from her law firm, yes."

"Oh, shit. Congrats," I say, feeling stupid. I saw Charlotte not that long ago and she looked like she was about to pop any second. "That must be keeping you busy."

The corners of his mouth turn up. "It's chaos, but we're loving it." The smile slides off his face. "Charlotte can't meet with you, but my step, uh, my president's wife can probably get it done. If not, she can recommend someone."

"The fuck you need a will for anyway?" Jigsaw runs his scary gaze over me. "What are you, fifteen? Need someone to leave your collection of Hot Wheels to?"

Next to me, Remy rumbles an annoyed sound. I kick my heel into his leg under the table.

"Thanks, Jiggy." I pat my cheeks. "Guess that new moisturizer is working wonders and I'm aging backward."

Teller snorts. Jigsaw's mouth even twitches.

"Seriously," I continue, "don't know if Dex mentioned it but I'm going to be on this reality show. They producers suggested I have a will drawn up." I shift my gaze to Jigsaw. "I don't have much, but what I *do* have I don't want my mother gettin' her hands on."

Jigsaw stares at me for a few seconds, then nods. "I get that."

"Reality show?" Teller's forehead wrinkles in disbelief. "You fuckin' serious? What're you gonna do? Prance around an island in a Speedo handing out roses?"

Remy ducks his head and cough-laughs.

"No." I lift my fists in the air. "It's supposed to be a competition for underground fighters. Who can battle it out to the final round."

Both Lost Kings stare at me for so long, I put my hands back down on the table and shrug. "There's a big cash prize if I make it to the end." I hold up one hand. "Dex already warned me not to mention the MC."

"How's it 'underground' if it's gonna be on TV?" Jigsaw asks.

I shrug again. "Chance to go pro."

Teller takes a sip of his drink. "You two know where the clubhouse is. Come up Sunday for family dinner night. I'll set things up with Hope for you, Griff."

"You sure she won't mind?" Last thing I want to do is piss off the wife of the MC's president. That guy makes Jigsaw seem cuddly.

"Nah." He waves a dismissive hand through the air. "She likes you for some reason."

Stunned, I sit back. Is he fucking with me? "She's only met me a couple of times."

"Don't get your meat wrench fully torqued," Jigsaw warns. "Hope likes you in the same way most kind-hearted ladies like stray puppies is all he meant."

I roll my eyes. "Thanks."

"I think you remind her of Murphy." Teller laughs. "He's her favorite son."

Jigsaw squints at him. "Nah, I think that's *you*."

I assume this is some weird MC brother inside joke but I like Murphy, so I'm not insulted by the comparison. "Well, if she's willing to do it, I'd appreciate it."

Teller picks up his phone and taps his thumbs over the screen. "I'll talk to her and text you a list of what she needs you to bring."

It'll be a relief to get this off my list of things I have to do. "Thanks."

"Not a problem." He slides his chair away from the table and stands. "Thanks for dinner. We gotta hit the road."

Jigsaw stares up at Teller with wide, sad eyes. "I wanted dessert."

"I'll bag up some chocolate chip cookies to go." Remy slides out of the booth.

"He doesn't need any cookies," Teller grumbles, shaking his head.

"Shut your mouth." Jigsaw stands and slaps Teller's arm.

"They're homemade!" Remy shouts.

Jigsaw grips the back of his chair and leans over it, getting way too close to my face. "Did *he* make them?"

I lift my shoulders but don't back away. "Doubt it. Lynette probably baked them today."

Jigsaw nods and releases the chair.

Still shaking his head, Teller walks over to the bar, pulls his wallet from his pocket, plucks a few bills out, and tucks them under the corner of the register.

Jigsaw follows his lead and adds a few dollars.

I pretend to see nothing.

Remy returns with two small white paper bags and hands them to the guys.

"Thanks." Teller lifts his bag and nods at Remy, then me. "See you two Sunday."

The way he says it sounds more like an order than an invitation.

Molly

CHAPTER TWENTY-FOUR

GRIFF

Sunday evening, Remy and I ride deep into the hills of Empire County to the Lost Kings MC clubhouse. If we hadn't already been here before, I doubt we'd be able to find the place. As it is, we miss the unmarked turnoff and have to find somewhere on the narrow country road to turn our bikes around.

We stop at the tall iron gate and wait for someone to open it and let us through. We back our bikes into spots at the bottom of the long driveway and walk to the clubhouse—which looks more like a luxury log cabin.

"You ever heard of a motorcycle club with property like this?" I say to Remy in a low voice.

"Place used to be some sort of Buddhist yoga retreat center or something."

I jerk my thumb over my shoulder. "Explains the big Buddha statue down there."

"They bought it for back taxes or something." He elbows me. "Like we bought The Castle."

"This is in infinitely better shape."

"Yeah, but we're landowners too—that's all I'm saying."

I guess that's true in the same way that Great Danes and toy poodles are both *canines*.

Bright security lights illuminate the entire area around the clubhouse. We follow the curved driveway to what I guess is technically the "front" of the building. It's full of neatly parked motorcycles, SUVs, and lifted trucks. Two huge garages stand adjacent to the main clubhouse. Farther back, I glimpse what looks like another house and a playground to rival what the richest school districts might have. Deep woods stand across from the clubhouse but through the trees, I catch glimpses of lights.

"I think most of the officers have built houses for their families back there," Remy whispers.

"So, *definitely* stay out of their woods."

"If we want to live, yeah."

The front door's open. But there's no music or smoke pouring out like there has been the few times we've been here for MC parties. Instead, it's all loud, rumbling male voices, women's laughter, and children's high-pitched squeals.

"Family night, indeed," Remy says, pulling the screen door open. The place is a huge, log-cabin sort of building. High ceilings, exposed beams. A large staircase to our left is lined with framed photos. A generous leather sectional takes up the entire back wall and corner. The room's full of bikers and their families.

Murphy notices us stepping inside first. The burly lumberjack-looking VP of the club grins and opens his arms wide. "Welcome."

Murphy's greeting draws everyone's attention to us. We face a lot of steely-eyed biker glares. Didn't Teller mention we were invited?

MCs are known for all their strict protocols and any perceived slight can get your ass kicked—or *worse*. While I try to be mindful and respectful of their rules, Remy approaches these gatherings with a *whatever the fuck* attitude that'll probably get us killed one day.

Rock, the president of this charter, approaches us first, hand outstretched. "Thanks for joining us." He shakes Remy's hand, then mine.

"Appreciate the invite, sir," I answer.

The corner of his mouth quirks. "Rock is fine." He turns toward the large open living room. "I think you two know pretty much everyone here."

I spot Wrath, the club's enforcer, in a back corner of the room with his wife. He lifts a hand and waves. The movement draws the attention of the redhead next to him. Hope flashes a bright, welcoming smile. For a second, she disappears in the crowd, then emerges holding the hand of a little girl who looks like her tiny carbon copy.

"Hi, Griff." Hope's warm voice carries above the rest of the noise. Rock moves closer and slips a protective arm around her waist. Her green eyes shift to Remy. "It's nice to have you guys up here finally."

"Hi!" the little girl chirps, waving her hands at us.

I smile at the little girl. "Grace, right?" I say to Hope, praying that's her kid's name.

She nods.

Rock leans down and picks up his daughter. "Mommy's got work to do." He kisses her cheek. "You're with me."

Grace beams at him.

"We don't have to right now," I protest.

Somewhere deeper in the clubhouse, a baby lets a scream rip. Then, another one adds to the noise. My eyes widen and I search the room.

"Let's go check on your cousins," Rock says to his daughter.

"Bye, Momma!" Grace waves to all of us. Hope waves back and watches her husband head up the long staircase to our left.

Grinder takes Rock's place, holding out a hand for Remy to shake, then me. "Good to see you two up here."

Have we been invited before and declined or something? Remy and I share a look. He must be getting that wandering-sheep-returning-to-the-flock vibe I'm picking up.

"Do you mind if I borrow him?" Hope says to Remy, resting her hand on my shoulder.

Remy flashes a flirty smile. "As long as you return him."

Hope's lips purse likes she's fighting off laughter.

Wrath somehow sneaks up behind Remy and wraps one of his tattooed, tree-trunk arms around Remy's neck, capturing him in a rear chokehold. "Ruthless. Just the man I was looking for."

"Why?" Remy gasps and tucks his chin.

Hope flicks an exasperated glance at Wrath. "Please don't toss our guests around like chew toys."

"Funny you should say that, Cinderella." Wrath reaches over and rubs his big hand over Hope's head, and she bats him away. "We got one of those attack suits to train the dogs. Z needs someone to wear it, and Ruthless looks like the right size."

"Wait, what?" Remy pivots, shifting his weight to his back foot, and throws his elbow back.

Wrath dodges the blow to his gut easily, and releases Remy. "Nice move."

"Thanks." Remy shakes it off and takes a deep breath.

"You done terrorizing the kid?" Grinder punches Wrath's arm.

"Yes, Grumpy...I mean, Grinder." Wrath grins.

I duck my head and swallow my laughter.

Hope lets out a heavy sigh. "Come on." She gestures to an open door to our right. "Be nice," she says over her shoulder to Wrath.

"I'll let him get into the protective gear before we release the dogs," Wrath promises.

"That's not what I meant," Hope mutters, shaking her head. "We're going to borrow the guys' office." She pushes the heavy wooden door open and motions for me to go in first. A desk rests against each wall of the office, leaving the middle of the room mostly open. A dog bed rests in one corner and a filing cabinet in another. A laptop and some folders or books sit on each one. Hope pulls out the chair at the largest desk. A yellow legal pad rests on top of a smaller laptop. This must be where the officers meet before "church."

She drops into the thickly padded executive chair and nods to a green leather chair across from her. "Take Murphy's seat."

"Dex doesn't get a desk?" I guess.

She shrugs. "I think the garages are his domain."

I nod, but damn, maybe I shouldn't have said that.

"So, Teller said you need to have a will drafted?" Hope prompts.

"I don't have much." I spread my hands in front of me. "This is probably pointless."

"Not at all." Hope reaches over and rests her soft, warm hand over mine. "It's smart to think ahead. Just in case."

"Thanks." I don't get the sense she's humoring me.

For some reason, I'm nervous. My leg won't stop bouncing. My gaze keeps straying to the closed door.

"This is confidential," she assures me.

"Remy already knows. It's not really a big deal."

"Well, that's your decision. But on my end, nothing you say in here leaves this room." She glances toward the door. "Rock understands that."

I relax into the chair and pull out the list I scribbled earlier.

"All right." Hope picks up her pen and legal pad. "So, tell me what made you decide to do this now?"

I tell her about the reality show, surprised Teller didn't mention it. She listens and jots a few notes. When I mention the contracts, non-disclosure agreements, and psych exam, she sets her pen down. Concern glints in her eyes.

"Are you sure about this, Griff? In theory you should have you own attorney look over the contract and negotiate the terms." She taps her pen against the pad.

"I don't have any bargaining power. If I try to change the terms, they'll probably just find someone else."

"True," she says slowly, as if maybe that wouldn't be a bad idea. "We could always argue later you didn't have your own counsel, but it's a hard battle to fight. The law rarely favors the little guy in cases like that."

Her questions don't provoke my defensive side like Remy's did. Her use of *we* reassures me even if what she said amounts to "we have a rat's chance in hell" of winning.

"You know what? It's never a bad time to have a will." She picks up her pen again. "Let's take care of that today. When it's time to sign the contracts, call me."

I blow out a relieved breath. "Yeah, that sounds good."

She works through a list of general questions: full legal name, date of birth, address, debts, family. A smile ghosts over her lips when I mention Molly.

All those things are easy to talk about. Then we get to my assets.

"Like I said, there's not much. My Harley should go to Vapor." My lips quirk up. "My collection of flannel shirts to Eraser."

Hope looks up from her notepad, a curious frown crinkling her forehead.

"It's...an inside joke," I explain. "He'll appreciate it."

A slight smile flickers at the corners of her mouth. "Got it."

"My car, Black Beauty, that goes to Molly. The Malibu is already in her name, so that's hers." I rub my fingers over my chin. What else do I have? I glance at the list in my hands, glad I brought it. "Money in my bank accounts goes to Remy."

"Good." She nods and scribbles another note.

"My half of The Castle goes to Remy too. Everything else in my apartment should go to Molly and Remy. Some cash. A watch from my grandfather." I shrug. "Not a whole lot."

"That's okay." Hope's pen hovers over the paper, and she flicks it back and forth. "Nothing to your mother?"

"No. She'll just shoot it in her arm." I mime jamming a needle to the inside of my elbow. I say it like it doesn't bother me—an automatic self-protection measure.

Compassion, not judgment, shines in Hope's eyes. She seems to be one of the few people I've met who doesn't assume the sins of the mother automatically land on the son.

"I understand," she says softly. "I'll draft this so it's clear what your intentions are."

"Thanks." Even though this seemed pointless at first, Hope seems to take it seriously and that's reassuring.

"The nature of the show..." Hope hesitates. "At your age it's not just *death* you have to worry about. What if you're injured or incapacitated? Who do you want making medical decisions for you?"

I blink and sit back. "Shoot. I don't want to burden anyone with that."

"You can think about it and let me know."

"Molly and Remy," I answer quickly. "She won't let him pull the plug on me too soon. He won't let me linger as a vegetable past my expiration date."

She doesn't laugh, but she writes it down.

The weight of all these decisions returns, settling on my shoulders like a heavy cloak of doubt I can't shake. The path in front of me seems like a maze of possibilities—some hopeful, some dangerous.

I just hope I don't slam into a dead end.

Molley

CHAPTER TWENTY-FIVE

Molly

The sharp bleat of an air horn slices the air. I jump and let out my own bleat of surprise.

"Welcome to The Castle!" my brother shouts over the noise.

My stomach flutters with fear and excitement.

The roar of conversation quiets. The jostling of bodies stops as people turn to locate the announcer.

Remy stands in the center of the cage on a chair. Pride fills my chest. That's *my* brother commanding the attention of an entire building full of brawlers and bettors.

"If you took a wrong turn in the woods and ended up here, now's your chance to run." Remy waits a beat as if he really expects people to dash for freedom. "My friend and I run this show. Say hi, Stonewall." He points to Griff standing on the steps just outside the cage. Griff raises his hand and waves. His broad shoulders and thick muscles straining against the sleeves of his T-shirt look even more impressive under the harsh, white lights. His sharp jawline remains tense. No hint of a smile. He's all business tonight.

A woman in the crowd lets out a shrill whistle, and another one follows. "Hi, Stonewall," they shout in flirtatious unison.

Hands off, ladies. He's all mine.

"We make the rules," Remy continues ignoring Griff's fan club, "and we'll determine the winners of tonight's fights."

I blow out a breath of relief. Griff already told me he wasn't fighting. But I wasn't sure about Remy. If he's calling the fights, he probably won't be in one himself.

"My man Eraser over in the corner will take your bets." Remy turns and points to a table against the back wall. Eraser stands with his arms crossed over his chest and throws a surly look at the room. He nods but doesn't wave or respond to the introduction. The money guy can't afford to look *too* friendly. Ella's sitting next to him with a more approachable smile. She doesn't stand and Remy doesn't acknowledge her. Knowing the guys, it's a safety issue, not a slight against Ella.

"Betting ends once the fighters are in the cage and the door closes," Remy continues.

With one quick, powerful movement, Griff shoves the door. It swings shut with a thunderous clang. A few people jump and back away from the cage perimeter.

"Maintain a respectful distance from the cage. Do not touch the fence." Remy jumps off the chair and slaps his palm against the chain link encircling the fighting ring. A soft clinking rustles through the air as the fence brushes against the steel poles embedded in the floor. Inside the cage, big foam pads cover the unforgiving metal. Outside, not so much.

"No refunds. No fighting outside the ring. No touching anyone or anything that doesn't belong to you. In our house, we congratulate the winners, shake hands with the losers, and leave the fight in the cage. Take your petty beefs off of our property. No whining if you lose—better luck next time." He stops and runs his gaze over the crowd, then moves onto the punishment phase of his lecture—which, if I remember correctly, is much shorter. "Punishment for breaking our rules will range from a simple beating to expulsion to permanent bans. Are we clear?"

Remy pulls the bullhorn away from his mouth, cocks his head, and cups his hand around one ear.

The deafening roar of spectators shouting, "Clear!" fills the building.

"Excellent! Tonight, we welcome a new challenger to our ring of chaos." Remy drones on about this newcomer, then runs through a list of the other matches. I tune him out and search the room, recognizing more people than I expected.

I recognize a few kids from school—some who graduated a couple of years before me. Others seem familiar, but I can't place them. There's a mix of men and women but it's definitely a more male than female audience overall.

At least eight or nine different girls who look like they took their fashion cues from a Victoria's Secret runway show mill around a large, garage-sized doorway. Ring bunnies. I'm fairly certain the tallest dark-haired one in a gold minidress worthy of a space-cowboy movie has come home with my brother once or twice. Three of the girls watch Griff with an interest that turns my stomach.

I slide my gaze away from the bunnies. A few guys wearing Lost Kings MC vests prowl through the crowd, keeping order just by the name of their club on their backs and the terrifying scowls on their faces. I recognize one Lost King—Jigsaw—since he's at Zips a lot. He probably doesn't remember me, so I don't bother waving or doing anything to call attention to myself.

While my brother continues his spiel, Griff pushes his way through the crowd. Most of the spectators seem to be headed toward the betting table, making Griff look like a fish swimming upstream.

There's no smile on his face when he reaches me, but he wraps me in his arms. "You okay?"

"Are you sorry I came tonight?" I tip my head back to see his face.

"No, but things get rough sometimes."

"I'm glad *you're* not fighting."

His lips tilt into a playful smile. "I thought you liked seeing me win?"

Shock holds my tongue for a few beats. Maybe I shouldn't have tuned out Remy's speech so early. Is Griff planning to get in the cage? "Remy said you two are calling the fights tonight."

His playful grin intensifies. "So, you *don't* want to see me in the ring?"

"Honestly? No." My heart pounds. "It makes me a little stabby every time you take a hit." *Stabby* makes me sound braver than I am. The last time I saw him fight, I almost threw up when he got kicked in the head.

"Good thing I don't take many hits, then." He brushes his knuckles against my cheek. "You'd be dangerous with a sharp instrument."

"When it comes to you, yes."

He hugs me against his body again, and this time I snake my arms around his middle and rest my cheek on his chest.

"I'm glad you're here tonight," he says.

Pressed so tight to his body, I both feel and hear his statement. I snuggle even closer. Even in amongst all this chaos and bloodlust, I'm safe with Griff. "Me too." I tip my head to peer up at him. "I'm proud of you two." I nod to the crowd surrounding the cage. "What you and Remy have built here."

"Our little operation's grown, for sure," he mutters.

"Hey," Remy's harsh voice interrupts, "if you're done molesting my sister in front of everyone, do you think you could do your job?"

"*Molest* implies he's bothering me," I say, hugging Griff tighter. "Which he absolutely isn't."

"My girl has spoken." Griff's body shifts to the side, his arm sliding up around my shoulders.

I open my eyes and pull away to find them in a staring contest. Remy breaks their eyeball duel first. His gaze shifts from annoyance to concern as it lands on me.

"You all right?" Remy asks. "Being here, I mean. I know you don't mind having this clown slobbering all over you." He jerks his thumb in Griff's direction.

Griff shakes with laughter.

"The only one clowning around here is *you,*" I snap back. "I'm fine."

"Well, when he's done marking you with his scent or whatever's going on here"—Remy circles his hand in front of both our faces— "I want you to go watch the fights from Eraser's table."

"But how am I going to see anything?" I twist my body away from Griff and scan the room. The area around where Eraser had been standing earlier is so crowded, I can barely make out the top of his head. I can't see Ella at all. "Are you sure the money table's the safest place to be during the fight?"

"During it, yeah. At the end of the night, maybe not." Remy scowls at Griff. I wish I'd been able to hear the discussion that went down when Griff told Remy I was coming here tonight. Remy seems off-balance and extra cranky.

"Jigsaw's covering the table," Griff says. "No one's gonna fuck with that scary bastard."

"Yeah, but he's here to protect the *money.*" Remy flicks his gaze to me again. His expression suggests he's close to ordering me to go home.

I stand straighter, jostling Griff's protective arm from my shoulders. "I can handle myself." I lift one knee, keeping my foot parallel to the floor. "Come closer so I can demonstrate my knee-to-groin move."

"Aw, look at that. We got our own mini-Amanda Nunes wannabe." Remy rubs his hand over my head and I bat it away.

"Hell yeah, she's a champion in multiple divisions." I raise my fists, tuck my elbows to my sides and throw a pretend jab.

"Put those away." Remy slaps one of his hands over my fists and pushes them down. "I don't need anyone thinking you're looking for a match."

Behind me, Griff wraps his arms around me again—the embrace closer to a straitjacket than a loving hug this time. I tip my head back and stare up at him. "Traitor."

"He's right." Griff kisses my forehead.

"I'll behave," I promise, shooting a glare at Remy who just laughs. When Griff doesn't release me, I try to wriggle free.

He leans down and brushes his lips against my ear. "I don't want to let you go. I kind of like you this way."

A blast of heat sears my skin. Why does the low, husky timbre of his voice have this effect on me? Sighing, I relax in his arms, wishing we were alone.

"For fuck's sake," Remy grumbles, stalking away.

I slide my head to the side, peering up at Griff. "Were you trying to piss him off?"

Griff slowly turns me in his arms, keeping us close. "No, but it *is* a bonus." He lifts his gaze to somewhere behind me. "What I really want is for every other motherfucker in this building to know you're with *me*. You're *my* girl."

That same melty, warm feeling slides over me. I loop my arms around his neck and lean up on my tiptoes. "Does it also mean your bunny fan club over there will stop eyeing you like you're a stack of banana pancakes with caramel drizzle?"

His lips quirk up but his head tilts in confusion. "I'm more like a Belgian waffle, no?"

"You know what I mean."

"No, I don't. The only girl I want drooling over me is you." He pats his stomach. "Although now I really want to stop for waffles somewhere. The thick, fluffy kind." He holds his thumb and index finger an inch apart to demonstrate. "Not those sad little things you slide in the toaster."

I shake with laughter and squeeze my eyes shut.

"That's better." He rests one finger under my chin, tilting my head, then slowly brushes his lips over mine. Blood thunders through my ears, drowning out the noise of the people shouting the names of who they think will win each fight.

He pulls away and I reach up to brush my thumb against the corner of his mouth. "You're wearing some of my cherry gloss now."

"Good." His tongue slides over his lip. "Tastes like you." He slides his arm around my shoulders. "Come on. Let me walk you over to E. Things are about to start."

"Griff!" a high-pitched voice shouts, accompanied by a rapid *clickety-clack* over the concrete.

Keeping his hand on the small of my back, and pushing me slightly ahead of him, Griff walks even faster.

Close to Eraser's table, the girl catches up to us, planting herself right in front of me like a traffic cop. Her tight pink dress seems to be made of latex and strings. Her golden skin glows under the lighting. Fine glitter dusts her shoulders, cleavage, and the tops of her breasts.

I glance down at my jeans, Chucks, and purple T-shirt with Griff's brass knuckles, flowers, and crown design stretched across my chest. The V-neck's cut low enough. Why didn't I think to glitter *my* boobs?

"Griff, where do you want me tonight?" The woman's breathy voice and eyelash batting make it sound more like she's asking about his favorite sex position than a job assignment.

Look at dollar-store Sydney Sweeney trying to hit on my boyfriend right in front of me.

Griff's hand moves from my back to my hip, drawing me closer. He doesn't bother to introduce us though.

"Uh, is Lyla here? Or Robin?" Griff gestures toward the door leading to other parts of The Castle. "Ask one of them what they need."

Her flawless face wrinkles with disappointment. "Okay." She shoots a glare at me and bumps me with her shoulder as she stomps away.

"She seems nice," I say, smiling sweetly at Griff.

The air horn screeches again. My entire body ducks as if a bomb's about to drop on my head.

"Wrap it up, everyone!" Remy calls. "We're about to start."

Griff nudges me toward Eraser and waves to get his attention.

"I'll be fine. Go before Remy bans me from ever coming back." I give Griff a playful shove toward the cage.

His gaze slides between me and the safety of the table as if he's the Terminator calculating the distance and risk to my safety.

"Go," I encourage.

"All right." He leans down and kisses my cheek. "I'll come check on you in a bit."

I'm maybe five feet away from Eraser when Pink Latex Girl pounces on me. "Who are you?" she shouts in my face.

I stop and stare at the stripes of highlighter along her cheekbones and down the center of her nose. Girl needs a blending brush, stat. "Who are *you*?" I counter.

"Dinah."

"Like the cat?" I ask, not sure I heard her right over all the noise.

Her cheeks squinch into something between a frown and a scowl. "What?"

Not a fan of Alice in Wonderland, I see. "I'm Griff's girlfriend." Wow, this is the first time I've introduced myself to anyone that way.

Her eyes widen and she slow-blinks. "Seriously?" She sneers and looks down her long, thin nose at me with such disbelief I want to shrivel into a raisin and be tossed in a vat of oatmeal cookie dough. "You're a little girl. Griff's a *man*. He needs a real woman to handle him right."

What in the bad-1980s-soap-opera nonsense is happening?

"You wouldn't know the first thing about handling him." I flick my gaze over her in the same dismissive once-over she gave me. "Right or otherwise."

"What'd you say?" She steps way too close into my personal space and raises one hand in the air.

Fear quivers down my spine. My mouth really shouldn't write checks my body's not prepared to cash.

On the other hand, I have a few self-defense moves in my

arsenal. Kneeing her in the crotch might not be the right one for *this* situation, but I'm willing to give it a shot.

A big hand wraps around her wrist before she has a chance to let loose, yanking her sideways so fast glitter flakes off her skin, floating in the air between us.

"The fuck you think you're doing?" Eraser growls loud enough for several people in the immediate area to turn and stare. "You touch Remy's sister, I'm gonna toss you out on your ass and let my wife back her car over you."

The girl's eyes widen and her gaze ping-pongs between Eraser and me. I pull my shoulders back and try to look like I wasn't five seconds away from peeing my pants.

"I didn't...You're...oh," she stammers.

Being Griff's girlfriend doesn't offer me much protection. Being Remy's sister does. *Interesting.*

Eraser releases Dinah and she stumbles away, mumbling an apology.

"You just got here. How are you already gettin' into trouble, lil' McMuffin?" Eraser teases.

I laugh and roll my eyes at the nickname. "Not my fault. Guess she feels a certain way about Griff?"

Eraser seems to read the question in my voice. "She's not his ex or anything, Molly. Just some chick who wishes she had his attention."

That must be his roundabout way of reassuring me Griff's never boinked her before. "Good to know."

"Come on." He slings his arm over my shoulder and gently guides me to his table.

Ella jumps up as soon as we make eye contact. "McMuffin! I was wondering when you'd get over here."

Eraser gestures for me to slide around to the other side where I can put my back against the wall and sit next to Ella.

"Boy, he really wants us trapped back here, huh?" I say to her.

"Nah. If anything goes down, we flip the table, brace it against the wall, and have ourselves a nice little fort to hide out in." She curls her fingers around the edge of the table as if she's about to demonstrate her plan.

"Uh, wow. You've put a lot of thought into that."

"We grab the cash box too, of course." She bends over and drags a small black backpack over. "And I've got a few tricks in here." Her hand disappears inside the bag and returns with a can of pepper spray.

"I thought that wasn't legal?"

She chuckles. "Look around you, Molly. *None* of this is legal. The pepper spray is the least of it."

Why'd I have to say something so good-girlish? Maybe I really don't belong here. "Uh, yeah. Good point."

"Anyway, I've never had to flip the table, but just in case, that's the plan." Her expression turns softer as her gaze lands on her husband. "He makes me run through a drill every time I come with him."

"You two are the cutest deranged couple ever," I tease.

"I know, right?" She grins.

"Hey, can I place a bet?" a guy on the other side of the table interrupts us.

Ella stands to help him.

While they're busy talking, I let my gaze wander the massive space. A lot of concrete and institutional tile. Maybe this was the cafeteria when this place was a correctional facility? Or a gymnasium? The big metal cage in the center makes it hard to tell.

"You with Stonewall?" a gruff voice from my left asks.

I tear my gaze away from the cage and glance up at the dark-haired man towering over the table. Something about his curly hair and bulky frame seems familiar but I can't place him. I glance at Ella for guidance on how to answer this stranger but she's still busy.

Good grief. I'm a big girl. I don't need Ella to protect me. I stand and cross my arms over my chest. "Who's asking?"

"Can I help you?" Ella turns and scowls at the intruder.

He flicks his dark brown gaze over her in an appreciative way.

One corner of his mouth curls into a seductive smirk. "You her mama bear or somethin'?"

Ella lifts her chin and glares. Even though she's probably a foot and a half shorter than him, he holds his hands in the air. "Easy, mama bear. Just wanna talk to your friend."

"So, talk." Ella shrugs, then crosses her arms over her chest, making it clear she'll also be part of the conversation.

"What do you need?" I ask, stepping around the table to stand next to Ella.

Dark Hair refocuses his attention on me. "I want to set up a re-match with your man."

Recognition slams into me. *Rico.* The guy who kicked Griff in the head, the night I went to see him fight in Ironworks. "I'm not his manager. Go ask him." I wave my hand toward Griff who's weaving through the people crowded around the cage.

Rico follows my line of sight. "He seems busy."

"Then talk to Ruthless," Ella says.

But Rico keeps staring at me like she didn't say a word. "Ruthless is your brother, right?"

"Don't worry about who she's related to. She's just here to watch the fights tonight and help me out," Ella says. "Talk to my husband. He'll get your message to Stonewall."

"Ah, you're Eraser's ol' lady, right?" Rico finally takes his intense gaze off me and shifts it to Ella.

"Yup."

The buzzer sounds and my brother shouts something into his bullhorn. My heart's pounding in my ears so loud, I can't make out the words.

Eraser muscles up to Rico. "We got a problem here?"

"Not at all, bro." Rico smiles wide. "Just looking to have a conversation with Stonewall."

"Well, he's in the opposite direction." Eraser points toward the cage.

Griff notices the gesture and lifts his chin. His gaze narrows and a frown creases his forehead. He climbs up the side of the cage and says something to Remy, then jumps into the crowd and hurries toward us.

"What's going on?" Griff inserts himself between Rico and me but reaches back to pat my hip. Eraser moves Ella toward the table.

Griff and Rico talk in low tones I can't make out. Griff's hand still rests on my hip. Tired of staring at his back, I curl my fingers around his and step next to him. The corner of Rico's mouth twitches as I reappear at Griff's side.

"You should've reached out sooner," Griff says, a low thrum of irritation running through his voice. "I can't tonight."

"Why not?" Rico smiles at me. "She was your good luck charm at our last match. I'm sure she'll bring you luck again."

As Rico's gaze lingers on my face, Griff's body goes completely still—a calm before the storm I've seen from him right before he delivers a punch or two to an opponent. Somehow this seems deadlier.

I gather all my courage together and force a confident smile on my face. "I wouldn't mind seeing my man hand you your ass again." I link my arm through Griff's and peer up at him.

His expression remains hostile and focused on Rico. "Not tonight," he repeats.

"Come on." Rico bends his knees. "I've been working on my striking technique." In a blur of movement, he throws a hook punch.

I squeal and duck to the side.

Griff catches the fist with one hand. A hard clap of Rico's knuckles against Griff's palm. Griff squeezes Rico's fingers and slowly twists his arm to the right. "I said, *not tonight.*"

Embarrassed that I shrieked like a little kid. I stand straight again and move slightly behind Griff.

Fear or shock widens Rico's eyes as he stares at where Griff's still holding him. Griff lets go, flinging Rico's hand away in disgust. "You ever pull that shit in my house again, I'll break your fucking arm."

"Sorry about that." Rico shrugs and shakes out his hand. "All right. Next time." He gives us a curt nod and backs away into the crowd.

Griff watches Rico until he stops to talk to two guys on the other side of the cage.

"Uh, is that normal around here?" I ask.

"No," Griff answers, still watching Rico. "He needs to learn some manners."

"You could've taken the fight. I know I said it makes me stabby to see you get hurt." I tug on his arm to recapture his attention. "But you don't have to say no because I'm here." While I'd secretly be thrilled if he never took on another match, I don't want to be the reason he gives up something he loves.

He slowly turns his head and stares at me for a few uncomfortable seconds. The corners of his mouth turn up, but the smile doesn't reach his eyes. "Nah. Not worth the risk." He cocks his head. "You don't want me to take you to prom with a black eye next weekend, do you?"

"Oh." Great, so it *is* my fault he's saying no to a rematch with Rico.

Griff

Lying to Molly sends ripples of agitation through my system. If it wasn't for Diane ordering me not to take on any fights until the show starts filming, I would've been more than happy to drop Rico to the floor in front of everyone. Yeah, I wouldn't love taking Molly to her prom with a busted lip or black eye. But I'm more than confident I could avoid any injuries. That little prick only got the kick to my temple because I was distracted. I wouldn't make that mistake again.

Molly frowns and glances at her sneakers.

"Hey." I press my finger to her chin, tipping her head up. "He was fucking around. There was no power behind that punch, Muffin. It was disrespectful but not dangerous."

"He was just trying to piss you off so you'd say yes?"

I lift my shoulders. "Probably. Doesn't matter, though. I'm not prepared to go in the cage tonight." I lift my chin in Rico's direction. "I would've been training a lot harder at Sully's every day this week if I was planning to fight him this weekend."

She hesitates for a second. "Okay."

"All good, bro?" Jigsaw asks, stepping next to Molly but focusing his intense stare on me. "You need me to rip off that kid's arm and beat him with it?" His face doesn't so much as twitch to indicate he's joking.

"Nah, just a guy looking for a rematch."

"And?" He lifts an eyebrow.

I shrug. "Not tonight."

He glances at Molly. *Fuck, no.* It's already obvious she thinks it's her fault I'm not taking the fight. I don't need him reinforcing that idea.

"I'll watch out for your girl," he offers.

Molly nods and jabs her thumb over her shoulder toward Ella and Eraser. "Between the deranged duo and Jigsaw, I'll be fine."

Surprised she's *that* comfortable around Jigsaw, I stare at her.

Jigsaw snorts. "Deranged duo?"

"It's an inside joke with Ella," Molly explains.

"Cute," Jigsaw says. He lifts his chin at me again. "You sure you don't want to get in more fight time before you—"

"Nope," I answer before he can mention the show. Jesus Christ, why the fuck did I have to tell *him* before I told Molly?

"Got it." Jigsaw turns and prowls around the outer ring of spectators.

As I roll my neck from side to side, it crackles and pops but does nothing to release the tension from turning down Rico's challenge and having Jigsaw almost spill my secret.

I don't back down from fights.

I don't lie to people I love.

Filming hasn't even started and already this show is changing me in ways I don't like.

Molly

CHAPTER TWENTY-SIX

Molly

GROWING UP ON A STEADY DIET OF MOVIES AND television shows where prom is the ultimate high school experience raised my expectations of this event to unnaturally high levels.

But over the last few weeks of listening to my classmates babble about nothing more interesting than spending a fortune on limos, dresses, dinners, and makeovers, or getting drunk, I'm a lot less enthusiastic about tonight's adventure.

I almost feel guilty for forcing Griff to take me. He's probably going to hate every second of it. If I hadn't already bought my tickets and promised my friends I'd be there, I think I'd ask Griff to take me somewhere else.

At least I like my dress. I fluff the skirt as I pace next to the front window. Every few seconds I peek outside, searching for Griff's car. I can't wait for Griff to see me in my dress.

"Sit down, Molly," Hayden scolds. "You're making me anxious."

"Your feet are going to be killing you if you keep walking in your heels now," Darcy warns from the dining room chair we moved into the living room. Ella's busy pressing and angling a flat iron into Darcy's long hair to create a cascade of mermaid waves. If I tried that, I'd probably end up with half my face fried off.

I hold out one foot to show off my shiny silver platform sandals. "They're pretty comfy."

Kyla steps out from behind one of the screens we've put up in the corners of the living room to give us privacy. Too busy smiling at the phone in her hands, she almost trips over her floor-length peach-colored beaded gown.

That's why I'm glad I chose a shorter dress.

"Walk much?" Hayden teases.

"Oh." Kyla's arm shoots behind her back, like she's trying to hide that she was texting someone.

The back door slams shut. "Is it safe to come inside?" Remy shouts.

"No!" I yell.

Darcy clutches my arm, stopping me from running into the kitchen. "Are you *sure* Remy won't go with one of us?" Her eyes stray toward the dining room, then she returns her attention to me. "Then Griff would have someone to keep him company," she adds in a forced, cheerful tone.

From across the room, Ella snort-laughs.

"Eh." I can't imagine anything worse than my brother coming to my prom with us. "It's not really his thing."

"Jenn, you're up next." Ella pats the back of the chair Hayden just vacated. Jenn minces over in her floor-length red sequin dress. I almost fell over when she picked red instead of something champagne or beige. She looks like liquid fire in it, and I can't wait to see what Ella does for her hair and makeup. We might not recognize Jenn by the end of the process.

"Can you ask him?" Darcy pleads, recapturing my attention.

Hell no. "Yeah, uh, sure."

I scurry into the kitchen before Darcy runs in there and asks him herself. My shoes *clackety-thud* over the hardwood floors. Maybe the girls are right and I *should* take these off until we're ready to leave.

Remy's at the kitchen sink scrubbing grease off of his hands with a small, bristle brush.

"What's up?" He glances over his shoulder, his eyes widening as he takes me in. "You look pretty."

Remy doesn't compliment me often. I stand straighter and fluff the layers of tulle that make up the lower half of my dress. "Thanks."

"Are you nervous about tonight?" He slaps the faucet handle off and reaches for a paper towel.

"Nervous? No." I lean over to slide the strap of my sandal off my heel, let the shoe drop to the floor, and then take off the other one. "It's the same people I see every day, just wearing nicer clothes." I scoop my sandals off the floor and hold them in the air like a trophy.

He snorts with laughter. "I love how practical you are. What about your friends?" He leans against the counter and lifts his chin toward the living room. "What are they expecting?"

I move closer to him and lower my voice. "We didn't make a pact to all lose our virginity for prom like that old *American Pie* movie, so you can chill."

Although I am very much looking forward to alone time with Griff at some point. That's definitely not Remy's business, though.

I swear his face turns a shade of green. He blinks rapidly and rears his head back. "So. Much. More. Information." He shakes his head. "Than I *ever* needed."

"Oh." I titter with laughter. "Sorry." Heat races over my skin as I realize how much I revealed with my off-hand jokey comment.

"You're all staying for the after-party thing at the hotel?" he asks.

"Unless it's totally boring, yeah." I clasp my hands together. "They're supposed to do a murder mystery game, though." My excitement falters. "But I think I'm the only one who wants to do that."

"Murder mystery, huh?" He rubs his hand over his chin. "Maybe we should hold a murder mystery dinner at the bar one night."

"Really?" I squeal and dance on my toes. "That would be so fun. Would you let me help you plan it? Please?"

"Yeah, maybe." He flashes a quick grin. "Research it for me tonight at the party. Let me know what works and what doesn't."

"Okay." I nod eagerly. "I can do that."

"Hey," he says more seriously, "I'm glad there's no *American Pie* pact with you and your friends." He turns to the side and sticks out his tongue, pretending to gag.

Burning with embarrassment, I slap his side with the back of my hand.

He straightens up and turns serious. "Given we've got all this alcohol-soaked generational trauma in our family, I'm more worried about your friends drinking and driving tonight."

"Ohhh." Now I understand his concern better.

"You'll be with Griff," he continues, "so I know you'll be safe. But look out for the other girls. Try not to let them do something dumb." His lips tilt into what I think he intended to be a smirk, but it seems more sad than sarcastic. "I don't want to see Hayden wrap that shiny new BMW around a tree or plunge it into a lake."

"That's, uh, oddly specific," I mutter.

He ignores my comment and continues. "If anyone needs a ride, call me. Okay? Doesn't matter what time it is." He holds up one hand. "No lectures or judgment."

Now I'm the one who's speechless. "Thanks, Remy. I appreciate that." I reach up and hug him, careful not to whack him with my heavy shoes. After a second, he returns the embrace.

"All right." He releases me and steps back. "I want you to have fun tonight."

"I will." I bite my lip. "I almost feel bad I'm making Griff go. He's probably going to be bored."

Remy shakes his head. "He's with you. He'll be fine."

I curl my finger, motioning him closer. "Darcy wanted me to ask if you'd go with—"

"That's a *hell no* from me. Sorry."

I blow out a quick, relieved breath.

He cocks his head. "You don't *want* me to go with one of your friends, do you?"

"Absolutely-the-fuck-not."

"Didn't think so."

I shrug, feeling dumb. "I said I'd ask, so…"

"Hayden's going with Wade, right?" he asks.

"Yeah," I answer slowly.

"So, Jenn, Kyla, and Darcy can all be solo together, right?" he asks, as if he'd reconsider his *hell no* if he found out only one of my friends would be dateless. It's sweet, but I still don't want him coming.

"Yup, they'll be fine," I assure him.

"Good." He blows out a breath. "But the ride thing still stands. Anyone needs a ride, call."

"Thanks. We will."

He turns toward the refrigerator and pulls out a tray of cold cuts, cheeses, and fruit. "Make sure you eat something before you go. Dinner will probably be served late." He carries the tray into the dining room and sets it on the table.

I follow him and dutifully grab a slice of salami, roll it, and pop it in my mouth without smudging my lipstick.

"Molly, can I talk to you for a sec?" Kyla asks.

"Yeah, sure." I pat Remy's shoulder and follow Kyla into the living room. She keeps walking until we're standing by the stairs and away from everyone else. Tension lines her forehead and she won't stop wringing her hands. "What's wrong?" I ask.

"Please don't be mad." Her forehead wrinkles like a sad, anxious basset hound puppy's.

A single warning bell clangs in my head. "About?"

"Well…" She hesitates and flicks her gaze toward Darcy. "I was talking to Wesley, and he wants to go with me."

"Wants to go with you *where*?" In my gut I already know the answer, but I need to hear the words from her mouth.

"To prom!" Her eyes sparkle with excitement that Wesley doesn't deserve.

"Why?" My question comes out much harsher than I intended.

"I dunno. He's home. And I guess because his brother's going with Hayden, he wants to go too." She scowls at me. "How's it any different than Griff going with you?"

"Uh, Griff's my boyfriend, and I asked him weeks ago. He isn't crashing the prom at the last minute. How are you even getting Wesley a ticket?"

"He was captain of the basketball team the year they went to state." She rolls her eyes. "I'm sure they'll let him in."

"All right." I lift my hands in the air, palms up. "So, what do you need my permission for?"

"Well, I know you liked him—"

"No, I didn't."

She stares at me. "Okay."

Someone knocks on the front door. *Please don't let it be Wesley.* "He's not coming now, right?"

"No, he and Wade are meeting us at Hayden's."

Thank God. I don't want that creep anywhere near my house.

She reaches out and traces her fingertips over my arm. "So, we're good?"

"Yeah. If you're happy about it." I bite my lip, debating whether I should warn her. What if she just tells me I'm being silly like Hayden did? "Then, I'm happy for you."

A frown creases her brow. I guess that wasn't a very enthusiastic endorsement.

"Molly!" Remy shouts.

"We're good," I reassure Kyla. Then, impulsively I add, "Just be careful, okay?"

Her frown shifts into confusion. "Duh." She shrugs and hurries over to share her news with Hayden.

The low rumble of voices from the foyer sends butterflies flapping through my stomach. Griff's here.

I hurry to slip my sandals on and meet him at the door.

Oh. Oh, wow.

My greedy eyes gobble him up. Something about his tux looks different than the faded, floppy ones I've seen my classmates renting. It's darker, crisper, fitted to Griff's body perfectly. Even under my brother's mocking scrutiny, Griff stands tall—broad shoulders back, chin lifted, and mild amusement rippling over his handsome face. Confident, even with Remy's sarcastic jabs.

"Did you escape from the Secret Service?" Remy steps back and slices his hand through the air. "You look like the bodyguard assigned to watch the president's daughter."

Griff's gaze shifts from my brother and lands on me. My heart beats faster.

"Molly," he rasps.

As if he forgot my brother's standing in his way, he brushes past him and walks toward me. His bow tie perfectly matches the deep purple satin of the bodice of my dress. In his hands, he holds a clear box with something red inside.

"What do you think?" I tug on the layers of tulle skirt tickling the backs of my thighs.

Griff's hot gaze slides over me from shoulders to toes. He stares for so long, I pluck at the bow on my shoulder. Did I tie it tight enough? I glance at my other shoulder. Are the bows even?

"Stop." Griff steps closer and rests his warm hand over mine. He pries my fingers away from the bow. "It's really nice." He closes his eyes and briefly shakes his head. "I'm struck dumb here, Molly. It's...perfect on you."

I tug at the skirt again.

"It's a little on the short side," Remy snarks, obviously trying to bait Griff.

Griff's eyes narrow, and he glances over his shoulder. "No one's asking *you* to wear it. Or for your opinion."

There's nothing but sweet, loving appreciation in Griff's eyes when he faces me again. His gaze drops to my bare legs. "Turn around for me."

I execute a perfect spin in my clunky shoes.

"You're..." He whistles. "Stunning. I'm really glad I never went to my own prom." He holds out his hand to me and I take it.

"You didn't?"

He shrugs and pulls me outside onto the front porch. "Things were too chaotic for me."

The late afternoon air cools my overheated skin. "It'll be silly. You'll probably be so bored." I shouldn't be dragging Griff to something so childish.

"No, I won't. I want you to have fun with your friends." He takes two steps back and sweeps his appreciative gaze over me again. "Trust me, I won't be bored as long as I'm looking at you."

"I don't know about that." I make two V shapes with my thumbs and index fingers and press them to my waist. "Kyla's dress has all sorts of strategically placed cut-outs."

He snorts as if he couldn't care less. "I'll still only be interested in you."

"Hayden went with bright pink sequins." I wave my hand toward the living room window. "You might be blinded before the night is over."

The corners of his mouth twitch. "She *does* love pink."

"I'm sorry you have to hang out with my friends all night," I mutter. Griff's high school days are way behind him. Hanging out with all my classmates will probably feel like torture. Although, I do have some things in mind to make up for it later. When we're *alone*.

"Molly." He grabs one of my hands and gently squeezes until I lift my gaze to his. "I'm just happy to be with you. I don't dislike your friends."

"They're kinda immature sometimes."

He cocks his head toward the front door where I still sense Remy's hovering out of sight. "You've met *my* friends, right?"

A giggle escapes me. "Okay, yeah."

"Good. Now, stop worrying so much." He lifts his eyebrows and glances at my feet. "Are you going to be comfortable in those all night?"

"I think so." I wave my thumb toward the front door. "I have sneakers and stuff to change into later."

Heat flares in his eyes for a second, stirring prickles of desire over my skin.

He holds out the clear box to me. "Here." A hint of excitement flickers over his lips. "This is for you."

Up close, I can finally examine the corsage. I pop the lid open and *squee* in delight. "It's so pretty!" Two red roses and two purple roses are nestled in silver metallic lace with purple ribbons. A tiny silver crown charm rests in the middle. The whole arrangement looks suspiciously familiar. "How'd you know?"

His lips curve up. "The woman at the flower shop asked me for my date's name and said she'd make sure they matched."

Laughing, I hold out the box to him. He takes the corsage out, and I offer him my hand. Shivers spark over my skin as he gently slides the flowers into place on my wrist. "Wow." I stare at the pretty arrangement. "It takes up a lot of real estate on my arm."

"Too much?" he asks.

"No! God, no. I love it." I wrap my arms around him. "Thank you."

He gives me a quick squeeze. "You're welcome."

"I feel like my surprise for you is ruined now." I grab his hand and tug him inside the house again.

The girls are crowded in the dining room, picking at the food.

"Whoa." Hayden stops mid-chew and stares at Griff.

"Er-nah-gawd," Darcy mumbles around a mouthful of ham and cheese.

Pride lifts my chin and I squeeze Griff's hand.

Ella's sitting at the head of the table, watching with an amused expression. She whistles at Griff. "Looking good, stud."

He grunts at her—a sound somewhere between a greeting and annoyance.

"All right. Stop staring at my boyfriend." I drag Griff into the kitchen.

He leans against the counter and tugs at the lapels of his jacket, then fusses with the cuffs of his shirt.

"You look good. That's why they're all staring," I whisper in his ear.

One corner of his mouth tilts. "Do *you* think I look good?"

I slide my gaze over him again. "Oh, yes."

He gives his left sleeve one final tug. "That's all I care about."

I hurry to the refrigerator and pull his boutonniere out. Carefully, I hand it over. Griff's lips turn up. "Confirmed. We match." He taps his lapel. "Pin it on me."

With shaky hands, I clutch the small stem of the red rose carefully wrapped with purple ribbon. The tiny crown charm catches the light, winking as I pin the flower into place.

He glances down. "Perfect. Thank you."

I lean up to kiss his cheek, but he turns his head, catching my lips. His arms slide around my waist, and his hand presses against the small of my back. I stumble closer, sighing into his mouth.

"Wooooo!" the girls scream.

"Get it, Molly!" Hayden shouts.

Pressing my palm to Griff's chest, I pull away. Red smudges outline his lips, and I reach up to wipe my lipstick off for him.

"Sorry," he whispers. "Couldn't help myself."

"I'm not complaining."

"All right, girls!" Ella claps her hands. "Final lipstick check! Then you're on your own."

"Where's your bag?" Griff asks me. "I'll go put it in the car."

"Uh, on my bed. I can go get it."

"It's okay." He kisses my cheek. "Sounds like Ella's planning to jet." He brushes his thumb against my bottom lip. "And I smudged this a little."

He casts a glance at the backyard, almost like he'd rather go outside and climb up the side of the house into my bedroom window than risk the girls twittering over him again.

I'm last in line for Ella to touch up my lips. "You two have fun tonight," she whispers.

"Guh," I mutter, trying to thank her without moving my lips.

When she's finished, I give her a quick hug. "Thanks for helping us out."

"Not a problem."

"Pictures, please!" Remy shouts.

"Hey, will you take a picture with me?" I ask Ella.

"Sure."

Remy must be in a good mood. He usually hates sitting still for pictures or being asked to take them. But today, he's turned into a professional, firing off a slew of combinations and poses for us to follow.

"Just the girls." He waves Griff and Ella to the side.

The five of us squeeze in tight and smile wide.

"Okay, Ella, join them," Remy directs.

Ella flicks her gaze to the sky but allows all of us to pile on until she's in the center of a big group hug.

Remy snaps a few more shots, then allows Griff to join me. I run over to Ella and hand her my phone. "Will you take a few? Just in case he cuts off Griff's head or something."

Laughing, she accepts the phone and waves me away.

Griff backs us up to the wide stairs of the front porch, and Remy spends more time than I'd expect framing the pictures.

"Go up a few steps, Molly," Remy directs. "Take her hand, bonehead," he says to Griff. "There ya go. Our very own Prince Charming."

Griff ignores the taunting from my brother by focusing all his attention on me. "You do look like a princess tonight," he whispers against my ear.

My heart flutters faster.

"All right. That's enough," Remy says.

Griff slaps Remy's chest. "Let me take a pic of you two."

"Get out of here," Remy scoffs.

"Please?" I pull the pout I know my brother can't resist.

"Fine." He slings his arm over my shoulders and allows Griff to take a few pictures. "Remember what I said," he says low against my ear.

"I will."

"Let's go!" Hayden shouts, her heels clacking over the sidewalk. "More photos to take at my mom's."

I cast a nervous glance at Griff, not sure how much more of all this pre-prom stuff he's willing to tolerate. But he only smiles at me.

As Hayden slides into her BMW, I notice the big, boxy, matte black Mercedes-Benz AMG G-Class parked behind her car. "Wait, where'd that come from?"

Griff dangles a black key fob in front of my face. "Ours for the night."

Remy chuckles.

"Really!?" My gaze darts between the Mercedes and my boyfriend's satisfied grin.

"I'll ride with you guys." Kyla's gaze swings between Hayden's car and ours.

Hayden doesn't seem to care—she's in too much of a hurry to leave. "Figure it out, ladies," she shouts through the open passenger-side window.

Darcy and Kyla end up in our back seat. I don't want to ask how Griff managed to procure such an expensive vehicle in front of them. Renting a tux was bad enough. I didn't want him to drop a fortune taking me to *my* prom.

He drives the unfamiliar SUV with the same mesmerizing ease he handles every vehicle. Thankfully, it's a short ride to Hayden's. Griff has barely stopped the car when the girls jump out and race over Hayden's front lawn.

"What's wrong, Muffin?" Griff places his hand on my leg.

"You didn't have to go out of your way to find a different vehicle." I flap my hands at the fancy dashboard. "I love the Chevelle."

"You said you didn't want to do the limo thing." The corner of his mouth tips up, and he lifts one shoulder. "I still wanted to upgrade my princess to a nicer carriage for her big night."

"But..."

He leans closer. "Do you like it?"

"Yes. But I didn't want you to spend a lot of—"

"I borrowed it." He tilts his head, and a cocky smile plays over his lips. "Well, I *won* it for the night."

"What? How?"

"At Zips. This guy who's been showing up to race a lot lately. I knew I could smoke him easily. Instead of racing for money, I asked him to race for the keys so I could take my girl to prom."

My jaw drops, and I stare at him. "Seriously?"

"Yup." He chuckles softly. "I think he was amused by my plight."

"I'm impressed by your resourcefulness." I frown, reconsidering his explanation. "Wait a second. What did *you* put up?"

"Don't worry about it." He glances away. "I wasn't in danger of losing."

"Griff!"

"I won." He kisses the tip of my nose. "I *do* have to return it Monday morning, though."

We get out and talk to Hayden's mom for a few minutes. After we've taken dozens of pictures, Wade's white Lexus rolls to a stop at the curb. He hurries out of the passenger side and Wesley slowly peels himself out of the driver's seat.

My stomach churns. I squeeze Griff's hand tighter, so happy he's here tonight to keep Wesley away from me. My eyes stray toward Kyla. Should I have warned her better? No. She seems to like Wesley and she's excited about tonight.

"I'm sorry." Wade apologizes to Hayden. "We had to run to the—"

"It's fine." Hayden forces a smile. "You're here. Let's take some pictures."

Kyla lifts the hem of her dress and hurries over to Wesley. "I told you my dress was pale orange."

It's only then I take in his dark green bow tie and cummerbund. *Yikes.* I enjoy some odd color combos myself but that green clashes with Kyla's pretty dress something awful.

Wesley holds the sides of his jacket open. "Yeah, but that's a girly color. My college's colors are green and white."

"What a skunk fucker," I say under my breath.

Griff chokes and laughs. "What'd you say?"

"Nothing." I press my lips tight.

Kyla's eyes are wide and shiny when she joins all of us for pictures. I slip my arm over her shoulders. "It's okay," I say against her ear. "You guys'll look like a freshly picked peach together. He's the leafy stem and you're the fruit." I add a silly grin to my ridiculous lemons-into-lemonade observation, and she finally smiles.

"Thanks, Molly."

The sun's almost set by the time we leave for the country club that's hosting our prom. Thankfully, this time, Griff and I ride together alone. Hayden's so eager to get to prom, you'd think she was head of the committee. We end up falling in behind her BMW.

"Isn't Wesley that douche canoe who bothered you at work?" Griff gestures to the white Lexus behind us. "How'd he end up with Kyla?"

I shrug and relay what Kyla shared earlier, leaving out the part where Kyla thought I ever liked Wesley.

We finally make the turnoff for the country club and travel slowly over the wide, gravel road.

Reluctantly, Griff hands the keys to the valet and accepts the slip. Music's already pouring out of the ballroom designated for our school. I spot Hayden at the top of the wide staircase leading into the building and wave.

"Aw, look! She and Wade are holding hands," I whisper to Griff.

A faint smile ghosts Griff's lips, and he curls his hand around mine.

"Darcy and Jenn went in to get us a table," Hayden explains when we reach her.

"Where's my brother?" Wade asks me.

I'm not his keeper. I shrug. "They were right behind us until we made the turnoff."

Hayden turns her head and giggles. "Let's go in."

I know I'm biased but Griff's easily the best-looking guy in the room. His tux fits his muscled frame perfectly and he has the sexy kind of confidence *none* of the boys in my class have mastered yet.

Unfortunately, that seems to put him on my teachers' radar as soon as we arrive. Ms. Johnson follows us around like I invited the neighborhood drug dealer to be my date instead of the love of my life.

Ignoring her, I walk closer to Griff. He nudges me slightly ahead of him as we work our way through the crowd but keeps his hand on either my hip or at the small of my back, a constant reassurance.

Our big round table's in the corner, and I hurry to slap my purse down on the chair closest to the wall. Griff chuckles and pulls out the chair next to it for me.

He leans down, his warm breath coasting over my shoulder. "You know me well."

"I do."

He hands me my purse and sits in the chair I claimed for him as the rest of my friends take their seats. Hayden drapes a shawl over the seat next to me to save it for Kyla.

Remy was wrong; dinner's served almost immediately. Rubbery chicken and some sort of fancy rice. I only try a forkful of the rice, knowing I'll end up dropping more of it in my cleavage than in my mouth.

Halfway through dinner, Kyla totters in and plops into her chair. Wesley's still nowhere to be seen.

Good.

"Grifffff," Kyla slurs, leaning forward to rest her boobs and elbows on the table. "You're old enough to buy us alcohol, riiiight?"

Seems like she's already had a few drinks.

"No." Griff's tone leaves no room for discussion.

I snort and slap my hand over my mouth.

Kyla smirks and jabs her finger toward Griff. "I see you."

Ignoring her, Griff drapes his arm over my shoulders and slides down in his chair. He lazily leans toward me and pulls me toward him at the same time. "Sorry, Wesley can risk an arrest to buy her alcohol if he wants, but I can't afford to take the chance."

"I don't *want* you to." I press my lips to his cheek. "You're *mine*. Not my friends' bartender."

Desire brightens his eyes. "That right, Muffin?" His low voice is only meant for me.

"Oh, yes."

He shifts his gaze to the ceiling.

"What?" I ask.

He slides his hand into his pocket and produces a flat black key card. "If you get tired of the after-party later, we have our own room." He glances around the table. "Although, Hayden said most of your class rented rooms on the same floor, so it might be too loud to sleep."

"You didn't have to do that." My friends only rented rooms at the hotel because they couldn't bring the party to their parents' houses. Griff has his own apartment.

He curls his arm around the back of my chair and rests his

hand on my shoulder. "I don't want you to miss out on anything."

Griff

For Molly's sake, I ignore the cold stares and watchful eyes of the teachers monitoring the prom. Yeah, I didn't end up graduating from *this* school, but I *did* graduate. I have a decent job—that nothing I learned here prepared me for. These teachers can shove their judgmental attitudes up their asses.

Besides, I'm not the only twenty-something here. That wanker Wesley somehow conned Kyla into letting him tag along. Poor girl looked heartbroken at Hayden's house when he showed up wearing a bright green tie that didn't even remotely match Kyla's peach dress. Didn't bother to bring her a corsage or even a damn flower. I wanted to punch him just for making one of Molly's friends unhappy.

Who am I kidding? My urge to use Wesley's face as a speed bag is there no matter what.

The asshole showed up and plonked himself into the chair next to Kyla just as dessert was served. And now I'm stuck sitting at the same table as him while the girls bop around to what Molly told me was "their song" right before she raced onto the dance floor.

Molly's so cute dancing and singing with her friends, I'll just watch her and ignore Wesley until the song's over.

"You want some?" Wesley shouts at me.

I take a deep breath and let it out slowly before turning to see what he's offering—although I already have an idea.

He holds out a silver flask. "You're gonna need it to get through the rest of the night." He rolls his eyes and mimics the girls' excitement with a high-pitched jumble of sounds.

"Why'd you come, then?" I ask, unimpressed by his attempt to make fun of the girls.

"Why not? Kyla's the hottest one after Hayden and Molly. My

brother's into Hayden, so she was off-limits." He points the flask at me. "Molly was going with you, sooo..." He shrugs as if that crude explanation makes any damn sense.

Anger roils my blood. This creepy perv rates his little brother's classmates?

"Hey, I *do* know you." Wesley leans forward and stares at me for longer than I'm comfortable having drunk dudes in my face. "Beggar! They used to call you beggar, right? Am I right?"

My stomach knots. Haven't heard *that* name since fourth grade. Figures—that's probably when Wesley stopped maturing. "They call me *Stonewall* now." I raise one hand. "Because getting hit with one of my fists is like running into a stone wall."

He's either drunk or dumb because he doesn't seem to recognize the threat. "Yes, yes! Stonewall. The Castle crew. My buddy Cannon says you're like a hurricane in the cage."

Cannon's actually a decent guy and a clean fighter. Would he really associate with this clown, or is Wesley name-dropping?

"Yeah, that guy's got a killer leg lock." That seems like a neutral response.

He nods quickly.

Two arms drape over my shoulders and a cloud of vanilla invades my senses. The heat of Molly's body presses against my back. "Are you okay?"

I take one of her hands and pull her into my lap.

She casts a nervous glance around. I follow her line of sight to one of her teachers making a beeline for us. Molly slides out of my lap and into the chair next to me, putting her back to the woman.

"I'm fine, baby." I take her hand again and rub my thumb over her knuckles. "Are you having fun?"

"Oh yeah." She beams a bright, happy smile.

"Molly!" Hayden screeches, her voice carrying over the music.

Molly turns and waves.

"Go ahead." I nudge her side with my elbow. "I'm fine. Really."

"Okay." Her gaze darts around for a second, then she leans in and kisses my cheek.

I can't take my eyes off her as she returns to her friends. She's the most beautiful girl in the room.

My phone buzzes, and I drag my gaze away from Molly to pull it out of my pocket.

Remy: Everything OK?

Me: Yes, Dad.

I snap a discreet pic of Molly dancing and send it to him. A few seconds later, he sends a middle finger emoji followed by a thumbs-up.

"You sure you don't wanna splash this in her drink?" Wesley waves the flask at me again. Jesus, my girlfriend sits in my lap for five seconds and the teachers are ready to call the cops. This jackass keeps waving a flask around at a high school prom and no one's even frowned in his direction.

"No," I growl.

"You do you." He snorts. "Just sayin'. Probably the only way you'll ever pry her legs open."

A slow burn of anger rolls through me. I turn so I'm fully facing him. "The fuck did you say?"

He flashes a trying-to-help-you-out grin. "If you wanna pop that cherry, you might wanna loosen her up a little." He shrugs. "I asked her for a blow job once and she got all offended. Whatever. She's probably all teeth, anyway."

Painfully aware of my surroundings, my body stills with slow, molten rage. My temples throb with the effort of not jumping out of my chair and punching the fuck out of him. But I'm not at Zips or The Castle. I can't yank Wesley out of his seat and smash his head into the nearest wall without consequences.

Ruin Molly's night.

Embarrass Molly.

Probably get arrested.

Possibly get Molly in trouble with the school for bringing me.

All the potential outcomes if I act on my need to beat this disrespectful windbag flash through my mind, one by one.

Getting arrested would be worth the satisfaction of seeing this motherfucker bleed. The rest of the possibilities are unacceptable. Fuck, if I get arrested, I might lose the reality TV contract too. There goes any hope of winning some money for us. Wesley's not worth risking Molly's happiness or our future together.

"Keep my girl's name out of your mouth." I growl.

He slowly blinks, as if he can't possibly understand why I'm not interested in his advice.

If I sit here one minute longer, I won't be able to control my fists. I stand and push in my chair. My gaze scans the room, landing on Molly. Her pretty face tipped toward the ceiling, eyes closed, cheeks flushed pink, and a smile is stretched across her lips as her body moves to the music. The fury threatening to blow the top of my head off drops several degrees.

The music switches to a slower song, and I head straight for my girl.

It takes a few seconds to weave through the throng of sweaty couples. But finally, I reach Molly, capture her hand, and pull her to me. Her eyes widen as her body hits my chest. She glances up and beams a bright smile.

"Sorry I've been out here so long," she says.

"Stop apologizing." I press her hand to my chest and wrap my arm around her waist, slowly moving us to the center of the floor. "Are you having fun?"

"Yes." Her happy expression fades. "But I didn't mean to leave you alone—"

"I was watching you the whole time." *Except for the few seconds when I almost beat Wesley senseless.*

Pink spots spread over her cheeks. "You were?"

"Mm-hmm." I lean down and press my forehead to hers. "Can I ask you something?"

"Sure." She glances up at me with expectation in her eyes.

"Did Wesley say something inappropriate that night you were

at Hayden's and came home early?" As I ask the question, the pieces click into place. Molly leaving her friend's house when she'd planned to stay the night. Her reluctance to tell me *why* she'd left. Wesley showing up at her job, trying to ask her out.

"He was drunk and dumb." Her shoulders jerk and she looks away. "I told him where to go."

"Why didn't you tell *me* what happened?"

"So you could beat him up and get in trouble?" She presses her body closer and lowers her voice. Her fingers gently stroke the back of my neck. "If I was going to be the cause of you getting into trouble, it was going to be for dating *me*, not punching that jerk."

I snort and kiss the top of her head. "You let me worry about that."

"What'd he say to you?" Her gaze strays over my shoulder. "Why are you asking about this now?"

I spin us so she's facing away from Wesley. "Like you said, he's a dumb drunk. But you need to tell me stuff like that."

Defiant as ever, she lifts her chin. "I took care of it. Told him where to go. He tried blaming it on the beer, and I basically said that excuse was invalid."

"Has he bothered you since that night he came to see you at work?" I ask.

"No, I haven't seen him since then." She rolls her eyes toward Kyla, Darcy, and Hayden slow-dancing together in a group-hug circle. "Until tonight. I don't even know why he bothered coming since he's barely paid attention to Kyla."

"I don't think he came for Kyla. I think she was just his way into the prom."

"Whatever." Molly wraps her arms around me tighter and squeezes. "I'm happy *you're* here."

"Me too, Muffin." I side-eye the teacher who seems to have a hard-on for me. "Although, that one teacher of yours seems to be looking for an excuse to toss me out on my ass."

She turns and scowls. "I don't know what her problem is. I'm not even in any of her classes." A wicked smile twists her lips. "Should I inform her that I'm eighteen?"

"No, don't make it worse." I stare at the woman. Was she a teacher when I went here? I didn't remember going to elementary school with Wesley. Maybe I forgot this lady too. "What's she teach?"

"English."

Nah, I had Ms. Pepper, and that sweet, aging hippie loved me. I'd gotten As on all my essays freshman year. Hers was the only class I liked besides gym and shop.

The music switches to something faster.

"Molly!" her friends scream at the top of their lungs.

Molly shakes her head.

"Go dance with your friends." I tilt my head toward the girls. "You *were* supposed to go with your girl gang, remember? Until I invited myself."

"But..." She flicks her gaze up. "I've wanted to go to prom with you ever since I knew what prom *was*."

Fuck that teacher. I lean down and kiss Molly. Press my lips to hers for a few seconds, brief and sweet. "Thank you for telling me that." I glance over at the girls. "It's your last big thing before graduation. Next year, the five of you will be scattered at different schools."

"I'll see them over the summer too."

I swallow hard. Molly's going to need her friends if I'm gone all summer. *Shit.* I *have* to tell her soon. I've been using prom as my excuse not to tell her. Well, come midnight, that excuse is toast. Maybe tomorrow? After we say goodbye to her friends.

Don't ruin tonight for her.

I pull her close again. "I'll have you all to myself later, right?"

"After mystery theater." Her eyebrows lift in a sweet, hopeful gesture.

As if I'd ever say no to her. "Yeah, okay."

"Yay!" She claps her hands. "Remy asked me to scope it out

and get some ideas. He's thinking of hosting a mystery dinner theater at the bar."

Suuuure he is. That fucker. Anything to keep Molly and me out of a bedroom.

There's no way I'd ever tell her what I think her brother's actually trying to do, so I force a quick smile. "Sounds like fun."

AFTER THE DJ announces the last song of the night, the girls rush back to our table. Molly throws herself into the chair, almost tipping it over, and lets out a loud sigh.

"You all right?" I ask.

She takes a sip from a plastic stemless wineglass in her hand. "I dunno."

"Look at me." I brush my knuckles against her cheek and turn her face. Her skin's warm to the touch. It's not the excitement of prom that's turning her eyes glassy, slurring her words, or coloring her nose a bright pink.

How could I fuck this up? *Watch Molly.* That was my only job tonight. It's not hard. She's barely been out of my sight.

"What's in this?" I tap my knuckle against the cup.

"It's a mystery!" Hayden giggles and hiccups.

I pry the cup of punch out of Molly's hand and take a sip. At first, I almost gag from the sickly sweet, thick liquid. Then the bitter burn hits the back of my throat.

Fuck.

"Who gave this to you?"

She gestures vaguely toward the table of drinks. "The punch bowl."

I reach for a bottle of water and uncap it. "Drink some of this for me."

She takes a timid sip, then a larger one.

"After-party!" Darcy bangs her hand against the table. "Let's go!"

After-party my ass. I glance at Molly. As far as I know, she's never been drunk before. With her dad's issues, she's never been interested. "How much of this did you drink, baby?" Thank fuck I realized her condition before one of the teachers did.

"Just that." Her eyelids drift closed.

Of course, she's a lightweight. The cup's still half full.

But our night's probably over.

Moller

CHAPTER TWENTY-SEVEN

GRIFF

Molly perked up on the way to the hotel but she's still tipsy. In the lobby, she stumbles over the hotel's slick marble floors. I bend down and scoop her into my arms.

"Weee!" She grins at me. "The party's that way!" She points at a window overlooking the parking lot.

"Sure, Muffin." I kiss her cheek. "Why don't we explore the room for a minute, then we can check out the after-party."

"Mmm." She drags her fingers over the back of my neck. "I want to explore some things in the hotel room."

I jab the elevator's *up* button. "Not like this, Muffin."

She pouts and frowns at the same time. "Why?"

"Because you're drunk." I kiss her forehead to take the sting out of my words.

"I'm not drunk." The outrage in her voice pulls a chuckle from me.

Outside our room, I gently set her on her feet and keep one arm around her waist while I press the key card to the door. Voices and pounding footsteps come from our right. *Stupid, slow key card. Please work.*

The light finally flashes green and the lock clicks. I push the door open and urge Molly inside.

I'd left a change of clothes and a few surprises for Molly here earlier in the day when I checked in. Everything looks untouched. I slide her backpack off my shoulder and set it on a chair next to the bed.

"Oooh!" Molly squeals. "Look, roses!" She hurries to the vase on the long, black dresser across from the bed and sticks her nose in the blooms.

"You like them?" I ask.

"Are they from you?"

"Who else?"

"Wow. You *were* busy today."

I step closer to her. "I wanted you to have a good night."

She straightens and pulls her long, curled hair over one shoulder. "It's been wonderful."

"Good."

She tries to turn around, tips to the side, and slaps her hand against the dresser to brace herself.

"Why don't we take your shoes off?" I suggest.

"Will you help me take off my dress?" She gathers her hair again and points to the tiny zipper down the middle of her back.

Have mercy on me. I rest my hands on her shoulders and tease the bows tying the straps together. "Can I untie these first?"

She glances at me over her shoulder. "Sure."

"Wanted to unwrap you like a present all night long." I tug and the left bow unravels. She shifts her hair to the other side and I untie the second bow. I lean down and brush a kiss over her shoulder to her neck.

She lets out a shivery sigh and sags against me.

"Now, how am I supposed to work this zipper loose?" I kiss her neck again. "Hmm?"

"Oh." She leans forward, resting her hands on the dresser. "Better?"

God, yes.

Undressing her while she's bent over sends my mind running in a hundred different filthy directions. *She's drunk. Control yourself.* I slide the zipper until it gets stuck in the middle of her back.

"That's good." Molly straightens and shimmies the dress off the rest of the way.

Fuuuuck me. Skin-tight black satin encases her from thigh to chest. "That's, uh, nice."

"Those thin straps were just for decoration." Molly cups her breasts and jiggles her body in a way that almost unhinges my mind. "I wanted to make sure my boobs didn't fall out on the dance floor."

"Uh, yeah." My brain's reduced to single syllable responses. "Good plan."

"It hooks in the back. Can you undo them?"

"Yup." I work the tiny hooks faster than the speed of light.

She wiggles out of the tight slip, letting it drop to her feet. "Ahh. That's better."

Yes, yes, it is.

She stands tall, turns, and places her hand on her hip. "What do you think?"

My hot gaze travels over her strapless bra and matching panties, loving everything in front of me. "How many purple bras do you have?"

She arches a brow. "Wouldn't you like to know?"

One corner of my mouth slides up. "Actually, yeah."

She laughs softly, then lets out a big yawn.

"You feel okay?" I ask.

She rests her hand on her stomach. "Kinda queasy."

"You want to lie down for a bit?" I tilt my head toward the bed and shrug my suit jacket off.

She flops onto the bed and curls up on her side. Not how I saw the night going but I'm relieved I got her to our room safely.

Keeping an eye on her, I strip out of the rest of my clothes, but leave my boxer briefs on. Between work, picking up the Mercedes from Quill, and getting everything else ready for tonight, I've been going non-stop since I woke up this morning.

The events of the day and night seem to sink into my bones, pulling me to the mattress.

I roll onto my back but slide closer to Molly. She's warm, soft, and smells amazing. I close my eyes and listen to her breathing. Beyond our room, rambunctious shouts and pounding footsteps from farther down the hallway seep through the walls.

We lie quietly together for a while. My mind hovers somewhere between sleep and awareness of Molly's every breath, sigh, and movement.

Hours or maybe only minutes later, the mattress dips, pulling me from my half-asleep state. I open my eyes, worried Molly needs something. She rolls over, colliding with me.

"Oh." Her eyes pop open. "Well, hello there, handsome."

I can't help laughing. "Hello."

She snuggles closer and I hold out my arm, encouraging her to rest her head on my chest. "Sorry. I'm too dumb to know when someone gives me spiked punch."

"Hey." I tighten my arm around her. "You're not dumb. Some of your classmates are dicks, though. I'm glad I was with you." Fuck knows I don't trust anyone else to look after her. I run my fingers through her hair. "You have any idea how many times I've wanted to sleep next to you?"

"Really?" She tilts her head back to look at me. "Is that *all* you wanted to do?"

"No."

She brushes her fingers over my chest, then down my abs. "I've dreamed about waking up next to you like this every day."

I grin down at her. "I love how much we have in common."

"Me too." She moves her hand lower. "You exceed all imagination."

Her fingers graze my cock. My entire body jolts. A deep groan rumbles through my chest. Why the fuck'd I go with compression boxer briefs under the tux? My dick's practically choking to death under the tight fabric.

"Careful," I warn in a strangled rasp.

I turn so I'm facing her, dislodging her hand. "Kiss me." I cup her cheek and press my lips to hers, cutting off her response.

Sweet, needy little moans vibrate from deep in her throat. She wiggles closer and throws one of her legs over mine. I slide my hand down her back to her hip, then squeeze her butt, drawing her impossibly closer.

Breathing hard, I pull away and stare at her face. "What do you want?"

"I want you to kiss me." She curls her fingers around the back of my neck and attempts to drag me close again, but I hold firm.

"Where?" I brush my thumb over her bottom lip. "Here?"

She doesn't move.

I lower my hand and cup her breast. "Here?" I sweep my thumb over the cup of her padded bra.

She gasps and pulls away to give me room.

"You like that?" I push the cup of her bra down and tease my thumb over her nipple. "Tell me."

"Yes," she whispers. "I like that. A lot."

I roll the hard little tip between my thumb and index finger, then lower my head to flick my tongue against it. "Like that?"

She whimpers and nods. I can't get over how sensitive she is. Every touch seems to overwhelm her. I roll her to her back and free her other breast.

"How about here?" I suck her nipple into my mouth.

"Ah!" She arches off the bed.

I release her with a soft, sucking *pop*. "Too much?" I feather one finger between her breasts, admiring a few scattered freckles dusting her skin.

"No. Please. Do it again."

"Yeah," I rasp, slowly dragging my tongue around one nipple, then the other. "That's what I want to hear."

"Oh." Her body tenses, arches, and twists under me as I continue kissing and licking each breast. "Griff."

"Hmm?" I kiss my way down her ribs and stop to dip my tongue into her belly button, then rest my cheek on her stomach.

"Do you want me to kiss you here?" I slowly stroke my fingers over the piece of satin between her legs. It's already soaking wet. I tilt my head to see her face. "It feels like you do."

She groans, bites her lip, and nods.

I need more words from her but taking the slow route is so much fun.

"You remember that night in my car? Parked in front of your house?" I stroke my knuckles against her slit, back and forth, back and forth.

"Uh-huh." She inhales a shaky breath.

"The way you ground yourself against me until you came?"

Pink splotches dot her cheeks. "Yes."

I close my eyes for a second, savoring the memory. "That was so fucking hot. I think about it all the time."

Jerk off to it three times a day is more like it.

"Really?" she whispers.

"Really."

"I...I think about it a lot too."

"Good." I slide lower and kiss her thigh but keep moving my fingers in the same slow rhythm. "Your birthday. In the garage." I squeeze my eyes shut for a second. "I still can't look at your car without getting hard."

She lets out a sound halfway between a gasp and a giggle. "That must...be uncomfortable...when you're working," she whispers between soft sighs and gasps.

"Worth it." I rest my cheek against her stomach again and dip my fingers under her slick satin underwear.

Her body jerks and I've barely touched her. I brush my fingers against her damp curls. "I want to make you come like that again. But on my tongue this time."

I tip my head back to see her face. Her half-closed eyes open wide. "What?"

I circle my thumb around her clit, not quite touching, but close. Her hips jerk in time to my movements. "My tongue." I stick it out and wiggle it at her. "Right here." I tap my thumb lightly against her clit.

She jumps, her breasts jiggling over the folded cups of her bra.

"Oh, oh." She squeezes her eyes shut.

"Would you like that?"

"I...I..."

"You're so sensitive." I slide my hand out of her underwear and stroke her over the fabric again. "I'll have to be careful not to give you too much."

"It's...oh...already..."

I smile like a devil. "What? Tell me."

"Griff." She twists her body and lifts her hips, needy and frustrated.

"Do you want me to make you come with my mouth?"

"Yes," she whispers.

"Say it."

She opens her eyes again, staring up at me. Desire and a hint of annoyance flicker over her face. I must be a bastard. That pissy lip curl gets me so fucking hard every time.

"Please, Griff." Her annoyed pout slides into a grin full of wicked amusement. "Try to make me come with your tongue. *If you can*."

Laughter rumbles out of me. I've created a little monster here. "You throwing down a challenge?"

"No." She lifts her hips and stares at me.

I hook my fingers in the straps of her underwear. "You want these off?"

She nods.

"Tell me."

She digs her heels into the bed and lifts her hips higher. "Please take off my panties, Griffin."

"*Fuuuck*, yes." I groan and squeeze my eyes shut for a second. "You've got it." I strip the tiny bit of satin down her legs and toss it somewhere over my shoulder. "God damn you're pretty." I hook my arms under her thighs and yank her closer.

She attempts to press her knees together. *Hmm. Don't like that.* I kiss and nibble her soft inner thigh to loosen her up. She sighs and giggles nervously. Not quite the sounds I'm after.

I kiss my way to her stomach again, then stretch out next to her. "Sit up."

"What?" she asks as she shifts her body.

I reach for her bra and unhook it, tossing it in the same direction her underwear went.

She kneels next to me, beautifully naked, and rests her hands on her thighs. "Where do you want me?"

"Come sit on my face." I squeeze her thigh, urging her closer.

"What?" Her eyes widen with shock. "No way. What if I hurt you?"

My forehead creases into a frown. "Hurt me how?"

"I don't know?" She rubs her hands over her thighs. "Smother you to death? These are more like pillows than earmuffs."

I snort, then laugh so hard she scowls at me.

"Baby, your thick thighs and beautiful eyes are two of my favorite parts of you." I grip one of her hips, urging her over me.

"Well, you can't *see* my eyes if my thighs are smothering you to death." She carefully lifts one leg and straddles my chest without lowering herself enough for our skin to touch.

I swallow my laughter and study her. Is she serious or screwing with me? The corners of her mouth are slightly tilted down, but her eyes sparkle with curiosity.

Maybe *sit on my face* was a bit much for the first time we do this. The crude motherfucker inside me can't be restrained much longer.

"Molly, I'm dying to taste you. If I really can't breathe, I'm more than strong enough to lift you off me." I slide my hands under her ass and demonstrate by lifting and holding her a few inches in the air.

She squeals and laughs, so I bounce her up and down a bunch of times. "See? I lift stuff heavier than you all the time."

"Okay! Okay!" She sputters and giggles some more. "Stop."

She curls her fingers around my forearms and leans over me.

"Nah, I like this." I lift her once more then drag her forward. "Brace your hands on the headboard."

Her knees land precariously close to my ears as heat from her center sears my skin.

"What?" She lets out a nervous laugh.

Time to show her. I spread her lips and take a long, slow lick, stopping to swirl my tongue around her clit.

"Holy shit!" Molly shrieks and bucks her hips, smashing herself against my face.

"That's it." My words come out muffled.

I don't let up though. I wrap my arms around her thighs, spread her wider, and yank her even closer, burying my tongue deeper.

"Gr...gr...oh." Molly continues babbling nonsensical sounds. Her thighs shake. She reaches for me, raking her fingers through my hair. I can't take the distraction. I shackle my fingers around her wrist, pull her hand away, and press it to her stomach.

"Stay," I mumble against her slick, wet flesh.

She lets out a sound somewhere between a moan and a giggle, then gasps. "Right there."

An encouraging growl rumbles from my throat.

"Griff. Oh!" Her hips roll faster. She grinds herself against my face harder. "Please!"

Her whole body violently shakes and shudders. I'm drowning in her and loving every drop.

Finally, she slumps forward, panting hard. Her body tilts to the side. "Oh no, did I hurt you?" She gingerly lifts her leg and throws her body to the mattress.

"Fuck no." I swipe my hand over my mouth and jerk my chin. "Only thing hurting is my dick."

I didn't mean it as some sort of weird I-did-you-now-you-do-me reminder to pay up, but she rearranges her body between my outstretched legs. I've never seen anything sexier in my life.

"Will you show me what you like?" Molly's big blue eyes stare up at me, bright with desire and curiosity. "Please?"

God damn, if that isn't the hottest question anyone's ever asked me. "Touch me."

Tentative, like my dick might have teeth, she reaches for the bulge in my shorts and strokes her palm over me. "Wow," she breathes out.

For some reason, her awed whisper pulls a sharp huff of laughter from me.

"What?" She snatches her hand away.

"Don't stop." If I don't get her hands on me again, I'm going to die.

This time she reaches for the waistband, curling her fingers in the elastic. "May I?" She lifts a not-so-innocent eyebrow.

"Fuck yes." I lift my hips and have to stop myself from yanking them all the way off. I need Molly to do it. Need to know she's in control and really wants this.

Her ticklish little fingers tease under the waistband and she slowly slides the briefs down. My cock springs up, proud, hard, and excited to finally meet her face-to-face.

I bite my lip to control myself.

"Holy frick." Molly stares. "That's supposed to fit inside me?"

I explode with laughter. "Not tonight, Muffin. But yeah, we'll be a perfect fit. Don't worry."

She frowns but doesn't take her eyes off my cock, which only makes him want to show off even more. "How?"

"Just touch me for now."

She wraps her hand around me and rubs her thumb over the head.

I suck in a sharp breath. "Just like that."

"Tell me."

Is she teasing me with my own words? Or does she really need instructions? Why can't I come up with an answer?

Her hand slowly dragging up and down the length of my cock keeps stealing the words from my brain.

"You're doing fine...without any...instructions from me," I

finally say between shaky breaths.

Hesitantly, she leans in and slowly swipes her tongue against the underside of my cock. Her gentle touch is both maddening and cautious.

"Fuck." I curl my hands in the sheets.

"You like that?" Her voice is so tentative. Curious about everything.

"God, yes."

"I don't know what to do next," Molly whispers. Her cheeks flush.

"I have a few ideas." A *few*. What a lie. A few *hundred* filthy fantasies starring my girl is more like it.

"Well, I know you've had better and, well, *more*." She lifts one shoulder and tilts her head, her hair tickling against my legs. "I don't want to disappoint you."

"You could never—"

Wait! What she actually said sinks into my sex-crazed brain. Her gentle stroking is way too much of a distraction. I sit up and grip her wrist, gently prying her hand off my cock so I can get out complete sentences.

This is too important.

"Molly, there hasn't been...*I* haven't...been with anyone else in a *long* time."

Her pretty face screws into something between a scowl and laughter. "I've seen the girls hang all over you at the racetrack. And I don't even want to think about what happens at The Castle on fight nights." Her cheeks redden and her shoulders jump up and down in a nervous shrug. "I've heard how the guys talk. Come on, Griff. I'm not dumb."

I tip her head back, forcing her to look me in the eyes. "Molly, I've known *you are it for me* for a while. If I couldn't have *you*, I didn't *want* anyone else."

"Griff," she protests, still clinging to whatever she thinks she knows. "I've been at some of those parties. And Remy always says..."

I glance down. *Huh, look at that.* My best friend's name is enough to deflate my dick.

"I let your brother *think* whatever he wanted." One corner of my mouth slides up. "Whatever helped distract him from knowing how much I wanted *you.*"

She frowns, clearly still not convinced. I'd be insulted, but she's right. Before I ever thought about us being together, I partied with ring bunnies after the fights all the time. Empty, meaningless encounters that never left me feeling good about myself the next day. Did I ever admit to Remy that those casual hookups left me feeling hollow? *Nope.* He loved it and I wasn't going to ruin his fun or make him feel bad about himself.

But also, Remy wasn't as fooled as I thought he was. Can't forget that priceless knowledge. "It didn't work, though. Your brother was starting to suspect something was going on between you and me."

"But he had those girls come over to the house—"

"He's an arrogant dick who wanted to force my hand and get me to admit my feelings for you." I bite the inside of my cheek. "And he thought if I screwed one of those girls right under your nose, it'd kill your crush on *me.*" Too bad for Remy there isn't another woman on this planet he could've brought home who would've made me risk losing Molly.

"What?" Outrage raises her voice. "That's so dumb. And *mean.*"

"It doesn't matter, Muffin." My voice remains calm, even though mild annoyance at Remy's childish plan still lingers. "There was never a chance I would've said yes. I only wanted you."

"I know that *now.*" She huffs but hurt shines in her eyes, betraying the tough-girl dismissal. "It stung that night because I wasn't sure..."

"It's my fault." Guilt pushes the air out of my lungs in a painful sigh. "I should've told him how I felt about you sooner."

She slides off the bed and unzips her backpack. After tossing a few things aside, she slips into a T-shirt that ends right below her cute, round little butt cheeks.

"Whoa, whoa, whoa." I swipe my hand through the air, reaching for her, but she's out of range. "What are you doing?"

"I need a do-over." She circles her hand in front of her lower half. "Talking about my brother has dried up my happy zone."

I burst out laughing. "Happy zone?"

Her lips tilt into a coy smile. "You seem pretty *happy* playing there."

"Baby, I'm not playing." Staring her down, I leap off the bed. She turns to run, but I grab her around the waist, lifting her in the air.

She lets out a sharp shriek that dissolves into giggles and kicks her feet.

I toss her on the bed, and she holds out her hand in a stop gesture. "You really want me to believe you spent how long of your most active sexual prime abstaining? For me?"

Active sexual prime? I stop at the foot of the bed and stare at her. "What?"

"It just seems..." She drops her gaze. "Unlikely."

I palm my cock and stroke a few times. Her wide eyes follow my every move, and she slides her tongue over her bottom lip. "Molly." My voice comes out low, close to a warning. "I have two hands and an incredibly *active* imagination."

"Imagination?" One corner of her mouth tilts up with more confidence. "Were you thinking about *me*?"

"I'd rather not incriminate myself." I wink at her.

Laughter bubbles from her lips. "I won't tell."

I place my palms on the bed and stare her down. "All. The. Time."

"You hid it well, Royal." She lifts one eyebrow. "I really thought you only saw me as—"

"Do *not* say 'little sister.'" I need her much closer. I press my knee to the mattress and as if she has the same need, she crawls to the end of the bed, meeting me.

She lifts her chin, her gaze searching my face. "One of the guys?"

"Absolutely not." I stroke my knuckles over her cheek. "I didn't want to be a creep and make you feel weird. Besides, I can control myself." I tease my fingers under her T-shirt and tug it up. "Sort of."

Molly

Am I an idiot for believing Griff?

I've known him for most of my life. Utter sincerity shines in his eyes.

I lift my arms, allowing him to strip off my T-shirt. "I wish I'd known sooner." It would've spared me a lot of pain if I'd known he wasn't hooking up with all those other girls.

"Molly." He tosses my shirt aside and cups my cheeks, his warm, rough hands so gentle against me. "I love you. Every single, little thing about you." His deep, hypnotic voice simmers over my skin.

"I love you too." The throb of desire pulses between my legs again. "No more talking about you-know-who though."

"It's just you and me here." His smoldering gaze traces the lines of my body. "You're all I want."

Griff probably knows me better than anyone. With him, my confidence soars. A deep, specific need to satisfy him thrums through my chest. To give him the same pleasure he gave me.

But damn, I'm not sure what to do. I reach for him, my fingers clumsily skating over his rigid cock. His body jerks, and he gasps against my lips.

Warmth spreads over my skin at the effect I have on him. "Please? I want to taste you. Will you show me what you like?"

"Yeah." He groans and closes his hand over mine, guiding me to grip him at the base.

His sharp exhale ricochets around our hotel room. "Your

hands on me are perfect." He pushes his hips forward, sliding against my grip. So smooth but hard.

My mouth waters. I've *never* wanted to do this before. Too much fear or embarrassment stopped me. Or Griff's the only person I've cared about enough to be this vulnerable with. I've certainly never trusted anyone more than I trust him.

Excitement shivers along my spine. He's large and thick. My fingers curl around him and squeeze, then slide. Again and again.

"Just like that," he whispers.

Eager, I lean in and slide my cheek along him, nuzzling and kissing.

His legs tremble. From just my small touches?

Without taking my hand off him, I move back. "Lie down."

He stretches out in the middle of the bed and tucks his hands behind his head. "Now what, Muffin?" The cocky edge to his voice returns, prodding something competitive inside me. I want to bring him to gasping, shuddering breaths again.

"Tell me what you like." I arrange myself between his legs and curl my fingers around him in a surer grip this time.

His hot gaze roams from my face to where I'm stroking him. "I like you naked and touching me."

Fire races over my skin, hardening my nipples.

"Everything you do," he continues. "Every movement you make turns me on."

Instead of answering with words, I lean down and swirl my tongue around the tip of his cock.

A gasping groan drags from his throat. He curls his fists in the sheets. His cock jerks against my lips. Heat rushes to my core. I open wider and suck the head into my mouth.

"Oh fuck," he groans.

"Do you have lube?" I curl my fingers around him and stroke.

"What?" His eyes flutter open. "Why?"

"Kyla said it makes it taste better." I lean in and slide my tongue along his length. "But I like how you taste."

His jaw clenches tight and his chest heaves. "Your mouth is

fucking heaven." He tilts his head. "Maybe the guys she's doing it with don't know how to wash themselves."

"Ewww." Laughing softly, I suck him back into my mouth.

"Fuck," he groans. "New favorite thing unlocked."

I try to laugh low in my throat again, but with my mouth so full it's more of a hum. Griff groans louder. His fingers graze the back of my head, trace my cheek and along my jaw.

"Keep going," he rasps. "So good, baby."

I swirl my tongue and use my lips to suck and kiss, careful not to graze him with my teeth.

His hips thrust up gently in time with the movement of my hand. "Can you take more? Hmm?" His low, silky tone sparks my deep need to do anything he wants.

I nod and relax my jaw.

He growls low in his throat and his muscles seem to clench with need. He rests his hand on the back of my head and drives up into my mouth harder and faster. The invasion prickles at the back of my throat and I gag. Fear sizzles over me. I back away, gasping for air, but keep my hand wrapped around him, stroking in an erratic rhythm.

"Fuck." Griff slows his movements and traces his fingers over my cheek. "Did I hurt you?"

"No." Keeping my gaze locked on his, I lean down and swipe my tongue over him. "Just surprised."

He sucks in a sharp breath. "You're doing so good. So good," he chants over and over between ragged breaths.

His fists curl tighter in the sheets. His body strains, muscles rigid. He's holding himself back, afraid he'll hurt me. It ignites my wicked desire to drive him mindless with pleasure until he snaps. Every time his body jolts, every groan, sigh, and hiss of breath, I catalog it so I can recreate the lick or touch that caused it.

"Molly," he gasps. His fingers twine in my hair again, snagging on the little rose clips. "Molly—"

Warm, salty liquid splashes against my tongue and I jerk my head away, sputtering.

"Fuuuck." He groans even louder.

Shit. I was supposed to keep my mouth on him, wasn't I? "I'm sorry."

He curls his hand over mine and prods me to keep stroking his cock. Much rougher than I was doing on my own. Fascinated, I watch him twitch, shudder, and moan through his release.

Panting, he falls against the pillows. I release him and hurry off the bed to grab a towel from the bathroom.

"Molly," he rasps.

"Be right there." I hurry into the bedroom and, unsure of what to do, hand him the towel.

"Why'd you leave?" He swipes at the mess on his stomach with the towel, then swings his legs over the side of the bed and stares at me. "You okay?"

"Yeah." I drop my gaze to my feet. "I messed up at the end... I...didn't..."

"Molly." He curls his fingers around mine. "You can't mess that up. Trust me." He groans and stands, wobbling like a newborn colt for a moment. "You sucked the balance right out of me."

Laughing, I wrap my arm around his waist. "I've got you."

"Come shower with me." He leads me into the bathroom.

"I..." *Oh, this is silly.*

"What?"

What a dumb, girly thing to worry about. I tug on my now messy curls and one of the long braids with the small rosettes woven into it. "I don't want to get my hair wet."

"This is a nice place. Let's see if they have one of those shower cap thingies."

I blink. My grandmother wore shower caps. It seems kinda unsexy to wear one in front of Griff.

In the bathroom, he finds a small box on the counter and pries one end loose. "Here we go." He slides a clear plastic cap out.

My nose wrinkles.

"What?" He holds it out to me.

"That's not very...sexy?"

He bursts into laughter. "Disagree. My gorgeous, naked girlfriend in nothing but a shower cap is pretty fucking hot." He motions for me to turn around. "Get over here. You got a clip or something?"

"My backpack." I hurry into the bedroom and unzip the front pocket, pulling out a medium-sized brown hair claw, which should hopefully hold most of my hair, and my cosmetic bag.

Griff has the cap stretched between his hands, waiting for me. Something about it seems so...familiar, intimate, or domestic. I can't quite put my finger on it, but it leaves warmth glowing in my chest as I turn and twist my hair into a loose knot and secure it with the clip. Gently he slides the cap over my head, tucking loose strands of hair under the thin elastic. For such a big guy, he's careful not to tug too hard on my hair.

"I think we got it all." He pats my behind, then turns toward the shower stall, opens the glass door, and twists the knobs. A powerful jet of water pelts the tile wall.

Damn, I'm going to have to wash all my makeup off too. I stare in the mirror for a second. My lipstick's wrecked, what's left of it smeared around my mouth. Black eyeliner's starting to migrate lower, and the little wings at the corners of my eyes have been smudged. The false lashes Ella so carefully applied need to come off. It's not like Griff hasn't seen me without makeup plenty of times. Most of the time, really.

"What's wrong?" he asks.

"Nothing. I uh...should wash my makeup off. I don't want you to watch, though."

That was the dumbest thing I could've said. It encourages him to walk closer. Staring at me with curiosity shining in his eyes, he asks, "Why?"

"Because." I twist the warm water on and run a washcloth under the faucet.

He chuckles softly. "Okay. I'm still gonna recognize my girl, right?"

I whap him with the wet washcloth. "Yes."

He laughs harder. "Don't make me wait too long."

As soon as the glass door whooshes closed behind him, I press the warm washcloth to my face. It's stiff and scratchy, not like the softer makeup removal cloths I'd use at home. Didn't think to pack one of those. I search through my cosmetic pouch and pull out a tiny bottle of face wash and the little tin Ella gave me to store the lashes in.

When I'm as clean faced as I can get, I head for the shower.

I'm going to shower with Griff.

How many times have I daydreamed about this? And I stopped to scrub off my makeup first? What's wrong with me?

The door nudges open. Warm, soap-scented mist swirls around me. "There's my little muffin." He holds out his hand.

My heart melts, and the long list of things I keep doing wrong tonight seems to disappear. "Sorry," I murmur as I step inside.

"Hey." He grabs my hips and backs me against the shower wall. "Stop apologizing."

I risk peeking up at him.

"You have any idea how happy I am to be with you right now?" he asks.

I tap the side of my head. "Shower cap and all?"

"It's a good look on you." He leans down and brushes his lips against mine. "Everything looks good on you."

Water rains down around us in relentless, warm, steady streams from several directions. Griff slides his slick hands from my hips over my ribs and cups my breasts. "You're so perfect. I could stare at you for the rest of the night." He touches my chin, tipping my head back.

I lift my gaze and meet his concerned stare.

"I didn't hurt you, did I?" He tilts his head toward the bedroom.

"God, no. I just feel bad I messed it up."

He shakes his head. "Please, stop saying that." His lips curl at the corners. "You blew my mind. Literally. My brain's still scrambled."

"But don't you like—"

He presses a finger to my lips. "I love you. Your hands on me. Your mouth on me. Fucking amazing, baby."

Finally, my embarrassment fades. I press my body closer. "So, you'll let me try again?"

His eyes widen and he lets out a soft huff of laughter. "Any time you want." He kisses my cheek. "How about you? You gonna let me taste you again?" He flicks his tongue against my ear, then sucks at a sensitive spot on my neck.

My breath stutters in my lungs. "God, yes."

"Mmm." He kisses my neck. "I like that answer."

He curls one arm around my back, protecting my shoulders from the cold tile. His other hand slides from my breast to my hip. I drop my gaze. His thumb brushes the crease of my leg, and he squeezes my upper thigh. My leg looks tiny under his big hand.

He moves his thumb closer to my center, and I automatically inch my feet apart.

A low noise of approval rumbles in his chest. "I want to make you come with my hands." His lips brush my shoulder. "Feel you squeezing my fingers."

As if to demonstrate, he slides one finger between my legs, slipping along my sensitive flesh. I gasp. A mix of fear and excitement shudders down my spine. "Your hands are really big."

"How're you ever gonna take my cock if you can't take my fingers?" He kisses my shoulder. "Hmm?"

A mindless thrum of anticipation pounds through my veins. Something hard pokes against my stomach. I drop my gaze. He's hard and ready again. "What about you?"

"We're not talking about me." His thumb finds my clit, and my body jerks.

I clasp his shoulder to hold myself up, my fingers digging into hard muscles. "Oh my."

"So sensitive," he murmurs, kissing my cheek.

"Is that weird?" I squirm and circle my hips, seeking more contact.

"No. It's fucking amazing." His lips graze my temple. "I need to taste you again."

"Already?" My eyes pop open. "You want to...do *that*...again to me?"

"Lick your pussy?" He slips his hand out from between my legs and reaches behind him to twist the handle, cutting off the water. "Yes. I could eat you all night, Molly."

My skin heats from forehead to chest at his plainer words.

He pushes the door open and grabs my hand, dragging me out of the shower.

Slightly disoriented, I stand on the tiles and cross my arms at the wrists.

Griff sweeps his gaze over me, his forehead wrinkling. "I'm happy to just hold you, though, too. If that's what you want." He plucks the shower cap off my head and tosses it toward the sink, then swipes one of the towels off the rack and gently rubs it over my shoulders.

"No, uh, I'm down for the pussy licking." I flash a quick smile.

His lips twist into a wicked grin. "That's my girl." He tosses the towel on the floor and grabs my hand, pulling us out of the bathroom. "Fuck it. Come on."

Laughing, I hurry to keep up with him.

In the bedroom, he stops. His wild gaze flicks around the space. He stares at the low dresser, a small round table and chair shoved in the corner, then finally, the mattress.

"What's wrong?"

"Nothing." He eyes the table again. "I want to spread you out on something a little higher."

"The table looks wobbly," I warn.

"Okay, so no to the table." He nudges me toward the bed.

I press my knee to the mattress and glance at him over my shoulder. "Is this where you want me?"

"God, yes."

I crawl into the center of the big bed, taking my time. He groans and mutters a curse. A white-hot bolt of arousal obliterates my last bit of hesitation.

"Lie back," he rasps.

"Like this?" I stretch my arms over my head, arch my back, lift my knees, and cross my legs at the ankles.

"Yes." The bed dips. "Hand me those pillows."

I grasp one of the big, fluffy white rectangles and toss it to him, then another.

He strokes his fingers along my calves. "Lift your hips for me."

It takes a second to work out what he's asking, but finally, I dig my heels into the fluffy comforter and lift enough for him to stuff the pillows under me. It's still not quite what he wants, though. He hooks his arms under my knees and drags me closer.

"Put your legs over my shoulders."

"Griff!" I protest, but he urges me forward and drapes my legs over his shoulders.

The slow tingle of embarrassment travels over my cheeks. I press my hand against my eyes.

"No." He squeezes my butt. "Watch me."

I peek through my fingers and find him staring at me from between my legs. He wiggles his tongue against me and electricity zips over my skin. My hips jerk. My eyes squeeze shut again.

"No. Eyes on me," he says in a firm but gentle tone.

I focus on him again.

"That's my girl." He squeezes my hips, holding me up. "Move your body. Show me what feels good."

He flattens his tongue against me and waits. Experimentally, I roll my hips, then circle while pressing my heels into his back for leverage.

"Mm-hmm," he encourages.

I circle once more, chasing a tingling sensation. "Oh."

He adds pressure and I gasp again. "There!"

He groans and closes his eyes, sucking gently like he's savoring a peach. His tongue...oh my...his tongue. I squeeze my eyes shut and concentrate on the rapid-fire pulsing in my core.

"Griff." I reach for his hand and he twines his fingers with mine. I'm lost. Overwhelmed. Melting into the hot, wet sensation of his tongue. My body coils tight, then I detonate against his mouth. Breathless and whimpering, I slump against the mattress.

Griff isn't finished. He kisses my thighs and gently lowers my legs. A cocky grin tilts his shiny lips, and he swipes his hand over his mouth and chin. "So good, Muffin."

The soft glow of his approval settles over me and I reach for him, running my fingers through his hair. He drops kisses against my stomach, teases his tongue over my ribs, then stops to kiss my breasts before finally stretching out next to me.

"I can't move," I whisper.

"You don't have to." He pulls me into his arms.

I tilt my head back to see his face and his lips crash into mine. Our breaths tangle, and his scent overwhelms me—a whisper of me on his tongue, the bright hotel shampoo clinging to his damp hair, and the familiar salt of his skin.

His free hand traces an electrifying path over my body, exploring every dip and curve. A restless desire inside me pulses awake. I blink. We're nose to nose.

The heat in his eyes scorches my skin.

He always stares at me like I'm the only one in the world. All night, I felt his eyes on me when I was dancing with my friends. At first, I'd thought he was annoyed with me. But that wasn't it. All I found in his eyes was burning affection and gentle possessiveness.

"You're so wet for me." His warm breath whispers over my cheek.

Why does that make me flush with embarrassment? Griff obviously likes my body's reactions. "Well, you *did* have your tongue all over me," I tease, my body tingling at the thought.

"This isn't me." He slides his finger through my slit. "It's all *you*."

"No," I whisper. "Still your doing. I only feel like this when I'm with *you*."

He feathers a sweet kiss over my lips as he slowly slides his finger inside me.

"Oh." I gasp at the invasion, the sound swallowed by his mouth hovering over mine. That's...*good*. I wriggle and shift my hips, adjusting. His thumb slides to my clit and works in slow, maddening circles. He nuzzles my neck, kissing and sucking. Sensations and pressure build. He presses inside me harder, deeper, a little faster. I can't help bucking my hips against his hand.

"Yes." He encourages me between kisses.

A tickling, tingling tension builds in my center. He presses deeper, stroking a certain spot over and over. My toes curl. Strobe-like bursts of pleasure heat my insides. My eyes roll back from the surge of ecstasy sweeping over my nerve endings.

"Yes." Griff groans, low and intense. "Give it to me."

All of his attention, his deep concentration on my every reaction, finally sends me over the edge. In the confines of his arms, I arch and twist, grinding myself against his hand, riding out the waves.

When I finally stop shaking and can take a full breath, I open my eyes. A warm, satisfied smile stretches his lips.

"That was beautiful." He kisses my cheek. "The way you squeezed my fingers..." His thumb brushes against my overly sensitive clit, and my body jerks.

He slides his hand from between my legs. Wetness coats my thighs. He flicks his gaze down. Something in his expression shifts but I'm too sleepy and floaty to question it.

"Give me a second." He pats my butt and rolls away. I lift myself off his arm so he can stand.

"Where you going?" Drowsiness slurs my words.

"Be right back." His fingers tickle the backs of my legs as he rounds the bed.

I close my eyes and drift on a cloud of bliss.

Molly

CHAPTER TWENTY-EIGHT

GRIFF

In the bathroom, I quickly wash the bit of blood from my fingers. It doesn't bother me, but I don't want Molly to freak out if she sees it. All right, maybe it bothers me a little. I feel like a bastard who's robbed her of her innocence or something. Which is dumb. She was loving every minute of what we did. Another asshole part of me wants to beat on my chest for being her first...*everything*.

Fuck. I squeeze my eyes shut and take a breath.

Grabbing another washcloth, I wet it with warm water and wring it out in the sink.

In the bedroom, Molly's in the same position I left her. Beautifully naked, facing away from me. My gaze travels up her long, toned legs—one bent at the knee, giving me a glimpse between her thighs. My cock's harder than a fucking crowbar. It'd be so easy to slip into bed behind her, lift her leg, and slide right inside her tight, wet heat.

But she hasn't asked me yet. Hasn't said those magic words.

My gaze lands on a smear of blood on her inner thigh, sobering me out of my lustful longing. I touch the washcloth to her skin, and she murmurs a sleepy sound.

"What's wrong?" She rolls to her back and stares up at me.

"Nothing." I quickly clean her up and ball the washcloth in my fist.

Bang! Bang! Bang! The door to our room rattles.

What the fuck?

Like someone's about to burst in and hold us hostage, Molly grabs the sheet and throws it over her naked body. We both stare in the direction of the door.

"Molly!" A muffled shout comes from the hallway.

"Fuck." I hurry into the bathroom and toss the washcloth in the sink.

"Molly, please!" *Bang! Rattle. Bang!*

"Is that Kyla?" Molly whispers from outside the bathroom.

I turn, and she's dressed in her T-shirt. She thrusts my shorts at me without taking her eyes off the door.

"Thanks." I grab the shorts and yank them on. "I think so." My gaze swings from the door to the short hallway leading to the bed. "I'll answer. Go back to the bedroom." Who knows what the fuck we're dealing with?

Her nervous eyes shift to the door and back to me. "Okay." She leans up and kisses my cheek, then scurries around the corner, out of sight.

I check the small, round viewing hole. The limited one-sixty range shows three girls huddled against the door. Based on hair color, I assume it's Hayden, Kyla, and Darcy.

I unlock the door and throw it open.

"Oh, thank God," Kyla wails, stumbling forward and crashing her wet face against my bare chest. I awkwardly catch her and pull her inside.

Hayden's tear-streaked eyes roam over me without comment. Darcy's the only one who seems sober and, given the twitch at the corners of her mouth, annoyed by the whole situation.

"What's wrong?" I tighten an arm around Kyla to keep her upright and step back to give the girls room. "What happened?"

Darcy smirks, rolls her eyes, and turns to close the door behind them.

"Where's Jenn?" I ask Hayden.

Her mouth flattens into a thin, irritated line. "She ditched us and went *home*. In *my* car."

At least she's not lost and wandering around the hotel.

Kyla continues sobbing and clinging to me. I twist, awkwardly searching for Molly. Where'd she go?

"What happened?" Molly turns the corner, gasps, and hurries toward us.

She took the time to change into her cute little PJ set and I can't even admire it. A putrid *scent* wafts off Kyla. My nose twitches, and I suppress the urge to gag.

I glance down, taking in her wild, matted, wet hair and stained dress.

"What—" Molly gingerly touches Kyla's shoulder then glares at Hayden. "What happened?"

Kyla wails—a high-pitched keening that stabs my eardrums.

Molly pries Kyla off me and hands me my shirt.

"Did you throw up, Kyla?" Concern heightens Molly's voice. "Are you okay?"

Christ, is *that* what's smeared all over my chest? I push past the girls into the bathroom, grab another towel, and wash myself off without verifying. With all the bodily fluids we've thrown around this room tonight, it could be considered a damn crime scene.

The girls are still crowded in the hallway when I return. Molly's the only one who seems to be trying to calm Kyla.

"Why don't you help her clean up?" I suggest, gesturing toward the bathroom.

Hayden rolls her eyes and pushes past me, throwing her duffel bag onto the table. "Aw, you got Molly roses?"

"Huh?" I glance at Hayden and nod. Flowers are the last thing on my mind.

"Sorry. We didn't know where else to go," Darcy says to me.

"Is someone going to tell me what happened?" I ask.

"Nooo," Kyla shrieks and glares at Darcy. "Don't you dare."

"Kyla," I say as patiently as possible. "Did someone hurt you?"

"No." She sniffs.

"Come on." Molly turns her friend toward the bathroom and nudges her inside. "Hayden!" she snaps over her shoulder. "Bring something clean for her to change into. I know you packed more than one outfit."

Hayden scowls. I cough to cover my laughter. The girls came to Molly, so now she's taking charge.

Not wanting to be anywhere near them while they clean Kyla up, I move to the farthest corner of the bedroom and wait for someone to tell me what the fuck's going on.

Molly's decisive voice cuts through the walls, even though I can't quite make out the words. A few seconds later, Darcy stomps out of the bathroom and throws the closet door open. She whips a plastic bag off one of the hangers and returns to the bathroom. A few seconds later, the full bag sails into the hallway, landing with a wet *thud*.

The shower blasts to life. There's more of Molly's murmuring. The other girls giggle but a terse "knock it off" from Molly silences them.

I grab my phone and text Remy.

Me: Something went down with one of Molly's friends. You around in case I need you?

Remy: Is Molly okay?

Me: Yes.

Remy: I'm home. Just say when and where.

Me: Thx.

No reason to drag him to the hotel yet, but knowing he's available reassures me.

That dickhead Wesley. Somehow, he's responsible for whatever happened. I just know it.

The shower cuts off and Molly's soothing voice seems to be reassuring Kyla.

Silently, I stand and move to the chair closer to the bathroom, straining to hear any bits of their conversation.

"Tried...choked...felt sick..." More crying.

Molly's comforting tone is full of patience as she tries to calm her friend. "It's okay. Shhh, you're okay now."

Love for Molly explodes in my chest.

Hayden giggles. "Worst sex story ever."

"Shut up," Molly hisses.

Darcy murmurs something I can't make out.

"He's going to tell everyone," Kyla whines. "I can't. I can't go back to school."

"No one cares." Darcy's sarcastic voice grates on my nerves.

A few seconds later, the four of them emerge from the bathroom dressed in T-shirts or pajamas. Kyla's in a hot-pink T-shirt that reaches her knees. *The Hell I Won't* is spelled out in pink rhinestones across the front. Definitely Hayden's shirt.

"Come on. Let's lie down. You'll feel better," Molly coos in Kyla's ear.

"Are you okay?" I ask Kyla.

"Better now." She flashes me a weak smile.

Still utterly confused, I search the girls' faces. Which one is most likely to tell me what the fuck happened? Of Molly's friends, I probably know Hayden the best. She doesn't seem to be in a chatty mood though.

I glance over as Molly helps her friend into the chair next to the bed. Kyla rests her elbows on her knees and her head in her hands. Molly kneels in front of her. "You okay?"

I grab a bottle of water from the fridge and hand it to Kyla. "Drink this, hon."

"Thanks," Kyla whispers, taking the bottle from me. She sips, then groans and clutches her stomach. "Everyone needs to stop staring at me."

"We're just worried," Molly says.

"What happened, Kyla?" I ask, desperate to drag the information from her.

Kyla groans and sets the water bottle on the floor. "You can tell him," she whispers to Molly.

Darcy and Hayden throw themselves on the bed.

Molly sighs and stands, keeping her hand on Kyla's shoulder. The corner of her mouth twitches, as if she's running over several ways to explain the situation and finding all of them inadequate.

"Did someone hurt her?" I ask Molly.

She stares at Kyla for a few seconds. "Not really."

"No," Kyla answers. "Just my pride."

I blow out a frustrated breath. All this waiting and inaction is killing me. *Just tell me who I need to punch.*

Molly sighs. "She and Wesley were in an...intimate moment... when she got sick," she explains in a delicate, halting voice.

"She choked on Wesley's dick, then puked in his lap," Darcy says in a dry tone.

"Darcy!" Molly scolds.

"Shut up, Darcy!" Kyla shouts and starts sobbing again.

Hayden falls against the mattress and sighs.

I've been in a few fucked up situations in my life. Nothing quite prepared me for this one.

"Did he force you, Kyla?" I ask as gently as possible.

She frowns. "Not really. I mean, I told him I didn't feel good, but..."

And here I thought my opinion of Wesley couldn't get much lower.

"All right, so then what happened?" None of this explains why they've all ended up in our room.

"Wesley got so mad he kicked all of us out of their suite." Hayden sits up and glares at Kyla.

Hayden and Darcy's attitude toward their friend is really starting to piss me off. "Kyla can't help getting sick, Hayden. Why're you taking it out on her?"

"Well, Wade and Wesley got into a fight over it! And Wade took off. Wesley kicked us all out! We didn't have anywhere else to go, so we came here," she says in a rush as if it explains her shitty behavior.

"Yeah, so? Wade's a pussy and can't stand up to his asshole brother." I sneer. "That's not Kyla's fault either."

"Thank you," Kyla whispers.

Hayden glares at me for a few seconds, then blows out a breath. "Sorry, Kyla," she murmurs. "I just wanted everything to be perfect tonight."

"Like I didn't?" Kyla screeches. "I'm mortified!"

"Okay, okay." I hold out my hands like I'm reffing a fight at The Castle. In fact, I kinda wish I was.

"Sorry we interrupted you guys," Kyla says to me.

"It's okay," I assure her. "You did the right thing coming to us."

They're not in any condition to leave, either.

Fuck. I can't stay here. Spending the night with my girlfriend is one thing. Staying in the same room with her *and* her drunk, underage friends is out of the question.

I grab my bag, then crook my finger at Molly, motioning for her to follow me into the bathroom. Once we're inside, I pull jeans, socks, and sneakers out of my bag.

Molly's gaze follows my every move. "I'm so sorry about this."

"It's okay." I try to ignore the way she watches me change out of the shorts but god *damn*, it's a turn-on having her eyes on me. "I'm going to run downstairs and see if I can find some saltines and ginger ale to settle her stomach."

"Thank you."

"Don't open the door for anyone except me." I nod toward the bedroom. "And don't let them leave."

"I'll do my best."

"Fair enough. I don't want *you* to leave the room, okay?"

"I won't."

"Good." I lean down and kiss her cheek.

Outside our room, more people than I'd expect to see at this hour are wandering the hallway. I double-check the door locked behind me, then head for the elevator.

Downstairs, the small hotel grocery store is manned by an irritated-looking employee. Ignoring his watchful glare, I pick up a box of crackers, a sleeve of Oreos, four small bottles of ginger ale, and a bottle of Tylenol. At the register, I grab two bananas out of the bowl on the counter.

The clerk recites a total equal to what I spend on a week's worth of groceries. I charge it to our room, grab the small paper bag he hands me, and return upstairs. I knock lightly, then use my key card to open the door. The security chain jerks the door to a stop.

"Hang on!" Molly says. "Sorry." She undoes the chain and opens the door.

"Don't apologize. I want you to keep that lock on." I hand her the bag. "Try to get them to eat something and take the Tylenol before you all go to sleep. There's more water in the fridge. Make sure you drink a lot, okay?"

"Okay." She peers into the bag, then gives me a soft smile. "Thank you."

"You got it."

"You're really going home?"

"Eh." I want her to get some rest, and if I tell her I'm planning to camp outside her door, she'll want to stay out there with me. "I might go sleep in the car."

"Griff," she protests.

"I'll be fine." I glance over her shoulder and lower my voice. "What room is Wesley in?"

She frowns. "Why?"

I stare at her, waiting for an answer.

She sighs. "I'm not sure. A suite on this floor, I think."

That shouldn't be too hard to figure out.

"What's going on, Molly?" Hayden joins us. "Hey, Griff."

"You feeling better?" I ask.

"Meh." She shrugs, then eyes the bag in Molly's hands. "What'd you bring us?"

"Nothing that exciting, but try to eat and drink something before going to sleep, okay?"

Hayden nods quickly. "This is so dumb. We're all crowding into one bed when Wesley has a whole two rooms to himself down there." She tilts her head to the left.

"Oh yeah?" I play dumb. "Two rooms, huh?"

"The last door on this side of the hallway is actually a two-room suite," she explains.

"You rent that? Or did he?"

"Wade got it." She pouts. "I feel so bad he left after spending all that money."

I couldn't give a fuck less about Wade's finances. "I'm sure he'll work it out with his brother."

Hayden shrugs, takes the bag from Molly's hands, and spins away, returning to the bedroom. "Snack time, girls!" she shouts.

Molly wraps her arms around my waist. "I don't want you to go."

"I know, Muffin." I return her embrace and rest my chin on top of her head. "Take care of your squad. They need you right now."

She chuckles softly and squeezes me tighter. "I love you."

"Love you too." If I don't go now, I'll never leave.

I need to call Remy and have him meet me here. There's a certain asshole we need to have a conversation with—of the fist-to-mouth variety.

Molley

CHAPTER TWENTY-NINE

GRIFF

"WHY ARE YOU SLEEPING OUT HERE IN THE HALLWAY like a hobo?" Remy's irritated rumble pulls me out of my semi-asleep state.

I lift my head and stare up at him. "I didn't think spending the night in a hotel room with my girlfriend *and* her underage friends was a great idea." I glance at the door. "But I didn't want to leave them unprotected."

He holds out his hand to me. "What happened, bonehead?"

I grab him and haul myself off the floor. "You won't believe me if I tell you." I run my hands through my hair.

"So..." He cocks his head in that dickishly annoying way he's perfected over the years. "Why exactly did you rent a hotel room with my sister?"

"That's what you're worried about?" I gesture to the long hallway. "Her whole class rented rooms. I didn't want her to feel left out."

"Uh-huh." Remy's eyes narrow.

I don't bother saying *nothing* happened—one, it'd be a lie, and two, it's none of his business.

"I thought she wanted to go to the mystery after-party thing or whatever?" He waves his hand toward the staircase. "Or was she lying about that?"

I flick my gaze to the ceiling and count to five. "She *did* want to go. But she was tired when we got here." *Then we got distracted giving each other orgasms and forgot all about the after-party.* "Then the girls showed up."

"All right. So, what happened?"

I give him the briefest possible version of the story that still gets across why Wesley needs his ass kicked.

"He booted them all out of his room?" Remy stares at me with his mouth hanging open. "Poor Kyla." He hangs his head and runs his hand over the back of his neck. "Molly told me Darcy asked if I'd go with her."

"Yeeesh." I let out a disgusted noise.

"Yeah, that was my response, too, jackass," he grumbles. "Now, I wish I had."

"I don't know if it would've mattered. Kyla was drunk before we even had dinner. And Darcy's been in a *mood*."

"Bullet dodged then." He rolls his eyes. "Is Molly okay?"

"Yeah." I snort. "She took charge and got everyone in line."

The corners of his mouth lift. "Of course she did." He glances down the hall. It's thankfully empty now. But who knows how much longer that will last? "All right. Let's go pay this twatwaffle a visit."

I smack my fist against my palm. "About time."

We walk the long hallway and finally stop at the last door on our left. "Pretty sure this is it." I rap my knuckles against the wood. I'd rather not bang on it and draw attention to us if I don't have to.

"Housekeeping," Remy says in a ridiculous, high-pitched voice.

I side-eye him. "You think this is funny?"

"Not yet."

I knock again, louder this time.

"Fuck off, you disgusting bitch!" someone shouts behind the door.

"This motherfucker," I growl.

"Don't get carried away," Remy warns me in a low voice. "I don't need you getting arrested. Half the town owes his father favors."

Fuck that. I knock again. Harder this time. Insistent.

The door swings open. Wesley stands there wearing nothing but sloppy boxer shorts and a stupid smirk. I step in front of Remy and let my fist fly, connecting with Wesley's cheek. The quick jab knocks him backward. Pain grazes my knuckles, but I ignore it and focus on the jackass in front of me.

Remy enters behind me, closing the door with a soft click.

Shock and wide-eyed outrage twist Wesley's expression. He clutches his cheek and stares at us. "What the hell was that for?"

I glare and don't say a word. Has he done so many awful things he really doesn't know why we're here? "You tell me."

His gaze darts around the room. "Kyla?"

"Bingo."

"Come on, man!" Wesley holds his arms out wide. "You have no idea what I've been through tonight. I've suffered enough." He shudders.

"Nah, sounds like Karma came to collect." I shrug. "Don't try to take advantage of girls you get drunk."

Remy chuckles—a dark, terrifying sound that snaps Wesley's head to the side.

"I didn't take advantage," Wesley protests. "She was fucking begging for it."

I kind of doubt that, but I wasn't exactly a witness to what went down either. Just the aftermath.

"You kicked her out when you should've taken care of her," Remy says. "The fuck is wrong with you?"

"Dude." Wesley's eyes bug. "She threw up on my *dick*." He points to his crotch, in case we're confused about what body part he's whining about. "I had to take the hottest shower possible." He turns his head to the side and retches.

"While you let her wander around the hotel, drunk and covered in vomit," I add.

"Hayden said they were going to Molly's room." He vaguely gestures at me and snickers. "Your girl's such a prude, they knew they wouldn't be interrupting anything."

His attempt to insult Molly doesn't faze me, but Remy chokes.

"What the fuck did you say about my sister?" Remy's jaw works from side to side as he takes a dangerous step closer to Wesley.

"Huh?" Wesley stares at Remy, wide-eyed. The hamster wheel of his brain turns slowly, but finally comprehension lights his vacant eyes as he makes the connection between Remy and Molly. "Ohhhh," he breathes out like a dumbass.

"I got this." I brace my hand against Remy's chest. Anyone else who tried that would probably get their arm snapped off. Remy just glowers at me.

"What'd I tell you earlier?" I say to Wesley.

He stares into the void, the moment stretching as he no doubt searches his fuzzy memory. Finally, his mouth turns down in an *oh, fuck* sort of way. "Keep her name out of my mouth?"

"Yup." I let loose with a fist to his jaw, snapping his head back. Pain sizzles through my fingers and up my arm. A split opens on his bottom lip and a trickle of red bubbles there. "That's for saying her name."

I'll give Wesley credit—this time, he puts up his fists and drops into a half-assed fighting stance. He thinks he knows how to fight, but I've trained to fight *to the death*. I'm hyperaware of the power behind my fists and how much damage I can do.

Remy chuckles, crosses his arms over his chest, and leans against the wall.

Wesley throws a lazy punch that misses my face by a mile.
Nice try.

I pop him on the other side of his jaw, whipping his head in the opposite direction. "That one's for Kyla."

He drops to his knees. "Fuck," he groans.

My legs tremble with the urge to smash my knee into his nose. But I restrain myself. I glance at Remy, and he nods. He steps closer to Wesley and grabs a fistful of his hair. Slowly, he tilts Wesley's head back. Wesley winces and stares up at Remy with pleading eyes. "Stay away from my sister," Remy seethes. "*And* her friends. Stick to college girls."

Wesley chokes and twists away from Remy. He leans over and spits blood on the carpet.

"What's wrong? College girls too smart for your bullshit?" Remy sneers. "Gotta prey on high school girls who don't know any better?"

I scowl in Remy's direction, but he ignores me.

Wesley holds up his hands in surrender. "I'm done with these little bitches. Trust me."

"Good." Remy slaps Wesley's cheek. Hard. "We don't want to have another conversation with you."

Wesley jerks his thumb over his shoulder. "Kyla left her bag here. You want it?"

"Yes." Remy nudges Wesley with his boot.

Wesley picks himself up from the floor without looking at either one of us. I track his movements carefully in case he's going for a weapon. But he returns with a small, sparkly peach purse and a pair of gold strappy heels and holds them out to me. Thankfully, they appear puke-free.

"She leave anything else?" I ask.

He glances around the room. "I don't think so."

"All right." I turn and head for the door. Once I have it opened, Remy joins me.

In the hallway, he shakes his head. "What the fuck? Why did he say that about Molly?"

I know him well enough to know it's not the comment itself bugging him—it's the *how* and *why* behind it. Shaking my head, I walk toward my room. "I think he hit on her and she turned him down once," I explain over my shoulder.

"Christ," he mutters. "He's not good enough to breathe the same air as my sister, let alone talk to her."

"Agreed."

"You should've punched him harder."

Now that we're away from Wesley, I recognize a stinging ache in my hand. I shake it out and glance at my knuckles. Two are bleeding. Must've scraped them on Wesley's teeth. "Fuck." I flex my fingers a few times. Luckily, Wesley can't throw a punch to save his life. Last thing I need is Diane finding out I got into a fight and kicking me off the show before it even starts.

"You've had worse." Remy claps my shoulder.

We stop in front of the door to my room. "Your compassion is heartwarming, really."

He chuckles and knocks. "You did good."

"Thanks." I pull out my phone and send Molly a text.

Me: At the door.

"When do you have to return Quill's Mercedes?" Remy asks me while we're waiting.

"Not until Monday."

"I still can't believe you had the balls to do that." He chuckles.

I shrug. "Molly liked it."

Finally, the door swings open. Molly blinks and yawns. Betrayal and shock register in her wide blue eyes when they land on Remy. "Why'd you call *him*?" She shoots a glare at me.

"Seriously?" Remy scoffs. "Get out here so I can talk to you."

She glances down at her PJs and crosses her arms over her chest. "No." She backs up, opening the door wider. "They're all asleep," she whispers.

Remy and I crowd inside. I hand her Kyla's stuff and she takes it without looking at me.

"I told Wesley to stay away from you," Remy says. "And them." He tips his head toward the bedroom.

"Remy—"

"Checkout is at eleven," he continues, steamrolling over her objection. "I'll be here to take the girls home. Don't keep me fucking waiting," he warns.

"Fine," Molly groans. "I doubt anyone's gonna feel like brunch, anyway."

"You can have them over at our place and cook whatever you want," Remy suggests, dialing back the dickhead older brother attitude. "Just make sure their parents know where they are."

"Okay."

"Come here." He slips his arm around her shoulder, pulling her closer, and kisses the top of her head. "Besides the vomit drama, did you have a good time?"

Molly's eyes stray to me, and a soft smile curves her lips. "Oh, yes."

Remy sighs and releases her. "Good." He slides his eyes my way. "At least you got that right."

"Don't pick on Griff." Molly pokes her finger in Remy's chest.

He chuckles and shakes his head.

"Give me a second," I say to Remy.

He rolls his eyes but heads into the hallway.

"Come here." I rest my hand on Molly's hip and pull her closer. "You all right?" I ask her in a low voice.

"Yeah, just tired." Her big blue eyes stare up at me. "It's been a long, long night."

"It has," I agree. "Try to get some sleep."

She snuggles closer to me, resting her hand on my shoulder. "I wanted to sleep next to you."

"Me too, Muffin." I kiss her cheek, then whisper in her ear, "Are you okay? Hurt anywhere?"

She frowns for a second, then pink spreads over her cheeks. "You mean *down there*?" she whispers.

I flex my fingers over her hip, digging into the fleshiest part of her backside. Fuck, these shorts are so thin. "Yes. Down there," I whisper back, widening my eyes for emphasis.

Her eyebrows pinch and she shifts her lower body, rubbing her thighs together. A groan drags from my throat as an image of my face between her thighs replays in my head.

"No, nothing hurts," she answers slowly. "More like my parts are *aware* that I had a visitor."

I snort, then chuckle at her description. "Visitor? Baby, I plan to move in and become a permanent fucking resident. And don't you forget it."

Molly

CHAPTER THIRTY

Molly

I SHOULDN'T BE PLAGUED WITH GUILT THE MORNING after prom. But the ugly prickliness in my stomach won't go away. Kyla had one of the worst sexual experiences last night. I had one of the best. I can't stop replaying each moment over and over in my head. And I can't even talk to any of my friends about any of it. Hayden's still mad she didn't get to fool around with Wade at all. Darcy's just mad at everyone in general. Kyla's eyes gloss over every time we mention the smallest detail about last night.

God, I'm the worst friend.

"Did someone get their period last night?" Hayden asks.

We all shake our heads or answer "no."

"Looks like blood on the sheets." Hayden wrinkles her nose and flips the covers over the bed.

"Ewww," Darcy moans. "Did we sleep in it?"

"Mollllly…" Hayden drags out my name and stares at me with wide, trouble-making eyes. "Did you get your V-card punched last night?"

Heat blasts over my cheeks. "No!"

"Who still says *V-card*?" Darcy scoffs.

I blow out a breath and force what I hope looks like a bored expression on my face instead of a guilty one. "When did we have time? You guys chased Griff out of our room."

"We didn't *chase* him away." Hayden tosses her hair off her shoulder and huffs at me. "He did the gentlemanly thing and let us have the room since we were roomless."

Kyla's sad, watery eyes focus on me. "Can we please not talk about all the awesome sex you had with your—"

"We didn't have sex!" *Get a grip, Molly. The louder you protest, the guiltier you sound.*

"Be honest. Does he have a huge wiener?" Hayden holds her thumb and forefinger like a pistol, then turns toward Darcy. "Have you seen the size of his hands? His dick must be *huge*."

Darcy snort-giggles and spreads the fingers of one hand wide, staring at it with a smile. "Hands, nothing. Did you see him in those shorts last night? He looked like he was smuggling an eggplant down there."

"Oh my God!" I explode. "Would you stop?"

"Guess we solved the mystery of the blood on the sheets." Darcy snickers into her open hand.

"Ignore them, Molly." Kyla wraps her arms around my waist and rests her chin on my shoulder.

I return the hug. "Thanks."

"But..." She lifts her face, a devilish smile curving her lips. "Take my advice: don't ever try to deep-throat his eggplant if you're drunk."

Darcy and Hayden erupt with laughter.

I shove Kyla away. "You guys suck."

"We need to live vicariously through you, Molly," Darcy whines. "What are we working with? A pickle or a cucumber?"

"Please stop comparing my boyfriend's anatomy to different vegetables." I glare at Darcy. "It's weird."

"Honestly, the size doesn't matter." Hayden lifts her chin like she's some sort of expert on the topic. "What matters is if he knows what to do with it. Bonus points if he's not afraid to use his hands and mouth."

If my face gets any hotter, I'm going to spontaneously combust.

"*Ohhh! Mollleee!*" Darcy squeals and points at me. "Your face is so red, Pennywise is going to inflate you and tie a string around your ankle."

I stare at her. "What the hell?"

Kyla frowns at her, then turns to me, wearing a face better suited for an investigative journalist. "Be honest. Does he go down on you?"

"Are his fingers magic?" Hayden asks. "I bet they are."

Darcy narrows her eyes on Hayden. "I never knew you had this weird hand obsession."

Hayden opens her mouth to protest, but I cut her off.

"Everything about Griff is magic," I say. "He's very...giving."

The three of them either groan or laugh.

As if our smutty conversation summoned him, a text from Griff lights up my screen.

Griff: In the hallway.

Me: K

"He's here. Please don't say any of this embarrassing eggplant stuff in front of him." I throw a warning glare at each of them.

I glance at my backpack, the bag and hanger I slipped over my dress, and the vase of roses. All ready to go.

Griff knocks and I hurry to answer.

"Hey." I open the door and take him in. Somehow, he makes a simple faded dark-red T-shirt and jeans look really hot.

He leans down and brushes a kiss over my lips. "Missed you."

"Missed you too," I whisper. My gaze drops to the three pink roses he's holding at his side, each individually wrapped in a piece of iridescent plastic.

"Don't be mad. I felt bad they had a shitty end to prom night," he whispers in my ear. "And they saw your vase of roses."

I throw my arms around his neck. "You're the sweetest."

"I don't know about that." His lips crash into mine again. My mouth opens and he gently sweeps his tongue against mine. I taste his warm, minty breath and press my body closer to his.

Someone clears their throat behind us. Loudly.

Reluctantly, I unwind myself from Griff.

"Morning, ladies." Griff curls his hand around mine, pulling me into the room. "How'd everyone sleep?"

"Like the dead." Hayden's eager gaze drops to the roses. "What's that?"

"One for you." Griff hands her a rose, then passes the other two to Kyla and Darcy.

"Aww, thanks, Griff." Darcy flashes a wicked smile at me. "Molly's right—you *are* a giver."

Griff nods but slides a confused glance my way. "I try."

The girls titter with laughter.

"I bet you don't have to try too hard." Darcy flutters her lashes and sticks her nose in the flower bud, inhaling noisily.

I blow out a slow, irritated breath.

"All right." Griff shakes off the weird comments and claps his hands together. "Everyone ready to go? Remy's waiting downstairs."

Darcy's eyes light up and she practically trips over the edges of her flared jeans to grab her bag.

"We can have brunch at my house, if you guys want," I offer, in the least inviting tone ever.

Hayden yawns. "No, it's getting late. My mom's gonna kill me if I'm not home soon."

"Same," Kyla adds.

In the elevator, the girls start pestering Griff about riding with us. I throw him a pleading look and curl my fingers around his.

He squeezes my hand. "We have to stop at the garage."

None of my friends are interested in *that*. "Never mind." Hayden dismisses the idea with a wave of her hand.

Outside, the sunlight stabs my eyes. The crisp air jolts me awake, helping me shake off the haze from so little sleep last night.

Remy's leaning against the back of his truck, flipping through his phone.

"Shotgun!" Darcy yells, running toward Remy's Bronco.

He glances up, a faint smile ghosting his lips. "Am I taking everyone home?"

"Yup." I squeeze Griff's hand and wrap my free arm around his to indicate everyone is riding with Remy except *me*.

Remy snorts and shakes his head.

Kyla stops in front of me, a weepy expression falling over her face. I release Griff's arm and I'm about to ask if she's okay when she throws her arms around my neck, hugging me tight.

"Thanks for not making fun of me last night," she whispers against my ear.

Emotion squeezes my throat and I hold her tight in my arms. "Never. Stuff happens. It's okay."

"Love you, babe." She releases me and her lips tilt up just a fraction.

"You too."

"I'll catch you at home, sis." Remy waves at me, then steps into the truck.

Griff walks me to the Mercedes and opens the passenger-side door. "Are we really going to the garage?" I ask.

The corners of his mouth tilt up. "We can. If you want."

"No." I curl my fingers in his shirt and pull him closer. "Let's go to my house. Remy will be busy for a while."

His nostrils flare and his eyes search my face for a few seconds. Then he frowns—it's brief, but I catch it.

"What's wrong? You don't want to be alone with me?"

"It's not that." He lifts his chin. "Get in."

I slide onto the buttery, quilted leather seat. Now that I'm not anxious about prom and my friends, I take time to admire the interior of the luxury SUV.

"This really is nice," I say to Griff when he settles behind the wheel. "Thank you."

"Anything for you, Muffin." He leans over and pops a kiss on my cheek.

Once we're on the main highway, he asks, "Did you get any sleep?"

"A little. Did you?"

Instead of answering, he yawns, then laughs. "Not enough, I guess."

"I'd almost rather go for a drive." I slide my hand over the complicated dashboard. "Before this turns into a pumpkin."

He grins. "Want to drop your stuff off at the house first?"

I nod quickly. "And maybe grab something to eat. I'm starving."

His smile falters. "Instead of buying the flowers, I should've brought you a breakfast sandwich or something."

"No." I rub my hand over his. "That was sweet." After the way my friends were talking about Griff's anatomy this morning, I'm not sure they deserved the roses, but I can't tell him that.

"You weren't mad, were you?" He glances over, worry creasing his brow. "I thought since they were pink and I'd—"

"No! Not at all." I cover my face with my hands. "This is so dumb," I mumble.

"What's wrong?"

Distress vibrates through his voice.

"Ugh. They were asking me...how, um, *big* you are. They have this theory that since you have big hands, your, you know, must be *huuuge*." I don't want to tell him Hayden's the one who started in with the hand comparison.

He snort-laughs. "All righty, then."

"I'm sorry." I hate the whiny tone my voice takes on. "I shouldn't have told you."

He reaches over and pats my leg. "It's fine, Muffin. No worse than the shit talk that went down in locker rooms when I was in high school."

"What? Really?"

"Yeah. The year I played football was awkward as fuck. Some

of the other dudes on the team were obsessed with checking out everyone else's equipment."

"That's, uh, creepy."

He snorts but his mouth flattens into a thin line. "They wanted to compare everything—dick size, ball size, ball stretchyness—"

"What?" I practically scream. "Why?"

"I don't fucking know," he scoffs. "They did all sorts of weird shit. This one fucker, Timmy Puck, snuck up on me in the shower once, then ran around telling everyone else mine was the biggest and had everyone call me Flagpole for the rest of the season."

I glance over and his face has taken on a pink hue. "That's deranged. No one ever pointed out it was *weird* to be peeping on your teammates?"

"Nope. They'd yell, 'Prank!'" Griff pitches his voice higher. "Or 'just for research!' but it was uncomfortable as hell."

"Ugh. I'm sorry." I wish I'd never started this conversation. The last thing I want to do is make him relive crappy high school memories.

"Given the choice, I'd rather have girls talking about me, than guys." He slides his hand over my leg. "Although, I won't ever be able to look any of your friends in the eye again."

"Girls aren't much better." I cross my arms over my chest. "In sixth grade, Cindy Adams stole one of my bras after gym class and showed it to *everyone.*"

"What?" He glances over. "Why?"

"Because she was a bitch?" Heat flames across my face. "I was already almost a C-cup and no one else in our class was, I guess?"

"Shit, Molly, I didn't know that happened."

"I sure as hell wasn't telling anyone." I lower my voice. "Mom hadn't been gone long. Nana's the one who had to take me bra shopping, which was embarrassing enough. I wasn't doing it again. I kicked Cindy's ass to get my bra back."

He chuckles. "Good girl."

"She didn't mess with me after that, but everyone still called me Boobzilla for weeks."

He mashes his lips together. "Kids aren't very creative, are they?"

"No. They suck." We're quiet for a few seconds. "Just so you know, I didn't confirm or deny my friends' guesses about your, um, size."

"Thank you, Muffin. That mystery belongs to you."

I snicker and stare out the window.

"Uh, just to be clear," Griff says. "Your brother and I *never* did weird shit like whipping it out and comparing ourselves."

"Gross." I stick out my tongue and gag. "I'm not surprised. Remy's so convinced that he's God's gift to women, I can't see him bothering to compare himself to anyone." I shiver with revulsion. "But don't worry—I've overheard some of the dingbats he likes to bang yapping about his 'stallion status.'" I lean forward and pretend to retch. "I needed a lobotomy after that."

Griff chokes and pounds his fist against his chest. "Shit, that's a disgusting thing for a sister to hear."

"Thank you! Sheesh!" I throw my hands in the air.

When we finally pull into my driveway, Griff asks me to wait and hurries to open my door, offering his hand.

"Thanks." I slide onto the sidewalk and stare up at Griff. "For listening to that and not making me feel bad. I never told anyone the Cindy Adams story." I roll my eyes. "I mean everyone in sixth grade knew, but..."

He leans down and brushes a kiss to my forehead. "I never told anyone the flagpole story," he whispers.

"Not even Remy?"

He shrugs and looks away. "He had enough going on. I'm sure he heard kids say it, but I just pretended I didn't know what they were yapping about."

"He would've killed them for making you uncomfortable."

"Yeah, and he didn't need to be in trouble." He glances at the back door. "Let me grab your stuff."

I'm keenly aware of him behind me as we walk up the porch steps and I slide my key into the front door's lock and open it.

"Where do you want this?" He lifts the vase snuggled in one arm.

"I'll put them in the kitchen for now." I take the arrangement from him and move into the dining room.

"Backpack and dress?" he calls out.

"By the stairs."

I set the roses on the counter. I should probably give them fresh water before bringing them upstairs to my room.

"Hey." Griff comes up behind me and rests his hands on my hips. "Can we talk for a sec?"

The grave undercurrent in his tone stops me from fussing with the roses. "Yeah, of course." My stomach rumbles. "Can we talk while we eat?"

"Sure." He rubs his hand over his chin.

It's almost noon, and I don't feel like cooking. In the fridge, I find the leftover cold cuts from yesterday's platter. I slap a few pieces of ham and cheese between two slices of bread and slide it in the toaster oven.

"Are you hungry?" I ask Griff.

He slides his gaze over my body. "I could eat."

I turn toward the tray.

"I'll have what you're having," he says quickly.

When we're seated at the table, I bite into my ham and cheese melt. *Oh, that's so good.*

Griff picks at the crust of his bread. "How do you feel today?"

"Me?" I chew faster, swallow, then take a sip of orange juice. "My head hurts a little, and I'm starving, but otherwise, great."

"Good."

I set my sandwich down and stare at him. "Why do you keep asking me that?"

He lifts his shoulders and won't quite meet my eyes. "I worry about you."

I flip through the events of last night and this morning, finally landing on the girls poking fun at me. How do I even word the question hovering in the front of my brain?

"Griff?" I can't do this over ham and cheese melts. Pushing my chair away from the table, I stand and step closer to him.

He leans back and tilts his head toward me. "What?"

I slide myself between his knee and the table, perching on his leg. His mouth tips into a smile and he curls his arm around my back, fully pulling me into his lap. "What's up, Muffin?"

"The girls said there was..." *Why is this so awkward after we shared such embarrassing stories in the car?* "Blood on the sheets. Did I...? Is that why you keep asking if I'm okay?"

He blows out a quick breath. "Yeah. I wanted to make sure I didn't hurt you. But I didn't want to freak you out either." One corner of his mouth tilts into a sexy smirk and he holds two fingers in the air, moving them in a crude gesture. "I didn't think I went at you that hard, but..."

Heat explodes over my cheeks. "You didn't hurt me," I whisper. "You need to be sure I can handle all of you, right?"

His breathing picks up, and he grazes his knuckles over my cheek. "You'll take me fine. When you're one hundred percent ready here"—he taps the side of my head— "and here." He slides his hand between my legs and strokes his fingers against my center.

Feeling brave, I reach down and rub my hand over the rapidly growing bulge in his jeans. "The sheets...that's *why* they started asking me about you."

He sucks in a sharp breath. "Careful, Muffin."

"You made me feel good last night. *So, so* good." I glance at the clock in the hallway. "Remy probably won't be back—"

"No." The desire burning in his eyes dials down to a simmer. "I need to talk to you about something before he gets home." He carefully circles my wrist with his fingers and pulls my hand away from his erection.

"What?" All the playfulness between us vanishes. Whatever he wants to tell me seems too serious for me to be sitting in his lap.

Carefully, I slide into the chair next to him and drag it close enough for our knees to touch.

"I didn't want anything to overshadow your prom." Griff glances away for a moment, then turns to me with a smile that looks more pained than joyful. "But it's been killing me not to share this with you."

An uncomfortable sensation slides down my spine. Griff's trying to appear cheerful, but it feels *off*. As if he's trying to talk *himself* into believing whatever he's about to share is positive.

"Okay," I answer with a slight hesitation to my tone. "You're not really selling it, though."

"No, no. In the long run, it's going to be good for us." He nods once, still looking like he's trying to convince himself. "Very good."

Still not feeling reassured. "What is it?"

He turns so he's fully facing me and curls his hands around mine. Now there seems to be more genuine excitement lighting up his eyes.

Why is only anxiety churning my stomach?

"This will sound wild, but I was approached to appear on a reality show about underground fighters—"

"What?" I squeal and throw myself forward and wrap my arms around his neck. "That sounds amazing. Wow...how did that even happen?"

"One of the producers saw some of the videos I've done for Sully's gym." He shrugs and ducks his head, but a smile still flickers over his lips. "I guess she thought I'd be a good fit."

I've spent more time than I'd ever admit out loud watching those thirst traps Griff's filmed to help promote his friend's gym. None of the ones I've watched had much to do with fighting. "But they're workout videos. How'd she know you fight too?"

He frowns for a second. "A lot of them are sparring videos where Remy and I discuss technique and stuff."

"Oh." A nervous giggle slips out of me. "I skip the ones that include Remy." A streak of boldness overtakes me, and I stare him dead in the eyes. "I wasn't watching for the fitness tips."

I swear an actual blush creeps over his cheeks. "No? What were you watching them for?"

"You." I reach for him and press my palm against his chest. He curls his fingers around my wrist and leans in, brushing a soft, ticklish kiss against my pulse point.

"I like that," he murmurs against my skin.

My heart flutters. *What were we talking about?*

"Tell me more about the show?" I prompt.

He sits straighter but keeps his hand on mine. "They offered me a spot on a new show. They're the real deal. They have a bunch of network reality shows."

"So, it'll be on television? Not some obscure website or app?"

"Yup."

"Griff, is that safe? Those shows push drama for ratings. I know the fights at The Castle aren't 'legal' but at least you have rules."

"This has rules." He stabs his fingers through his hair. "Trust me, I went through pages and pages of the rules in the contract."

"Wait. A contract?" I slip my hand out of his grasp. "This is a done deal?" There's more he isn't sharing. I feel it in my soul.

"It looks like it." He glances away. "I don't have exact dates yet."

"Dates? For what?"

"When I'll be away."

"Away?" I sit back in my chair with a thud. "For how long?"

He looks me right in the eyes. "Up to eight weeks."

"Eight weeks...Two *months*?" I fight to calm myself. This is important to Griff. Huge for him. "Well, okay. I guess I'll be getting adjusted to college and—"

"Shooting could start as early as the beginning of the summer."

That soon? "But...you'll be here for my graduation, right?"

He doesn't look away. No, Griff touches his fingers to my

chin and his steady gaze remains focused on me. "I'm not sure. Probably not," he says gently.

"But it's my graduation," I insist, waving my hands around in frustration. "They'll let you leave for something like that, right?"

"No. The set's locked down. I'll be able to call you once a week, but—"

"Once a week?" Tears sting my eyes. I work hard to swallow the lump threatening to close off my throat.

Then the truth rattles into me like a rusty shopping cart to the shins.

This is already in motion. It didn't happen overnight. It had to be planned way in advance. Griff signed papers and has details.

All without ever saying a word to me.

"How long have you known about this?" I ask with a chilling calmness.

"A while," he admits.

"Since before we got together?"

He runs his hand over the back of his neck. "Ah, officially? Or unofficially?"

"I don't believe you." Do I really mean so little to him? "How could you consider something so big and not even mention it to me?"

"I wasn't sure I was going to do it at first. I needed to arrange some things. Make sure Remy would be okay without my help at the—"

"Wait, so Remy already knows?"

"Molly, we're partners in The Castle. I can't just up and leave without—"

"And what am I? Your dimwitted girlfriend who's still in high school? The one you don't have to tell about monumental decisions?"

"No! Molly, we—"

"*'Officially'* we've been friends a lot longer than we've been dating, or at least I thought we were friends. I would've been excited for you." A painful wave of embarrassment almost knocks me out of my chair. "How could you not tell me at all?"

He scowls and genuinely seems puzzled.

"Wow." I draw out the word with as much sarcasm as I can gather. "I see how it is. We're *not* really friends. My opinions don't matter. You expect me to accept all your decisions."

"Calm down—"

Those two words are a lit match tossed on the gasoline in my veins. "Don't tell me to calm down!" I jump out of my chair so fast, it skids backward several inches. "Eight weeks is almost the entire summer. I might already be starting classes by the time you get back."

"It'll be okay." He stands and reaches for me, but I dodge to the side, out of his grasp.

"No, it won't." Pressure builds behind my eyeballs. *No, no, no.* I can't cry in front of Griff. I *won't.*

"Can you go?" I point toward the door.

"What?" Shock twists his face and raises his voice. "No."

"I don't want to talk anymore." The tip of my nose stings. I push past Griff. "I'm tired."

"Molly."

I can't look at his face or I'll cave.

I all but run for the staircase, praying he won't chase me.

He's leaving.

He's been lying to my face for weeks.

Crying in front of him—acting like a baby when he already has so little respect for me—that's unacceptable.

I gather my humiliation and hold onto it tight all the way up the stairs. Once I'm in the safety of my room, I quietly close the door, and burst into tears.

All by myself.

Griff

Despair wraps around my chest as I watch Molly run up the

stairs, fighting off tears. She didn't want me to see, but I know my girl. Every sign that she was about to cry was written on her face and ripping up her voice.

A magnetic force tugs my body toward the staircase, instinct to go after her and say anything that will chase away her tears.

To repair the damage I caused.

Why didn't I tell her sooner? She was happy for me at first—before she realized I'd been lying to her for so long.

"So, how'd that work out for you?" Remy steps out of the kitchen with an angry scowl twisting his face, and nods toward the stairs.

I shouldn't be surprised he caught some of our conversation. Or hell, maybe he's listened in on the whole disaster. "Not great, but thanks for showing up to gloat."

"I warned you to tell her."

I blow out a long, annoyed breath. "I think she would've been pissed no matter *when* I told her."

"Eh." He lets out a sharp mocking sound. "I dunno about that."

"Yeah, because you're some sort of relationship expert?"

"Maybe not." He tilts his head toward the stairs and walks around the table to stand in front of me. "But I know my sister pretty damn well."

"Then get out of my way so I can go talk to her." I step toward him, and he blocks my path.

"No." He lifts one hand in a *stop* gesture but doesn't touch me. "Let her cool off."

"Are you fucking serious?" I slap his hand away.

"Go home," he insists in a lethal tone. "Give her some breathing room."

The stubborn part of me wants to tell him to *fuck off*. Stay out of our relationship. But deep down, I know he's right. There's no way I'm giving him the satisfaction of saying that, though. His ego's big enough.

"Fine." I lift my chin in stubborn defiance. "Just tell her—"

"No, you'll tell her yourself. *Later.*"

"Remy," I plead. "You know the only reason I considered this is to give us—"

"I understand why you think it's a good idea." Above us, the pipes screech and water rushes through the house's ancient system. Remy tips his head back, staring at the ceiling for a few seconds.

I follow his gaze and try not to picture Molly wet and naked in the shower. Or think of her last night, all cute in the little shower cap and nothing else while I ran my hands over her slick body.

"She actually loves your dumb ass for some reason," he finally says in a sharp voice that snaps me out of my showering-with-Molly fantasy.

"Thanks," I grumble. "You know I love her too."

He dips his chin in agreement. "Being away from you for that long probably seems like an eternity to her right now." He shrugs. "Give her some time to digest the information. It's a pretty big secret you kept from her. "

How did I *not* anticipate the damage keeping a secret like that would cause? Of course Molly feels betrayed.

I just hope I haven't fucked things up beyond repair.

Molly

CHAPTER THIRTY-ONE

Molly

Later, when I'm calmer and I'm sure Griff isn't around, I venture downstairs. Stillness fills the house. There's no chatter from the television or music humming out of the speakers.

A steady *thwack, thwack, thwack* from the backyard echoes as I enter the kitchen. I stop at the sink and fill a glass of water, take a few sips, then head outside.

Remy's in the back corner of the yard—where our grandmother used to keep her most prized flowers.

After she died, no one had the skill or heart to maintain the garden. Remy keeps saying he wants to clear it out, but he never has the time.

I stop a few feet away and watch him wrestle with an overgrown hydrangea bush. "Remember Grandpa used to say the garden was so pretty because the flowers were afraid to disappoint Nana?" I say softly.

Remy chuckles and snips a brown, hollow sprig. "I think he was onto something." He stops messing around with the bush and sets the clippers on a large rock Nana used as a bench before she got so thin sitting on it hurt her "old bones," as she used to say.

"How are you doing, kid?"

The stubborn part of me doesn't want to confide in Remy about my fight with Griff. And maybe a little bit of me also wants to protect Griff from my brother's wrath. Or I want to protect our relationship from Remy's criticism.

I shrug and don't say anything.

"You can tell me." Concern and patience shine in Remy's blue eyes. Of course, he already knows Griff's plan. He's known for a while.

And never said anything to me.

"A heads-up that my boyfriend was planning to get beat up on television all summer would've been nice." I cross my arms over my chest and glare.

He releases a slow breath and wipes the back of his hand over his forehead. "It wasn't my information to share."

"That's a weak excuse, Remy."

"Did you have fun at prom?" he asks. "Until all the stuff with Kyla later."

"Why does it matter?"

"It matters. It's something you were looking forward to."

"Prom was great. We had a lot of fun." Especially *after* the dance. Alone in our hotel room. My skin warms, and I look away from Remy. "But now I find out the whole time he had this big secret he was hiding." How long has Griff *actually* known?

"He wasn't hiding it," Remy says. "He was trying to find the right time to tell you." He lifts his gaze to the sky. "As much as it nauseates me to admit it, you're the only person that could stop him."

"Is that why he waited until he'd already signed a bunch of papers and couldn't back out?"

Remy shifts his gaze to me again. This time his eyes are wide with surprise. "I didn't realize it was finalized. I think *I've* been hoping he might decide not to do it myself."

"Oh." For some reason, that admission steals the wind out of my anger at Remy. "Really?"

"Of course." He forces a cocky grin onto his face, but it doesn't quite sit right. "I depend on him for a lot of stuff."

As if he won't miss Griff. "That's it?"

"No," he says with exaggerated patience. "But I can't even guilt him about abandoning me because he went behind my back and asked Dex for help while he's gone. Before he even told *me* he was considering this."

If I wasn't still stung over everything, I might laugh at Remy's indignant tone. "Good."

"You two will be fine," Remy says.

I sniffle, hating this so much. "It feels like we just...we barely got to be a couple out in the open—"

Oh, shit. Too late, I realize what I just admitted.

"You think I didn't know you two were up to something?" Remy chuckles.

Oooh, that's right. Griff said Remy tried to set him up with those girls on purpose. I should be furious with him, but it seems insignificant now.

"I don't care," Remy continues. "But I wish he hadn't felt like he had to sneak around. You're not a secret to be kept."

"He didn't make me feel that way." Not too much anyway. "You're important to him, and he didn't want to wreck your friendship if you went all crazy big brother."

"Yeah, I know," he answers in a dry tone. "Am I really that awful?"

"You've been surprisingly chill."

He runs his hands through his hair like he's having some internal battle. "He doesn't *want* to be away from you all summer. You realize that, right? He's not running *away* from you —he's trying to run *toward* a future for the two of you."

I sniffle, hating how pathetic I sound. "What do you mean? How?"

"He didn't tell you?"

Shame crawls over my skin. "We didn't get into a lot of details."

"There's a cash prize if he makes it to the final four." He frowns and cocks his head. "Or final two? I don't remember." He waves it off as if it's not important. "It's a lot of money, though. More than he can make restoring cars in Johnsonville."

"But I don't *want* him to put himself in danger and say it's for us. You said Grandpa left me money for school. I'll graduate and find a good job." I wish I *felt* as confident as I sound. "Together, we'll be fine."

"That's not how Griff operates. He'll never accept sponging off of you." He tips his head back and runs his hand over the top of his head. "Christ, he barely wanted to take the small amount of money Gramps left him."

"Why? Nana and Grandpa loved Griff."

"Yeah, they did. And that's how I convinced him to accept it. Then we turned around and bought The Castle with that money."

"You have to have earned that back by now." For a while, it seemed like they hosted fight nights there every weekend.

"Yes and no. It's...a lot." Remy shakes his head. "What I'm trying to say is, Griff doesn't have a family who gave him any kind of head start." He pulls a disgusted face. "If anything, his parents left him in a deficit. With his mom's issues, she's basically an emotional *and* financial vampire. He barely got to be a kid at all."

"As bad as Dad is, we had Mom for a little while. And our grandparents," I whisper in agreement.

Remy nods. "I'm not saying this so you'll throw him a pity party. I want you to have some context. As hard as it's been to maintain, Nana and Gramps left you and me with *something*—the bar and the house. If I wasn't so stubborn and sentimental, I could sell the bar." He glances over my shoulder toward the house. "The house...that's something you and I will have to talk about when you're older."

Sell our grandparents' house? Pain squeezes behind my eyes. So many happy memories live between those walls. How can Remy even suggest we sell it?

"You don't want to live with me forever, do you?" Remy cocks an eyebrow as if he's reading my mind.

"Sure." I force some teasing cheer into my voice. "Griff and I will get married. He'll move in here and you can be the manny to our kids."

He rumbles with laughter. "Male nannies get paid, little sis. I ain't working for free."

At least he didn't freak out about his future nieces and nephews. "I don't know. I haven't thought that far ahead."

"Right, because it's not your job to worry about houses and finances right now." He steps closer and lowers his voice. "Your job is to finish school and go to college. Your brother's job is to start working smarter instead of harder."

"I hope that means less fighting, not *more*. I worry about you getting brain damage." And now I'm right back to fretting over *Griff*. "What kind of reality show is this, anyway? Isn't the point of your underground fights to keep them *underground*? Not bleed on television?"

He shrugs. "Lots of guys have come up that way. Do what they can, earn some money, then turn legit."

Turn legit? Like travel all over, fighting professionally? "Is *that* what Griff wants?"

"I didn't think so. But I don't know what they promised him."

It finally occurs to me that for the first time in their long friendship one of them made a huge decision without the other's input.

"You okay?" Remy asks.

"I guess so."

"Good." He blows out a breath. "I'm going to miss him too. And I'm worried about him." He glances at the hydrangeas and almost seems on the verge of changing the topic.

"Worried? Why?"

"I doubt it's only a reality show about guys training for a fight. Those shows thrive on drama. All the emotional highs and lows force viewers to take a side and get them invested in watching every single week." He crosses his arms over his chest. "Watching a bunch of guys prep for fights every episode will get boring quick."

For the first time since I learned about it, I realize Griff has the potential to be exposed to thousands, if not hundreds of thousands, of women who will fall for his looks without caring one bit about what a good man he is on the inside.

I don't *want* to share my boyfriend with the world.

I don't want to lose him.

"They like to cast unstable people in those shows and manufacture drama by fucking with the contestants' heads," Remy continues, oblivious to the new fears invading my mind. "The kind of behavior Griff hates. He's been ducking and weaving away from that kind of shit his whole life."

Shame washes over me. I've only been thinking of myself and *my* insecurities. Not what participating in the show might cost *Griff.* If he really wants to do this, he'll need my support.

"If you're done abusing the hydrangeas, do you think you could take me to the store and then drop me off at Griff's?" I have to see him and actually listen to him this time.

Remy drills me with an unreadable stare. "Why?"

"So I can apologize and let him finish telling me about the show."

"Okay." He snorts. "But promise me you'll make him apologize to *you* for keeping it under wraps for so long first."

My desire to see Griff is so overwhelming, I'll agree to pretty much anything right now. "Deal."

Molles

CHAPTER THIRTY-TWO

GRIFF

How the fuck am I going to fix this with Molly? I didn't want to ruin her prom, so instead, I ruined the day *after* prom. *Smooth.*

I can't lose her.

I don't think I can back out of the show either.

Worse, I don't *want* to back out of the show. I need to explain to her that this is a once-in-a-lifetime opportunity for me. For *us.*

After leaving Molly, I stop at Strike Back and work out my frustration in the gym. Sweaty, exhausted, and no more sure how to work through this than I was before, I return to my place and hop in the shower.

As I step out to dry off, a steady thumping echoes through my apartment. I shut off the fan and step into the hallway.

Thump. The sound is coming from my front door.

I wrap a towel around my waist and run my hands through my wet hair. Whoever it is will have to wait a fucking minute. I hurry into my bedroom and slip into a clean pair of gym shorts.

Thump. Plastic rustles. Another thud.

"Be right there!" I shout. Why can't this impatient asshole take a hint and get lost? I don't even bother to look and see who it is, just fling the door open.

Molly. On my doorstep, holding two big colorful reusable grocery bags. Wearing tight black leggings and a shoulder-baring cropped black sweatshirt with pink skulls and flowers all over the front. I couldn't ask for a better surprise visitor.

"Oh, wow." She gasps and lets her gaze roam over my torso, then lower. "I brought dinner, but there you are, looking like dessert."

"What?" I laugh and grab the bags out of her hand. "How'd you get here?"

"Remy dropped me off." She steps inside, her curious gaze darting all over the place.

"He let you carry all this shit up here by yourself?" I jerk my head toward the kitchen, indicating she should follow me.

"Nooo," she answers slowly. "He brought the bags upstairs and *then* I told him to get lost."

Wish I'd seen *that*. "No you didn't."

"Believe what you want."

I hoist the bags on the counter and peer inside one of them.

"No peeking." She presses her arm over the top of the bag, flattening the sides down to obscure the contents.

Warm herbs and spices tease my nose—a scent that could only be one thing. My mouth waters in response. "Is there a rotisserie chicken in one of those bags?"

"Maybe." Her serious blue eyes focus on my face. She reaches up and brushes her fingers through my damp hair. "Did I interrupt your shower?"

I'm tempted to say *yes* and invite her to join me, but we have too many things to talk about. "Not really. I was getting out when I heard you pounding on the door."

"I tried knocking like a civilized person at first."

"I should've given you a key." I pull open the kitchen drawer closest to the door where I keep a bunch of crap and locate the spare key. "Remy has one somewhere. But you should have your own." I hold it out to her, but she just stares at it.

"Really?" She slowly reaches for the key dangling from my fingers. "You're...okay with that?"

I reel in my arm, forcing her to step closer. "What're you going to do? Sneak in here and steal my collection of gym shorts?"

She drops her gaze to my groin. "Never. They look *way* too good on you."

Nope. Can't let those curious, big blue eyes distract me.

I hold out the key to her again. "Yes, I want you to have it. I trust you."

She curls her fingers around the key. "Thank you."

"So, what are you making?" I gesture to the bags on the counter.

"Well, it depends on what kind of cookware you own." She bites her bottom lip. "If you have a baking dish, I thought I'd make buffalo chicken enchiladas. If not, it's going to be soft chicken tacos."

Laughing, I lean over and open one of the bottom cabinets. "We're in luck because the first option sounds awesome." I pull out a heavy, green glass baking dish and set it on the counter. "Will that work?"

"Yup." She grabs it and sets it on the other side of my oven, then starts unpacking the bags, neatly laying everything out over my counters and kitchen table.

"Let me grab a shirt, then I'll be back to help you."

Lost in thoughts of meal prep, she only nods at me. Her eyes dart around as if she's trying to figure out where I store everything.

"Silverware in there." I point to a drawer next to the stove. "Dishes up there. I have a frying pan and a saucepan for cookware down there." I point to a lower cabinet next to the stove.

"Perfect."

Chuckling to myself, I hurry into the bedroom and grab the first clean shirt I find. I peer in the mirror next to my closet and run my fingers through my hair, taming a few spiky pieces.

Molly's in my kitchen, making dinner for us. Why am I fucking with my hair?

I thought for sure I'd screwed things up with us before. But she's here. I hate that it seems to be some sort of apology dinner she's putting together, though. She's not the one who needs to apologize. I am.

The scent of sizzling onions greets my nose in the hallway. Molly's humming to herself and flitting around my tiny kitchen like she owns it. I lean on the doorframe and watch her for a few seconds. She stripped off the sweatshirt and draped it over the back of a chair, leaving her in a tight pink tank top and black leggings.

How am I supposed to leave her for two months?

Because hopefully when I get back, I'll have enough money to take care of us for *years. Short-term pain for long-term gain.*

"Smells good," I say.

She turns and smiles.

"Need help?"

"Sure." She waves her hand over the short assembly line of fixings in a neat row on my counter. "We're going to spread that mixture in the tortillas, stuff them with cheese, chicken, and the veggie mix, then roll 'em up and nestle them in the baking dish."

"Sounds easy enough." I move closer. "Which end do you want me at?"

She studies the ingredients, as if she's really concerned about what point in the process my skills will be most valuable.

"Hmm...how about I'll do the spreading and you do the stuffing."

"Happy to stuff your tacos anytime, Muffin." I flash a dirty smile at her.

She attempts a stern side-eye, but the corners of her mouth twitch. "En-chil-a-das." She pronounces each syllable slowly.

"Even better." I pick up the spoon and run my gaze over her body. "Where are we smearing this again?"

"Not on me," she scoffs. "It has hot sauce in it."

"Okay, yeah. Let's definitely keep that away from our sensitive parts."

"All right, funny guy." She nods at the spoon in my hand. "You spread, I'll stuff."

"Works for me." I dip the spoon in the orange mixture and smear it over a softened corn tortilla, then pass it to Molly.

While I'd probably sloppily toss everything together, throw it in the oven, and hope for the best, Molly artfully arranges each layer, then neatly rolls each enchilada and carefully places them seam-side down in the baking dish.

"Kinda feeling like a slacker here." I wave the spoon at her after handing over the final tortilla.

"Yours is the tastiest step of the process, so it's important." She pours buffalo sauce over the enchiladas, sprinkles more shredded cheese, and drizzles blue cheese dressing over the whole thing.

"It looks good just like that," I say.

She wiggles her fingers over the top of the dish like she's the prettiest witch, casting a delicious spell. "But we want the cheese to get all melty, gooey, and bubbly."

"That *does* sound better." The dish has to be heavy, so I grab it before she does. She lowers the oven door and heat blasts over us. "Huh. Who knew the oven actually works?" I slide the pan onto the middle rack.

"I'm as shocked as you are." She pats the top of the stove like it's a dog she's rewarding for sitting on command.

"How long?"

She taps her watch. "I'm setting my timer for fifteen minutes."

Good. That gives us time to clear up a few things. "Let's talk." I wrap my hand around hers and tug her over to the table.

She chooses the chair wedged into a spot between the stacked washer/dryer combo in the corner and a window that looks out onto the parking lot. I grab the empty laundry basket in the middle of the table, set it on the floor, then sit across from her.

She's so solemn as she rests her elbows on the table and clasps her hands in front of her. "I'm sorry I cut you off earlier."

I hold up one hand to stop her apology. "*I'm* sorry." I reach across the table and rest my hand over hers. "You are *so* important to me, Molly. Please, don't doubt that." I blow out a long breath, trying to arrange my words in the right order. "I didn't mean to make the decision without talking to you about it. I...I'm not used to asking permission—"

"You don't need my permission." She squeezes my hand and rubs her thumb over my knuckles. "But I wish you'd told me sooner."

So do I. She's the first *person I should've told.* But thank fuck she's willing to listen now. "There's a cash prize if I make it to the final four. That's the main reason I said yes. The only reason, really."

"You don't want to get a manager to book big fights for you and turn into a professional UFC fighter?"

Is that what I want? "Not really."

Disappointment slides over her face. Was she hoping for a yes or a no to that question?

"I learned to fight out of necessity," I explain, without diving into gory details. "I've had some formal training here and there—"

"Griff, I can count on one hand how many fights you've lost."

"Yeah, that's *here*. Backwoods New York. Against little punks with more money than motor skills."

"You're selling yourself short," she argues. "You're disciplined. Quick on your feet. Strategic."

"You want to be my manager?" I tease.

"No." She taps my hand. "Go on."

"I'd like to see what I can do against other skilled fighters."

"Remy's not enough of a challenge?"

A huff of exasperation eases out of me. "We're too aware of each other's weaknesses. Besides, I hate...he's my best friend. Even when he has it coming, making him bleed kinda sucks."

"Aww," she sighs.

"Don't tell him I said that." I turn serious again. "I want the money for *our* future, Molly. Yours and mine."

Her lips slowly curve. "What kind of future?"

"Any one you want." I already know what I want. *Her.*

She seems to turn that over in her mind. "I'll have that internship this summer. When I'm done with school, I should be able to find a decent job."

"Yeah, and I'd like you to be able to go to school without worrying about how the tuition's gonna get paid, or buying your books, or any of that other stuff that might distract you." The corner of my mouth slides up. "I need you to get good grades so you'll have your pick of job offers."

"I can't ask you to do that."

"You're *not* asking. That's what couples do."

"What do *you* want, Griff?"

"You."

She shakes her head. "What do you want to *do*?"

I take a deep breath and let it out slowly. "I want to buy Jerry's garage when he retires. We joked around about it, but Ella's got her welding cert, now. She could be a big help at the shop. So can Eraser. Vapor does solid auto body work—"

Something that looks like relief passes over her face. "So you want to make it a family business?"

"Yeah, why not? If I can't help my friends, what's the point of any of this?"

"What about me? What can I do?"

"Fit us all for hearing aids when we go deaf from listening to Eraser's shitty music all day long?" I shrug.

"You're terrible." Her watch buzzes and she pushes away from the table to stand.

"I've got it. It was too heavy for you to put in cold—I definitely don't want you lifting that pan when it's three-hundred-and-seventy-five degrees."

She stays put but doesn't sit again.

I grab a dishtowel and lower the oven door. A cloud of steam rushes out and mists my face. "Fuck, that's hot." I swipe the towel over my forehead and grab the dish by the closest handle and drag it out, then set it on top of the stove.

"Griff, what if you meet someone else?" Molly asks in a small voice.

"What?" I turn so fast, the edge of the still-open oven door sears my calf. "Ow, fuck!" I kick the door closed with a hard bang.

"Are you okay?" Molly asks.

"I'll be fine." I twist to look at my leg. A small red line's seared my skin. Nothing serious. "Now what are you talking about?"

"On the show."

"Uh, it's gonna be ten or eleven other dudes, Molly." I open the top cabinet and pull down what I hope are two clean plates. To be safe, I rinse them off in the sink. "In case you haven't noticed, I'm only interested in one specific woman—*you*."

"You said the producer was a woman."

"Trust me, I'm not her type and she's not mine." I glance over my shoulder. "You gonna show me how to dish this out? I don't want to mess up all the cheesy goodness."

"Oh." She laughs and hurries over.

I hand her a spatula, then slip my arm around her waist and lean down. "I don't want anyone else. The whole time I'll be away, all I'll be thinking about is coming home to you."

She nods and slides the spatula under a layer of cheese and sauce. "But it's a television show. You'll probably meet lots of people. You're so charming, and sexy. You'll have lots of fans. Older, experienced, sophisticated..." She squeezes her eyes shut and clutches the spatula tight in her hand. "I don't know."

I kind of get where she's coming from. "You don't think I'm worried you'll meet some college boy who'll sweep you off your feet?"

"What?" She sets the spatula down on the counter so hard, bits of cheese and sauce splatter against the Formica. "That's crazy."

I shrug and poke my fork into the enchilada. "No crazier than what you said." I shift my gaze to her face. "You're smart. Beautiful. You might meet other guys and realize you can do a lot better than a greasy gearhead who knocks people around for fun."

"You really think that?" she whispers.

"You're eighteen," I say as gently as possible, even though the thought of losing Molly makes me want to carve my insides out.

She bites the inside of her cheek. "Nana and Grandpa were sixteen and twenty when they met. And she said she knew she wanted to marry him even then."

The corners of my mouth turn up. "I know. He also wanted her to finish college before they got married."

"I'm going to college." She picks up the spatula and thrusts it into the enchiladas, scooping two and dropping them on a plate. She dishes out another one, grabs both plates and returns to the table.

I grab the silverware and join her. "That's all I get?" I wave my fork at my dish. "Two?"

"You can have as many as you want." She stabs her fork into her food and touches the tip of her tongue to a small amount. "It's hot," she cautions.

"You're hot," I mutter, digging into my own food.

Her lips quirk but she keeps her gaze focused on her plate.

The food's so good, for the next few minutes, I just concentrate on shoving it in my mouth, then grab seconds.

"You can take the leftovers to work if you've got a microwave there," Molly says.

"Leftovers?" I snort. "You better grab what you want now before I eat it all."

"You like it?"

I wave my fork over my almost-clean-again plate. "Ya think?"

She coughs and waves her hand in front of her face. "I might've dumped too much Frank's in it."

"Never too much hot sauce." I turn and open the fridge, then pull out a can of seltzer and a can of Coke.

"You keep black cherry seltzer here?" she asks.

I shrug. "I drink it from time to time." Because it reminds me of *her*.

She pops the tab and takes a quick sip. "Thanks."

When we're finished, we stare at each other for a few beats.

Molly jumps up and grabs the dishes. "I don't want to leave you with a mess."

"Stop." I stand and take the plates. "You brought the food *and* made it. I'll take care of this."

"I'm going to run to the bathroom, then." She slips her sweatshirt off the back of her chair and shrugs it on.

By the time I finish clearing the table, she still hasn't returned. I find her in the living room, pacing in front of my couch.

"What's wrong?"

Her gaze snaps to mine. "I'm sorry I didn't let you tell me about the show before. Will you tell me now?"

We'll make it through this. She understands. "Yeah, Muffin. I'll tell you what I know."

A brief smile flickers over her lips.

I lead her to the couch, and she drops into the corner, turning her body to face me. Shit, some of this I'm really not supposed to tell anyone. "I had to sign a thing saying I wouldn't disclose any details, so you can't talk about it to your friends."

Her eyes widen for a second, then she nods. "Okay."

I explain everything I can from the moment Diane found me at Strike Back Studio to the trip I took to the city to sign some papers. I leave out the part about seeing Hope for a will, since I'm still not sure how I feel about it myself.

Molly's quiet and doesn't interrupt but she slowly pulls away from me. She crosses her arms over her middle, shrinking herself into a tight ball.

"That's it," I finally finish.

"You...did a lot and never said a word about it." Her brows knit together. "Jerry will be okay with you taking the time off of work?"

"Yeah, he's kinda psyched I might be on TV." As I say it, her frown deepens. *Fuuuck,* he's another person I told before her. "I had to explain it to him to ask for the time off."

"Do you know *where* you'll be filming?" she asks in a small voice.

"I think it's a house. Sounds like downstate somewhere. Maybe Long Island? They won't tell me, yet."

"And you don't know who else will be living there with you?"

"Not yet."

"Are you nervous?"

I stare at her for a few seconds. "Honestly?"

She nods.

I reach over and rest my hand on her ankle. The time for acting cocky and putting on a good front is over. Molly deserves the truth. And she's probably the only person I can share this with. "Yeah, Muffin. I'm nervous as hell about the whole thing."

Her tense expression softens. She unfolds her arms and reaches for my hand, linking our fingers together.

"You're the *only* person I've admitted that to," I add.

"Remy's worried about you too."

I cock my head. "Really? Afraid I'll get my ass kicked on television and ruin The Castle's rep?"

"No." She scowls but shifts closer to me. Her gaze weighs heavily on my skin. "He's worried the people who run the show will try to fuck with your head. He says that's what they do."

Isn't that a punch to the gut? I thought Remy was just trying to talk me out of the show when he brought that up, but it's obviously bothering him if he talked to Molly about that aspect. "I've been careful what information I've given them." No matter how much I think I've concealed, these people aren't dumb. If they want to dig and find dirt, it won't be hard. "Didn't mention my mom's issues. Not sure they can access my juvenile records. But if they do, there might be info in there about her." I shrug. "That's the only thing they could really use against me. I mean, the underground fights...that's kind of the reason they want me on the show, so it'd be dumb if they made a big deal out of it. The betting on the fights—it's not like that's a shock. Dex warned me not to mention the MC, but why would that ever come up, you know? I'm not in the habit of dropping names for clout."

"Keep your head down. Be friendly but don't think you're going to bond with any of the other guys." Her voice drops into something low and cold-blooded—very unlike my usually sweet Molly. "The minute you do, they'll probably stab you in the back."

I stare at her.

"What?" She lifts her shoulders. "If you're doing this, you need a strategy."

"Thank you." I swallow hard. "For understanding."

"I'm still...upset." She meets my eyes, and fuck if there's not a ruthless edge to her baby blues I've never seen before. What's happening here? "But if we have to spend our first summer as a couple apart, you better win this thing."

"First of many, many summers, baby." I tug on her leg. "Come here."

She carefully shifts away from her corner of the couch and when she's close enough, I drag her into my lap.

Mistake. My body responds immediately to having her snuggled so close. She turns so she's straddling me and rests her hands on my shoulders. "Is this better?"

I groan and slide down a little, taking some of the pressure off my balls. "Yes and no."

"Thank you for such a great prom last night." She drills me with an intense stare. "I really did have a good time. I'm so happy you went with me."

"I loved every minute I spent with you." I trace my finger over her cheek. "Did I tell you how beautiful you looked?"

Her cheeks push into a smile, and she leans into my hand. "You mentioned it."

"Prettiest girl in the room."

"I don't know about—"

"I can't even remember what anyone else was wearing. Just you."

A happy sigh passes her lips.

I jerk forward and press my mouth to hers. My hand cradles the back of her head, dragging her closer.

She sighs a whispery breath and falls against my chest. Our tongues meet and slide against each other. She tastes spicy from the chicken with a hint of her sweetness.

"Oh." She pulls away and covers her mouth. "Do I reek of onions?"

"Fuck no. Get back here." I cup her face and smash my mouth against hers.

She laughs softly, and I swallow each little sound like the greedy fucker I am.

"Griff." She moans and wriggles against me. Her hips start that slow, maddening roll she does when she's in my lap.

Fuck. This time we're alone. In my apartment. My bedroom's only a few feet away. I slide my hands under her butt and plant my feet to lift us off the couch.

Thud. Thud. Thud.

What the fuck?

Molly's so into kissing me, she doesn't seem to hear the knocking at my door. Maybe I'll follow her lead and ignore it too.

"Griff? Honey, it's me." My mother's pleading voice filters through the door. The artificial motherly tone should be an immediate boner killer, but Molly's still grinding in my lap.

I yank my head back, breaking our kiss. "She can see my car in the parking lot." I groan and sit straighter. "I'm sorry."

She braces herself with her hands on my shoulders and slides out of my lap. Her gaze fixes on the boner turning my shorts into a damn circus tent. Having her eyes on my dick isn't resolving the situation.

"Uh." She swipes her tongue over her bottom lip.

Not helping, baby.

"Griff?" *Bang. Bang. Bang.*

Molly frowns. Her desperate eyes ping around the room like she's looking for an escape route.

Of all the motherfuckin' times for Tanya Royal to show up.

"I'll get the door," Molly offers, even though it's clear she'd rather go hide under my bed than deal with my mother. "You go..." She gestures toward my bedroom. "Take care of *that*."

"Thanks." I jump off the couch and pop a quick kiss on her cheek.

Molly

Griff's mom. The last person in the world I want to see or talk to. Especially when Griff and I were in the middle of such an amazing moment.

I check the peephole. Maybe it's some other unbalanced woman shrieking Griff's name out in the hallway?

How would that be better?

Just answer the door!

A gasp catches in my throat as I peer through the tiny fish-eye lens. The haggard woman on the other side looks familiar but...maybe it's the distortion of the peephole or the dirty glass making her look so...bedraggled.

I unchain the lock and open the door. Blinking, I force a smile and try not to show my shock at her disheveled appearance.

"Hi, Mrs. Royal. How've you been?"

Her hard, gaunt face takes on an unpleasant pinch as she stares at me. "What are you doing here, Molly?" As usual, she pronounces my name *Mahllly*, her harsh voice dripping with familiar disdain that I easily ignore.

Mrs. Royal has never liked me no matter how polite I am, how much I smile, or try to find the right things to say. All for Griff's sake. Because she's his mother. He's such a good person, and she gave birth to him, so surely there must be some goodness lurking inside her too? Somewhere way deep down under her awful exterior.

"She's here with me." Griff steps up behind me, resting his hand on my hip—a reassuring touch announcing that he won't let his mother bully or disrespect me. "What do you need, Mom?"

I blow out a relieved breath, thankful he's rescued me so quickly.

She swings another annoyed glance over me, then focuses her glassy eyes on Griff. The stale scent of beer and something more chemical I can't identify crawls up my nose. Griff wasn't kidding about her condition. Death seems to loom over her shoulder.

"Are you going to let me in or not?" she snips.

Griff's reluctance is clear in the way he hesitates to take a step back and open the door wider. He keeps his hand on my hip. "Come in."

He closes the door behind her and shoots an apologetic look at me.

His mom moves slowly but still somehow seems to be in constant motion. She compulsively rubs her hands over her thighs while her gaze darts all over the apartment. Casing it for things to steal and sell?

That's mean, Molly.

Finally, she perches on the edge of the couch. She bounces on the cushion a few times like she can't sit still.

Griff narrows his eyes at her, then sits at the opposite end of the couch.

"Do you want something to drink, Mrs. Royal?" I ask, praying for an excuse to leave.

"Water. Thanks," she answers without glancing my way.

Griff nods and mouths *thank you* to me.

"I'm going away for a bit..." Mrs. Royal murmurs as I turn toward the kitchen.

Bon voyage!

Stop it—that's Griff's mom.

But I can't silence my mean thoughts. Tanya Royal royally *sucks.*

I take my sweet time putting away some of the extra groceries and supplies I brought over but hadn't unpacked yet. Then, I find a glass, fill it with tap water, and return to the living room.

"You can help your mom out, right, baby boy?" Her sickly-sweet voice activates my gag reflex.

Griff flashes a pained frown at me, as if he wishes I'd stayed in the kitchen longer.

I hand the water to his mom, and she sets the glass on the floor, ignoring me.

You're welcome.

Unsure of what to do next, I stand behind the couch, wringing my hands, awkward as a deer on the highway at midnight.

Griff leans back and shoves his hand in his pocket, then pulls out his tattered leather wallet. Hmmm…he definitely didn't have his wallet on him a few minutes ago when I was in his lap. Did he grab it when I opened the door, knowing his mom was here to ask for money?

Discomfort rolls off of him in waves, but I don't think he's looking for my support or even my presence. Since Mrs. Royal hasn't acknowledged me, it shouldn't be rude to duck out of the room again. Skirting around the end of the couch, I dash toward the hallway. It's a small, simple apartment. There aren't many places to hide, so I choose Griff's bedroom. It seems safer than hanging out in the kitchen.

Everything in his room is tidy. Sparsely furnished. A plain wooden chest of drawers leans against one wall. A framed photo of Remy, Griff, and me in my grandparents' driveway sits in a leather tray on top of it. A watch, money clip, pile of quarters, and a bottle of cologne are also in the tray. I pick up the photo and smile. I clearly remember the day it was taken. Griff had just gotten his driver's license. I'm sitting on the hood of my grandfather's truck with Griff and Remy on either side of me. They're grinning like fools, while I seem to be practicing some sullen pout Hayden probably told me would make me look more mature.

Voices from the living room rise, then cut off. A few seconds later, Griff's bedroom door swings open. As soon as our eyes meet, his troubled expression shifts into relief.

"You okay?" he asks.

"Are *you*?"

He nods slowly and closes the door, leaning against it and swiping his hands over his face. "Yeah. I'm sorry about that."

"It's okay. I knew she lived downstairs. Figured I'd run into her eventually." Tentatively, I add, "Is everything all right?"

"No." He pushes away from the door and walks over to me. "What're you looking at?" He takes my hands and turns toward the photo. "Ah, that's one of my favorites."

"Obviously." I take a teasing glance around his bedroom. "It's the only personal decoration in here."

He leans down and presses his lips to my forehead, stopping and inhaling me. "When we have our own place, you can decorate at it any way you want."

"Oh yeah? What if I want every room to be a different shade of purple with glitter accents?"

He chuckles and pulls away. "If it makes you happy, I'm down for a purple house."

My heart flutters. A house with Griff. "I'll be happy as long as we're together."

"Me too." He blows out a long breath and runs his hand through his hair. "I don't have time for this right now."

I try not to flinch at his words. "I can go home."

"No." He rests his hands on my shoulders, gently squeezing. "Not you. Sorry." He slowly jerks his chin toward the bedroom door. Exhaustion seems to dull his movements. "I don't have time for my mother's bullshit."

"Is she okay?"

"I don't fucking know. She wants to move again." He flicks his gaze to the ceiling. "'Get her head on straight,'" he adds in a sarcastic imitation of his mother's voice.

"Where?"

"Jersey Shore?" He shrugs.

Not far enough. "With her boyfriend?"

"Yeah. She says he has a job lined up."

Honestly, this sounds like the best possible news to me. "Are you worried about...?" It feels wrong to ask about his mother's addiction. Even though he's opened up to me about it before, prodding at something that's so painful doesn't seem right.

But he seems to understand exactly what I'm asking. "I don't know. When she was living up north, she did okay." His brows dip. "Actually, she didn't relapse this bad until she moved back." He lets out a humorless laugh. "I'm starting to think being around *me* is her main problem."

"Don't say that." I reach out and squeeze his biceps. "It has nothing to do with you." Unless being around Griff makes his mom realize what a shitty mother she's been and that's what drives her to use. But still, that's no one's fault but Tanya's.

"I know." He taps the side of his head. "In here." He taps his chest. "In here? Not so much."

"Well, *I'm* telling you. You're a good son. You do as much as you can for her." *When she's done so little for you your whole life.* I leave that part unsaid. It seems cruel.

"Maybe that's the problem. I enable her or something." He runs his hands through his hair again. "It doesn't matter. She's going." His lips slide into a pained smirk. "I didn't exactly try to talk her out of leaving. I'll lose the security deposit on her place, but whatever. I probably wasn't getting it back anyway." He snorts. "I'll have to box all her shit and store it somewhere."

"Wait, she's leaving right *now*? And not...taking care of that stuff herself?"

"Nope. Live in the moment. The sea is calling her name." He scrubs his hands over his face. "I'll get it done between my job and all the stuff I'm doing to prepare for the show."

Great, now we've moved on to my second least-favorite topic. "I know your mom doesn't like me, so maybe she won't want me

going through her stuff, but I can help you out after school."
Only because I care about Griff and hate to see him so stressed.

"No." He shakes his head. "No," he says with more force as if
he really hates the idea. "I don't want you doing a damn thing for
her. Most of the stuff I'll probably toss in the dumpster. Anything
sentimental she got rid of a long time ago. Anything of value she's
sold."

"I'm sorry."

"It's not your problem, Molly." His jaw tightens with
stubbornness. "I shouldn't even—"

"Griff, I *love* you." I use my sternest tone. "If I can ease some
of this stress for you, I want to help."

"Maybe." Regret clouds his eyes. "If there's anything left I
need to box and store here, maybe you can help me do that," he
concedes.

"Okay." I rub my hand over his arm. "Maybe she's right and a
change of scenery will be good for her." It'll definitely be good for
Griff not to have to worry about her every day when he has so
many other things to do.

"I hope so."

"Jersey? I guess maybe she'll be closer to you when you're
filming." I swallow hard and try to keep an upbeat tone.

"Christ, I hope not. I didn't even tell her about the show. The
less she knows about what I'm up to, the better."

Ah, that explains why she seemed so surprised to see me. I'm
not even offended he hasn't told his mother about us. He
probably wants to protect me. Out of reassuring things to say, I
wrap my arms around his middle and hug him tight.

He rests his chin on the top of my head and hugs me back.
"Thank you," he murmurs.

All out of words, we stay that way for a long time—saying
nothing but feeling everything.

Molley

CHAPTER THIRTY-THREE

Molly

After I finish my shift at Miller's Farms on the weekends, I've been heading straight to Griff's shop to help him work on my car. Today, I asked my friend Becky to drop me off after we clocked out.

She squints through the windshield, staring at the darkening sky. "Looks like rain. That sucks. I wanted to go to the drive-in tonight."

"What are they showing?" I had *other* plans with Griff tonight, but maybe he and I can go to the drive-in tomorrow.

"Horror double-feature."

"Oooh. I think I'd be too freaked out to watch horror movies in my car." I laugh. "I need a blanket to hide under."

She chuckles. "I thought you liked horror movies?"

"I do. In a controlled environment." I cover my face with my hands and peek between two fingers. "Where I can hide." *Or cuddle close to Griff.*

She laughs harder. "Please tell me you're not planning to quit Miller's after graduation. I know you're starting your internship, but it'll be so boring without you."

A mixture of warmth and sadness spreads through my chest. "No, I'm taking your lead and going to try to work two jobs over the summer. I'll work days at the office and take as many nights and weekends as they'll give me at Miller's." Anything to earn as much money as possible for school and to keep myself occupied so I don't miss Griff while he's away. And whatever free time I have, I plan to help Remy at the bar whether he likes it or not.

"Oh yay!" She bleats a happy little noise. "We should tell Stacy we have the same availability, so she puts us on the schedule together."

That would make the dreary shifts go by faster. "Let's do it." I point to the right. "It's up here."

"I can't wait to see your Chevelle when it's finished." She flips on her blinker and slows the car.

"Me too."

She pulls to a stop in front of the office, and I reach down to hook my arm through the straps of my backpack. "Thank you."

"See you Monday!" She waves as I close the door.

I hitch my backpack over my shoulders and stare at the building. One of the garage bay doors is up. Griff's low rumble reaches my ear. I can't make out the words, but I follow his patient-but-annoyed voice.

At the threshold, I stop. Griff has a car up on the lift and seems to be mounting a tire on a Trans Am. Or at least he's trying to. A man, who I assume is the owner of the car, keeps yammering at Griff while my man's trying to pay attention to his work. Anxiety trickles through me. Doesn't this guy know the garage is dangerous, and he should leave Griff alone to do his job in peace?

Should I interrupt? Maybe draw the man away from Griff so he can finish the job without being annoyed?

"So, this chick is a seven at best, but she's got major attitude," the man says.

"Can't imagine why," Griff mutters.

The man lets out a hearty chuckle. "Right?"

Lines of tension bracket Griff's mouth and crease his forehead as he tightens a bolt.

"We're at the restaurant and she's talking about this movie she wants to see. And I mean, honestly, after dinner, I thought we'd go back to her place."

"Sounds like she wasn't interested," Griff says.

"Yeah, so I ask her about work and she's a nurse, so I make a joke about giving me a sponge bath."

Gross.

"And she gets all offended. So I try again, like, 'Oh do you have access to the good drugs?'" He punctuates that awful question with an equally terrible laugh. "'Can you get your hands on some Oxycodone for us?' And she just…"

I tune out the moronic guy's babbling. The tension in Griff's face shifts from annoyance to anger as the guy keeps joking about illicit painkillers. Given his mom's history, I can't blame him. Griff's fingers grip the wrench so tight, his knuckles turn pale. His arm muscles pop and strain as he cranks another bolt into place.

"I pick up the shaker and ask where does salt come from anyway, and she looks at me like I'm stupid—"

"Google is free, Glen," Griff says through clenched teeth.

I have to say something before Griff beats this guy to death with the wrench. "Salt mines and evaporated seawater," I blurt, taking a few steps closer.

Genuine relief and happiness smooth out the harsh edges of Griff's face when his gaze lands on me. "Molly."

The older man turns around. His cheeks pull into a feral smile as he takes me in. "What's that, young lady?"

"Salt," I say. "The majority comes from salt mines or evaporated seawater." I'm almost positive that's true.

"Look at that." The man points at me. "Now, *she's* a ten. Pretty, smart, *and* polite."

Just listening to this guy makes me want to run home and rinse my ears with bleach. He has to be around my dad's age, if not older, and everything about his tone sounds condescending, not complimentary.

"This is my girlfriend." Griff shoots a hard look at his customer.

"Lucky man," Glen continues, grinning and sliding his pervy gaze up and down my body. "Bet she treats you right." His voice oozes sliminess.

Griff finishes with the tire, adjusts something, then sidesteps Glen. "You want to set your stuff down?" He tilts his head toward the bay where my car's waiting. "I'll be done in a few minutes."

"Okay." I want to kiss him but Glen's watching as if he expects a free show. Instead of a kiss, I settle for squeezing Griff's hand. He seems to sense my unease and returns the gesture.

The rest of the bays are empty, the doors closed. My lips curve when I reach my car. It's come a long way since my birthday. We've replaced or fixed most of the interior. The exterior is all one color now—matte black. I pop the trunk, pull out my coveralls, and fling them over my arm.

I hoist my backpack onto the long counter running along the back wall of the garage. From the other end of the garage, a mechanical whir and clinking breaks the silence. Glen shouts something over the noise. I hope that means Griff's almost done.

While I'm waiting, I step into the coveralls and zip the front. Griff must've organized the items we're using today. I find two shiny side mirrors laid out with a bunch of brackets and tools. Technically, the passenger side wouldn't have had a side mirror, but Griff said adding one or not was up to me, and I'm more interested in safety than historical accuracy.

An engine revs somewhere behind me. The garage door rattles and hums its way into place.

My heart pounds an excited beat. Griff must be finished and on his way to me.

The familiar scrape and scuff of his boots over the concrete echoes through the garage. I spin around. Weariness seems to slow his steps but warmth hovers in his eyes.

"Hey, baby. Sorry about that." He jerks his thumb over his shoulder. "That dude's got the personality of parsley but suffers under the delusion he's a ghost pepper."

I snort, then burst out laughing. "You must really dislike him to come up with something so specific."

He stops in front of me and rests his hands on my hips. "I've had time to think on it since he never shuts the fuck up. Always a bad date story. One of these days I'm going to point out that the common denominator is *him*." He glances over his shoulder again. "But he's a friend of Jerry's..."

"So, you keep your opinion to yourself."

"Pretty much."

My gaze slides to Griff's arms, barely contained by the short sleeves of his button-up shirt with the Jerry's Garage logo on the left side. I wrap my fingers around his biceps. It's like squeezing granite. "Maybe he's intimidated since you're younger and manlier, so he's trying to impress you."

He lifts one eyebrow. "Manlier, huh?"

"You know what I mean." My cheeks heat, and I pull my hand away.

"Get back here." He gathers me in his arms, hugging me tight, and buries his face against my neck. "Been looking forward to seeing you all day."

"Me too."

"How was work?" He kisses my cheek and loosens his hold on me.

"Long. Boring. I'm very excited to spend the rest of the night with you." I lower my voice, hoping he'll take the hint that I mean *spend the night*.

"So am I." He presses a kiss to my forehead. "Would you rather go get dinner instead of working on the car?"

"No, I came to work," I answer quickly. Griff's already done so much of the restoration himself.

"All right."

"Unless you're tired?"

"Nope. Got my second wind as soon as I saw you."

We work steadily, finding the fasteners and removing them

from the door panel. Griff uses a special tool to pry the panel loose.

"The mirrors don't have power functions, so that'll be easier," Griff murmurs. "Hold this for me."

He hands over a gasket and oval-shaped bracket, then grabs one of the mirrors.

"Place the bracket right here." He taps his finger against two perfectly drilled holes along the top of the door. I hold the bracket and mirror while he fastens them tight.

"It's nice having an extra set of hands." He tickles his fingers against the back of my leg once the mirror is secure.

"Yeah? I'm not slowing you down?"

"No." His lips tilt into a smoldering mile. "Distracting me? Yes."

"Distracting how?"

"You're hot in coveralls."

"I'm hot all right." I wipe a bead of sweat from my forehead.

He chuckles and lifts one of the panels, clipping it back into place on the door. I help him reinstall the other fasteners. Then we install the second mirror.

"I think the car is close to being finished." Griff walks around it, slowly studying every inch. "Just need Vapor to work his magic with the paint."

I stare at it and try to visualize what he's seeing. The inside's been transformed, for sure. But it's still missing door handles, and some other essential elements.

"It's hard to see it now," Griff says.

Thunder rattles overhead, and the garage lights dim for a second. Griff tips his head and stares out the window. "Let's clean up and get going. I have my bike. Don't want to get caught in the rain."

"Okay." I shimmy out of the coveralls. The cooler air is a relief on my skin.

I lean into the car to stuff my things in the back seat. "We're going to spend the day here tomorrow, right?"

Griff doesn't answer, but a solid wall of heat presses against my butt and legs. "If that's what you want."

Still bent at the waist and half in, half out of the car, I peer over my shoulder. "I want a lot of things."

He slides his hand under my T-shirt, skimming his fingers along my spine. "Like?"

I crawl onto the wide bench seat in the back of my car. The black, textured vinyl's cool against my palms.

"What are you doing?" Resting his arm on the roof, Griff ducks his head inside.

"Come here." I crook my finger at him, then pat the seat.

One corner of his mouth tilts and he laughs softly. "Okay." He slides into the seat next to me. "Now what?"

"I want to do this." I swing my leg over his and settle into his lap, resting my hands on his shoulders. "And this." I swoop down and slide my lips against his.

"Mmm." He inches lower in the seat and tangles his fingers in my hair while palming the small of my back, holding me in place. "I can get on board with this," he says against my lips.

"When the car's done, can we take it to the drive-in one night?" I run my fingers through his hair and kiss his cheeks.

"Sure." He rubs my back. "We can go in my car, too. Any time you want."

"What about tomorrow night?"

He tilts his head and squints at me. "You've got school Monday morning."

"So?"

For a few heartbeats, neither of us say anything. Then Griff nods. "Okay. Do you know what's playing?"

"Something scary, so I'm going to need you to protect me." I grin and kiss him again.

"I'll do that no matter what."

A blast of thunder rattles outside.

"We better go." Griff squeezes my hip, urging me up.

With a sigh, I twist and roll in a not-at-all graceful way out of the back seat.

"I need to check on things and lock up. Grab your stuff and meet me in the front office."

I nod and hurry through the shadowy garage. Instead of going into the office alone, I stand by the door, waiting for Griff. One by one, the overhead lights wink out. Low lights from the office and the security lights from outside provide a soft glow, so I can make out Griff's form coming toward me.

"Ready?" he asks, zipping up his jacket.

I hoist my backpack on and nod, then follow him into the parking lot.

Outside, the wind picks up, swirling leaves into a quickly passing funnel.

"Shoot." Griff glances up at the sky. "It's supposed to storm. Let's go back to my place. We can drop off the bike, then go out for dinner somewhere." He reaches for my hand.

I curl my fingers around his. "Or we can stay in?"

"Not a lot of DoorDash options around but we can do that too," he suggests.

Food's the last thing on my mind.

At the bike, we put our helmets on.

Thunder crashes and a zigzag of lightning splits the sky.

"Hurry." Griff straddles the bike and I climb on behind him as quick as I can, which isn't fast at all. But he waits until I'm situated to fire up the bike. More bolts of lightning and earth-shaking thunder follow us to Griff's place, but no rain.

Not until Griff makes the turn into his parking lot.

The sky unloads. What feels like buckets of water splash over us. Griff mutters a string of curses and guides the bike to a stop by the sidewalk.

"Go on!" Griff shouts.

My foot slips as I dismount. For a second, I wobble, thrown by the weight of my backpack. Griff's arm shoots out and he catches me around the waist, steadying me.

My wet clothes cling to my skin in the most uncomfortable way as we make a run for the front door of Griff's apartment building.

"Sorry!" he shouts as we tumble into the entrance. "I thought we'd make it home in time." Drops of water glisten on the tips of his hair, and I reach up to brush the wet strands off his forehead.

"It's okay." My nose wrinkles. "I feel gross though."

He holds out his keys to me. "Go on upstairs and get dry. I want to cover my bike and move it to a different spot. You can borrow one of my T-shirts to change into."

"Don't leave me waiting too long." *I plan to change but into something with a whole lot less material than a T-shirt.*

Dear Griff,

Molly

GRIFF

Now that the sky's let loose, the storm rages like a living thing, trying to keep me from Molly. The wind and rain batter my back as I race into my apartment building, splashing through puddles.

Finally, I'm inside, and I slam the door shut behind me.

My phone buzzes and I pull it out of my pocket.

Remy: Is Molly with you?

Me: Yes.

Remy: OK.

He doesn't need more detail than that.

The building's quiet. A sense of relief slides through me as I pass my mother's now empty apartment. I've only heard from her once since she left for Jersey. No news is usually good news where she's concerned.

I stop outside the door to my apartment to unlace my boots and leave them to dry in the hallway. Inside, I find a towel folded on the back of the couch. Assuming Molly left it for me, I grab it and swipe it over my head and face.

"Where you at, Muffin?" I peel my jacket off as I cross the living room into the kitchen. I toss my phone on the counter. The whir of the dryer spinning draws my attention. I open it, strip off my clothes, and toss them in. A bolt of lightning illuminates the kitchen. I take the towel and wrap it around my waist.

I cock my head. No sounds above the wind and rain outside. Where'd Molly go?

Another bolt of lightning brightens everything, blinding in its intensity.

The lights blink out and darkness blankets everything.

"Shit," I grumble, feeling around for the drawer where I keep odds and ends. "Molly, you okay? Give me a second. I'll grab a flashlight or some candles."

Even though I know my place well, moving through it when it's pitch-black isn't the easiest. I fumble my phone off the counter and click the flashlight app on, then carefully sift through the drawer where I usually keep a bright tactical flashlight. Nothing. *Fuck.*

Molly gave me a candle when I moved in. Where'd I put it? *Cabinet.* My fingers brush against the heavy glass jar, almost knocking it on my head. I grab it and rummage through the drawer for a lighter. Once it's lit, I return to the living room.

"Molly? Where you at?"

"In here."

Bedroom.

All my blood heads south.

I hated telling her we had to go earlier when we were tangled up together in the back seat of her car. Even getting caught in the raging storm hasn't stopped my mind from replaying her body pressed up against me over and over.

Now we're alone. In my apartment. And she's in my bedroom. During a blackout.

Every nerve in my body thrums with anticipation.

I cross the threshold and at first can't make out any details. A soft glow from what looks like several small candles on my nightstand provides some guidance. Another flash of lightning illuminates the room.

There she is. Sitting on the farthest edge of my bed, facing the window.

My gaze slips over her bare shoulders. Her long curtain of dark hair spilling down her back obscures my view. Can't tell if she's completely naked or not.

Can't wait to find out.

I set the candle on my dresser and slowly make my way around the bed until I'm standing in front of her. "What are you doing in here all by yourself?"

"Waiting for you." She holds her hand out, inviting me closer.

No, wait, she's handing me a piece of paper.

The corners of my mouth tip up. "What's this?" I take the folded note.

She stretches, resting her hands on the mattress and arching her back, letting me get the full view of the sheer bra and panty set covering almost nothing.

My mouth waters, and I can't stop my gaze from gliding over all her curves. She lifts one leg and rests her foot on the edge of the mattress but angles her knee to obstruct my view.

"Read it." She encourages me.

Read? I'm not sure I remember how. Not when I'm dying to slide my tongue over every inch of her exposed skin.

The paper crinkles as I unfold it.

Molly's girlish print fills the page with a very simple message.

Dear Griff, I'm ready. Please make love to me. Love, Molly

And in case my brain was too scrambled to read the words, she doodled a cherry on its stem and written "yours" with an arrow pointing toward the fruit.

"You said you needed it in writing," Molly teases.

Laughing, I fold the note and set it on my nightstand. I want to laminate it and carry it in my wallet for the rest of my damn life except if anyone ever accidentally saw her sweet, personal note to me, I'd have to carve out their eyeballs.

"Actually, *you're* the one who wanted to put it in writing," I remind her. "But I'm not complaining."

Just thinking of Molly taking the time to write those words and the intention behind them has me harder than a fucking hammer. I reach for her, cup her cheek, and rub my thumb over her bottom lip. "I still want to hear you *say* a certain phrase."

Her skin warms and she glances down. "Griff, will you—"

"Look at me," I demand.

Her chest rises and falls as she slowly drags her gaze to mine. "I want to learn how to come on your cock."

"Fuuuck," I groan, "Yes."

I cup her cheeks with my hands and encourage her to kneel at the edge of the bed, then lean down to press my lips to hers. "Thank you," I whisper.

"I haven't done anything, yet."

"Yes, you have." More than I can put into words.

"Hmmm." She slides her hands over my shoulders and down my chest. My skin's still damp from the rain but my cock's straining against the thick terry cloth towel. Molly cups me and purses her lips. "You really liked hearing me say that."

I grunt out a sound that's meant to be a *yes* but words are too difficult when she's rubbing and exploring. With monumental effort, I shackle my hand around her wrist and stop her.

"I'm going to come if you keep doing that," I warn. "Stand up for me. Let me look at you."

With a slow gracefulness only Molly's capable of, she slides off the bed and stands so close the heat from her skin ripples over mine.

Oh, Christ. In the flickering light, she's extra beautiful. "I wanted to undress you slowly." I slip my fingers under the strap of her bra, playing with it.

"And *I* wanted to surprise you."

"I'm surprised." I can't stop my gaze from roaming over every beautiful inch of her. Even in the dancing golden light, I'm able to see through the sheer material of her bra. Hard pink nipples press against the netting. I step back and soak in every inch. The simple triangle of her pale purple lace underwear leaves her looking both innocent and wicked. *Wait a second.* My gaze zeroes in on the small dots scattered over her underwear. Little red and green embroidered cherries. I lift my eyes to her bra. Same little decoration. How the fuck'd I miss that?

I rub my thumb over one of the little cherries. "You really did plan this night, didn't you?"

"Down to the last detail. Well, except for the blackout." She nods to the little candles carefully arranged into a heart shape on the nightstand. "You just noticed?"

Gently, I place one hand on her hip and cup her breast with my other. "Forgive me. I'm pleasantly overwhelmed here." My thumb brushes over the hard tip of her nipple, and her body jolts.

"You're forgiven," she whispers through shaky breaths.

Her hands settle on my chest. At first, it's as if she wants to push me away but then her fingers curl over my shoulder. Her forehead pinches into a frown and she lowers her lashes. "How many girls have you had here, Griff?"

Huh? What kind of question is that?

"None." More heat than I want enters my voice, and I try to smooth out my tone. "I told you there hasn't been anyone else for a long time. And definitely not in this apartment." Calmer, I add, "I made up my mind a long time ago. You're all I want. I rented this place *for us.*"

The tension that gathered seems to drain out of her, replaced by something else. The need to have her hot skin against mine overwhelms me. She places her palm on my stomach, then slides it to the knotted towel at my hip.

"You remember the night I came to see you fight in Ironworks?" She teases her fingers against the edge of the towel.

First time I finally kissed her. "How could I forget?"

"You were in a towel then too." She tugs at the knot and slides her tongue over her bottom lip. "I wished I was brave enough to rip it off you."

"Do it now." My hand tangles in her hair, drawing her closer. "I'm all yours."

She hooks her fingers in the terry cloth and tugs. The towel releases, and cool air drifts over my skin.

"Oh yes." Her hushed amazement lights a fire inside me.

"Lie down."

She eases onto the edge of the bed, then slides backward into the center and stares at me, waiting so patiently.

I place one knee on the bed and pull her closer. Her legs part, and I wedge my knee between them, hovering over her.

"Tell me you still want this, Molly." I kiss along her collarbone to her neck. A sense of panic slams into me. How am I supposed to leave her this summer? Nope. *Not the time.* "Tell me to stop if you want me to."

Her body shivers against mine. "Keep kissing me."

That's it. I can't wait another second to devour her perfect, pouty lips. Her soft moan against my mouth says she wants me as much as I want her. She parts her lips and I dip my tongue inside. She opens wider and I deepen the kiss.

Her fingers thread into my hair and I groan at the sensation. "Molly," I whisper, desperate for her to understand what's inside me. "I love you so much. You know that, right?"

She lifts her gaze to mine. "I love you, too."

I kiss lower, running my tongue over her collarbone, dragging the straps of her bra down. I trail my tongue over the peaks of her nipples straining against the sheer fabric. Something hard pokes my tongue. A clasp at the front.

"I really like this bra, Molly," I whisper. "But it has to go."

She arches her back as if begging me to undo the clasp. "I'll wear it for you again."

I barely touch the clasp and it pops open, freeing her breasts into my eager hands. "Best bra ever," I murmur, nuzzling my face against her skin.

"I thought you'd like it." She laughs softly, then sighs and runs her fingers through my hair. "Please."

"What? What do you need?"

"I want to touch you."

"Touch me, baby."

She slides her palms down my sides, over my back, and up to my shoulders again. "You're so strong," she whispers.

"So I can protect you."

The corners of her mouth tilt down. "I don't want to share you."

"Share me?" I glance over my shoulder in an exaggerated search of the room. "With who?"

"The world."

It takes a few heartbeats for her meaning to click in my brain. "No one else in the world is *you*."

"I..." She hesitates. "But I'm always worried you'll find someone older or prettier or—"

I press my lips to hers, cutting off that nonsense. My hands cup her cheeks, framing her face and forcing her to meet my eyes. "There is no one else more beautiful. No one I want more than anything in the whole world. I swear, a few months will never change that." I kiss her again. "I'm doing this *for* us."

"I know," she whispers, not sounding convinced at all. She hooks her fingers around my neck and draws me close again.

"No, wait." I stop and pull back. "Is this because you're worried about losing me?" I circle my hand in the air, indicating the candles, the outfit...everything. "We don't have to—"

"Oh. No." Her eyes shine with indignation and she loops her arms around my neck. "I've waited long enough."

"I'll be thinking about you the whole time I'm gone." I kiss her neck. "You're going to kick ass at your internship and learn all sorts of new things." I drag my tongue to her breast and circle her nipple.

She twists her body and wiggles lower.

"Where you going?"

"I want to touch you." Her hand grazes my cock, and a shudder races through my body. She grips me tight, and I bite back a moan.

Molly remembers everything I told her the night of her prom. For someone with so little experience, she has me ready to black out from the intense pleasure of her perfectly timed strokes.

I really might come all over her leg if she keeps that up.

Gently, I grip her wrist and pull it away.

Embarrassment flashes across her face, as if she thinks I didn't like what she was doing or she did something wrong. The flickering light catches the shine in her eyes.

"Shhh," I soothe. "Your hand feels so good, this'll be over before we even start." My thumbs brush her nipples. "I want to focus on you first."

"Oh." Her body relaxes and her hands return to my hair, pulling me down for more kisses.

A soft moan passes her lips when my mouth closes over her nipple. I suck gently, teasing my tongue over the tight peak. Moving to the other breast, I taste and explore. "So perfect," I murmur against her skin.

I lift my gaze and find her watching me with a sultry expression I've only gotten glimpses of before. It hits me hard and washes away any lingering hesitation about taking this next step with her.

"Have you touched yourself since prom night?"

Her forehead wrinkles. "No."

"Why not?"

"I wanted to save that for you."

Done.

I'm so done.

Never wanted anyone or anything as much as I want Molly for the rest of my life.

My dick throbs, begging for release.

"I can't say the same." I kiss her stomach and squeeze my eyes shut tight. "But I've been thinking of you every time."

"About what?"

"How you taste." I rub my chin against her underwear. "How you felt coming on my tongue. You want me to touch you here?" I tease my knuckles against her slit. Through the thin lace, wet heat sears my skin.

"Yes." She presses her feet into the mattress, lifting her hips to emphasize her request.

I lightly sink my teeth into her hip. Her body ripples with laughter. Then I sit up and grip her thighs, pushing them apart. The tiny candles barely throw enough light and I really want to see every inch of her, but it doesn't seem like the power's coming back on any time soon.

I press a kiss to her mound through her panties and inhale her scent.

She shifts and tries to close her legs.

"No," I warn, gripping her tighter. "I thought you wanted me to kiss you here again?"

"I do," she whispers.

I press another kiss over her clit, closing my teeth over the fabric and tugging the damp, sheer netting from her skin.

Her breath stutters, and she curls her fingers in the blankets.

I run my tongue along the crease of her thighs. She wriggles and moans.

"I'm taking these off now." I hook my fingers in the thin band at her hips.

"Okay." I glance up. She has her eyes squeezed shut, her teeth nibbling at her lower lip.

I take a second and run my thumb up and down her slit, feeling how wet and hot she is. Gently, I massage the spot right over her clit until I'm grinding my thumb in slow circles there.

Her breath hitches and her hips follow my movements. "Oh."

"That feel good?" I ask, pressing a kiss to her inner thigh.

"Yes."

I drag her underwear down her legs slowly. Even in the low light, her pussy glistens with how turned on she is. Her soft, dark curls, damp and beautiful.

Her hand comes down, covering herself.

Gently, I remove her hand. "You're beautiful."

"I should have—"

"Stop talking, Molly. I can't wait another second to get my mouth on you."

"Oh." She giggles nervously then moans as I run my finger along her slit.

"Look at me."

Our eyes meet as I slide a finger inside her tight heat. I've never been with someone I loved or wanted so much. Part of me regrets that this won't be the first time for *both* of us.

I slide my finger in and out of her. She's so wet, it makes these sexy, obscene noises, and she wiggles again. My girl's embarrassed.

"That's so sexy, Molly." I add another finger and move the two of them in and out in a slow, steady rhythm. "Hear that?"

Her body trembles but she doesn't answer.

"You weren't this shy prom night." Then it hits me—she was tipsy then. Now, I feel like an asshole.

She gestures toward the window. "There wasn't a thunderstorm and power outage."

Relief spirals through me, easing out in a huff of laughter. "You don't have anything to be afraid of with me."

I hit that spot inside that seems to make her forget everything else. She gasps and spreads her legs wider.

"That's it." I rub the spot harder. "You're so wet for me, Molly. I love it. That's how much you want me."

She lets out a little moan, and her body melts against the mattress. "I do. I really do."

"Good." I move in closer, dying to run my tongue through her slit.

"Ah!" She jolts as I take my first lick.

"So good, Molly." I use my free hand to reveal her clit. "I'm going to kiss you right here."

"Yes, yes."

I feather the softest kiss there, then gently tongue her clit while sliding my fingers in and out of her.

Her fingers tunnel into my hair, gripping hard. "Oh my...oh, Griff."

"Hmmm," I encourage, not wanting to take my mouth off her for even a second.

"Griff, oh my God." She keeps chanting over and over as I kiss and lick and finally suck her little clit into my mouth.

She cries out in pleasure, all shyness obliterated as she shoves herself against my face. I take what she offers, sucking at her clit while my fingers curl up inside her, rubbing harder against her G-spot.

"Oh! Griff, I'm..." The rest of her words are swallowed up by moans of pleasure as her pussy tightens around my fingers. I keep working her until she lets out a loud sigh.

"That was intense. Oh my God," she whispers.

I slip my fingers from her and wrap my hands around her waist, pressing another kiss over her clit before moving to her belly. She ripples with laughter when I flick my tongue into her belly button and kiss my way up her ribs.

"You're so quiet," I tease. "I wanted to hear you scream."

Her lips curve into soft, satisfied affection. "I couldn't think. I blacked out or I don't know—it was so amazing."

"Mmm, I like that." I brush my lips against hers. She opens and teases her tongue against my mouth.

"Is that me?" she asks, so innocently.

"That's your sweetness."

"Oh," she whispers. Her fingers brush my cheek. "I want…"

"More?"

"Everything. I want you." She arches and rolls underneath me, like she's as desperate to have me inside her as I am.

I groan when my cock brushes against her damp curls. "Give me a second." I raise myself and reach for my nightstand.

"Wait." She curls her fingers around my forearm.

I snag the knob of the top drawer, yank it open, and dig around inside. "What?" My fingers graze the plastic-sealed box I'm after.

"We don't need… You don't have to."

I stop my search and glance at her.

She sinks her teeth into her bottom lip. "I went to the doctor and asked, well, I started taking the pill. I've been on it for a while now."

Jesus Christ. I might not last long enough *to* squeeze inside her.

I drop the box and slap the drawer closed.

"Are you sure?" I cup her cheeks, framing her face with my hands so she meets my eyes. "I get tested for the fights regularly. Always been negative for everything."

"If you want to that's fine." She angles her head back to glance at my nightstand. "You can… I didn't mean… You don't have to."

"I want to make love to you with nothing between us."

"Okay." She hooks her arm around my neck. "I'd like that."

I lean down and fuse my mouth with hers, groaning as she slicks her tongue against mine.

Underneath me, she spreads her legs wider, then lifts and wraps them around my waist, inviting me inside. Making me lose my mind.

"I don't want to hurt you," I say between kisses.

"You'll be gentle."

Our mouths meet again, and I kiss her long and deep. Wrapping my arms around her, I roll us so she's on top.

Deep affection burns in her eyes as she smiles down at me. "What are you doing?"

"I want you on top for your first time. You set the pace." I flash a cocky grin. "Decide how much of me you can handle."

Her eyes widen as if she had never thought of that but likes the idea. "Show me how."

Fuck, yes, I will. "Sit up."

She straddles my hips while I grip my cock, holding steady. My free hand fits into the curve of her waist. "Up." I guide her slowly.

She shifts and moves her hips, slowly lowering herself.

"There you go."

Her breath hitches as the tip grazes her entrance.

I flick my gaze to her eyes. "Still okay?"

She nods once.

"Touch me," I rasp, barely hanging onto control. "Put me inside you."

She raises again, reaching for and finally grabbing my cock.

"That's it," I encourage.

Time unravels so gradually as she slides down, my brain's dangerously close to melting into a puddle. Inch by torturous inch, she takes me. My body's dying to slam up into her, but I'm also determined to enjoy every second of our first time together.

She's squeezing me tighter than fucking tight. *So fucking amazing with no barrier.*

"Fuck," I breathe out. "That's it, baby."

She whimpers but keeps easing down, then rises up a fraction. "Ohhh."

The way her body clamps around me sends heat shooting across my body. She slides down again. And again, repeating the same experimental motions. Testing what feels good. Pausing and frowning when it's too much. Oh, fuck, I want to watch every second. But with every slick squeeze and flutter, I'm flirting with coming. I'm trying so damn hard to hold back for her.

"Griff?"

"Yeah, Muffin?"

"Am I hurting you?"

"God, no." My voice grinds like tires on gravel. "You feel like heaven."

She takes more of me until I'm finally buried to the hilt. I take a chance and open my eyes, finding a curious expression on her face.

My fingers brush her cheek. "You okay?"

"I think so." She wiggles.

I grit my teeth. *Five, four, three, two...fuuuck.*

"It hurts a little..." She rolls her hips. "But also feels good."

"Take your time."

She presses her palms against my chest and raises her hips. "Like this?"

"Yeah. Just like that." I cup her breasts, squeezing and gently pinching her nipples. She sucks in a sharp breath. "Do you like that?"

"More please," she begs.

I roll and pinch her nipples while she raises and lowers herself again.

And again.

I slide my hands down her sides and curl my fingers around her hips, guiding her movements, urging her to go faster. "Still feel good?"

"Y-yes." Her hands wrap around my forearms, nails digging into my skin. "Less hurt. More good. Really good."

I'd laugh if I didn't think my balls would explode. I work one hand between us, my thumb finding and flicking her clit.

"Oh, that's nice." She gasps and moves faster.

She rocks back and forth, until she's grinding into me hard. *Wild.*

Losing herself in the pleasure of us.

"Griff." Her cries turn urgent and sharp.

"That's it." My jaw's too tight to say much. "Keep riding me. Come on my cock."

"I…" Her head falls back, and she works her hips slower and slower until she stops and lets out a deep sigh. The ends of her hair tickle my thighs. I flex my fingers, squeezing her hips.

"Come here." I pull her down over me, wrapping my arms around her. Her soft, warm body fits mine so perfectly. "Kiss me."

Her lips find mine and I press my palm to her lower back, allowing my fingers to brush her ass. Holding her tight while I pump up into her. She wiggles and tilts her hips, moaning against my neck. I'm so fucking close. Pressure more intense than anything I've ever felt gnaws at the base of my spine, shooting straight to my balls.

Takes maybe ten more seconds before I explode. Primal satisfaction roars through me as I empty myself inside her.

"Molly, Molly, Molly," I whisper. My hands brush her hair out of her face so I can kiss her. She falls to her side, our legs entwined, still joined together. My cum leaks out of her, making me want to fuck her all over again. I reach down, feeling our combined wetness. My spent cock slips out of her and more cum slowly falls free. I rub my fingers through it, marveling at the mess we've made.

"Mmmm," she hums. "That feels good. I'm still all tingly down there."

I bring my fingers up, rubbing her clit gently until her back arches and she lets out a breathy cry.

"Stop, stop." She wriggles and pushes my hand away.

I reach up, dragging my wet fingers over her nipples.

"Griff," she protests.

"That's us, baby. You and me."

She laughs softly and kisses my shoulder.

"Are you okay?" I ask. "Did it hurt?"

"Just a little at first. Then it was incredible." She cracks open one eye and gives me a half-smile. "I'm glad you broke me in on prom night."

I chuckle. "Good. I couldn't stand hurting you. Not for a second."

She shivers and I run my hands over her. "Let's go clean up, then get under the covers."

I slide out of bed first, holding my hand out to her. She gingerly rolls over then grimaces when she stands.

"Hurt?"

"No." She points to her thigh where my semen runs down her leg.

"That's so fucking hot."

Her nose wrinkles and I take her hand.

"Power's out so there won't be much, if any, hot water," I warn her.

"That's okay." She hurries to keep up with me. "You'll keep me warm."

"You know it."

The water's tepid at best, but we climb in the shower anyway. I wash her clean, kissing every inch of her.

"What are you doing?" she asks.

"I want to be thorough."

Her laughter echoes in the darkened bathroom. The water's quickly turning ice-cold. I rinse us both off one more time before shutting the water off.

As I rub a towel over her skin, she follows my every movement with her eyes.

When I glance at her face, I find one tear silently rolling down her cheek. "What's wrong, baby?"

She sniffles. "Nothing. I'm going to miss you."

One of my T-shirts hangs from the back of the door, and I pluck it off the hook.

"Arms up." I coax her.

I slip the shirt over her head and love the way it pools around her curvy frame. "It's a crime to cover your beautiful body, but somehow you're even hotter wearing my shirt."

The corners of her mouth turn up in a sad smile.

I take her hand, leading her into the kitchen. My mind's

racing, rolling over all the things I want to say. I pour a glass of water and hand it to her. "Drink."

Eagerly, she grips the glass and swallows while I down my own.

A shiver works over her body as she sets her glass on the counter.

"Let's get back under the covers." I turn her toward the door. "Unless you're hungry?"

She shakes her head. "Chilly."

In the bedroom, I flip the blankets back and settle her on one side, then search my closet for an extra blanket. I find an old, heavy but soft gray-and-white blanket with two kittens on the front of it.

Molly smiles as I spread it over her and rubs her fingers along the worn edge. "I remember this. You used to bring it when you slept at our house."

I let out a sad laugh. "Yeah, probably."

Once I'm under the covers with her, I wrap her tight in my arms. "Talk to me."

"About?"

I brush my knuckles over her cheek. "Why are you sad? I wanted to make you come, not cry."

She laughs softly. "I came." She reaches under the covers and presses her hands between her legs. "I still feel all shivery and tingly."

"Maybe I didn't do a good enough job." I throw the covers over my head and slide down.

"No!" She giggles and tugs on my arms. "Get back here. Give me a few minutes to recover."

I kiss my way up her body again and pull her against me. "Talk to me."

She's silent for a few minutes, but I'm patient when I need to be.

"We've never been away from each other for so long," she whispers.

"That's not true. I was at Castle Correctional for longer than two months," I remind her. Although, comparing the reality show to the time I spent in kiddie prison isn't exactly making me feel better about the situation I've put myself in.

"That was different. You didn't have a choice then. And at least I could write you letters." She squints at me. "Sometimes you even wrote me back."

I squeeze her tighter. "I didn't write much because there wasn't anything good to share. But I loved every letter from you."

She's silent for a minute. "I want to support you. I *do* support you. I can't help being sad, though."

"I need to make it to the finals." I run my hand over her hair. "But I'd really like to win. It might be enough for a down payment on a house for us and for me to buy into the garage."

"You're sure you want to be a mechanic more than a fighter?"

"I can't fight forever. Not the underground fights." *One day, it might get me killed.* But I don't dare say that to Molly. "I want to have something more substantial to support you with."

"I told you, I'll have a decent job. It's not all your responsibility to support us."

I squeeze her again. "So, we'll work at jobs we love all day long. Then come home and make love all night."

Her soft laughter vibrates up my arms, warming my heart. "Sounds like a plan." She nuzzles my neck, kissing me.

"Don't start something you can't finish," I warn her.

"Who says I can't finish?"

I run my hand under her shirt, gripping her hip. "Are you sore?"

"A little."

I press a kiss to her forehead and snuggle her closer.

"Griff?"

"Hmm?"

"Was I...was it good for you, too?"

"How can you ask me that?" I pull away and stare at her face. "I thought I was going to blow the second I squeezed inside you."

"Okay."

"Don't ever doubt that." I kiss her cheek. "You're exactly what I want. In every way."

The way Molly sounds and feels when she comes is forever carved into my brain.

I'll need to hold onto every one of those memories to survive an entire summer without her.

Molley

CHAPTER THIRTY-FIVE

GRIFF

Sweet vanilla tickles my nose. My eyes blink open. Sunlight stretches through the curtains, highlighting the empty space next to me.

"Molly?" I rasp.

Music drifts from somewhere in my apartment. Something upbeat. A clink and sizzle. Power must've come back on sometime in the middle of the night.

What's Molly doing?

Why isn't she in bed with me?

I toss the covers back, make a quick stop in the bathroom, then stumble into the kitchen. My sleepy brain slowly processes the scene in front of me. Molly's curvy body swallowed whole in one of my T-shirts. A gadget I don't recognize on my counter that she's pouring batter onto. Bowls of fruit, a carton of eggs, and a box of waffle mix lined up next to where she's working.

Molly twitches her hips in time to the music as she sprinkles blueberries onto the batter, then closes the waffle maker. A red light glows on the front, and it lets off a quick muted *beep*.

If this is a dream, I'd rather not wake up, but I have to ask, "Where did you find waffle supplies in *my* kitchen?"

Molly jumps and turns. Then the smile that sets my whole body on fire slowly spreads over her face.

"I brought them over last time I was here." She laughs and points to the mint-green waffle maker. Steam pours out of the sides, and batter drips over the edge. "How'd you miss it?"

"Must've been too happy you were at my place to notice anything else."

"Well, I *knew* you'd have plenty of eggs—"

I return her grin. "Eggs are nature's—"

"Perfect protein." She flicks her gaze to the ceiling, a teasing smile playing over her lips. "You and Remy with your eggs."

"Hey, it's a cheap meal." The total from my last grocery bill flashes in front of my eyes. "Or at least it *used* to be."

"Well, I brought vanilla and cinnamon last time." She points to one of the cabinets. "And left them up there."

"I never noticed." I sniff the air. "Is that why it smells so good in here?"

"Yes."

I glance at the washer/dryer combo in the corner of my kitchen. It rocks slightly and hums in a steady rhythm. "You did laundry too?"

"No choice. Our stuff was still wet and kinda smelly from sitting in the dryer all night." She tugs the shirt away from her body. "I had a waffle maker stashed here, but no clothes."

My lips curve up. "Fine by me." I rest my hands on her hips and pull her closer. "You look good in my shirt, Muffin."

"Mmm." She sighs and leans back against me.

I kiss the top of her head. "You can leave clothes or whatever you need here, though." Better yet, she could move in with me. Or we could get a nicer place together.

No. I can't ask her to move in then take off for two months and leave her by herself in a new place. That'd be a dick move, for sure.

"You wouldn't mind?" Molly asks.

"Nope."

Why couldn't this show have approached me last year? I finally have my girl. How am I supposed to leave her for two months? It's not just the physical separation I'm dreading. Only being able to talk to Molly once a week *and* having our phone calls monitored—it's going to be brutal.

Stop it. I can't let worries ruin the time we have left.

I tighten my arms around her. "How do you feel after last night?"

She turns and loops her arms around my neck. A playful grin flickers over her lips. "How do *you* feel? Once I got the mechanics down, I rode you pretty hard."

I choke on my laughter. *That* was unexpected. "Yeah, you did." I lower my voice and kiss her cheek. "Loved every second."

"Mmm." She rubs on me like a kitten, then drops her hand to my cock. "What do we have here?"

"Morning wood. Can't help it when I wake up and find my beautiful girlfriend making waffles in my kitchen."

"This isn't morning wood." She curls her fingers around me through my shorts and squeezes. "It's a morning maple tree."

Good God, her low, throaty whisper is an even bigger turn-on than her hand on my cock.

Focus, fucker.

"Hey, seriously." I brush my lips against her cheek. "How do you feel today?"

She sways from side to side as she rubs her thighs together. Her face pinches into a thoughtful expression. "A bit sore, but a good kind."

Good or not, I don't like hurting her.

"No complaints. My body goes haywire when you touch me." She closes her eyes and slicks her tongue over her bottom lip as if just the memory of my touch has her close to orgasm.

"Touch you where?" I slide my hand along her thigh, drawing her shirt up, up, up.

She leans back, bracing her hands on the counter. "Anywhere

you want." She flicks her gaze to mine. "It even turns me on when you look at me like that."

"Like what?"

"Like you want more than waffles for breakfast."

I laugh, low in my throat, then grasp her waist and boost her onto the counter. "I'm going to eat those waffles right after I make you scream." I lift her T-shirt out of my way. "No panties. I like it."

"They're lost somewhere in your room."

"We'll find 'em." I pat the counter next to her thigh. "Put your foot here."

"What?" She glances toward the window. "No."

"No one can see us from that angle."

She hesitantly lifts one foot. "Are you sure?"

"Unless someone can levitate, they're not seeing all the way to this corner of the kitchen."

I wrap my fingers around her other ankle and guide it to the counter, revealing glistening skin. "God damn, I can't get over how pretty you are."

I bury my face against her inner thigh and nibble at her soft skin. Up close, I notice a red patch against her pale flesh. That hadn't been there last night. "Must've given you a friction burn or something." I gently brush my finger over it. "Does this hurt?"

"What?" Her body shifts as she peers down to see what I'm looking at. "No."

I press my hands against her thighs, pushing her open wide to accommodate my face and not give her beard burn. I squeeze my eyes shut and inhale. The urge to stand and impale her on my raging morning wood seizes me.

Control yourself.

I turn and rub my mouth against her pussy, parting her lips with my tongue.

"Ohhh." Molly moans and drags her fingers through my hair.

"That's it." I take another long, slow lick, then stop to kiss her swollen clit. I'm gentle as can be, but her body jolts, and she moans louder. I feather the softest touch of my tongue to her clit over and over. My hands press against her thighs, holding her wide open so I can tongue the hell out of her.

Her thighs tremble against my palms. Her arousal drips down my chin. I increase the pressure.

She lets out a sharp scream and yanks my hair. Her hips wiggle and push against my face. I stop moving and let her work herself against my tongue, groaning noises of encouragement.

"Oh, God. Gr...Griff, don't stop. Please!"

I shake my head and she screams louder. Her whole body trembles and curls forward. I risk suffocation and take my hand off her thigh, slowly pushing two fingers inside her.

"Yes, yes, yes." She tugs harder on my hair. I twist my fingers, searching for the spot that makes her really lose it.

The waffle maker bleats a series of high-pitched beeps, like it's congratulating us on our performance.

"Oh!" Molly shakes and tightens, her pussy so tight around my fingers. I lick and suck harder, greedy for her to give me everything.

She's still clenching around my fingers when I stand. For a second or two, I work them in and out of her, slowly bringing her down. Then, I lean over and yank the waffle maker plug out of the wall.

"What?" She blinks up at me.

"I need you." I lift her off the counter. "Need to fuck you. Right now."

She seals her mouth over mine and wraps her legs around my waist. Good thing I had practice moving through the apartment in the dark last night. I can't break our kiss to look where I'm going. Somewhere along the way, Molly uses one hand to start shoving my shorts out of the way, like she's just as crazed to have me inside her as I am to be there.

The second I cross the threshold into my room, she tugs her T-shirt off and throws it.

"Good girl." I kiss her cheek, her jaw, attack her neck. My

shorts slip down my legs and I lift her. As if she's reading my mind, she curls her fingers around me and guides me to her entrance.

I groan as my cock slips against her wet flesh. Fucking torture.

"I've got you," I promise.

She whimpers and struggles, not quite getting the right angle. My arms shake as I gently lay her on the bed. Her back barely touches the sheets, and I thrust inside her.

"Yes." She wraps her legs around my waist, tilting her body. "That feels so good."

Thank God. I don't want to be rough with her, but I can't stop the animal side that's in control of my body now. I've never been so turned on, so desperate to connect with someone in my life. "Molly."

She wraps her arms around my neck and raises herself enough to smash her lips against mine. "I love you," she whispers against my mouth. Or maybe she's pushed the thought into my brain. We're so deeply connected I'm not sure what either of us are saying, but I feel everything.

Her fingers trail down my back, her nails dig into my ass, and I thrust harder.

"Oh, shit!" She arches and tilts her hips. I slow my frantic pace, stopping to grind myself against her every time I'm deep. Her body trembles and her eyes roll back.

"Yeah," I groan, watching in fascination as she comes undone. Her pussy squeezes around me.

And I'm lost.

My body cinches tight, ready to explode. *Fuck.* I'm not ready to stop, but my balls don't care. I drive into her harder.

The tension in my body breaks, bliss blinding me for a few shattering heartbeats. I bury my face against her neck, licking the sweat from her skin. Her nails dig into my ass, sharp little pricks encouraging me to grind deeper as I release. *Sweet fucking relief.* I groan and squeeze my eyes shut, coming so hard it almost fucking hurts.

Underneath me, Molly's panting just as hard as I am. She gently slides her fingers along my sides up and down, like she's soothing a wild animal.

Finally, I'm able to open my eyes. I press a sloppy kiss to her cheek. "Thank you."

"Thank *you*." She lifts her head and grazes her lips against my jaw. "I lost count of how many times you made me..." Her cheeks glow pink. "You know."

Still semi-hard, I rock into her again. "No, I don't. Tell me."

"Come." The word rolls off her tongue a bit awkwardly. "Orgasm." That comes out easier. "See stars." She lifts her eyebrows. "Is that better?"

"Fuck yeah." I ease myself out of her. This morning, she doesn't wince or seem to even notice the new mess we've made. She eagerly cuddles close to me, throwing her arm across my chest and kissing my shoulder.

"I thought people who talked about sex as some out-of-body experience were being poetic," she whispers. "But I swear I floated out of my body to the stars and back that last time."

Life doesn't get much better than this.

"Better than being on top?" I peer down at her.

She squints like this is a complicated question. "Not better. Different. You just hit something at that angle that felt *really* good."

"Told you we'd fit together just right."

She laughs softly, her breath floating over my skin. "Are there other ways you want to try?"

"Uh, only about a thousand."

More laughter. "Juliet said someone gave her this hundred-and-one-sex-positions guidebook or something..."

Now, I shake with laughter. "I think I heard that story once. Pretty sure we can look all those positions up online if you want."

Her nose wrinkles. "I'm afraid we'll find something gross, not sexy." She taps her fingers over my chest. "Tell me, is there anything *you* want to try?"

An immediate picture forms in my mind. "You know that dresser we had in the hotel room? With the long mirror running behind it?" I bite my lip and rub my hand over my chin. "When you bent over to take off your shoes that night, I so badly wanted to bend you over the dresser so I could fuck you from behind while I watched your face in the mirror."

"Oh, wow," she breathes out, staring at me with wide eyes. "That's hot." She sits up and glances around my room. "Why don't you have a low dresser like that here?"

I sit up, my head doing a quick spin. "Uh, if I'd known, believe me, I would've bought one and carried it up the stairs myself."

"Let's try the bathroom." She stands and holds out her hand, wiggling impatient fingers at me.

"What?" My brain struggles to catch up, but I curl my hand around hers.

"The mirror over your sink," she explains like a dirty little scientist, eager to conduct her newest naughty experiment.

Gorgeous and an excellent problem-solver—I've won the girlfriend lottery. "You're a genius."

Molly

In the bathroom, I press my hands flat against the sink and thrust my butt out, wiggling my hips from side to side. "Is this what you had in mind?" I tease.

Griff's big hands clamp around my waist, yanking me toward him. He uses one foot to tap the insides of my ankles. "Spread your legs for me." He presses his palm against the middle of my back. "Arch."

As sweet and patient as Griff's been with me, now he seems determined to teach me two lessons.

One—he's in charge.

Two—he wants to discover every single possible way to make my body sing.

I grip the sides of the counter around the sink and lift up on my toes, offering myself to him.

"Fuck, Molly. I thought I'd need a few minutes to recover." His cock prods my entrance. "But I'm harder than a fucking baseball bat."

"Oh!" I squeak as he eases inside me. "Yes, you are."

He stops. "You okay?"

Our eyes meet in the mirror. Concern and restraint furrow his brows. "Go slow," I whisper.

He lets out a growly noise. "You got it."

His hands slide from my hips to my waist as he leisurely pushes forward. Fascinated, I watch his reflection. He pins his gaze where we're joined, his mouth forming into a fascinated "O." He glances in the mirror and catches me watching him. His lips tilt.

"I wish the mirror was bigger." He bends, trying for a different angle. Our height difference seems to be making things difficult. "And you were wearing those cute boots from your birthday."

"Oooh, remind me to grab them when we stop by the house later."

"Yeah," he groans, sliding all the way in, so I'm forced up on my toes. "A little extra height would be nice."

I laugh and grip the counter harder. "Do that again."

"This?" He moves faster.

I arch my back and wiggle, chasing the slight tingling sensation below.

Griff pulls out all the way and spins me around.

"What are you doing?"

Instead of answering, he lifts me and pins me against the wall opposite the sink. He kisses my neck. "Wrap your legs around me."

I hitch and raise my legs, crossing my ankles over his butt.

"That's it." He thrusts inside me, stopping to grind into my pelvis. My body shudders with pleasure.

"Yeah, much better," he says against my neck.

Our lips meet and we breathe each other in, panting and sighing. He withdraws, then flexes fully inside me again. Over and over.

"Griff," I gasp. He pounds into me so hard, I'm vaguely aware of a steady *thump, thump, thump* as we knock against the wall.

Tension builds and twists inside me.

"Right here, Muffin." He kisses and sucks at the spot below my ear. His fingers squeeze my thighs and butt. "Come for me."

My back slides against the wall. I wrap my legs around him tighter. Pleasure pinches at my core. My heartbeat thunders through my ears. *So close.*

"Keep doing that," I pant between shaky breaths.

"Yeah? You like that?" He lifts me higher, grinds into me slower, taking his time.

"Yes, yes." Liquid fire shoots through my veins. Relief and pain tangle together as I finally find release, leaving me moaning and trembling in Griff's arms.

A few seconds later, he squeezes his eyes shut and stops moving, keeping me pinned to the wall.

"Fuck, ah, fuck, Molly!" He lets out a tortured groan, his face contorting with agonized pleasure. He's never looked more beautiful. Warmth spills inside me. I'm so oversensitive, I swear I feel every drop. A rush of pride spreads through me. *I* have the power to make Griffin "Stonewall" Royal lose control, to make his strong legs shake and his muscled body tremble.

His cock twitches with the last of his release.

"I love you." I kiss his shoulder. Our sweaty bodies cling to each other.

His mouth finds mine for a long, slow kiss.

"Love you," he mumbles against my lips. "So much, baby."

After a few heartbeats, his fog seems to clear. He searches my face. "You okay?"

I blink up at him. "I'm queen of the universe."

His cheeks lift. "Yeah, you are."

Carefully, he slips out of me and sets me on my feet. *Whoa.* My legs wobble. Warmth trails down my thigh.

"Come on. Let's shower." He rubs the pads of his fingers over my scalp. "Let me wash your hair."

"You need to wash more than my hair."

He rumbles with laughter. "You got it."

I hug him from behind, plastering myself against his sweat-slicked back as he adjusts the shower for us. When the water's just right, he pulls me inside.

"Much better today." I sigh and step under the warm spray.

Behind me, there's a click and a familiar creamy, cherry-vanilla scent fills the shower.

"Tip your head back." Griff's quiet rasp rises above the pattering water.

I sluice more water through my thick hair, thoroughly wetting it, then lean back. Griff carefully scrubs and massages shampoo into my scalp.

"Mmm. I could go back to sleep," I murmur.

"I'm not opposed to spending the day in bed together."

"But I should go home and get those boots." My lips curve into a teasing smile, and I turn to see him.

"Yeah?" He raises an eyebrow and nods toward the sink. "You sure you want to try that again?"

"I'll keep trying anything with you until we get it right."

"How'd I get so lucky?" He reaches for my hair. "Rinse."

I tilt my head and squeeze my eyes shut.

"Conditioner?" I ask, groping blindly for a bottle.

"I got you." A cap clicks and Griff's hand on my shoulder guides me to turn around again. He slowly works the conditioner through my hair.

"Your turn." I stick my face under the spray, rinsing suds from my eyes. "I want to let this sit before washing it out."

He chuckles. "You can't reach my hair."

"Sure I can. Bend over." I reach for the few bottles lined up on the shelf. A jumbo-sized dark-green bottle. *Evergreen and cedar all-in-one.* That explains Griff's woodsy scent. My gaze lands on two small gold bottles. "You use the same shampoo I do?"

"No." He grabs the big green bottle and pours a generous amount in his palm. "But I know you're particular about what you put in your hair."

I swallow hard, overcome by a rush of emotion. "Thank you."

"Unfortunately, I only have one option for bodywash." He holds up his foamy hands.

I giggle and lift my arms over my head. "Soap me up, Stonewall."

"Yes, ma'am." He moves in close, thoroughly rubbing and sliding his hands over me.

"Did you ask Remy what I use?" I nod to the bottles.

He frowns. "You think that's a conversation I wanted to have with him?" He pitches his voice in a deep, fake-conversational tone. "Hey, bro, give me a list so I can stock my apartment with Molly's stuff for when she sleeps over." He motions for me to turn around. "After he specifically said, 'no sleepovers.'"

"That was *before* my birthday," I scoff.

"He never lifted the ban." He presses his body against my back and cups my breasts. "We're breaking the law, Ms. Holt," he says against my ear.

"Ooopsie." I lean back against his slick, warm body. "Too bad, so sad."

He rumbles with laughter. "I know he's a pain sometimes, but he really wants what's best for you."

"Why do you think I haven't smothered him in his sleep, yet?"

"Brutal." He chuckles. "Final rinse. We're losing hot water." He pulls the showerhead down and floods my hair, then sprays my body while I shut my eyes and hold my breath.

Outside the shower, Griff hands me a fluffy purple towel. "Darcy told me the college guy she was dating didn't even own towels," I say as I wrap my hair into a neat beehive on top of my head.

He snorts. "I'm grimy all day at work. I like to come home at night and get clean."

He hands me another towel and I quickly rub it over my body, then pull it around and tie it over my chest. "Thanks."

He hooks his fingers around the edge of the mirror and pries it away from the wall with a screech of metal. "Made sure I had this here for you too."

I drop my gaze to the small, clear bottle in his hand. My favorite hair serum. "Griff, that stuff's expensive," I protest.

"So?" He shrugs. "Told you I want you to feel comfortable when you're here." His lips quirk. "And take *lots* of showers with me."

Laughing, I pour a nickel-sized amount in my palm and smooth it through my hair. Griff searches through a drawer and hands me a wide-toothed comb. Thank God. I was scared I'd have to use his fine-toothed one.

"What I *don't* have is a decent blow-dryer." His lips pull into an apologetic smile, and he holds up an ancient-looking black-and-red blow-dryer. "This was here when I moved in. It works, I think. But it's gotta be older than I am."

"That's okay." I run the comb through my wet hair. "I like letting it air-dry sometimes. Actually, maybe I'll braid it. I have hair ties in my backpack."

He ties the towel around his hips. "You want me to go plug in the waffle maker again?"

"Oh my God! The waffles." I wrinkle my nose. "You think the batter is still okay?"

"I'm sure it's fine." He turns and reaches for the door.

"Griff?"

He stops and faces me. "Hmmm?"

I rush closer and loop my arms around his neck. "Thank you for being so patient with me."

His eyebrows draw down, but one corner of his mouth slides up. "Patient, how?"

I tip my head toward the bedroom. "Waiting...you know, for me until I was ready."

"Molly." He slips his arms around my waist and stares at me with loving eyes. "I want us to spend the rest of our lives together. A couple months—years if you needed them—was nothing." He flicks his gaze toward the ceiling, like he's searching for the right words. "I didn't want you to ever look back and regret anything about us. Or feel like I talked you into something."

"I'd never regret *you*, no matter what."

That doesn't seem to reassure him. His frown remains as he studies my face. "I wanted our first time to actually be *good*, too."

"Oh, it was *good*." I lean up and kiss his cheek. "Very, very good. Like I'm-still-tingly-all-over good."

Genuine amusement lights his face, chasing away the concern. "I'll never get tired of hearing you compliment my skills."

I glance at the mirror and warmth spreads over my skin. "You think maybe we can stay at that hotel again?"

He groans. "You're killing me."

"What?" I grin up at him.

He hugs me tighter. "Baby, we can do anything you want when I get back. We'll go away for a weekend. Just you and me. Okay?"

The reminder that he's leaving me soon sucks all the fun out of our moment. My heart crackles with pain. I don't want to be without him for so long.

We've already talked about it. It's a done deal. Support him.

I force a big smile. "I can't wait."

Molly

CHAPTER THIRTY-SIX

GRIFF

My ego wouldn't let me tell Molly that my legs were still shaking after our naked workout in the bathroom. Showering with her. Letting her find all the things I've been storing here for her to use one day. All that made the explosive sex even sweeter.

Not wanting to be away from her for more than a few seconds, I end up wearing my towel to breakfast. Molly's in one of my shirts that reaches her knees. While the waffles cook, she twists her hair into two long braids.

"I have sausage in here." I stand and yank the freezer door open.

"Oh, yum." She takes the package out of my hands and tears into it.

"Hungry?" Damn, I never fed her dinner last night, did I?

"Staaarving." She peers at me over her shoulder. "I had an intense workout session. Several of them."

"Want me to make you a protein shake?"

She wrinkles her nose. "No. But I sprinkled some of your protein powder in the waffle mix."

Could she be more perfect? "You're the best."

The waffle maker's slow. We have the eggs and sausage ready before half the batter's been used.

"We'll start with these." I hold up the plate of two waffles. "And let those keep cooking."

"Maybe I'll make chicken and waffles for dinner."

"You think those will last until dinner?" I wait until Molly's seated, then set a plate of sausage and eggs in front of her and the waffles in the center of the table.

"This is nice." She reaches across the table and rests her hand over mine.

"I like having you here." I dig into my waffle. "So good," I mumble around a mouthful of crisp, fluffy sweetness.

"It's cold and overcooked." She pokes her fork in the corner of my waffle. "Here, take mine."

"No." I brush her fork away. "Careful. It's dangerous trying to touch food on my plate, girl."

She laughs and pulls her fork back to her side. "I'm trying to put food *on* your plate, you ravenous beast."

I growl at her, and she laughs hard, shaking her head.

"You've really never had anyone over here?" she asks causally. Almost too casual, like she's holding her breath while she waits for the answer.

I sit back. "You. The guys." I snap my fingers. "I lied. I *have* had girls here."

Her eyes widen.

"Juliet and Ella," I say, cutting off the images she's probably conjuring in her mind. "They've been here too."

"Oh. Yeah. I knew that."

"It's just a place to sleep. I'm usually out, busy doing other stuff. Over at your place." I chew on a piece of sausage, swallow, and take a swig of orange juice. "But I'm hoping when I get back, we can look for a house."

She stares at me with concern wrinkling her forehead. "What if I go to school a couple of hours away?"

The question hits me in the gut. I knew it was a possibility. I was just hoping she wouldn't go that far.

"Then you'll have somewhere to come home to on weekends and breaks." I take another sip of orange juice. "Or I'll bank the money and when you're done with school, we'll figure out where we want to live."

She blows a relieved breath and pokes her fork into her eggs.

"Molly, I want you to go to school wherever you want. I'm not gonna be the guy holding you back. I want to help you soar, not keep you chained down."

Her bottom lip trembles. "I...I want to do the same for you. You want to buy the garage—"

"The world is *full* of garages, Molly. If you want to move somewhere else, I'll find another one."

A relieved smile slips over her face. "Remy mentioned he might want to sell the house one day."

"Shit, really?"

She grins. "I said you were gonna move in with us and he can be a manny to our kids."

I choke on a piece of sausage. "How'd he respond to *that*?"

"He laughed." She shrugs.

Huh. Not the reaction *I* would've gotten from Remy if I'd made the same joke.

We finish eating. Every few minutes, she grazes her foot against my calf under the table, then shyly glances away.

"Do you want another waffle?" she asks.

I glance down at the towel I'm still wearing. "I think I'm gonna get dressed. You're welcome to come help."

"I'll finish the waffles, then come find you."

"Deal." I lean over and kiss her cheek.

Molly

I stand and drool over Griff's legs as he pads out of the kitchen. Shaking my head, I clear the table.

"Leave the dishes. I'll do them!" Griff shouts.

I stack the dishes in the sink. The waffle maker beeps, and I pry the sweet, golden, fluffy disk out of the griddle and set it on a plate. Then I pour the rest of the batter into the griddle and snap it shut.

Someone knocks on the apartment door. I whisk a towel off the counter and wipe batter off my fingers.

"I got it," I call to Griff.

Please don't be Tanya again. Griff said his mom made it to Jersey and seems happy there. She can't be back already, right?

I press my nose to the door, peering into the peephole. Bright light sears my eyeball. I wince and jerk away. *What the heck?*

"Griff, I'm not sure who it is." I reach for the knob and twist.

"Hang on!" Griff shouts.

I try to twist the knob but the lock scrapes and doesn't close all the way. The door flies open, hitting my shoulder.

"Ow!" I jump back, pressing my hand to the sore spot. Thank God it missed my face.

The blinding light bobs closer. I squint against the glare. The glowing orb seems attached to a large camera held by a man with a pointy beard. Two more people follow him inside.

"We're here for Griffin 'Stonewall' Royal." A short, older woman with pink hair stops and peers up at me. "Are you the girlfriend?"

What the hell is happening? "Uh, yeah. And you are?"

"Diane? What the fuck?" Griff says from somewhere behind me. A few seconds later, he drapes a protective arm over my shoulders and pulls me against him.

"Griff?" Trembles of fear travel up my legs. "What's happening?"

"She even legal?" The man behind Diane runs his dismissive gaze over me and scoffs.

Was that directed at *me?*

Diane's gaze narrows on me. "Do you live here?"

Griff squeezes me tighter with one arm and reaches for the

camera, pushing it out of my face with his free hand. "Leave her out of this. She's not part of the show."

The show. This is the woman responsible for recruiting my boyfriend onto a reality show and taking him away from me all summer. My fingers curl, desperate to wrap around her throat and squeeze really hard.

Diane tilts her head but doesn't repeat her question. She focuses her energy on Griff.

"We decided to accelerate the schedule." Her chipper tone grates against my nerves like pebbles in my shoes. "The surprise pick-up adds excitement." She grins, wide and amused. "One of our other producers already got punched in the face. It'll make a *great* episode."

Her gaze lands on me again, and a sick feeling slithers through my stomach. "Although, barely legal teen girlfriend might be an even better hook. Please tell me you're at least eighteen, sweetheart? Do your parents know you're here?"

Griff says, "Don't," at the same time that I say, "Yes, I'm eighteen."

"Oh, thank God." She presses her palms together like she's in a church and raises them toward the ceiling. "We want a bad boy, but not a statutory rapist."

"The age of consent is seventeen in New York," I mutter, remembering Hayden's advice about dating Griff.

"Molly," Griff warns in a low voice.

"I love it!" Diane claps her hands. "Good lord, aren't you an adorable thing, too." She reaches for my hair, pulling one of my long braids like she wants to film a shampoo ad next. "Smile, sweetie. Aren't you excited? Griff's going to be on television." Her voice takes on the babyish tone you might use to train a golden retriever puppy.

Gritting my teeth, I force my cheeks up, but I doubt what my face is actually doing resembles a smile.

"Look at those perfect, straight, white teeth." She pats the side of my face. "Such a pretty girl." Her gaze swings to Griff then back to me again. "You make a stunning couple."

Officially creeped out, I glance at Griff again.

"Diane, I have a job. I need to give notice," Griff says, instead of protesting the way she's studying me like I'm a racehorse she wants to load into a trailer and haul to Saratoga.

"We took care of that. Jerry was very excited for you," Diane gushes. "What a nice man."

"He's a good boss," Griff mutters. I can only imagine how stressed Griff is, thinking he's leaving Jerry in the lurch. He continues glaring at Diane. "I'm not packed, yet."

"It was in your contract. You should be ready to go at a moment's notice," Diane says.

"Yeah, and this is *weeks* ahead of the time frame I was given," he counters.

This is all so unfair. Ridiculous.

My eyes prickle and my nose stings. Pain wraps around my throat, and I force myself to wheeze in an agonizing breath.

Oh no.

I'm not crying in front of these people.

"I'll help you pack," I mutter, ducking out from underneath Griff's arm. I hurry toward the bedroom without waiting for a response.

"Thanks," Griff says. In a lower voice, he says, "No."

That "no" wasn't meant for me.

Afraid the creepy camera dude might chase after me, I run to Griff's bedroom and quietly close the door.

Is this really happening?

My heart pounds wildly. I count to five and then ten, desperate to get my breathing under control and not cry.

My gaze strays to the bed. Still rumpled from last night. The first night we...

Scalding tears roll down my cheeks, and I brush them away with the back of my hand.

Everything was so beautiful. So perfect. We had plans today.

Hurry. There isn't much time.

A ragged sob tears out of my throat. I stuff my fist in my mouth and bite hard to muffle the noise.

Bed. What if they come in here and film? Absurdly worried it'll look like we had sex, I hurry to straighten the sheets and comforter. I scoop up our scattered clothes, folding them into a neat pile on one side of the mattress.

My frenzied gaze pings around the room. Pack. I came in here to help Griff pack.

What will he need for the next *two months*?

Clothes. *Closet.* Griff rotates through a collection of T-shirts and shorts in the summer. Some sleeveless shirts—*God, I love when he wears those*—and a bunch of work shirts. I doubt he wants anything with his job embroidered on the front, so I flip by those. What about Zips? I know the guys race and gamble illegally there, but Uncle Pax hosts legitimate car shows and stuff too. Griff would want to support the racetrack if he had a chance. I set that shirt in the maybe pile.

A T-shirt with the crown, brass knuckles, and flowers logo Griff and Remy use to represent The Castle crew. It doesn't have any writing on it. I toss that on the maybe pile.

Support your local LOKI MC, Port Everhart Virginia. Why does he have one for Virginia but not New York? *Doesn't matter. No time!* Griff said he wasn't supposed to mention the Lost Kings MC on the show. I leave that shirt on its hanger.

There's a T-shirt with *Clary's Tavern* emblazoned on the front. Remy can use all the publicity he can get for the bar. I throw that one in the definite pile.

A muscle tank with *Strike Back Studio*. Doing those promo videos for Sully's gym are what got Griff into this mess. Sully's gym could use the free advertising too. I toss that shirt on the definite pile.

I throw a bunch of plain T-shirts on the bed, then go through the rest of his wardrobe. Lots and lots of flannel shirts. Long-sleeved Henley's, hoodies. His wardrobe is pretty basic. A crime, since he looks so good in a tux.

Focus.

This feels too intimate. Personal. Pawing through his clothes. Trying to figure out what he'll feel most comfortable in when he's in a strange environment. What he'll need for the next eight weeks. He'll have access to a washer and dryer, right? Will they let him run to a store and grab something if he forgets it?

So many unknowns.

On the top shelf, a large backpack peeks over the edge. I hook my finger in the strap and drag it down, grab a few pairs of shorts, then carry everything to the bed. The front of the backpack has tons of little stash pockets. I unzip one outer pocket and find another inner pocket nestled inside. I hurry to the nightstand and grab the tube of cherry lip balm I tossed there last night. Griff once told me how much he liked the taste of it on my lips.

Paper? My frantic gaze searches his room. A black pen from the garage rests on top of his dresser but there's no paper in sight. I grab a crumpled receipt. That'll have to do. I scribble a quick note on the back of the receipt, then roll it around the lip balm and stuff it inside one of the inner pockets of Griff's backpack. Hopefully he finds it.

What if the show's producers search his bag and they laugh at my note?

Let them.

I pack a few more essentials he'll need and one more surprise, then start folding and rolling T-shirts into tight bundles, stacking everything in a pyramid shape.

The door opens and Griff slips inside. He carefully twists the flimsy lock on the handle and presses a finger to his lips.

He hurries toward me and backs me up to the far wall.

"Listen." His low, urgent voice sends more fear pumping through my veins.

He presses his palms to my cheeks and leans down to stare

into my eyes. "If anything happens to me, Hope Kendall has all my info."

I frown, recognizing the name but not understanding. "The Lost Kings' president's wife? Why? What info?"

"She's an attorney. She drafted a will for me."

A hot spike of fear stabs me between the ribs. "A will? Like, if you *die*?" I can barely get the words past my lips.

"You never know. I wanted to make sure my mother doesn't get her hands on anything." He flicks one hand in the air as if it's inconsequential. "My rent's paid up through the end of October. One way or another, I should be home by then."

"October! You said eight weeks."

"It's just in case. You have my keys. Stay here if you want."

"Alone?" *Is he nuts?* "I don't know if I can stay here all by myself, but I'll check on things for you."

"Thank you. Jerry already agreed to let me store your car in one of the outbuildings, so don't worry about that. Vapor will take care of moving it when he works on the paint. The keys for Black Beauty are on the peg in the kitchen. It's yours to drive while I'm gone if you want."

"Griff, I can't take your car—"

"I'm serious. I thought we'd be done with the Malibu before I left, so take the Chevelle." He forces a quick smile. "I'll feel better knowing you're driving it instead of having it sit idle for weeks. If you're not comfortable behind the wheel on your own, park it at your house. Remy can look after it."

My brain's struggling to keep up with all the information being thrown at me while my heart's splintering into a thousand pieces.

"Remy's storing my bike at your house. He and Eraser will come over and pick it up. Keys are—"

"On the peg in the kitchen," I finish for him.

He smiles and kisses my forehead. "Yes. Thank you."

Just help him get through this. Break down later.

Griff studies the items on the bed.

"I didn't know what you might want to wear." Since everything's in a neat roll, I describe what I pulled together.

"That's fine." He shakes his head. "I can't think straight."

"Phone charger." I snap my fingers.

He shakes his head. "I think they're gonna take my phone when I get there." His eyes widen. "Hang on."

He hurries to the closet and kneels, reaching way back into the darkest corner. His shoulder jerks as he pries something loose. He slides a box out and flips the lid off. "Burner phone I keep for emergencies," he whispers, holding up a small, silver, oval-shaped phone with a little antennae. "At least I can send you a text here and there to let you know everything's okay. I assume cameras will be rigged all over the house, so I'll have to be careful." He lifts his gaze, meeting my eyes. "I'll *only* use it to reach out to *you*."

I bite my lip and nod once.

He unwinds a cord from the box and plugs the phone in. "Still got juice." He flips it open and taps on the keypad.

My phone vibrates from the nightstand, and I hurry to pick it up.

Unknown: It's me.

"Got it." I add the number to my contacts.

"Hopefully they don't confiscate it." He shuts it down, wraps the cord around it, and stuffs the bundle into a sock.

"You've got lots of hidden pockets." I gesture to the backpack.

"I'm so sorry, Muffin." He slides the phone into a side pocket I hadn't noticed when I examined the backpack. Hopefully that means no one else will notice it either. "I never expected them to come today. I thought there was a chance I might still be here for your graduation."

Griff won't be there to see me graduate. "They really won't let you leave to come to my *graduation*?"

He shakes his head sadly. "Once I'm in, I'm in. Total lockdown, except for once-a-week calls."

Once a week. All the fun things I thought we'd finally get to do this summer—gone. No parties at Zips. No riding on the back of his bike. No movie nights at the drive-in. All the things I've wanted to do with Griff for years.

It's one summer. You'll make up for it next year.

But what if we don't survive this separation? What if Griff doesn't want to come back to Johnsonville? What if he doesn't want *me* if he does come home?

"Molly, I know how much this sucks," he says as if he's reading all my thoughts. "I wanted to do so many things with you this summer. But I should be home in time for the haunted carnival. We'll go to Picking Ladder Farms for apple cider donuts. The drive-in is still open on the weekends through most of October. There will be bonfires at Zips until snow starts flying. We'll finish the Malibu, race it, and win some money."

Every word's meant to reassure me. I nod slowly. Smile. I don't want to do anything to make this harder on him.

But I can't seem to smother the sense of impending doom squeezing the air from my lungs. My fears for Griff's safety and my anxiety about our future have combined into a sinister force taking up permanent space in my chest.

Molley

CHAPTER THIRTY-SEVEN

Molly

Someone knocks on the bedroom door. "Long ride, Griff. We need to roll out," Diane shouts.

"Shit." Griff stares at the pile of clothes and starts scooping things into his backpack.

"I'll wrap up a waffle for the road." I squeeze his shoulder.

"I warned them not to film you."

"It's okay." I wrap my arms around him and squeeze. "If it will help you. Give you an edge. Humanize you to the audience. To know you have loved ones cheering for you at home..." I shrug. "It can't hurt, right?"

He frowns and shakes his head. "No. I don't want you exposed to that."

"Griff!" Diane calls.

"I'll deal with them." I pat his shoulder.

In a daze, I step out of the bedroom and close the door behind me. The camera guy returns with the light in my face.

"Did ya squeeze in a quickie?" he asks.

"What? No."

"Knock it off." Diane shoos him away. She threads her arm through mine and steers me into the kitchen. "Dear, I need you to sign a release form so we can use your footage in the show. You *are* eighteen, right?"

"Yes," I snap, tired of this question. "What if I don't *want* to be in the show?"

"Of course you do!" She slaps a piece of paper on the kitchen table and sets a blue ballpoint pen next to it.

I sweep my gaze over the document, and it snags on my name already typed in several spots. She sure came prepared.

"Come on. Won't all your friends be jealous when they see you on the show?"

Not really. This lady exists in some alternate reality where everyone's dying to be famous. "It's not our thing."

"Honey..." Her voice loses its fake niceness and takes on a harder edge. "If you don't sign it, we'll need to re-shoot Griff's intro or cut it."

No, no. I don't want to be the reason he gets off to a bad start on the show. "It will help Griff if I sign it?"

"Yes! My gut says he's going to be very popular with our audience. And part of that will be his commitment to his loving girlfriend waiting at home for him."

False sincerity oozes through her words. But I sigh and take the pen she forces into my hand. "Can I read it first?" *My Nana didn't raise a fool.*

"Sure, sure. It's all standard."

Molly Holt—background actor—releases Sidespeed Salmon Productions and assigns permission to license all video recordings in any packaging and promotion for Ultimate Underground Fighter...

My vision blurs with boredom. I ignore the nagging sensation in my gut and sign where Diane points.

"Great! That's covered. I think your man's going to be the star of the show, Molly."

I force a quick smile.

"What are you doing?" Griff snaps at Diane. "I told you to leave her out of it."

"Griff, it's fine. Molly understands. She wants to help you win." Diane takes out her phone, scans the document, then slips it into a folder. She pats his shoulder. "You ready?"

"I don't know, I—"

"We'll get you whatever you need. Sponsors will be dropping off clothes and gear by the crate. Anything you forget, I'll have someone run out and buy for you." She nudges him toward the door.

My stomach twists. This is all happening so fast. "Wait."

I push past Diane and grab one of the leftover waffles on the counter and wrap it in plastic, then turn to hand it to Griff.

His lips tilt. "Thank you, Muffin."

He drops his bag, and it hits the floor with a thud. "Come here."

Frantic, I rush into his arms and cling to the safety of his body. "Griff." I curl my fingers into his shirt and inhale his scent. "I'm going to miss you so much."

"I know, baby. It's going to be okay." He shifts and turns us to the side. "Come on. Not now!" he barks.

I open my eyes. The blinding light burns my eyeballs again and I squeeze them shut. "They're filming us?" I whisper.

"I guess." He growls. "I love you, Molly. A few weeks are nothing. We can do this."

I gather my courage and pull away from him. Straightening my spine, I lift my chin and try to give him a reassuring, confident smile. "I'll be sending you winning vibes every day."

"Don't worry about me. Kick butt on all your finals. Don't let any of this distract you, okay? I'll be back before you know it."

I nod quickly. "We'll finish my car?"

"Yup. And take it to the drive-in." He leans in and kisses my forehead, stopping to take a deep inhale.

"Win for us," I say.

He seals his mouth over mine, taking a long, slow kiss.

"Niiiice," the camera guy says.

Griff curses, and we pull away.

"We gotta go, Griffin." Diane waves at me. "Molly, it was nice to meet you. I'm sure I'll see you again at the reunion show or something."

Reunion show?

Does that mean this goes on for *more* than eight weeks?

I turn my questioning gaze on Griff, but he's picking up his bag.

"Call Remy," Griff says. "Have him come get you."

"You can follow us downstairs," Diane says to me.

"No." Griff and I answer at the same time.

If I go downstairs with them, I'll throw myself on the car and try to force them to stay.

"Stay here. Lock the door behind us," Griff says.

"Okay," I agree.

The crew gathers their stuff and follows Griff with their cameras. Diane's careful to stay out of the shots. I follow her lead and keep to the side.

At the door, Griff turns. I rush to him and give him another kiss.

"Love you," he says.

"Love you too."

Then they move into the hallway. I can't watch. Griff's blank expression chills me from the inside out. It's the same face I've seen on him when he's in the ring. I close the door and put my back to it, silently sobbing.

In the hallway, I still hear the crew talking but I can't make out their words. I run into the bedroom, kick the door closed, and fling myself onto the bed.

Everything was so perfect. Last night. This morning.

Now he's gone.

WHAT SEEMS LIKE HOURS LATER, I peel myself off the bed and send Remy a text to come get me. I run through the apartment, straighten up and empty the garbage cans—anything I can think of to stop the tears from falling.

Griff said I could stay here. But there's no way I can be in his space without him.

Someone knocks on the door. Painfully aware that I'm alone, I creep to the door and peer into the hallway.

Remy.

Judging by the angry scowl on his face, walking home might've been a better option.

I open the door, and he storms inside.

"What the fuck is going on? You don't come home last night." He holds his phone up. "Griff sent me some cryptic message—"

"He did?"

"What's going on?"

I explain everything from the time Diane and her camera-toting minions showed up to Griff's departure.

"What do you mean they showed up and told him he had to leave?" Remy crosses his arms over his chest and glares at me.

I sob and hiccup at the same time.

"They said it was better for the show. I helped him pack and..." I work hard to wrangle my sobbing into submission. The harder I cry, the more Remy's anger seems to build.

He steps closer and pushes my hair off my shoulder, staring at my neck. "Wait a second. He had you...he let you spend the night here, then fucking left you all alone the next day?" he grinds out in a lethally low voice.

Embarrassment blasts my skin. Remy doesn't know we slept together. It's none of his business anyway.

"He didn't leave me!" I shout. "They *took* him. He didn't know today was the day. He didn't have a choice."

"The fuck he didn't. He signed up for this shit!" Remy clenches his fists. "I could fucking kill him right now."

"Remy, stop."

A tortured expression twists his features. "I don't know how to fix this for you, Molly."

"You can't." I take one breath, then another. The tears finally stop. "I don't need you to fix it. Just be here with me."

"Okay, okay." He gathers me in his arms, holding me tight. "I'm here." After a few seconds, he rocks us back and forth, the way he did when I was little, and we hid in the closet together during one of Dad's tirades.

Even though I'm safe with my brother, without Griff here, it feels like half of my heart is missing and I don't know how we're going to survive this separation.

Molley

CHAPTER THIRTY-EIGHT

GRIFF

Being without Molly is already its own special hell. I crave her hot skin against mine. An overwhelming need. Finally making love to her the night before I had to leave is probably the shittiest thing I've ever done. I swear, the minute I'm home, I'm taking her to bed and we're not leaving for at least a week.

My whole apartment would fit into the room I've been assigned. White-and-gray wallpaper lines the walls. The big, white, fluffy comforter tossed over the king-size bed seems like a poor choice for a sweaty fighter's bedroom, but as long as I'm not paying for the dry cleaning, I don't care. From what I saw when Diane walked me to my room earlier, every guest room in this wing of the house is basically the same. Maybe the production company got a discount for buying the bedding and furniture in bulk. At least there's no tacky hotel art on the walls.

I toss my bag on a purple velvet chair in the corner. My lips curve up. Molly would love this chair.

Molly. I can't stop thinking about her. This is so messed up. I feel like the biggest fucking asshole. I can't even call to see if she's okay. They took my phone as soon as I got into the "limo" for the insufferable ride to Long Island.

I unzip the largest pocket of my backpack and start pulling out clothes. Hell, I don't even know what I brought with me. Molly laid out a bunch of choices and I blindly chose whatever was closest. Having her pack for me had been a good thing. Even in all the chaos, she took time to roll my clothes into neat little bundles to maximize my packing space. How'd she get so good at packing? The longest trip she's ever taken is to visit Hayden's grandparents in Vermont.

Shaking my head, I explore the small walk-in closet and hang my meager wardrobe. I return to the pack and pull a pair of sneakers from the bottom pocket. Molly had rolled and stuffed socks inside them. Diane had said something about sponsors giving us all sorts of free shit and that she'd need my measurements and sizes for clothing. They probably don't want me to look like a stray dog who wandered onto the set.

Once I put the clothes away, I explore the smaller pockets of my backpack. My hand brushes against a sharp edge, and I pull out the framed photo from my dresser. Remy, Molly, and me. I trace my finger over her face. She knew I'd want something to remind me of home. I set the frame on the nightstand so I can see it first thing in the morning. Not even annoyed I'll have to look at Remy's smug face too.

Paper crinkles against my fingers in the next pocket. A crumpled receipt? I pull it out and something hard hits the floor.

"Dammit." I hurry to scoop it up before it rolls away.

I snag the bright red tube. *Cherry vanilla EOS lip balm.* Molly's favorite. I stare at the receipt in my hand and frown. It's for a car part I bought last week. I flip it over and find Molly's neat handwriting on the back.

Griff,

Use this when you need a kiss from me. I'm so proud of you. You've got this!

Love always,

Your Muffin

My throat tightens. I know damn well how much she hates

that I'm doing this. Hates that I'll be away for so long. But she still wanted to be brave and encourage me. Give me the only thing she could think of during a chaotic shitstorm we never expected.

I uncap the balm. The inner tube's a bright purple. No wonder it's her favorite brand. I smooth the balm over my lips. It's not Molly, but the scent *is* comforting in a way. I curl my hand around the tube and set it on top of the nightstand next to the photo, so it doesn't get lost.

Jesus. Are the cameras in the house already on? Diane mentioned that there were cameras everywhere. Even in the bedrooms. Good God, are they going to air footage of me getting sentimental over a damn lip balm?

Sure enough, above the closet door, I find a small camera mounted to the wall, aimed at the bed.

The fuck? They hoping to catch me jerking off every night?

I scowl at the camera but it's impossible to tell if it's actually recording. Could be fake. Meant to fuck with my head.

Would they put cameras in the bathroom too? I snag my backpack off the bed and walk into the adjoining bathroom. Bet the hot water in this shower never runs out. The damn thing looks like a car wash with so many nozzles and knobs pointed in every direction.

I shut and lock the bathroom door, then do my best to scan the space for hidden cameras. When I'm satisfied no one's gonna watch me take a piss, I dig into one of the hidden side pockets along the edge of my pack. I pry the slim zipper open and dig for the flip phone I stashed in there earlier.

It buzzes to life, and I clamp it between my hands to muffle the sound. God damn, these things are so annoying to send a simple text. But I manage to tap out a few words to Molly.

Me: Got here safe.
Thank you for the picture and kisses.
I miss you so bad.
I'm so sorry I had to leave like that.
I love you.

That about covers it. I stare at the screen for a few seconds. Did Remy pick her up like I asked? Is she home with him now? Is she crying? God, I hope not.

I hesitate over the keypad. Should I text Remy too? I can't risk anyone finding out I have a phone. The more people who know and try to reach me, the bigger the risk of getting caught.

I flip it shut and tuck it back into the secret pocket, then leave the bathroom and store the backpack on a top shelf in the walk-in closet. No one should have a reason to go in there. I stand back and stare. The backpack isn't visible unless someone's really looking for something.

After the ugly way I had to leave Molly this morning, I'm more committed than ever to making all this misery mean something.

I'm staying till the bitter end and winning the big prize.

Molly

CHAPTER THIRTY-NINE

GRIFF

On the first night we're all officially in the mansion—or "training house" as they keep calling it—we're summoned downstairs for "cocktail hour." Since I have no idea what one wears to that kind of thing, I throw on a T-shirt with the Zips logo on the front and a pair of cargo shorts.

Diane said they wanted me for my looks and fighting skills, not my fashion sense.

In a short amount of time, I'm introduced to so many people, my head's spinning. I can't keep the names of the other contestants straight. Nine other guys, probably ranging from eighteen to thirty. A mix of ethnicities. Everyone seems on edge. Sussing out the competition. Lots of *cocky asshole* vibes cloud the air. Nothing I haven't dealt with before.

On *my* turf, I run the show. People know not to fuck with me. Here, it's like starting from scratch. Like prison, someone will probably pick a fight with the biggest guy just to try and prove they're the top dog.

I'm certainly not small. But there are at least four other contestants bigger than me. One of them looks like he came straight from the *Icelandic League of Heavy Lifters.*

I'm here to win, so I plan to hang back and assess the situation until it's time to make my move.

Another guy, maybe a few years older than me, seems to be taking the same approach. Diane had introduced him to me as Venom earlier. *That* name I remembered. I'd internally scoffed when Diane said it, but the more I observe, the more it fits—he's silent and his movements are slow, but his calculating eyes seem to radiate deadly intentions. He's one I need to watch.

I bypass the grand living room, a large, open-air space with cameras hanging from every available spot. Two large sectionals are set up in the middle, facing each other—like an annoying Tetris puzzle that can't be cleared. A massive flat-screen takes up the wall across from the couch, making it impossible to sit and see the screen without craning your neck. Just looking at the configuration makes my neck hurt.

On the far end of the grand room, there's an L-shaped corner to the right. A normal-sized sectional and built-in bookcases full of a variety of reading material fill the space. Looks like someone raided a used bookstore and threw everything on the shelf for decoration instead of potential reading interest. The cozy area reminds me of Molly, so that's the territory I stake out. If I win, I'm going to buy a house for us with a book nook just like this for Molly to fill with all her favorites.

"Avoiding the inevitable pissing match, too?" someone asks.

I glance up from a shaggy copy of *The Fighter's Mind.* Venom's big frame takes up the immediate area. I'm not sure I'm willing to share my corner with him, so I answer with a disinterested, "Yeah."

"I think Diane wants us to make friends."

I snort. "I'm sure she does." *Fuck Diane.* After ambushing me at my apartment and giving me less than an hour to pack and say goodbye to Molly, she can kiss my ass.

"She spring that shock-and-awe ambush with the film crew at your house, too?"

It's like he stole the thought from my brain. Some of my

indifference thaws. I set the book on the end table and nod. "Yeah."

He sits in the chair across from me. "My wife was hysterical," he confesses. "She wasn't thrilled about this in the first place. Then them coming with no warning..." He glances away. "They won't let me use a phone to call her until Tuesday, either."

My contraband flip phone is right upstairs.

No. You just met this dude. What if he's working for the producers? He could be trying to figure out if we're breaking any rules and get me kicked off the show before it even begins.

"Yeah, my girlfriend was really upset," I say. "They filmed her, then tricked her into signing a release so they can use the footage. I'm not thrilled."

"That's not cool. Kelly signed a lot of the same stuff I had to sign." He shrugs. "I guess 'cause we're married or whatever. They wanted to know we're both on board."

That's where I might've messed up. Wanting to protect her from any reality show drama, I downplayed Molly's significance in my life when I interviewed with the other producers.

Although Diane *had* shown up to my apartment prepared with that contract.

"Boys." One of the producers, whose name I haven't bothered to learn, steps around the corner and snaps his fingers at us. "We're doing icebreakers in the main room. Come, come."

He snaps those fingers at me again, he's gonna lose 'em.

Venom slides his gaze my way and seems to be having the same amputating-the-producer's-fingers thoughts. "I wasn't a fan of being called 'boy' when I was one," he grumbles.

"Same." I push to my feet and follow him into the main room.

We join the loose circle, standing behind one of the couches. Some of the guys are sprawled out on the fluffy white furniture. Some of them chose to stand like Venom and me. With all the perfectly angled bright lights and the white furniture, my eyes won't stop twitching. A low, painful throb pounds through the top of my skull.

Someone passes out bottles of beer. I stare at the fancy IPA in my hand and my lip curls. This isn't gonna help my headache. And the last thing I need is to lower my inhibitions my first night in the house. I walk over to the kitchen/bar area and set the bottle down. In the fridge, I find rows of bottled waters, and I grab two of those instead.

"You Mormon, Royal?" someone shouts behind me.

"No." I uncap the bottle, checking first to make sure it's sealed. "Lights are giving me a headache. Don't want to make it worse."

I return to the group and hold out the extra bottle to Venom. I must be feeling guilty for not loaning him my burner to call his wife. He accepts the drink and nods his thanks.

"All right!" Diane stands in front of the fireplace and claps her hands like a maniacal cheerleader. "How's everyone feeling?"

"Pumped!" someone shouts.

"Let's do this!" someone else adds.

Caution and distrust still rule me. I can't help it. I'm not wired to trust *anyone* outside of my chosen family. But a bit of excitement wedges its way inside my chest. I've never done anything like this before. It's different. I'm eager to pick up some new skills.

And I definitely want to win that money.

I want to make Molly proud and return home as a champion.

"Let me introduce your host." Diane extends her hands like she's welcoming a revered cult leader into our midst. An older man in a black suit, with a shaved head, joins us. He has the frame and posture of a retired athlete and even looks vaguely familiar. Hard to tell underneath the layers of orange foundation someone spackled over his leathery face.

Venom leans closer and murmurs, "Someone's had one too many eye lifts or Botox."

I mash my lips together to contain my laughter. Now that

Venom mentioned it, my attention's drawn to the host's almost cat-like squint.

The host—Matt—recites a long list of the belts and championships he's won. His record's impressive, actually. I'm just having a hard time taking him seriously when he's wearing so many layers of foundation that don't match the rest of his skin.

"Here's what it comes down to, boys." Matt takes a long, dramatic pause.

I cross my arms over my chest and rock back on my heels.

"Great moments in your life are born from great opportunities," he says in a low, melodramatic tone that tickles my *get-the-fuck-outta-here* laughter response.

"That's what you've been given with the chance to be part of this show. Opportunity." Matt draws out the word and widens his eyes as much as the laws of Botox allow.

For fuck's sake, it's reality television. It's not that deep.

"Whether you stay until the end or get sent home the first round, you're *all* champs. You've been given an opportunity to do something great, and you seized it!" Matt lifts his hand in the air like he's reciting the speech from *Braveheart*. "Be proud of that! Most people don't seize the opportunities they're given. They let fear hold them back or they're not smart enough to even recognize what's in front of them."

He drones on about fear, opportunity, and fighting, working a different variation of those three themes into every sentence. Is he trying out a few different speeches that they'll edit later? Or does he really love the sound of his own voice that much?

"Okay. Let's go around and introduce ourselves. Ring names only," Matt says, wrapping up the inspirational speech. "We'll film your individual intros later." He points to a guy perched on the arm of the couch.

The fighter jumps to his feet. He's about my height and build. Once he opens his mouth, that's where our similarities end. "Got the name Naptime 'cause when my fist hits you, it's lights out, sucka." He dips and rips like he's in the ring, evading his opponent's attack, and then he throws a counterpunch.

I open my mouth and let out a loud, obnoxious yawn.

Naptime zeroes in on me and thrusts his fist in my direction. "Got something to say, pretty boy?"

"No, that's impressive," I deadpan.

The guy frowns as if he can't tell if I'm making fun of him or not.

The corner of Matt's mouth twitches. "Spicy. I like it."

The next few names are so generic, I realize I shouldn't have judged Naptime so fast—Rumbling Thunder, Snorting Bull, Powerful Pirate, Bear Trap, Hammer Fists. I guess mine's not much more creative but at least it's simple.

When it's my turn, I nod to the other guys. "Stonewall— when my fists hit you, it's like running into a stone wall."

Naptime scoffs and rolls his eyes. Yeah, I guess I deserve that.

Another guy steps up, waving his arms around like he's trying to scare away a flock of seagulls. "Deadass, cuz I ain't fuckin' around in the cage."

"Bro, *Deadass* has a punchable face," Venom whispers.

I bite my lip and nod.

A big guy with the squarest jaw I've ever seen and a perfectly round puff of white-blond curls raises his hand. If his arms and legs weren't covered in the same white-blond fuzz, I'd assume he'd bleached his hair. "Woolly Mammoth."

I would've guessed Merino Sheep, but okay.

"Because my fists will send you back to prehistoric times," he finishes.

Are you sure, bud? I study Woolly's face but there's no hint of humor in his earnest expression.

Venom goes last. "I got my name from the joint locks and chokes I use to immobilize my opponent."

So serious and specific. Assuming his background is in Brazilian jujitsu or aikido, I study him closer. His quiet, thoughtful approach should be scaring the shit out of these other guys. But they seem to dismiss him quickly. Must've never been put in a nerve hold. That shit *hurts.*

"That's great," Matt says, raising his voice over our chatter. "Do we all feel like we know each other better now? You're going to be living and training together for weeks. So get comfortable with your housemates."

Behind us there's a clanging and shuffling. The whole group turns toward the sound. A guy behind a camera throws a hand signal to Matt.

"All right, gentlemen, we have a surprise for you."

A deafening *clickety-clacking* echoes through the marble entryway.

Five women in short dresses and high heels strut into the room like they're auditioning for a Vegas show. *What the fuck?*

"What's going on?" Venom rumbles.

"Yeah, baby!" Deadass shouts, punching his fists in the air. "That's what I'm talkin' about."

I hope I square off against Deadass first. Can't wait to wipe the floor with his obnoxious face.

"No cage or octagon is complete without the lovely ladies who hold up the placards," Matt says with a cheesy grin.

Ring girls. I can't even protest. We employ plenty of them at The Castle. But no one ever mentioned they'd be part of this show.

"And if a few of you happen to find love, won't that be romantic?" Matt adds.

What. The. Fuck? This is so not what I signed up for.

"But the numbers are uneven, so you'll be competing against each other in the ring. And *outside* the ring, you'll compete for the ladies'...*affection.*" The emphasis he puts on that last word makes my skin crawl.

"I didn't sign up to be a fuckin' john," Venom sneers. "This isn't cool."

"The girls are here to *elevate* the fights," another producer says with an indignant sniff that seems fake as fuck. I can't take this dude seriously—his perfect eyebrows look like they were lacquered on with a toothbrush. "Not *service* you."

"Bullshit," I mutter. My gaze searches the room for Diane. She might be a sneaky bitch, but I respect her more than these other producers. Did she even know about this?

"Cool, then they don't gotta stay in the house with us," Bear Trap says.

"What he said." Venom points at Bear Trap. At least I'm not the only one lacking enthusiasm for this new arrangement.

"The romantic aspect is an extra bonus for our contestants. And an element of suspense for your viewers," Matt insists.

"Hard. Pass," Bear Trap rumbles.

Deadass rubs his hands together and licks his lips, staring at the women like he's ordering off a menu. "More for us."

"Jesus Christ." Venom groans. "I told my wife this was a serious show. Not some twisted *UFC-Bachelor* mashup."

"Same," I grumble. "This isn't what I came for."

"It's a distraction technique." Woolly taps his forehead. "Stay mentally strong. You can resist any temptation."

"I'm *not* tempted. I have a girlfriend." How could I be tempted by any woman other than Molly? I'm only *here* to win money for our future. If I wanted a mindless fuck, I could've done that at home. Not on the set of this twisted show where I have no doubt the producers will exploit any hookup to the max.

As if she's ignored our protests, one of the girls makes a beeline for Venom, Bear Trap, and me. If she moves any quicker, her boobs are gonna explode out of her tight red satin dress.

They might've dressed her up like a tart, but her hazel eyes are sharp and assessing. "Venom, Stonewall, Bear Trap, right?" she says pointing at each of us. "I'm Kiki."

"Congratulations," Venom says in a dry tone.

"Not. Interested," Bear Trap adds.

Who knows if she wasn't tricked into being here? Maybe she was told she'd auditioned for a date-an-athlete show. "Sorry. I think we're all spoken for." I glance at Bear Trap to confirm but he just keeps glaring at Kiki.

"Where the fuck is Diane?" Venom twists around, his gaze searching the vast house. He storms off, and Bear Trap follows him.

Kiki steps closer to me. "Don't go." She pouts. "We watched the pickup videos for all the guys. Your little girlfriend was so cute." Her tone turns a shade mocking.

Danger prickles over the back of my neck. My expression hardens. I didn't want to be a dick, but my relationship isn't up for discussion. With anyone. Not for any price.

She glances to the side, then lifts her gaze to mine again. She rests her hand on my chest. "I've got a question for you, though."

I wrap my hand around her wrist and pry her hand off me. "Yeah? What's that?" I sneer.

"Why are you letting some little girl back in your hick town lock you down so young, Griff?" Her hazel eyes drill into mine but there's no genuine curiosity or kindness. "You have so much potential. Why shackle yourself to one girl when you can have your pick of any *woman*?"

She wants to bait me into an argument. And I'm not biting.

I lean down to make sure she hears every word. "You wouldn't understand. She's not my prison. She's my peace."

Molley

CHAPTER FORTY

GRIFF

Everything I thought I knew about fighting up to this point in my life was a lie.

I've never trained harder. In school, I learned to fight on the playground to protect myself and later to protect my friends. In the dank basement of the detention center, I started out fighting to gain special privileges from the sick guards who pitted inmates against each other. Later, it became a battle just to survive that hellhole.

Once I left the correctional facility behind, I never fought dirty. Hard—yes. Dirty—no.

Remy and I formed our fight club to keep our skills sharp and earn extra money. I thought I was hot shit. I rarely lost a fight at The Castle. Respect was earned with blood, sweat, and fists.

At the "training house," I'm way the fuck out of my depth. The little underground fighting ring I run with Remy might as well be a playground happy hour.

Half of these guys are street fighters. Dirty fighters. The kind of guys Remy and I would ban from entering the ring at The Castle.

Despite the upscale surroundings, it reminds me way too much of my time in the basement.

Venom, Bear Trap, Woolly, and I form a sort of alliance. Together, we've avoided the "romantic drama" element that was introduced to the show.

They're all serious fighters. Venom's clearly above all our skill levels, but instead of dogging us for it or using our lack of knowledge against us, he's been showing us different techniques. Each of us adds a little something to our group.

Unfortunately, one thing I know a lot about is avoiding strikes. I can advance, and dodge, and throw some vicious punches. The day before our first matches, we huddle in the gym and talk strategy.

"Your reflexes are unbelievable," Venom says.

I tilt my head. "I've conditioned myself to respond without thinking."

"I see that. You've got a useful toolbox of moves."

I snort. Sounds like something Eraser would say. "I have a friend back home that would agree with you."

"He fight too?"

"Sometimes." Only out of necessity.

"You're going up against Hammer Fists. You need to use your evasive moves," Woolly says.

No shit. That guy's built like the side of a mountain.

Venom nods. "He'll bulldoze you easily if you try to engage him at long range."

"I don't know about *easily*," I protest, mildly insulted. "But yeah, I plan to get close, cut loose, withdraw."

"Resist the temptation to blast him with a flurry of body shots," Bear Trap says.

I roll my eyes his way. "Do I look suicidal?"

"He's heavy on the back leg," Venom says with a thoughtful tilt of his head. "A quick step in and chop is something he probably won't expect."

"He's heavy *period*," Woolly says. "Make him move so he's out of breath. Use those quick feet to dart away and cut some angles. Make him keep moving to defend himself."

"I will." I've fought bigger guys before, and that strategy's worked well.

On fight night, I'm bubbling over with confidence. Maybe too much. The air in the arena we're using tonight is thick with anticipation.

Hammer Fists is huge and not much of a talker. We shake hands before entering the cage but that's about it. While the producers fuck around with the lights, I take a moment to close my eyes and breathe.

You've got this. You know what you're doing. Keep moving. Don't let him grab you. Stay off the cage wall.

I open my eyes and bounce on my toes. Adrenaline thunders through my veins. Across from me, Hammer Fists is formidable. But his expression's blank. He could be assessing my strengths and weaknesses or pondering how long it takes grass to grow. It's hard to tell.

As soon as we're given the signal, Hammer Fists lunges for me with his thick arms.

"You tryin' to bear hug me, bro?" I dart away.

He grunts. We circle each other. I see an opportunity and weave in at an angle. I throw a quick shot that lands in his solar plexus. I'm too keyed up and my fist doesn't connect as well as it should've. He drops his elbow, catching my shoulder, and I rock sideways.

Fuck no.

I dart away. Too far. He whips out a powerful roundhouse kick to my midsection. The thud reverberates through my body. I grit my teeth and move in closer.

The arena's quiet. Too quiet. I'm used to a crowd cheering or talking shit as background noise. Hammer Fists' heavy breathing and slow steps trigger something at the back of my mind.

Gas this big fucker.

I cut in close and pop him once, twice. He moves to defend. I weave away. I hit him again. He moves to kick again, and I switch and come in with a kick to his back leg. He grunts and grabs me in a clinch.

Fuck.

I posture up and move in tight so he can't knee me.

Keep him busy. Don't let him apply force.

I distract him with my hands and angle my feet for better leverage and dump him on the floor.

Breathing hard, I back away.

"Cut!" someone yells.

Huh? Even though he's still on his back, I don't want to take my eyes off Hammer Fists.

"Hold on!" one of the producers yells.

Bright light sweeps through the cage. Hammer Fists groans and rolls to his side.

"Stonewall! Move in closer!"

To what?

Is the fight over? Hammer Fists didn't really tap out.

Confused, I move closer to the center of the ring. The ref steps inside and squats next to Hammer Fists, talking too low to hear him.

The ref stands and raises my hand in the air, turning me toward the brightest lights.

To make the outcome even more muddled, the ref has Hammer Fists stand and do the same raised hand, turn-toward-the-camera thing.

Did we tie?

"You're a fast fucker," Hammer Fists says to me with a respectful chin lift.

"Knew I couldn't let you grab me."

A sinister grin spreads across his face.

"Is that it?" I ask the ref.

"We got what we needed."

I glance at Hammer Fists and he shrugs.

THE NEXT DAY, we all have to sit through a ceremony where Matt and some other "expert judges" criticize our moves and performances. None of it is constructive or helpful critique.

Then we're forced to watch Bear Trap get the axe.

"Shit." I drop my head and sigh. I was hoping none of my guys were leaving yet.

I haven't known him long, but it sucks.

Venom, Woolly, and I huddle around Bear Trap to say our goodbyes.

"This shit's fucked," he says, shaking his head.

He gives me a hug. "Stay vigilant, Stonewall."

"I'll try."

"Hit me up when you get out."

I pull away and shake his hand. "Will do."

He says a similar goodbye to Venom and Woolly, flips everyone else the bird, and storms off the set.

"And then there were three little monks." Deadass pulls a sad face at us and mockingly rubs his fists against his eyes.

I glare at him but don't respond to the taunt. *Why couldn't I have gone up against him instead of Hammer Fists?*

"Center," Woolly reminds me. "Ignore him."

Kiki—persistent as ever—hurries to console us. No one's confirmed it, but I've gotten the impression she was "assigned" to us or something. I rarely interact with the other girls, but somehow Kiki's always in my face. Wandering the hallway outside my room, bumping into me outside the gym, in the kitchen.

"I'm going to the gym," I say.

Venom pats my back.

Working out to avoid the drama going on with the other contestants is the only thing preserving my sanity. It keeps me from missing Molly. When I think about her, I train. When the pain becomes too much, I picture Molly's smile, replay her laugh in my head. Think about our last night together. The note she gave me. The little cherries embroidered on her underwear that she picked out just for me. That only makes me miss her. So, I jump on the treadmill and run until my body's as limp as overcooked spaghetti.

For a show dedicated to fighters training, Venom, Bear Trap, Woolly, and I were usually the only ones in the gym. Guess now it'll just be the three of us.

The days after the match are a never-ending monotonous routine of physical punishment and mental gymnastics. Forming the alliance helps. But I'm still on my guard—which one of the guys will stab me in the back? Will I see it coming? Betrayal always comes from the ones you least expect.

Finally, I get my weekly phone call.

I swear I had more access to outside communication when I was in kiddie prison.

"Remember, no details about the show," the producer reminds me.

I haven't talked to Diane since that first night. She didn't even show up for my first match. And she wasn't at the *fuck off* ceremony, either.

"Yeah, yeah," I answer.

"Keep it short. If she asks about the show, cut her off or we'll cut *you* off," the producer warns.

I flick an irritated glare at him. How the fuck did I ever let myself get roped into this bullshit?

"I got it." I jerk my chin toward the door to the room that's barely bigger than an old-time phone booth. "Now get out."

Once the door's closed, I pick up the phone and punch in Molly's number. Part of me doesn't even want to talk to her. To expose her to any of this madness. But I miss her so damn much. It's selfish but I need to hear her voice. Know that she's okay. That she's still my girl.

"Griff?" Excitement rings through her greeting.

"Hey, baby." I refuse to call her Muffin with all these creeps listening in on our phone calls. "How are you?"

"I miss you." She sighs. "How are you?"

"Missing you too." I clear my throat and flick my gaze in the direction I think the "hidden" camera is located. "I can't talk too long. Tell me what you're up to." I hesitate. "Remember, they're recording my calls."

"I know." She sighs. "Well, finals are next week and I'm freaking out about Pre-calc. I wish I'd never taken it."

Damn, I wish I could see her face. Or do something to reassure her. "Can any of your friends help you out?"

"Maybe." She groans. "I don't know."

"What else?"

"Well, I took the week off from work to focus on finals and I almost think I'd rather be ringing up groceries than studying." She laughs, then stops abruptly. "I miss you."

"I miss you too."

"Enough about tests," she says. "How is the training? Are you learning all sorts of killer new moves? You're allowed to tell me about *that*, right?"

"It's good. One of the other guys is into—"

Click.

"Molly?"

No answer.

I stare at the phone. "God dammit, I didn't say anything!" I shout into the camera. "What the fuck?"

The door opens again. "We warned you, bro. Nothing about the show. Nada."

Rage swirls inside me. I wanted to do the show *for* Molly. Now I can't even talk to her for five uninterrupted minutes?

I'm not sure how much longer I can handle this before I snap.

Molley

CHAPTER FORTY-ONE

Molly

I JERK MY CAP OFF MY HEAD AND TOSS IT IN THE AIR with the rest of my classmates. For a second, I watch all the shining green and gold rise above us, then I throw my arms around Hayden's neck.

"We did it!" we both squeal at the same time.

She squeezes me back, and we jump around in a circle together. Caps rain down on us. Classmates push and dive to grab the right cap. As if it matters. Someone shoves one into my hands. A tag with *Holt* is pinned inside. *Okay, it matters.* I have to return this if I want my deposit back.

Hayden scoops her cap off the ground and hugs it to her chest. "Wade's speech was amazing. He's brilliant, right?"

If by amazing and brilliant she means long-winded and used a lot of big words to say nothing, then yes, he was *brilliant* as our valedictorian.

"It was a good speech." I force a quick smile to bolster the weak compliment. My girl accepts no criticism of her beloved.

Stop it. I'm salty because Griff can't be here. I can't even talk to him without someone listening in and cutting us off. But I shouldn't take it out on Hayden. She and Wade make a cute couple. Even if I still think his brother's a creep.

Jenn, Kyla, and Darcy barrel into us, and we form one big circle-hug.

"What a relief. We're finally out of here!" Kyla shouts, tipping her face toward the sky.

"I'll toast to that." Darcy lifts her cap in the air like a wineglass.

Jenn leans into Hayden and whispers something in her ear. Kyla starts talking about all the parties she wants to stop by tonight.

"We're all coming over to watch Griff's show at your place Sunday, right?" Darcy asks me.

An uncertain smile flickers over my lips. At first, I appreciated the support of my friends. But the show's taken such an awkward and gross turn, I'm almost embarrassed to watch it with anyone else.

The week before finals, when the first episode aired and all my classmates saw my tear-streaked goodbye to Griff, had been mortifying. While I didn't get bullied the same way I had as a kid, the relentless whispering and laughing behind my back made the last few days of high school unbearable.

Then the second episode aired, and the ring bunnies were introduced. One of them—Kiki— always seemed to be hovering around Griff. After that, several of my classmates made a point to tell me they were *Team Kiki,* which made me want to vomit.

Horrible stuff was posted about me online from people all over the country watching the show. Remy would've committed murder if he knew where to find these people.

"Molly?" Hayden places her hand on my arm. "Is that okay? Should we still come over?"

"Sure," I answer in a less than enthusiastic tone.

Kyla stops rattling off classmates' names. "Did you see the ads they've been running for this week's show?" Her nervous gaze shifts to Darcy, Hayden, then finally me.

"No, I was too busy worrying about this." I wave my hands in the air to indicate the graduation ceremony.

"Oh..." Kyla's gaze drops to the ground.

Well, that's not good. "Why? What's—"

"Hey, graduate." Remy taps my shoulder.

I turn, and he holds out his arms. At least *one* family member came to see me. The only one I have left as far as I'm concerned. "Thanks for sitting through all this," I say against his ear.

"Wouldn't have missed it for anything." He squeezes me tight. "Proud of you."

"Thanks." Over his shoulder, I spot Juliet, Vapor, Ella, and Eraser. "You made them come too?"

He laughs and holds me at arm's length. "Made them? Are you kidding? Juliet pitched a fit this morning. I'm pretty sure she robbed some eleventh graders of their tickets."

"He's exaggerating. Congratulations, Molly." Juliet glides next to Remy and nudges him aside to pull me in for a hug. "I thought you'd be a little sad Griff's not here and might need some extra voices cheering you on," she says, low enough for only me to hear.

"I thought I recognized your whistle." I grin and step back. "Thank you."

"Girl, that was *me*." Ella pushes in next to Juliet and squeezes me with more strength than someone her size should be capable of. "Congrats."

"Thanks."

Eraser and Vapor offer quick hugs and congratulations, then step to the side with Remy.

Juliet squints at me and presses the back of her hand to my cheek. "You're so red, Molly. Did you wear sunscreen?"

Now that she mentions it, a stinging sensation prickles my cheeks.

"Here." She opens her giant purse, pulls out a metal water bottle, and shoves it toward me. "Drink some water."

I accept the cool, slick metal and smack my dry lips together. "Aren't you the one always telling me *not* to accept strange drinks?"

"I'm not a stranger." She rolls her eyes. "And it's ice water."

"She's got like six of those in there." Ella taps a piece of masking tape with a black M scribbled on the front of the bottle in my hands.

Vapor lifts his hand. "Can confirm. I carried that bag into the stadium." He flashes a quick smile at his wife who grins back at him.

Grateful for the drink, I flip the cap open and take a deep sip. Cool water slips down my throat. I'm more parched than I realized and take several long swallows before capping the bottle. "Thank you."

Juliet takes it from me and sticks it back in her purse.

"You're such a mom," Ella teases.

"Duh." Juliet shrugs.

Vapor wraps his arms around Juliet's waist and hugs her to him, leaning down to kiss her cheek. "My girl's always prepared."

"At least one of us is," Remy says, holding up his empty hands. "I brought myself and nothing else."

Eraser slaps my brother's shoulder. "That's why I always say you're as useful as an ashtray on a motorcycle."

"I don't see *you* carrying anything." Remy points his wide eyes at Eraser's empty hands.

"Wrong. So wrong, bro." Eraser pulls a white envelope out of his back pocket and hands it to me. "For our little graduate."

"Aw, thank you." I take the envelope. "You guys didn't have to do that."

"*He* didn't," Ella teases. "Open it at home."

"Uh, okay." I tuck it into the little purse at my side.

"Come on, Molly." Hayden tugs on my arm. "We're all headed to my house before we start hitting the parties."

I glance at Remy, hoping he'll save me. But he's busy bullshitting with Vapor and Eraser again.

"I'm going to run home and change first." I tug on my gown. "I'm all sweaty."

Hayden pouts for a second, then nods. "All right. But don't disappoint me, girl."

HAYDEN WAS right to be skeptical. Once I'm home, the thought of leaving is intolerable. I just want to crawl into bed and sleep.

"Come on. You should go have fun with your friends," Remy insists.

My heart's not in it. "Honestly, I'm really tired." I touch my forehead. "I think I got sunstroke out in the heat all afternoon."

Remy cups my cheek and frowns. "You *are* really red."

"Juliet already lectured me about sunscreen," I warn, too tired for a scolding.

He chuckles and pushes me toward the kitchen. "Drink a glass of water, then I'll let you go upstairs and sleep."

"Thanks, *Dad*." I smirk.

Hydrated, moisturized, and in my pajamas, I finally settle under the covers and stare at my phone. It buzzes in my hand and I drop it, the hard edge smacking my chin.

"Ow, dammit," I grumble, picking it up and flicking open the message.

G: Congratulations, baby.

Me: I miss you!

G: Miss you too.

I stare and wait but nothing else comes through. I'd give anything to hear Griff's voice tonight.

Did someone catch him texting on an unapproved phone? From the show, it looks like there are cameras stashed all over the house—even in the bedrooms.

Exhausted and sad, I set the phone down and close my eyes.

I'm finally done with school. I had friends and family there to see me walk the stage. More than some of my classmates had. I'm grateful. I am.

But the one person I needed the most wasn't there. I know Griff said he was doing this show for our future. That it was what was best for *us*.

Without him here, alone in the dark stillness of night, I'm finding that harder and harder to believe.

Molly

CHAPTER FORTY-TWO

Molly

"All right!" Kyla punches her fist in the air. "Let's watch Griff kick some butt!"

"Woo!" Darcy and Hayden answer.

"Or watch him embarrass himself more thoroughly," Eraser says in a dry tone.

"Hush," Ella teases, snuggling close to him on our couch.

Remy glares at the television. "This show is such bullshit."

I agree but don't want to criticize Griff. Especially to my brother. Remy's been livid since the show aired the footage of me. Every week, they've flashed my face on the screen at some point—no doubt to remind the audience of Griff's poor, pathetic teenage girlfriend pining away for him in our small, sheltered, upstate town. They got a lot of mileage making fun of the photo I sent with Griff. He didn't seem to care what anyone said, though, and left it right on his nightstand. At least that was something.

I understand it's a television show. I can't even call it a *reality* show because so far, nothing that's aired has anything to do with the real Griff or our relationship.

I miss him so much.

I graduated near the top of my class, but the way this show

portrays me, I look like I don't have two brain cells to rub together. Sweet, naive, virginal, and *dumb*.

Some of the charming comments I've read online scroll through my head. *He probably cheats on her all the time. How pathetic. She's the kind of girl you marry, not fuck. Bet she's a starfish in the sack. She's kinda cute but probably dumber than a bag of hair.* If it's not the too-stupid-to-live narrative, other people say I'm probably a whore, sleeping my way through town while Griff's "working hard" to earn money for us. I can't win.

Remy's threatened to lock up my phone in the gun safe in his room at night so I don't stay up until dawn, doom scrolling for shitty comments about myself.

Worse, I know everyone in this room has read that stuff. Even if they don't believe it, and they're on my side, I want to claw my way out of my own skin from the humiliation.

I don't want to watch this week's episode. But I can't *not* watch it, either. And I don't want to be alone when I do.

I sit on the floor with my back to the couch. Kyla drops down next to me. Hayden sits above me, absently weaving her fingers through my hair. It's oddly comforting.

"How about a French braid?" Hayden asks in a chipper tone.

As if a different hair style could cheer me up.

"Sure," I mumble.

Darcy takes up the old love seat, farthest from the television, and scrolls through her phone. I hope she's not going to read out every crappy thing that gets posted about me again. Remy's in his usual recliner, but he turns to stare at me for a minute.

"You sure you want to watch this?" he asks. "We can catch it later." Sounds like he wants to watch the episode first to make sure nothing in it will upset me.

"I'm not a baby." I pout, negating my words. I hug my knees to my chest and rest my chin on them.

"Stay still," Hayden murmurs, tugging on my hair.

The opening begins with a recap of the previous episodes. The guy Griff seemed to be friends with who got booted in the second episode flashes on the screen. Griff's scowl burns into the camera. God, he's so handsome it hurts to look at him. Voice-overs explain past events. The show's a mishmash mess. One week it seems to be focused on fighting. Venom spoke rather passionately about his martial arts training during the first episode. The next, it focused on the dramatic introduction of a bunch of ring bunnies to the show. Griff was hyped as "the bad boy trying to stay faithful to a good girl" back home. "Will he resist the tempting Kiki?" was flashed across the screen as she put her claws on his chest.

"Stay mentally strong. You can resist any temptation," Woolly said to Griff.

Was Griff really fighting temptation? Kiki *is* pretty. Mature and stylish, I guess. A lot of shots seem to be of her staring at Griff from afar. Or Griff working out.

The other contestants all seem to have their assigned roles. Deadass is the delusional douche canoe who no one takes seriously and everyone in the house seems to hate. Naptime's the one with the catch phrase. It's not even a good one. He just yells, "time for a nappy nap" every time he lands a punch.

Venom's the fatherly advisor, even though I don't think he's that much older than Griff. Woolly's the spiritual, hippie guy who tosses out motivational quotes. Rumbling Thunder's a judgmental goody-two-shoes who critiques everyone's moves—whether they've asked for his opinion or not. The girls seem to have their own characters assigned to them too. One wants to be a singer. Another one's the quirky, not-like-other-girls girl. Kiki's presented as an empty-headed bimbo but in one of the solo interviews, she dropped the airhead act and talked about wanting to open her own nail salon. Someone driven. Who wants to run a business doing something she loves—like Griff.

It bugs me. It bugs me a lot.

The rest of the ring girls are some variation of slutty temptress. If anything, I guess the show's equally insulting to everyone in every way possible.

As soon as Griff comes on the screen, I perk up. He's being fitted for a suit, which seems odd. The episode follows all the contestants to some fancy dinner.

"So they *are* allowed to leave the house?" I shout.

"None of this makes any damn sense," Eraser gripes.

"No kidding," I mutter.

Kyla leans against me. "Griff looks good all dressed up, though."

"He does." I hug my legs tighter.

"I fuckin' hate this." Remy stands and walks behind his chair. "What was he thinking?"

"Remy, calm down. Griff's doing fine," Ella says.

"You had to let him leave the nest some time, Papa Bear," Eraser adds.

"Bears don't live in nests," Hayden says.

Remy chuckles. "Tell him, Hayden."

Eraser rumbles with laughter. "Fine, he had to lumber out of the *cave* sometime."

"Better," Hayden praises.

After the dinner, the camera cuts to the living quarters. Watching black-and-white, grainy footage shot from a high angle gives the show an extra-creepy voyeuristic feel that's made me uncomfortable from episode one.

"Is Kiki going to make her move tonight?" the voice-over artist asks.

I roll my eyes.

"And will Griff give into temptation just this once?"

On the screen, Griff's at his door and Kiki walks up behind him.

My pulse spikes. I hate her being so close to my boyfriend. Talking to him like she has the right. And I'm all the way here in Johnsonville. So far away from him.

It's just a TV show. Griff's only there for us. Nothing to be alarmed about.

Next, Kiki's in his arms.

The screen cuts to a commercial.

Did I see what I think I saw?

"What the fuck?" Remy shouts.

"Bro, chill," Eraser says. "We should've watched it later so we could fast-forward through all these erectile-dysfunction ads. Why are there so many broken dicks in this country? That's the real mystery."

I huff out a sad laugh.

Eraser leans over and squeezes my shoulder. "You okay?"

"I'm fine." I glance at the screen. "I know who Griff is." *At least I thought I did.*

Whatever he's doing is just a strategy. To make sure he wins. For us.

The sinking feeling in my stomach seems to disagree with my mental pep talk.

The show returns and follows Deadass and two of the ring girls while they frolic in the pool under the moonlight. My stomach clenches as I wait for some update on Griff.

The show stops at Venom in the phone booth, talking to his wife. The show's sort of framed her as a nag, which honestly, I think I'd prefer to dumb virgin slut.

Bull and Pirate spar in a cage.

The screen switches to the grainy black-and-white footage again.

"Wait a minute," the dramatic voice-over says. "Did Griff invite Kiki into his room after all?"

The camera zooms in on the door, then jump-cuts to a dark, shadowy bedroom.

Two people are in the bed.

Under the bright white comforter.

Moaning.

"Looks like Griff has a difficult conversation with his girlfriend coming up."

The camera focuses on Griff's back. A woman's long nails digging into his shoulders. His body moves over the woman.

"Shhh," he keeps saying every time the girl moans too loud. Then a harsh, whispered, "Hurry up."

Bile burns the back of my throat.

Everyone in the living room stops breathing or moving. No one says a word as we all stare in horror. I can't look directly at the screen.

Don't cry. Don't throw up.

I suck in a deep breath, fighting the tears stinging my eyes and the pain in my throat.

How could I have been so dumb?

I really thought Griff and I were destined to be together. Our years of friendship meant that we had a deep connection. I believed him when he said he was competing on this reality show to secure our future. When they introduced the girls into the house, I wasn't worried.

I trusted him.

Our love is strong.

Strong enough to withstand weeks apart.

But not strong enough for Griff to resist temptation.

My chest hurts, and I drag in a ragged breath. How can his betrayal physically *hurt* so much? Never mind the embarrassment of my friends and family surrounding me while we all witness the love of my life cheating on me on national television.

I trusted him with *everything*.

On wobbly legs, I walk out of the house and onto the front porch. Fog dulls my brain. My thoughts tumble in a painful circle. If anyone calls after me or follows, I can't hear them.

Air. Oxygen. I can't breathe.

Griff...with another woman.

Those grainy, black-and-white images. The voices. *His* voice. Shushing her. *Hurry up.*

That's not the sweet, loving, patient way he treated me.

That doesn't ease any of my pain, though.

I squeeze my eyes shut but the images won't go away. My mind fills in the gaps of what I couldn't make out on the screen.

Griff's face, his body. The other woman, who's been yapping to the cameras about how hot he is for weeks, touching him.

Pain slices through my heart, and I double over. A deep, ragged sob tears out of my throat. Blindly, I thrust my hand forward, searching for the railing. Tears scald my eyes and trail over my cheeks.

My Griff. My first love. The man I'd thought would be my only love. My forever.

How could he do this to us?

"Molly." Remy's solid voice offers no comfort—only more pain. He'll take his best friend's side. Tell me to get over it. Or that we shouldn't have been together in the first place. I'm too young for Griff. We're too different.

I hate that maybe Remy's right.

I sniffle and stand straight but still cling to the railing, too embarrassed to turn around and face my brother.

"Molly." He rests his hand on my shoulder and turns me to face him. I duck my head and curse the tears rolling down my cheeks.

He wraps his arms around me, pulling me close into his solid, protective embrace. "I'm so sorry," he rasps.

"Why?" My voice cracks, and I sob even harder. "Why would he do that?"

Remy's body stiffens for a moment, but he keeps hugging me. "I don't know. But everything's going to be okay, Molly. I promise."

"Nothing will ever be okay again."

"Shh," he soothes, running his hand over my hair and down my back. "Yes, it will."

"How?" I cry.

"Because when I get my hands on him, I'm going to murder him for doing this to you," Remy swears.

"W-what?" I stutter and pull away from Remy. "You don't mean that. He's your best friend."

"Oh, yes I do." Murderous intent shines in my brother's eyes.

"I fucking warned him if he pulled something like this what would happen."

"Something…like *this*? How could you predict he'd cheat on me on national television?"

"I meant cheat on you in general. Or hurt you in any way."

"Wait, what?" My voice rises into screaming range. "You talked to him about cheating on me?"

"No. When he told me his intention to date you, I warned him if he ever hurt you, I'd hurt him."

Any other night, under any other circumstances, I might find that sweet. But right now, my anger and heartbreak execute a swift detour and aim at the man in front of me. "That's humiliating." I lift my arms to shove him, but he catches my hands mid-air. "Why can't you mind your own business?"

"You *are* my business." He grips my shoulders and shakes me. "Like it or not, you'll always be my business, Molly. Someone hurts you, they hurt me. And no one gets away with that unpunished." His voice breaks, and he shakes his head. "Not even him."

"You're insane." I jerk out of his hold and step around him, then barge into the house.

Hayden rushes to meet me in the foyer. "Are you okay?"

"No."

She focuses on the door like she's planning her escape. Can't say I blame her. "The teasers for next week…just look like they all discuss 'the aftermath.' Griff says to the camera he 'doesn't know what to tell Molly.'" She screws her face into a furious scowl. "What a load of crap."

"Aftermath." I let out a pathetic laugh that sounds like a sob. "Yeah, can't wait for whatever he has to tell me."

"Don't answer the phone."

Why'd I agree to have everyone over to watch this again? So there'd be witnesses to my humiliation? It's been a shitshow from the first episode. How could I think it'd get any better?

Thank God school's over. I can't imagine trying to walk through the hallways and look at my classmates after this.

But I don't have to.

I don't have to look at anyone ever again.

Maybe I'll just leave town. Tell no one where I'm going. Disappear and start a new life.

Except that stupid show flashed my face in every episode. But who cares? It's just some dumb reality show. The only reason it matters here is because everyone in Johnsonville knows Griff. Everyone in my class met him at prom.

If I leave town, problem solved.

"Molly?" Hayden touches my elbow. "Are you okay?"

The thought of leaving town is like a runaway train. I have a little money saved up. How hard can it be to find a job at another grocery store?

I force a weak smile. "No, but I will be."

I just need to make one stop before I leave Johnsonville for good.

Molley

CHAPTER FORTY-THREE

Molly

After everyone went home and Remy went to bed, I snuck outside. Griff said I could drive Black Beauty while he was away. I'm not doing anything wrong.

Sliding into the front seat brings on a wave of nausea even though I haven't eaten anything in hours. I can't be in this car without thinking of Griff.

Lock it down, Molly.

I twist the key. The powerful engine grumbles to life. Yikes, that's loud in the middle of the night. Remy's room is on the other side of the house. *Please don't let him come outside.*

Carefully, I ease off the brake and apply slight pressure to the gas pedal. Just how Griff taught me.

Don't think about him. It's just a car. Metal and rubber. Mechanical parts to propel me forward—nothing more.

I back the car into the street and tap the gas. The engine roars and the car shoots forward. Barely touching the pedal, I steer the car toward Jerry's garage.

Jerry won't open up for hours.

My Malibu is in a separate garage behind the shop now. Vapor moved it there to prep it for some work a few days ago. I ease the Chevelle next to that building and kill the engine.

For a few stinging minutes, I can't breathe. There's no air. Just pain exploding in my throat and stabbing my eyes.

Finally, I calm myself. Without turning around, I reach behind the seat, searching the floor for the bat that Griff keeps for protection.

I gave Griff everything. And it wasn't good enough.

I'm not the girl he wants. This is the first time we've been separated, and he couldn't control himself. Was he lying when he said he hadn't been with anyone else in a long time before we slept together? Probably.

I step out of the Chevelle and heft the bat in my hands. On the key ring, I find the one for the garage door and open it. My car sits there in its unfinished state. Mocking me. A present from Griff. Something we shared and built together.

My mind flashes back to the day he gave me the car. Each moment we spent in the garage, restoring it. Building our relationship. Creating memories. Kissing on the hood. How happy we were. How much fun we had together.

Disgust and embarrassment well up inside me. How could I be so stupid?

I lift the bat, testing the weight of it in my hands. I never played softball in high school. Maybe I should've. I pull the bat back, twisting at the waist. Every bit of hurt and anger slides from my chest, down my arms, and into my fingers as I grip the bat tighter and swing forward.

Smash!

The bat crashes through the driver's side window. Glass shatters and tinkles on the concrete floor. Bits spray back, scratching and prickling my skin, but I barely notice.

I lift it again and bring it down hard. *Crack!* It slams into the side mirror with a jarring but satisfying metallic *clang*. The mirror flies into the back wall, leaving a shiny trail of mirrored glass like tears on the concrete floor.

Home run.

Griff kissing that woman.

I smash the passenger side mirror.

Her moans.

The bat punches into the headlights with a satisfying crunch and crackle.

Their bodies twisting under the covers. Her nails digging into his skin.

The bat connects with the A-pillar holding the windshield in place instead of the windshield I was aiming for. The impact jars my bones and rattles my teeth.

My arms shake and throb.

Breathing hard, I turn, stumble out of the garage, and stand in front of the Chevelle. Griff's pride and joy. My arms wobble like spaghetti as I lift the bat.

I sat in the garage and watched him restore it from scraps. He's let me race it at Zips. I had my first orgasm in that front seat.

I lift the bat higher, aiming for the headlights.

No.

I can't seem to force my arms to move.

He's had this car for years. Long before we were a couple.

It's not mine to destroy.

I lower the bat and turn to stare at the mess I've left behind. My car was going to be so beautiful. Now it's shattered. In pieces.

Just like my heart.

Tears stream down my cheeks but I ignore them as I toss the bat into the trunk of the Chevelle. I pull the car into the bay next to the ruined Malibu, leave the keys inside, and slam the door shut.

Now what?

It doesn't matter.

The sun's coming up.

Exhausted and throbbing with pain, I stumble onto the main road and start walking toward the sunrise.

Griff and Molly's story continues in:
<u>Repairing the Wreckage (Ruthless & Royal #2)</u>

Hello!

If you're new to my books, welcome! Thank you for taking a chance on an unknown author. If you're familiar with my Lost Kings MC world, welcome back! Thank you for your willingness to try something a little bit different than my usual bikers. It's the same world and of course many of the same characters you've come to know and love, so I hope you enjoyed catching up with everyone!

Fighting the Forbidden is a story I've been dying to write for at least five years. I'm *so* excited and even a little sad that I'm finally releasing it into the world!

For the last nine months, I've completely immersed myself in Griff and Molly's lives and loved every minute. Their story turned out a little differently than I first envisioned way back when they first whispered in my ear, but I love it so much more now. I hope you enjoyed spending time with Griff, Molly, and the rest of the Castle Crew, too!

I hope you'll return for *Repairing the Wreckage,* it's sure to be a wild ride. After that, Jigsaw is finally getting his book—#24 of the Lost Kings MC series. After Jigsaw's story, I plan to write Remy's and I can't for the twisted adventure that will be. I chose to weave in and out of the Ruthless & Royal series and the Lost Kings MC series for a reason and I am so excited for all the things to come!

If you want regular updates about what I'm working on and sneak peaks into my writing, the best place to do that is my Facebook Group. You can also sign up for my newsletter, although I don't really send it out as often as I probably should.

I hope 2024 is treating you well so far.

xoxo,

Autumn

ALSO BY AUTUMN JONES LAKE

The Lost Kings MC Series

Slow Burn (Lost Kings MC #1)

Corrupting Cinderella (Lost Kings MC #2)

Three Kings, One Night (Lost Kings MC #2.5)

Strength From Loyalty (Lost Kings MC #3)

Tattered on My Sleeve (Lost Kings MC #4)

White Heat (Lost Kings MC #5)

Between Embers (Lost Kings MC #5.5)

More Than Miles (Lost Kings MC #6)

White Knuckles (Lost Kings MC #7)

Beyond Reckless (Lost Kings MC #8)

Beyond Reason (Lost Kings MC #9)

One Empire Night (Lost Kings MC #9.5)

After Burn (Lost Kings MC #10)

After Glow (Lost Kings MC #11)

Zero Hour (Lost Kings MC #11.5)

Zero Tolerance (Lost Kings MC #12)

Zero Regret (Lost Kings MC #13)

Zero Apologies (Lost Kings MC #14)

Swagger and Sass (Lost Kings MC #14.5)

White Lies (Lost Kings MC #15)

Rhythm of the Road (Lost Kings MC #16)

Lyrics on the Wind (Lost Kings MC #17)

Diamond in the Dust (Lost Kings MC #18)

Crown of Ghosts (Lost Kings MC #19)

Throne of Scars (Lost Kings MC #20)

Reckless Truths (Lost Kings MC #21)

Deeper You Dig (Lost Kings MC #21.5)

Rust or Ride (Lost Kings MC #22)

Agony to Ashes (Lost Kings MC #23)

Twist the Knife (Lost Kings MC #24)

Collect the Pieces (Lost Kings MC #25)

Lost Kings MC World

Ruthless & Royal Series

Fighting the Forbidden (Ruthless & Royal #1)

Repairing the Wreckage (Ruthless & Royal #2)

The Hollywood Demons Trilogy

Also in audio!

Kickstart My Heart

Blow My Fuse

Wheels of Fire

Stand-Alones in the Lost Kings MC world

Renegade Path

Bullets & Bonfires

Warnings & Wildfires

THE LOST KINGS MC® WORLD

by *USA Today* bestselling author
Autumn Jones Lake

Fighting the Forbidden is the first book of a new series and can be read without reading any of my other books. But if you're curious about how it fits into the Lost Kings MC World, this is my suggested chronological reading order.

1. Kickstart My Heart (Hollywood Demons #1)
2. Blow My Fuse (Hollywood Demons #2)
3. Wheels of Fire (Hollywood Demons #3)
4. Renegade Path (A Lost Kings MC World Novel)
5. Slow Burn (Lost Kings MC #1)
6. Corrupting Cinderella (Lost Kings MC #2)
7. Three Kings, One Night (Lost Kings MC #2.5)
8. Strength From Loyalty (Lost Kings MC #3)
9. Tattered on My Sleeve (Lost Kings MC #4)
10. White Heat (Lost Kings MC #5)
11. Between Embers (Lost Kings MC #5.5)
12. Bullets & Bonfires (A Lost Kings MC World Novel)
13. More Than Miles (Lost Kings MC #6)
14. Warnings & Wildfires (A Lost Kings MC World Novel)
15. White Knuckles (Lost Kings MC #7)
16. Beyond Reckless (Lost Kings MC #8)
17. Beyond Reason (Lost Kings MC #9)
18. One Empire Night (Lost Kings MC #9.5)
19. After Burn (Lost Kings MC #10)
20. After Glow (Lost Kings MC #11)
21. Zero Hour (Lost Kings MC #11.5)
22. Zero Tolerance (Lost Kings MC #12)
23. Zero Regret (Lost Kings MC #13)
24. Zero Apologies (Lost Kings MC #14)
25. Swagger and Sass (Lost Kings MC #14.5)
26. White Lies (Lost Kings MC #15)
27. Rhythm of the Road (Lost Kings MC #16)
28. Lyrics on the Wind (Lost Kings MC #17)
29. Diamond in the Dust (Lost Kings MC #18)
30. Crown of Ghosts (Lost Kings MC #19)
31. Throne of Scars (Lost Kings MC #20)

...and many more to come!

ABOUT THE AUTHOR

Autumn Jones Lake is the *USA Today* and *Wall Street Journal* bestselling author of over twenty novels, including the popular Lost Kings MC series. She believes true love stories never end. Her past lives include baking cookies, bagging groceries, selling cheap shoes, and practicing law. Playing with her imaginary friends all day is by far her favorite job yet!

Autumn lives in upstate New York with her own alpha hero.

www.autumnjoneslake.com

facebook.com/autumnjoneslake

goodreads.com/autumnjoneslake

pinterest.com/autumnjoneslake

instagram.com/autumnjlake

bookbub.com/authors/autumn-jones-lake